THE ▮▮▮▮▮▮▮▮▮▮

They went ▮▮▮▮▮▮▮▮▮▮▮▮▮▮▮▮▮ mirrored passageway. "▮▮▮▮▮▮▮▮▮▮▮▮▮▮▮," Quillan warned. "We just could get ja▮▮▮▮▮▮▮▮. think so, though. They'd have to get past the Commissioner."

"Oh, he's here, too?"

She didn't hear what Quillan answered, because she had an after-effect from the drugs her recent captors had given her, and things faded out around then. When they faded in again, the passageway with the mirrors had disappeared, and they were coming to the top of a short flight of low, wide stairs and into a very beautiful room. This room was high and long, not very wide. In the center was a small square swimming pool, and against the walls on either side was a long row of tall square crystal pillars through which strange lights undulated slowly. Trigger glanced curiously at the nearest pillar. She stopped short.

"Galaxy!" she said, startled.

Quillan reached back and grabbed her arm with his gun hand. "Keep moving, Trigger! That's just how Belchik keeps his harem grouped around him when he's working. Not too bad an idea—it does cut down the chatter. This is his office."

"Office!" Then she saw the large business desk with prosaic standard equipment which stood on the carpet on the other side of the pool. They moved rapidly past the pool, Quillan still hauling at her arm. Trigger kept staring at the pillars they passed. Long-limbed, supple and languid, they floated there in their crystal cages, in tinted, shifting lights, eyes closed, hair drifting about their faces.

"Awesome, isn't it?" Quillan said.

"Yes," said Trigger. "Awesome. One in each—he *is* a pig! They look drowned."

"He is and they aren't," said Quillan. "Very lively girls when he lets them out."

IN THIS SERIES:

Telzey Amberdon
T'n T: Telzey & Trigger
Trigger & Friends
The Hub: Dangerous Territories (forthcoming)

BAEN BOOKS BY ERIC FLINT:

Mother of Demons
1632

The Belisarius series, with David Drake:
An Oblique Approach
In the Heart of Darkness
Destiny's Shield
Fortune's Stroke

with Dave Freer:
Rats, Bats & Vats

TRIGGER & FRIENDS

The Complete Federation of the Hub

Volume 3

JAMES H. SCHMITZ

EDITED BY ERIC FLINT

co-edited by Guy Gordon

Trigger & Friends

"Harvest Time" was originally published in *Astounding Science Fiction* in September 1958. "Lion Loose" was originally published in *Analog* in October 1961. "Aura of Immortality" was originally published in *IF* in June 1974. "Forget It" is an adaptation by Guy Gordon of a story originally published under the title "Planet of Forgetting" in the February 1965 issue of *Galaxy*. *Legacy* was first published in 1962 by Torquil Books, under the title *A Tale of Two Clocks*. It was re-issued in 1979 by Ace Books under the title *Legacy*. "Sour Note on Palayata" was originally published in *Astounding Science Fiction* in November, 1956.

Afterword, © 2000 by Eric Flint; "The Psychology Service: Immune System of the Hub," © 2000 by Guy Gordon.

A Baen Books Original

Baen Publishing Enterprises
P.O. Box 1403
Riverdale, NY 10471
www.baen.com

ISBN: 0-671-31966-3

Cover art by Bob Eggleton

First printing, January 2001

Distributed by Simon & Schuster
1230 Avenue of the Americas
New York, NY 10020

Produced by Windhaven Press, Auburn, NH
Printed in the United States of America

CONTENTS

Harvest Time

1

Senior Assistant Commissioner Holati Tate sat comfortably on a high green hill of the Precolonization world of Manon, and watched Communications Chief Trigger Argee coordinating the dials of a bio-signal pickup with those of a recorder. Trigger was a slim, tanned, red-haired girl, and watching her was a pleasure from which neither her moody expression nor Holati Tate's advanced years detracted much. She got her settings finally, swung around on her camp chair and faced him. She smiled faintly.

"How's it going?" the S.A.C. inquired.

"It's going. Those bio-patterns aren't easy to unscramble, though. That to be expected?"

He nodded. "They're a mess. That's why I had to borrow a communications expert from Headquarters."

"Well," said Trigger, "if you just want to rebroadcast the strongest individual signal, we'll have a usable transcription in another ten minutes." She shielded her eyes and peered up at the late afternoon sky. "Can't see more than a green tinge from here. The Drift's about nine miles up, isn't it?"

"At nine miles you're barely scratching the bottom layer," Holati Tate told her. "The stuff floats high on this world."

Trigger looked at him and smiled again, more easily now. She liked Holati, a weather-beaten little Precol veteran who'd come in as a replacement on the Manon Project only six months before. Assistant commissioners were mostly Academy graduates nowadays; he was one of the old guard the Academy was not too gradually shoving out of the supervisory field ranks. Trigger had heard he'd been in the Space Scouts until he reached the early retirement age of that arduous service. "What's this beep pattern we're copying supposed to be?" she inquired. "Sort of a plankton love call?"

Holati admitted that was as good a guess as any. "At the Bio Station we figure each of the various species keeps broadcasting its own signal to help the swarms keep together. This signal is pretty strong because the Drift's mainly composed of a single species at the moment. When we set up the food-processing stations, we might be able to use signal patterns like that as a lure."

Trigger smoothed her red hair back and nodded. "Dirty trick!" she observed amiably.

"Can't be sentimental about it, Trigger girl. Processed plankton could turn out to be Manon's biggest export item by the time it's a colony. The Federation's appetite gets bigger every year." He added, "I'm also interested in the possibility it's the signals that attract those Harvester things we'd like to get rid of."

"They been giving you trouble again?" Trigger's duties kept her close to the Headquarters area as a rule, but she had heard the Harvesters were thoroughly dangerous creatures capable of producing a reasonable facsimile of a lightning bolt when disturbed.

"No," he said. "I won't let the boys fool with them. We'll have to figure a way to handle them before we start collecting the plankton, though. Put in a requisition for heavy guns last month." He studied her thoughtfully. "Something the matter? You don't seem happy today, Trigger."

Trigger's thin brown brows slanted in a scowl. "I'm not! It's that boss we've got, the Honorable Commissioner Ramog."

Holati looked startled. He jerked his head meaningfully at the recorder. Trigger wrinkled her nose.

"Don't worry. My instruments are probably the only thing that isn't bugged around the Manon Project Headquarters. I pull the snoopies out as quick as Ramog can get them stuck in."

"Hm-m-m!" he said dubiously. "What's the commissioner doing to bother you?"

"He slung Brule Inger into the brig yesterday morning." Brule was Trigger's young man, Holati recalled. "He'll be shipped home on the next supply ship. And I don't know," Trigger added, "whether Ramog wants Brule out of the way because of me, or because he really suspects Brule was out hunting Old Galactic artifacts on Project time. He wasn't, of course, but that's the charge. Either way I don't like it."

"People are getting mighty touchy about that Old Galactic business," Holati said. "Biggest first-discovery bonus the Federation's ever offered by now, just to start with."

Trigger shrugged impatiently. "It's a lot of nonsense. When the Project was moved out here last year, everyone was saying the Manon System looked like the hottest bet in the Cluster to make the big strike. For that matter, it's why Ramog got the Manon Project assigned to him, and he's been all over the planet with Essidy and those other stooges of his. They haven't found a thing."

Holati nodded. "I know. Wouldn't be at all surprised, though, if the strike were made right here on Manon eventually. It's in a pretty likely sector."

Trigger regarded him skeptically. "So you believe in those Old Galactic stories, too? Well, maybe—but I'll tell you one thing: it wouldn't be healthy for anyone but Commissioner Ramog to make that kind of discovery on Commissioner Ramog's Project!"

"Now, now, Trigger!" Holati began to look alarmed again. "There's a way in which those things are handled, you know!"

Trigger's lip curled. "A foolproof way?" she inquired.

"Well, practically," the S.A.C. told her defensively. He was beginning to sound like a man who wanted to convince himself; and for a moment she felt sorry for disturbing him. "You make a strike, and you verify and register it with the Federation over any long-range communications transmitter. After that there isn't a thing anybody else can do about your claim! Even the . . . well, even the Academy isn't going to try to tangle with Federation Law!"

"The point might be," Trigger said bleakly, "that you wouldn't necessarily get near the transmitters here with that kind of message. As a matter of fact, I've seen a couple of pretty funny accidents in the two years I've been working with Ramog." She shrugged. "Well, I'm heading back to the Colonial School when my hitch here is up—I'm fed up with the way the Academy boys are taking over in Precol. And I've noticed nobody seems to like to listen when I talk about it. Even Brule keeps hushing me up—" She turned her head to a rattling series of clicks from the recorder, reached out and shut it off. A flat plastic box popped halfway out of the recorder's side. Trigger removed it and stood up. "Here's your signal pattern duplicate. Hope it works—"

While Holati Tate was helping Trigger Argee load her

equipment back into her little personal hopper, he maintained the uncomfortable look of a man who had just heard an attractive young woman imply with some reason that he was on the spineless side. After she had gone he quit looking uncomfortable, since it wasn't impressing anybody any more, and began to look worried instead.

He liked Trigger about as well as anyone he knew, and her position here might be getting more precarious than she thought. When it became obvious a while ago that Commissioner Ramog had developed a definite interest in Trigger's slim good looks, the bets of the more cynical elements at the Bio Station all went down on the commissioner. No one had tried to collect so far, but Brule Inger's enforced departure from the Project was likely to send the odds soaring. While Ramog probably wouldn't resort to anything very drastic at the moment, he was in a good position to become about as drastic as he liked, and if Trigger didn't soften up on her own there wasn't much doubt that Ramog eventually would help things along.

Frowning darkly, Holati climbed into his own service hopper and set it moving a bare fifty feet above the ground, headed at a leisurely rate down the slopes of a long green range of hills toward the local arm of Great Gruesome Swamp. Two hundred miles away, on the other side of this section of Great Gruesome, stood the domes of Manon's Biological Station of which he was the head.

He had a good deal of work still to get done that evening, but he wanted to do some thinking first. Nothing Trigger had told him was exactly news. The Precol Academy group had been getting tougher to work with year after year, and Commissioner Ramog was unquestionably the toughest operator of them all. The grapevine of the Ancient and Honorable Society of Retired Space Scouts, which counted slightly more than twelve thousand members scattered through Precol, credited the commissioner with five probable direct murders of inconvenient Precol personnel, though none of these actions stood any chance of being proved after the event. Two of the victims, including an old-time commissioner, had been members of the Society. Ramog definitely was a bad boy to get involved with—

The hopper began moving out over the flat margins of Great Gruesome, a poisonous-looking wet tangle of purple and green and brown vegetation, gleaming like a seascape in the rays of Manon's setting sun. There were occasional vague motions and sudden loud splashings down there, and Holati cautiously took the vehicle up a couple of hundred feet. The great chains of swamp and marshy lakes that girdled two-thirds of the planet's equator contained numerous unclassified life-forms of a size and speed no sensible man would have cared to match himself against outside of full combat armor. Precol personnel avoided unnecessary encounters with such brutes; their control would be left to the colonists of a later year.

His immediate problem was the ticklish one of establishing the exact circumstances under which Commissioner Ramog was to murder Holati Tate. It was an undertaking which could only too easily be fumbled, and he still wasn't at all certain of a number of details. Brow furrowed with worried thought, he kicked the hopper at last into a moderately rapid vertical ascent and unpackaged the bio-signal record Trigger Argee had transcribed for him. He fed it carefully into the hopper's broadcast system.

Floating presently in the tinted evening air of the lower fringes of Manon's aerial plankton zone, Holati Tate sat a while scanning the area about and above him. A few hundred yards away a sluggishly moving stream of the Drift was passing overhead. A few stars had winked on; and hardly a thousand miles out, a ribbon of Moon Belt dust drew thin glittering bands of fire across the sky. Here and there, then, Holati began to spot the huge greenish images of mankind's established competitors for the protein of the Plankton Drift: the Harvesters of Manon.

In a couple of minutes he had counted thirty-six Harvesters within visual range. As he watched, two of them were rising until they dwindled and vanished in the darkening sky. The others continued to hover not far from the streams of the Drift, as sluggish at this hour as their prey. The sausage-shaped, almost featureless giant forms hardly looked menacing, but three venturesome biologists had been electrocuted by a Harvester within a week after the Project was opened on the planet; and the usual hands-off policy had been established until Project work advanced to the point where the problem required a wholesale solution.

Holati tuned in the bio-receiver. Around midday both Harvesters and plankton were furiously active, but there was only the barest murmur of signal now. He eased down the broadcast button on the set and waited.

He'd counted off eight seconds before he could determine any reaction. The plankton stream nearest him was losing momentum, its component masses began curving down slowly from all directions towards the hopper. Holati was not sure that the nearest Harvesters had stirred at all; keeping a wary eye on them, he gradually stepped up the signal strength by some fifty per cent. The hopper was a solid little craft, spaceworthy at interplanetary ranges, but he was only slightly curious about what would happen if he allowed it to accompany a mass of plankton into a Harvester's interior. And he wasn't in the least interested in stimulating one of the giants into cutting loose with its defensive electronic blasts.

The Harvesters were definitely moving toward him when the first streamers of the plankton arrived, thumped squashily upon the hopper's viewplate receivers and generally proceeded to plaster themselves about the front part of the machine. Blinded for the moment, Holati switched on a mass-scope, spotted an oncoming Harvester at five hundred yards and promptly stopped the broadcast. Somewhat nervously, he watched the Harvester drift to a stop while the butterfly-sized plankton life, dropping away from what had become an uninteresting surface again, made languid motions at clustering into a new formation.

He hesitated, then eased the hopper backward out of the disturbed area. A mile off he stopped again and swept his glance once more over what he could see of the gliding clouds of the Drift. Then he jammed down the broadcast button, sending the bio-signal out with a bawling force the planet had never experienced before.

Throughout the area, the Drift practically exploded. Great banks of living matter came rolling down through the sky toward the hopper. Behind, through and ahead of the sentient tides, moving a hundred times faster than the plankton, rushed dozens of vast sausage shapes, their business ends opened into wide, black gapes.

Holati Tate hurriedly knocked off the hopper's thunderous Lorelei song and went fast and straight away from there. Far behind him, he watched the front lines of the plankton clouds breaking over a converged mass of Harvesters. A minute later the giants were plowing methodically back and forth through the late evening snack with which he had provided them.

The experiment, he decided, had to be called a complete success. He got his bearings, turned the hopper and sent it arrowing silently down through the shadowy lower air, headed for Warehouse Center on the southern side of the local arm of Great Gruesome Swamp.

Supply Manager Essidy was a tall, handsome man with a small brown beard and a fine set of large white teeth, who was disliked by practically everybody on the Project because of his unfortunate reputation as Commissioner

Ramog's Number One stooge. Perhaps to offset the lonely atmosphere of his main office at Warehouse Center, Essidy was industriously studying the finer points of a couple of girl clerks through his desk viewer when he was informed that Senior Assistant Commissioner Tate had just parked his hopper at Dome Two.

Essidy clicked his teeth together alertly, lifted one eyebrow, dropped it again, cleared the viewer, clipped a comm-button to his left ear and switched the comm-set to "record." Of the eight hundred and thirty-seven people on the Manon Project, there were nine on whom the commissioner wanted immediate reports concerning even routine supplies withdrawals. Holati Tate was one of the nine.

Essidy's viewer picked up the S.A.C. as he walked down the central corridor of Dome Two and followed him around a number of turns, into a large storeroom and up to a counter. Essidy adjusted the comm-button.

" . . . Not just for atmospheric use," Holati was saying. "Jet mobility, of course. But I might want to use it under water."

The counter clerk had recognized the S.A.C. and was being respectful. "Well, sir," he said hesitantly, "if it's a question of pressure, that would have to be a Moon-suit, wouldn't it?"

Holati nodded. "Uh-huh. That's what I had in mind."

Back in the office, Essidy lifted both eyebrows. He couldn't be sure of the Bio Station's current requirements, but a Moon-suit didn't sound routine. The clerk was dialing for the suit when Holati added, "By the way, got one of those things outfitted with a directional tracker?"

The clerk looked around. "I'm sure we don't, sir. It isn't standard equipment. We can install one for you."

Holati reflected, and shook his head. "Don't bother with it, son. I'll do that myself . . . Uh, high selectivity, medium range, is the type I want."

✧   ✧   ✧

" . . . That's all he ordered," Essidy was reporting to Commissioner Ramog fifteen minutes later, on the commissioner's private beam. "He checked the suit himself—seemed familiar with that—and took the stuff along."

The commissioner was silent for almost thirty seconds and Essidy waited respectfully. He admired the boss and envied him hopelessly. It wasn't just that Commissioner Ramog had Academy training and the authority of the Academy and the home office behind him; he also had three times Essidy's brains and ten times Essidy's guts and Essidy knew it.

When Ramog finally spoke he sounded almost absent-minded, and Essidy felt a little thrill because that could mean something very hot indeed was up. "Well, of course Tate's familiar with Moon-suits," Ramog said. "He put in a sixteen-year hitch with the Space Scouts before getting assigned to Precol."

"Oh?" said Essidy.

"Yes." Ramog was silent a few seconds again. "Thanks for the prompt report, Essidy." He added casually, "Keep the squad on alert status until further notice."

Essidy asked no foolish questions. The matter might be hot right now, and it might not. He'd hear all he needed to know in plenty of time. That was the way the boss worked; and if you worked the way he liked, another bonus would be coming along quietly a little later to be quietly stacked away with previously earned ones. Essidy looked forward to retiring from the service early.

Commissioner Ramog, in his private rooms at Headquarters, let the tiny beam-speaker slip back into a desk niche and shifted his gaze toward a slowly turning three-dimensional replica of Manon which filled the wall across the room. The commissioner was a slender man, not very big, with a wiry, hard-trained body, close-cropped blond hair and calm gray eyes. At the moment he looked intrigued and a trifle puzzled.

The obvious first item here, he told himself, was that there simply wasn't any spot on the surface of this planet where the use of a Moon-suit was indicated. The tropical lakes were too shallow to present a pressure problem—and the fauna of those lakes was such that he wouldn't have cared to work there himself without both armor and armament. He could assume therefore that Senior Assistant Commissioner Tate, having checked out neither armor nor armament, wasn't contemplating such work either.

The second item: a directional tracker had a number of possible uses. However, it had been developed as a space gadget, and while it could be employed on a planet to keep a line on mobile targets, either alive or mechanical, it looked as if Tate's interest actually might be centered on something in space—

Nearby space, since the only vehicles available to personnel on Manon had a limited range.

Dropping that line for the moment, the commissioner's reflections ran on, one came to the really interesting third item—which was that Tate was an old-timer in Precol service. And as an old-timer, he knew that a requisition of this kind would not escape notice on an Academy-conducted Project. In fact, he could expect it to draw a rather prompt inquiry. One had to assume again that he intended to accomplish whatever he was out to accomplish with such equipment before an inquiry caught up with him—unless, of course, he had a legitimate explanation to offer when the check was made.

In any event, Commissioner Ramog concluded, no check was going to be made. At least, none of the kind that the senior assistant commissioner might be expecting.

Ramog stood up and walked over to the viewwall.

There were two other planets in the system of Manon's great green sun. Giant planets both and impossible for a man in a hopper to approach. Neither of them had a moon. There would be stray chunks of matter sprinkled through the system that nobody knew about, but Tate didn't have the equipment for a planned prospecting trip. He had the experience: his record showed he'd taken leave of absence a half dozen times during his Precol service period to take part in private prospecting jaunts. But without equipment, and the time to use it, experience wouldn't help him much in sifting through the expanses of a planetary system.

And that left what really had been the most likely probability almost to start with. The commissioner switched off the image of Manon and replaced it with that of Manon's Moon Belt.

The planet had possessed a sizable satellite at one time; but the time lay far in Manon's geological past. What was left by now was debris, thick enough to provide both a minor navigational problem and an interesting night-time display, but not heavy enough to represent a noteworthy menace to future colonists. So far there had been no opportunity to survey the Belt thoroughly.

But anyone who was using a hopper regularly could have made an occasional unobserved trip up there.

He couldn't, however, have left his vehicle. Neither to make a closer investigation, nor to pick up something he thought he'd spotted. Not unless he had a Moon-suit.

The commissioner felt excitement growing up in him, and now he could allow it to come through. Because there was really only one reason why an old-timer like Tate would violate Precol regulations so obviously. Only one thing big enough! The thing that Commissioner Ramog had come to Manon to find. An Old Galactic artifact—

He noticed he was shaking a little when he switched on the communicator to the outer office of his quarters. But his tone was steady. "Mora?"

"Right here." A cool feminine voice.

"See what you got on Tate during the day."

"The S.A.C.? He was out with Argee for two hours this afternoon. No coverage on that period."

Ramog frowned a little, nodded. "I have her report here. A Project Five item. What else?"

"Afterwards—Warehouse Center . . ."

"Have that, too."

"I'm scanning the tapes," Mora said. And presently, "Seems to have been in his hopper alone since early morning. Location checks to his station. Nothing of interest, so far. Hm-m-m . . . well, now!"

"What is it?"

"I think," Mora told him, "I should bring this in to you. He's going to be gone two or three days."

"I'll come out." Ramog already was on his feet. "Get me a current location check on that hopper of his."

Mora looked around as he came hurriedly into the office. "No luck, commissioner. Hopper can't be traced. He's gone off-planet."

Ramog's eyes narrowed very briefly as he dropped into a chair at her desk. "Start up the playback. And don't look so pleased!"

Mora smiled. She was a slender quick-moving, black-haired girl with big eyes almost as dark as her hair. "That's my little blond tiger!" she murmured.

His face was flushed. "What do you mean?"

"I mean," she said, "that I feel very, very sorry for the S.A.C." She started the playback. "The other one talking is Chelly. Ecologist. Tate's unofficial second-in-command at the station."

Ramog nodded impatiently. There weren't more than a dozen sentences to the conversation between Holati

Tate and Chelly. Mora shut off the playback. "That's all there is to his tape." She waited.

Ramog had had a bad moment. The S.A.C. had simply put Chelly in charge of station operations for the next two or three days, until he returned. No explanation for his intended absence, and Chelly seemed only mildly surprised. But obviously he wasn't involved in what Tate was doing.

What had bothered Ramog was the sudden thought that Tate might have arranged for an off-planet rendezvous with an FTL. But a second or two later he knew it wasn't possible. The Precol patrol boat stationed off Manon would spot, report, and challenge anything equipped with a space drive before it got close enough to the system for a hopper to meet it. The patrol-boat's job was a legitimate one: a planet undergoing orderly processing became a Federation concern and closed to casual interlopers. But in this case it insured that wherever Holati Tate was heading, he would have to return to Manon eventually.

The commissioner had relaxed a little. He smiled at Mora, his mind reverting to something she'd said a minute or so ago. A thrill-greedy, sanguinary little devil, he thought, but it would be regrettable if he ever had to get rid of Mora. They understood each other so well.

"You know," he told her, "I seem to feel very sorry for the S.A.C., too!" He added, "Now."

She gurgled excitedly and came over to him. "Are you going to tell me what it's all about?"

"Don't be stupid," Commissioner Ramog said tolerantly. An operation like this was a game to Mora. But she wasn't stupid. She was the most valuable assistant he'd ever developed.

"How many possible lines of action?" she persisted.

Ramog already had considered that. "Three," he said. "And I don't think we'd better waste any time."

❖   ❖   ❖

As it happened, it was Ramog's third line of action with which Holati Tate became involved when he dropped back into Manon's atmosphere two and a half planet days after his departure. Had he set the hopper down then in some wild section of the planet it would have been a different story. Ramog had been obliged to consider the possibility that the S.A.C. would be so lacking in human trustfulness that he might bury some item of value where it would never be found by anyone else.

An electronics specialist by the name of Gision was, therefore, on Holati's tail in an armed hopper as soon as he was spotted again, and he followed the S.A.C. around the curve of the planet as unobtrusively as one hopper could follow another. However, Holati Tate was merely heading by the shortest route for his Bio Station. When he settled down there, Gision took up a position halfway between Headquarters and the Bio domes and waited for developments.

At the Bio Station Essidy took over. For the past eighteen hours Essidy had been conducting an unhurried inventory of the station, assisted by a small crew of husky warehouse men. Holati locked his hopper when he got out, and it wasn't Essidy's job to do anything about that. He merely reported to Ramog that the S.A.C.— looking a little travel-worn and towing a bulky object by a gravity tube—had gone to his personal quarters. The object appeared to be, and probably was, the packaged Moon-suit. A few minutes later, Holati re-appeared at the hopper without the object, climbed in and took off. Gision reported from his aerial vantage point that the S.A.C. was going toward Headquarters now and was told by Ramog to precede him there.

Essidy was chattering over the private beam again before Gision signed off. Holati Tate had left his quarters sealed, but that had been no problem. "We got the thing unwrapped," Essidy said. "It's the Moon-suit, all right, and nothing else. He's got the directional tracker installed. It's activated. And that's the only interesting thing in these rooms."

"Go ahead," Ramog said quietly. "What's the reading on the tracker?"

Essidy checked again to make sure. "Locked on Object," he reported. "At two to twenty thousand miles."

And that was all Ramog had wanted to know. For a moment he was surprised to discover that his palms were slippery with sweat.

"All right, Essidy," he said. "Seal up his rooms and bring the suit over here, immediately." He added with no change in inflection, "If anyone has tampered with that reading before I see it, I'll burn him and you personally."

"Yes, sir," Essidy said meekly. "Shall I have the boys go ahead with the inventory to make it look right?"

Ramog said that would be fine and cut him off. The commissioner was actually enormously relieved. His third line of action was unreeling itself smoothly, and even if Tate got suspicious and panicked now it wouldn't present a serious problem, though it might still make the operation a little messy.

One could even hope for the S.A.C.'s own sake, Ramog thought, smiling very faintly now, that he wouldn't panic. The third line of action was not only the least risky, it was by far the most humane.

Holati Tate set the hopper down a hundred yards from the Headquarters vehicle shelter entrance. The service crew chief's voice said over the intercom, "Better bring her in, sir. We're on storm warning."

Holati obediently turned the hopper, slid her into the shelter and grounded her. The entrance door closed a hundred yards behind him.

"Want her serviced, sir?"

"No, no; she doesn't need it." Holati set the hatch on lock, got out and let it snap shut behind him. He looked at the crew chief. "I'll be taking her out again in thirty minutes or so," he said. Then he walked off up the dome tunnel toward the office sections.

The crew chief looked around and saw the hopper's hatch open. He frowned.

"Hey, you!" He went up to the hatch. "Who's that in there? She don't need servicing. How'd you get in?"

The man named Gision looked out. He was a large man with a round face and a sleepily ferocious expression.

"Little man," he said softly, "just keep the mouth shut and take off."

The crew chief stared at him. Gision was tagged with a very peculiar reputation among the best-informed Project personnel, but the crew chief hadn't had much to do with him personally and he habitually ignored Project rumors. Rumors about this guy or that started up on almost any outworld operation; they could usually be put down to jumpy nerves.

He changed his mind completely about that in the few seconds he and Gision were looking at each other.

He turned on his heel and walked off, badly shaken. If something was going on, he didn't want to know about it. Not a thing. He wasn't an exceptionally timid man, but he had just realized clearly that he was a long way from the police of the Federation.

Mora was in temporary charge of the communications offices, though Holati Tate didn't see her at first. He walked up to a plump, giggly little clerk he'd talked to before. She was busy coding a section of the current Project reports which presently would perform some fantastic loops through time and space and present themselves briskly at the Precol Home Office in the Federation.

Holati looked around the big room. "Where's Trigger Argee?" he inquired.

The clerk giggled. "Visiting her boy friend—" She

looked startled. "My . . . I guess I shouldn't have said that!"

So Holati discovered Trigger had been offered a special four-day furlough from the commissioner to go console Brule Inger in the brig, which was stationed in the general area of Manon's southern pole. He could imagine Trigger had been a little suspicious of the commissioner's gesture, but naturally she'd accepted.

He pulled down worriedly on his left ear lobe and glanced over to the far end of the room where three other clerks were working. "Who's in charge here, now?"

"Mora Lune's in charge," said the little clerk. She giggled. "If there's something . . . maybe I can help you?"

"Hm-m-m," Holati Tate said dubiously. As the little clerk told the others afterwards, he looked mighty nervous at that moment, hesitating as if he didn't know what to say. As a matter of fact, he felt rather nervous. "This Mora Lune," he went on at last. "Who's she?"

"The commissioner's secretary," explained the girl. "Mostly. She does all kinds of things, though. Sort of his assistant."

The S.A.C. stood stroking his chin and gnawing his lip. Finally he frowned.

"Well," he said with a sigh, "guess I'll go see Mora."

The little clerk giggled brightly and jumped up. "I'll show you to the office," she offered. Because, as she explained afterwards, she could just feel that something exciting was up.

That was all she had to tell. Mora sent her back to her work as soon as the two of them reached the door of the Central Communications Office. Mora didn't look excited except that her eyes had become nearly black. One would have had to know Mora to interpret that correctly, but Holati Tate made a fair guess. Like a man who's reached a decision, he explained his purpose almost curtly, "I want to send a personal message by long-range transmitter."

Mora indicated restrained surprise. "Oh . . . you'll want privacy, I suppose?" She added, "And I'm sure you're aware of the expense factor?"

He nodded. Just getting the long transmitters started up came to around three months of his salary.

Mora looked arch. "Perhaps congratulations are in order? A registration?"

At that, Holati Tate chuckled nervously. "Well, I'll say this much . . . I'll want to use the Notary!"

"Of course." Mora rose from behind the desk. "I'll attach it for you myself," she offered graciously. She floated ahead of him down a short hall and into the communications cabinet, dealt deftly there with switches and settings, connected the Notary machine with the transmitter, floated back to the door. "It's expensive, remember!" She smiled at him once more, almost tenderly, and closed the door behind her.

"How'd he take it?" Gision inquired a few minutes later.

Mora shrugged. They were in her own office and both were bent intently over a profile map of the area. On the map a small yellow dot moved out from the sprawl of Headquarters domes toward the southern swamps. Gision's large thumb rested lightly on a button at the side of the frame. Map and attachments were his own creation. "He just clammed up completely when he discovered it was to be a canned message," she said. "Refused to make it, of course—said he'd be back tomorrow or whenever the transmitters were working again. But I'm not even certain he was suspicious."

Gision grunted. "You can bet he got suspicious! The transmitters don't cut out that often."

"Maybe. He'd already checked out positive on the Notary anyway. It was a registration, all right." Mora moved a fingertip toward the thumb that rested on the button. "If you let me do that, I'll tell you what he was going to register."

Gision shook his big head without looking up. "You're too eager. And I'm not interested in what he was going to register."

She smiled. "You're all scared of Ramog."

Gision nodded. "And so would you be," he said, "if you had any sense."

They sat quietly a few minutes; then Mora began to fidget. "Isn't that far enough? He'll get away!"

"He can't get away—and it's almost far enough. We want him right out over the middle of those swamps."

She looked at his face and laughed. "I can tell you're going to let me do it. Aren't you?"

Gision nodded again. "And now's about the time. Put the finger up here."

She slipped her finger over the button and wet her lips. "Like this?"

"Like that. Now push."

She pushed down. The yellow dot vanished.

"Is that all?" she said disappointed.

"What did you expect?" Gision said. "An explosion?"

"No," Mora said dreamily. "But there's not much to it. If the old boy had been a little sharper, we might have had a questioning."

He shrugged. Sometimes Mora gave him the chills. "Questionings are what you try when you can't figure it out," he explained. "In a setup like this they can get pretty risky. So the boss likes to figure it out." He added his own basic philosophy, "When they're dead, they're safe."

Holati Tate was sweating under his clothes when he slid the hopper back out of the vehicle shelter entrance and lifted into the air. Actually, as far as he could tell, everything was rolling along very smoothly, and he could reassure himself with the thought that he was dealing with a group of people who appeared to have proved their competence at this sort of business more than once in the past. If their thinking was up to par, he would be quite safe for the next eight minutes.

But one couldn't be sure.

Somewhat shakily therefore, he gave the hopper its accustomed fix on the Bio Station and put it on automatic. Then taking a coil of wire out of his pocket, he slipped its looped end over the acceleration switch, secured the loop and gave the wire a tentative tug. The hopper responded with a surge of power.

Holati patted another pocket, which contained a package of emergency rations, and sat back to sweat out the remaining minutes. A persistent fluttering started up in the pit of his stomach. His gaze went wistfully once to the collapsed escape bubble on his left. He was getting a little old for field and track work, he thought; the bubble looked very attractive. But he had no way of knowing just how thorough Ramog's preparations had been, and no time to check. So the bubble was out, like the grav-tubes and the heavy rifle in the hopper's emergency locker. Field and track stuff, as if he were a downy cadet! He groaned.

Wooded stretches passed under him and Great Gruesome's lowlands moved into view ahead. Holati cut the hopper's speed to a crawl, dropped to twenty feet and opened the hatch. He edged out, breathing hard and hanging on to his wire with one hand, and as they passed over the first patch of marshy ground he gave the wire a firm tug and jumped. The hopper zoomed off, slanting upward again.

The ground was much wetter than Holati had estimated, but he floundered and waded out in three and a half minutes. A pair of hippopotamus-sized, apparently vegetarian, denizens of Great Gruesome followed him part of the way, bellowing annoyedly, but undertook no overt action.

As he sat down on the first piece of dry earth to pour the mud out of his boots, there was a moderately bright flash in the noonday sky over the approximate center of the swamp-arm behind him. Holati didn't look around but he grunted approvingly. Clean work! Even if someone had been interested in going hunting for fragments of the hopper, they weren't going to invade the center of Great Gruesome to do it. Not very long.

He worked his boots back on, stood up, sighed, and set out squishily on what was going to be a two-day hike back to the Headquarters Station.

2

When the long-awaited announcement of the first artifacts of the legendary Old Galactic civilization finally was flashed from Precol's Manon System to the Federation, the Precol home office and Academy showed an uncharacteristic lack of enthusiasm. The fact that one of their most able and respected field operators had just been lost off Manon in line of duty might have had something to do with it. In the wave of renewed high interest in space exploration which swept the Federation, this detail remained generally unnoticed.

For the discovery was a truly king-sized strike. The riches of robotic information alone which it provided for a dozen interested branches of human science might take a century to be fully utilized. The Old Galactic base on an obscure planetoid circling far beyond the previously established limits of the Manon System was no dead relic; it was a functioning though currently purposeless installation. The best guess was that approximately thirty-two thousand standard years had passed since the constructors of the base had last visited it. Automatically and efficiently since then the installation had continued to reap and process the cyclic abundance of plankton life from Manon's atmosphere.

When the ships which once had carried away its finished products no longer came and the limits of its storage facilities were reached, it piled up the accumulating excess on the little world's lightless surface. But its processing sections remained active, and back and forth between the planetoid and Manon moved the stream of Harvesters, biological robots themselves, and performed their function until a human discoverer set foot on the little world and human hands reached for the controlling switches in the installation that turned the Harvesters off.

So scientists, technicians and reporters came out by the shipload to the Manon System, and for a few months Manon's new Acting Commissioner was an extremely busy man. One day however he summoned his secretary, Trigger Argee, to his new office on what was now popularly though inaccurately known as Harvest Moon and said, "Trigger, we're going for a little trip."

"You're scheduled for three more interviews in the next six hours," Trigger informed him.

"Chelly or Inger can handle them," the Acting Commissioner said.

"Not these," said Trigger. "Reporters. They want more details on the Space Exploits of the Gallant Scout Commander Tate in His Younger Days."

"Hell," Acting Commissioner Tate said, reddening slightly, "I'm too old to enjoy being a hero now. They should have come around thirty years earlier. Let's go."

So they rose presently from the surface of the dark worldlet, with Trigger at the controls of a spacecraft not much bigger than a hopper but capable nevertheless of interstellar jumps, though Trigger hadn't yet been checked out on such maneuvers. It was, as a matter of fact, basically the ferocious little boat of the Space Scouts rebuilt for comfort, which made it a toy for the fabulously wealthy only. The Acting Commissioner, having observed recently that, on the basis of his first-discovery claims to Harvest Moon and its gadgetry, he was now in the fabulously wealthy class, had indulged himself in an old man's whim.

"Here's your course-tape, pilot," he said complacently and settled back into the very comfortable observer's seat on Trigger's right, equipped with its duplicate target screen.

Trigger fed in the tape and settled back also. "Runs itself," she said. "Practically." She was a girl who could appreciate a good ship. "What are you looking for, out in the middle of the Manon System?"

"You'll see when we get there." Trigger gave him a quick look. Then she glanced at the space-duty suit he had brought from the back of the ship and laid behind his seat. "I'm not so sure," she said carefully, "that I'm going to like what I see when we get there."

"Oho!" Holati Tate reached up and tugged down on his left ear lobe. He looked reflective. After a moment he inquired, "How much of this have you got figured out, Trigger girl?"

"Parts of it," Trigger said. "There're some missing pieces, too, though. I've been doing a little investigating on my own," she explained.

Manon's Acting Commissioner cleared his throat. He reached out and made an adjustment on his target screen, peered into the screen, muttered and made another adjustment. Then he said, "What got you going on an investigation?"

"The fact," said Trigger, "that Precol Academy seems willing to let you get away with murder."

"Murder?" He frowned.

"Yes. It didn't take much digging to find out about the Ancient and Honorable Society of Retired Space Scouts. First I'd heard of that outfit." She hesitated. "I suppose you don't mind my saying it doesn't sound like an organization anyone would take seriously?"

"Don't mind at all," said Holati Tate.

"I believe you. In fact, after I'd found there were around twelve thousand of those retired Scouts scattered through Precol—and that you happened to be their president—it occurred to me the Society might have selected that name so nobody *would* take it seriously."

"Hm-m-m." He nodded. "Yes. Bright girl!"

"There may be bright people at the Academy, too," Trigger said. "Bright enough to work out that Commissioner Ramog's departure from our midst was a well-planned execution."

"I'd say I like 'execution' better than 'murder'," Holati remarked judiciously. "But it's still not quite the right word, Trigger girl."

"You prefer 'object lesson'?"

"Well . . . that'll do for the moment. So what did you mean about it's being a well-planned object lesson?"

Trigger shrugged. "Wouldn't it have been a remarkable coincidence if you'd made the Old Galactic strike at just the right instant to help close out Ramog's account?"

"I see." Holati nodded again. "Yes, you're right about that. A few of us discovered Harvest Moon almost three years ago, on a private prospecting run—" He leaned forward suddenly. "Brake her down, pilot! There's a flock of those Harvester things ahead right now. I want to look them over."

She brought the ship to a stop in the middle of a widely scattered dozen of Harvesters, drifting idly through the system as they had been doing since Holati Tate had disconnected the switch that energized them, in an airless underground dome on Harvest Moon, three months before.

Peering out against the green glare of Manon's sun,

Trigger eyed the nearest of the inert hulks with some feeling of physical discomfort. It was very considerably bigger than their ship, and it looked more like some ominously hovering dark monster of space than like an alien work-robot. She became aware that her companion's hands were moving unhurriedly about an instrument panel on the other side of his target screen. Suddenly, first one and then another of the Harvesters was glowing throughout its length as if a greenish light had been switched on inside it. The glow darkened again, as the invisible beam that had been scanning them from the ship went on to others of the group.

"Looks like this bunch was about four weeks out from Manon when the power went off," Holati remarked conversationally. He cut the scanbeam off. "It would have taken them close to two months to make the run to Harvest Moon at the time."

Trigger nodded. "I've seen the figures. Shall I get us back on course?"

"Please do. There's nothing here."

Trigger remained silent until she had gone through the required operations. Then, feeling unaccountably relieved at being in motion again, she said, "I suppose it was your Society that started the rumors about the Manon System being the most likely place for an Old Galactic strike to be made."

"Uh-huh. Sound data back of the rumors, too. We felt that with a sharp operator like Ramog the situation we set up had better be genuine." After a moment, he added, "There really wasn't any way of doing it gently, Trigger girl. That Academy outfit was too cocksure of its position; it needed hard processing. One of the things they had to learn was that—away from civilization, anyway—the members of the Society can play rougher and dirtier than any commissioner they can send out. After all," he concluded mildly, "we've had the training for that. Years of it."

Trigger looked at him curiously. "What puzzles me is that they seem to have got the idea so quickly. I wouldn't have thought Precol Academy would let itself be impressed too much by just one object lesson."

"They might have missed some of the implications," Holati admitted. "However, we gave them a helpful hint."

"Oh?" she said. "What?"

"A formal complaint from our Society, signed by its president. It listed Society members and others who had been killed on Precol Projects in the last ten years, because of the inefficiency, let's say, of specific Project commissioners. The commissioners in question—all members of the Academy—were also listed. Ramog's name happened to be at the head of that list ... and they got the complaint the day after Ramog was reported lost."

Trigger's eyes widened. "Well," she acknowledged, "that's as broad as a hint can get!"

"We weren't trying to be subtle. Murder gets to be hard to prove under Project conditions—there're too many possibilities. So the Academy group is safe enough that way; we aren't accusing anyone of anything worse than inefficiency. But the complaint suggested that the people we listed be withdrawn from active service, as they were obviously unfit for such work."

She smiled briefly. "And since the Society has taken the precaution of turning its president into an extremely famous man, the home office can't resort to obvious counteraction—like firing the whole twelve thousand of you from the various Projects?"

"That would raise a terrible stink, wouldn't it?" Holati said cheerfully. "And, who knows, we might even publish our complaint then. With additional data we could— Slow her down again, will you? We should be pretty close to course end by now."

"A few minutes off," Trigger said reluctantly. "What is it—more Harvesters?"

He was fiddling with the target screen again. "Uh-huh," he said absently. "But we'll move on a little farther. Slow and easy now!"

Trigger kept it slow and easy, ignoring the dark shapes they slid past occasionally. After a while, she said, "There's one thing the Academy must have thought of trying, though—"

"To pin Ramog's disappearance on me?"

She glanced at him. "Perhaps not on you personally. There's evidence enough you'd just started walking back from the edge of the swamps when Ramog climbed into a jet suit, took off for the Moon Belt on an undisclosed mission, and vanished. But it wouldn't be too unreasonable for the Academy to assume that some retired, but not so decrepit Space Scouts, were waiting for him up there when he arrived."

"You know," Holati said with some satisfaction, "that's exactly how they did figure it." He kept his eyes on the screen as he went on. "Naturally, they wouldn't expect us to leave a body floating around, but a really capable investigator doesn't need anything as crude as that in the line of evidence. The Academy had some very good boys combing over the Moon Belt and other parts of the system the past couple of months. There were times when we had to be careful not to trip over them."

"Oh?" said Trigger. "What did they find?"

"Nothing," Holati said. "Naturally. They gave up finally."

She frowned. "How do you know?"

"I get the word. The word I got last week was that the bad eggs in Precol we named on that list are resigning in droves and heading for the Federation. And the men that are being moved up are men we like. Just today," he added, "an Academy courier came in with an official notification for me. I'm confirmed in rank as commissioner now, in permanent charge of the Manon Project."

Trigger Argee sat thoughtfully silent for a while. "So

there really wasn't anyone waiting up in the Moon Belt for Ramog?"

Holati shook his head. "No," he said almost casually. "We never laid a finger on him. Wouldn't have been quite ethical—we had no proof."

Her face began working curiously. "And there was that plankton signal you had me copying for you—Did you ever find out whether it attracted the Harvesters, too?"

He nodded. "Chow call, pure and simple. Now, pilot, do you spot that singleton on your screen over there?"

Trigger's head was swimming for a moment; then she saw the distant dark blob. "Yes," she said faintly.

"Move in on it, adjust to the drift, and stop." She heard him stand up.

"Holati!" It wasn't much more than a gasp. "Are you going out?"

"Well, what else? It won't take long."

Trigger closed her eyes slowly, opened them again and grimly maneuvered the sluggishly gliding boat in on its dark target. From behind her came a series of vague metallic sounds, followed by the snaps of the magnetic suit clamps. She stopped the boat and stared out at the shadow shape swimming like a whale in the tides of space beside them. Soft heavy footsteps passed behind her, moving toward the lock. Waves of horror began crawling over her skin.

The lock hissed, and presently stopped hissing. She was alone. The boat turned slowly, and she found herself staring again at the green blaze of Manon's sun. But the dark thing still floated at the edge of her vision, and now and then it seemed to move slightly. She felt like screaming. Then the lock began hissing again, and stopped again.

He came in slowly and turned to the back of the ship. Something went dragging and bumping heavily across the floor behind him.

She nodded slowly, though he couldn't see that from the back of the ship.

Riding a directional beam, she thought—and the beam pre-set to cut out when he hit the altitude where the Plankton Drift is thickest. So there he hangs wondering what's happened, while the suit is broadcasting to those— *whew!*

"Holati," she said evenly, "I think I'm going to faint."

"Not you," his voice came from the back of the ship. "Or I wouldn't have picked you for the trip." He was breathing heavily. "You can start us back to base now."

Trigger didn't faint. The ship began to move and the thing outside vanished. The thing he had brought inside went with them. Holati made no stir for the moment; she guessed he was glad of a chance to rest.

The happy little monster is right, her thoughts ran on. It wasn't a murder; it wasn't even an execution. They couldn't prove Ramog was a killer, so they tested him. He couldn't climb into that suit until he'd got Holati Tate out of the way. And once he'd done that, he couldn't send anyone else because, with stakes that big there was never anyone else a man like Ramog could trust.

The Society had it set up, all right—

There was a loud metal clang from the back of the ship, and a pale purple glow grew in the dark behind Trigger. The little fuel converter door had been opened. At the same time, something seemed to shut off her breathing.

Holati said conversationally, "Precol Service was a pretty fair organization before the Academy took over, Trigger. Shouldn't be long before it's back in good shape again now—" He stopped and grunted with effort, and there was a sharp cracking sound like a stick of dry wood being broken.

"The Academy's all right," he went on, breathing unevenly again, "for raising funds and things like that. We'll keep it around. But it's out in the field where the fun is, and we intend to keep the fun clean from now on."

The purple light faded; the converter door clanged shut. The little boat's interior lights came on. "All right," Holati said. "You can look around now."

Trigger looked around. There were dark streaks on the floor before the converter door, but the thing that had been brought in from outside was gone. Holati Tate was climbing out of his space-duty suit. He looked at her and closed one eye in a wink that was not, in the slightest degree, humorous.

"Processed!" he said.

Lion Loose

1

For twelve years, at a point where three major shipping routes of the Federation of the Hub crossed within a few hours' flight of one another, the Seventh Star Hotel had floated in space, a great golden sphere, gleaming softly in the void through its translucent shells of battle plastic. The Star had been designed to be much more than a convenient transfer station for travelers and freight; for some years after it was opened to the public, it retained a high rating among the more exotic pleasure resorts of the Hub. The Seventh Star Hotel was the place to have been that season, and the celebrities and fat cats converged on it with their pals and hangers-on. The Star blazed with life, excitement, interstellar scandals, tinkled with streams of credits dancing in from a thousand worlds. In short, it had started out as a paying proposition.

But gradually things changed. The Star's entertainment remained as delightfully outrageous as ever; the cuisine as excellent; the accommodations and service were still above reproach. The fleecing, in general, became no less expertly painless. But one had *been* there. By its eighth year, the Star was dated. Now, in its twelfth, it lived soberly off the liner and freighter trade, four fifths of the guest suites shut down, the remainder irregularly occupied between ship departures.

And in another seven hours, if the plans of certain men went through, the Seventh Star Hotel would abruptly wink out of existence.

Some fifty or sixty early diners were scattered about the tables on the garden terraces of Phalagon House, the Seventh Star Hotel's most exclusive eatery. One of them had just finished his meal, sat smoking and regarding a spiraling flow of exquisitely indicated female figures across the garden's skyscape with an air of friendly approval. He was a large and muscular young man, deeply tanned, with shoulders of impressive thickness, an aquiline nose, and dark, reflective eyes.

After a minute or two, he yawned comfortably, put out the cigarette, and pushed his chair back from the table. As he came to his feet, there was a soft bell-note from the table ComWeb. He hesitated, said, "Go ahead."

"Is intrusion permitted?" the ComWeb inquired.

"Depends," the guest said. "Who's calling?"

"The name is Reetal Destone."

He grinned, appeared pleasantly surprised. "Put the lady through."

There was a brief silence. Then a woman's voice inquired softly, "Quillan?"

"Right here, doll! Where—"

"Seal the ComWeb, Quillan."

He reached down to the instrument, tapped the seal button, said, "All right. We're private."

"Probably," the woman's voice said. "But better scramble this, too. I want to be very sure no one's listening."

Quillan grunted, slid his left hand into an inner coat pocket, briefly fingered a device of the approximate size and shape of a cigarette, drew his hand out again. "Scrambling!" he announced. "Now, what—"

"Mayday, Quillan," the soft voice said. "Can you come immediately?"

Quillan's face went expressionless. "Of course. Is it urgent?"

"I'm in no present danger. But we'd better waste no time."

"Is it going to take real hardware? I'm carrying a finger gun at the moment."

"Then go to your rooms and pick up something useful," Reetal said. "This should take real hardware, all right."

"All right. Then where do I go?"

"I'll meet you at your door. I know where it is."

When Quillan arrived, she was standing before the door to his suite, a tall blonde in a sleeveless black and gold sheath; a beautiful body, a warm, lovely, humorous face. The warmth and humor were real, but masked a mind as impersonally efficient as a computer, and a taste for high and dangerous living. When Quillan had last met Reetal Destone, a year and a half before, the taste was being satisfied in industrial espionage. He hadn't heard of her activities since then.

She smiled thoughtfully at him as he came up. "I'll wait outside," she said. "We're not talking here."

Quillan nodded, went on into his living room, selected a gun belt and holstered gun from a suitcase, fastened the belt around his waist under the coat, and came out. "Now what?"

"First a little portal-hopping—"

He followed her across the corridor and into a tube portal, watched as she tapped out a setting. The exit light flashed a moment later; they stepped out into a vacant lounge elsewhere in the same building, crossed it, entered another portal. After three more shifts, they emerged into a long hall, dimly lit, heavily carpeted. There was no one in sight.

"Last stop," Reetal said. She glanced up at his face. "We're on the other side of the Star now, in one of the sections they've closed up. I've established a kind of emergency headquarters here. The Star's nearly broke, did you know?"

"I'd heard of it."

"That appears to be part of the reason for what's going on."

Quillan said, "What's going on?"

Reetal slid her arm through his, said, "Come on. That's my, hm-m-m, unregistered suite over there. Big boy, it's very, very selfish of me, but I was extremely glad to detect your name on the list of newly arrived guests just now! As to what's going on . . . the *Camelot* berths here at midnight, you know."

Quillan nodded. "I've some business with one of her passengers."

Reetal bent to unlock the entrance door to the indicated suite. "The way it looks now," she remarked, "the odds are pretty high that you're not going to keep that appointment."

"Why not?"

"Because shortly after the *Camelot* docks and something's been unloaded from her, the *Camelot* and the Seventh Star Hotel are scheduled to go *poof!* together. Along with you, me, and some twelve thousand other people. And, so far, I haven't been able to think of a good way to keep it from happening."

Quillan was silent a moment. "Who's scheduling the poof?" he asked.

"Some old acquaintances of ours are among them. Come on in. What they're doing comes under the heading of destroying the evidence."

❖   ❖   ❖

She locked the door behind them, said, "Just a moment," went over to the paneled wall, turned down a tiny silver switch. "Room portal," she said, nodding at the wall. "It might come in handy. I keep it turned off most of the time."

"Why are you turning it on now?" Quillan asked.

"One of the Star's stewards is working on this with me. He'll be along as soon as he can get away. Now I'll give you the whole thing as briefly as I can. The old acquaintances I mentioned are some boys of the Brotherhood of Beldon. Movaine's here; he's got Marras Cooms and Fluel with him, and around thirty of the Brotherhood's top guns. Nome Lancion's coming in on the *Camelot* in person tonight to take charge. Obviously, with all that brass on the job, they're after something very big. Just what it is, I don't yet know. I've got one clue, but a rather puzzling one. Tell you about that later. Do you know Velladon?"

"The commodore here?" Quillan nodded. "I've never met him but I know who he is."

Reetal said, "He's been manager of the Seventh Star Hotel for the past nine years. He's involved in the Beldon outfit's operation. So is the chief of the Star's private security force—his name's Ryter—and half a dozen other Star executives. They've got plenty of firepower, too; close to half the entire security force, I understand, including all the officers. That would come to nearly seventy men. There's reason to believe the rest of the force was disarmed and murdered by them in the subspace section of the Star about twelve hours ago. They haven't been seen since then.

"Now, Velladon, aside from his share in whatever they're after, has another reason for wanting to wipe out the Star in an unexplained blowup. There I have definite information. Did you know the Mooley brothers owned the Star?"

"Yes."

"I've been working for the Mooleys the past eight months," Reetal said, "checking up on employees at Velladon's level for indications of graft. And it appears the commodore has been robbing them blind here for at least several years."

"Sort of risky thing to try with the Mooleys, from what I hear," Quillan remarked.

"Yes. Very. Velladon had reason to be getting a little desperate about that. Two men were planted here a month ago. One of them is Sher Heraga, the steward I told you about. The other man came in as a bookkeeper. Two weeks ago, Heraga got word out that the bookkeeper had disappeared. Velladon and Ryter apparently got wise to what he was trying to do. So the Mooleys sent me here to find out exactly what was going on before they took action. I arrived four days ago."

She gave a regretful little headshake. "I waited almost a day before contacting Heraga. It seemed advisable to move very cautiously in the matter. But that made it a little too late to do anything. Quillan, for the past three days, the Seventh Star Hotel has been locked up like a bank vault. And except for ourselves, only the people who are in on the plot are aware of it."

"The message transmitters are inoperative?" he asked.

Reetal nodded. "The story is that a gravitic storm center in the area has disrupted transmissions completely for the time being."

"What about incoming ships?"

"Yours was the only one scheduled before the *Camelot* arrives. It left again eight hours ago. Nobody here had been let on board. The guests who wanted to apply for outgoing berths were told there were none open, that they'd have to wait for the *Camelot*."

She went over to a desk, unlocked a drawer, took out a sheaf of papers, and handed one of them to Quillan. "That's the layout of the Star," she said. "This five-level building over by the shell is the Executive Block. The

Brotherhood and the commodore's men moved in there this morning. The Block is the Star's defense center. It's raid-proofed, contains the control offices and the transmitter and armament rooms. About the standard arrangement. While they hold the Executive Block, they have absolute control of the Star."

"If it's the defense center, it should be practically impossible to do anything about them there," Quillan agreed. "They could close it up, and dump the air out of the rest of the Star in a minute, if they had to. But there must be . . . well, what about the lifeboats in the subspace section—and our pals must have a getaway ship stashed away somewhere?"

"They have two ships," Reetal said. "A souped-up armed freighter the Brotherhood came in on, and a large armed yacht which seems to be the commodore's personal property. Unfortunately, they're both in subspace locks."

"Why unfortunately?"

"Because they've sealed off subspace. Try portaling down there, and you'll find yourself looking at a battle-plastic bulkhead. There's no way of getting either to those ships or to the lifeboats."

Quillan lifted his eyebrows. "And *that* hasn't caused any comment? What about the maintenance crews, the warehouse men, the—"

"All the work crews were hauled out of subspace this morning," Reetal said. "On the quiet, the Star's employees have been told that a gang of raiders was spotted in the warehouse area, and is at present cornered there. Naturally, the matter isn't to be mentioned to the guests, to avoid arousing unnecessary concern. And that explains everything very neatly. The absence of the security men, and why subspace is sealed off. Why the Executive Block is under guard, and can't be entered—and why the technical and office personnel in there don't come out, and don't communicate out. They've been put on emergency status, officially."

❖   ❖   ❖

"Yunk," Quillan said disgustedly after a moment. "This begins to look like a hopeless situation, doll!"

"True."

"Let's see now—"

Reetal interrupted, "There is one portal still open to subspace. That's in the Executive Block, of course, and Heraga reports it's heavily guarded."

"How does he know?"

"The Block's getting its meals from Phalagon House. He floated a diner in there a few hours ago."

"Well," Quillan said, brightening, "perhaps a deft flavoring of poison—"

Reetal shook her head. "I checked over the hospital stocks. Not a thing there that wouldn't be spotted at once. Unless we can clobber them thoroughly, we can't afford to make them suspicious with a trick like that."

"Poison would be a bit rough on the office help, too," Quillan conceded. "They wouldn't be in on the deal."

"No, they're not. They're working under guard."

"Gas . . . no, I suppose not. It would take too long to whip up something that could turn the trick." Quillan glanced at his watch. "If the *Camelot* docks at midnight, we've around six and a half hours left, doll! And I don't find myself coming up with any brilliant ideas. What have you thought of?"

Reetal hesitated a moment "Nothing very brilliant either," she said then. "But there are two things we might try as a last resort."

"Let's hear them."

"I know a number of people registered in the Star at present who'd be carrying personal weapons. If they were told the facts, I could probably line up around twenty who'd be willing to make a try to get into the Executive Block, and take over either the control offices or the transmitter room. If we got a warning out to the *Camelot*, that would break up the plot. Of course, it wouldn't necessarily save the Star."

"No," Quillan said, "but it's worth trying if we can't think of something better. How would you get them inside?"

"We could crowd twenty men into one of those diner trucks, and Heraga could take us in."

"What kind of people are your pals?"

"A few smugglers and confidence men I've had connections with. Fairly good boys for this sort of thing. Then there's an old millionaire sportsman, with a party of six, waiting to transfer to the *Camelot* for a safari on Jontarou. Old Philmarron isn't all there, in my opinion, but he's dead game and loves any kind of a ruckus. We can count on him and his friends, if they're not too drunk at the moment. Still . . . that's not too many to set against something less than a hundred professional guns, even though some of them must be down on the two ships."

"No, not enough." Quillan looked thoughtful. "What's the other idea?"

"Let the cat out of the bag generally. Tell the guests and the employees out here what's going on, and see if somebody can think of something that might be done."

He shook his head. "What you'd set off with that would be anywhere between a riot and a panic. The boys in the Executive Block would simply give us the breathless treatment. Apparently, they prefer to have everything looking quiet and normal when the *Camelot* gets here—"

"But they don't have to play it that way," Reetal agreed. "We might be dead for hours before the liner docks. If they keep the landing lock closed until what they want has been unloaded, nobody on the *Camelot* would realize what had happened before it was too late."

There was a moment's silence. Then Quillan said, "You mentioned you'd picked up a clue to what they're after. What was that?"

"Well, that's a curious thing," Reetal said. "On the trip out here, a young girl name of Solvey Kinmarten attached herself to me. She didn't want to talk much, but I gathered she was newly married, and that her husband was on board and was neglecting her. She's an appealing little thing, and she seemed so forlorn and upset that I adopted her for the rest of the run. After we arrived, of course, I pretty well forgot about the Kinmartens and their troubles.

"A few hours ago, Solvey suddenly came bursting into the suite where I'm registered. She was shaking all over. After I calmed her down a bit, she spilled out her story. She and her husband, Brock Kinmarten, are rest wardens. With another man named Eltak, whom Solvey describes as 'some sort of crazy old coot,' they're assigned to escort two deluxe private rest cubicles to a very exclusive sanatorium on Mezmiali. But Brock told Solvey at the beginning of the trip that this was a very unusual assignment, that he didn't want her even to come near the cubicles. That wouldn't have bothered her so much, she says, but on the way here Brock became increasingly irritable and absent-minded. She knew he was worrying about the cubicles, and she began to wonder whether they weren't involved in something illegal. The pay was very high; they're both getting almost twice the regular warden fee for the job. One day, she found an opportunity to do a little investigating.

"The cubicles are registered respectively to a Lady Pendrake and a Major Pendrake. Lady Pendrake appears to be genuine; the cubicle is unusually large and constructed somewhat differently from the ones with which Solvey was familiar, but it was clear that it had an occupant. However, the life indicator on 'Major Pendrake's' cubicle registered zero when she switched it on. If there was something inside it, it wasn't a living human being.

"That was all she learned at the time, because she was afraid Brock might catch her in the cubicle room. Here in the Star, the cubicles were taken to a suite reserved for Lady Pendrake. The other man, Eltak, stayed in the suite with the cubicles, while the Kinmartens were given other quarters. However, Brock was still acting oddly and spending most of his time in the Pendrake suite. So this morning, Solvey swiped his key to the suite and slipped in when she knew the two men had left it.

"She'd barely got there when she heard Brock and Eltak at the door again. She ran into the next room, and hid in a closet. Suddenly there was a commotion in the front room, and Solvey realized that men from the Star's security force had arrived and were arresting Brock and Eltak. They hauled both of them away, then floated the cubicles out on a carrier and took them off too, locking the suite behind them.

"Solvey was in a complete panic, sure that she and Brock had become involved in some serious breach of the Warden Code. She waited a few minutes, then slipped out of the Pendrake suite, and looked me up to see if I couldn't help them. I had Heraga check, and he reported that the Kinmarten suite was under observation. Evidently, they wanted to pick up the girl, too. So I tucked her away in one of the suites in this section, and gave her something to put her to sleep. She's there now."

Quillan said, "And where are the prisoners and the cubicles?"

"In the Executive Block."

"How do you know?"

Reetal smiled briefly. "The Duke of Fluel told me."

"Huh? The Brotherhood knows you're here?"

"Relax," Reetal said. "Nobody but Heraga knows I'm working for the Mooleys. I told the Duke I had a big con deal set up when the *Camelot* came in—I even suggested he might like to get in on it. He laughed, and said he had other plans. But he won't mention to anyone that I'm here."

"Why not?"

"Because," Reetal said dryly, "what the Duke is planning to get in on is an hour of tender dalliance. Before the *Camelot* arrives, necessarily. The cold-blooded little skunk!" She hesitated a moment; when she spoke again, her voice had turned harsh and nasal, wicked amusement sounding through it. "Sort of busy at the moment, sweetheart, but we might find time for a drink or two later on in the evening, eh?"

Quillan grunted. "You're as good at the voice imitations as ever. How did you find out about the cubicles?"

"I took a chance and fed him a Moment of Truth."

"With Fluel," Quillan said thoughtfully, "that *was* taking a chance!"

"Believe me, I was aware of it! I've run into card-carrying sadists before, but the Duke's the only one who scares me silly. But it did work. He dropped in for about a minute and a half, and came out without noticing a thing. Meanwhile, I'd got the answers to a few questions. The bomb with which they're planning to mop up behind them already has been planted up here in the norm-space section. Fluel didn't know where; armaments experts took care of it. It's armed now. There's a firing switch on each of their ships, and both switches have to be tripped before the thing goes off. Part of what they're after is in those Pendrake rest cubicles—"

"Part of it?" Quillan asked.

"Uh-huh. An even hundred similar cubicles will be unloaded from the *Camelot*—the bulk of the haul; which is why Nome Lancion is supervising things on the liner. I started to ask what was in the cubicles, but I saw Fluel was beginning to lose that blank look they have under Truth, and switched back to light chitchat just before he woke up. Yaco's paying for the job—or rather, it *will* pay for the stuff, on delivery, and no questions asked."

"That's not very much help, is it?" Quillan said after

a moment. "Something a big crooked industrial combine like Yaco thinks it can use—"

"It must expect to be able to use it to extremely good advantage," Reetal said. "The Brotherhood will collect thirty million credits for their part of the operation. The commodore's group presumably won't do any worse." She glanced past Quillan toward the room portal. "It's O.K., Heraga! Come in."

Sher Heraga was a lean, dark-skinned little man with a badly bent nose, black curly hair, and a nervous look. He regretted, he said, that he hadn't been able to uncover anything which might be a lead to the location of the bomb. Apparently, it wasn't even being guarded. And, of course, a bomb of the size required here would be quite easy to conceal.

"If they haven't placed guards over it," Reetal agreed, "it'll take blind luck to spot it! Unless we can get hold of one of the men who knows where it's planted—"

There was silence for some seconds. Then Quillan said, "Well, if we can't work out a good plan, we'd better see what we can do with one of the bad ones. Are the commodore's security men wearing uniforms?"

Heraga shook his head. "Not the ones I saw."

"Then here's an idea," Quillan said. "As things stand, barging into the Executive Block with a small armed group can't accomplish much. It might be more interesting than sitting around and waiting to be blown up, but it still would be suicide. However, if we could get things softened up and disorganized in there first—"

"Softened up and disorganized how?" Reetal asked.

"We can use that notion you had of having Heraga float in another diner. This time, I'm on board—in a steward's uniform, in case the guards check."

"They didn't the first time," Heraga said.

"Sloppy of them. Well, they're just gun hands. Anyway,

once we're inside I shuck off the uniform and get out. Heraga delivers his goodies, and leaves again—"

Reetal gave him a look. "You'll get shot down the instant you're seen, dope!"

"I think not. There're two groups in there—around a hundred men in all—and they haven't had time to get well acquainted yet. I'll have my gun in sight, and anyone who sees me should figure I belong to the other group, until I run into one of the Brotherhood boys who knows me personally."

"Then that's when you get shot down. I understand the last time you and the Duke of Fluel met, he woke up with lumps."

"The Duke doesn't love me," Quillan admitted. "But there's nothing personal between me and Movaine or Marras Cooms—and I'll have a message for Movaine."

"What kind of a message?"

"I'll have to play that by ear a little. It depends on how things look in there. But I have a few ideas, based on what you've learned of the operation. Now, just what I can do when I get that far, I don't know yet. I'll simply try to louse the deal up as much as I can. That may take time, and, of course, it might turn out to be impossible to get word out to you."

"So what do we do meanwhile?" Reetal asked. "If we start lining up our attack group immediately, and then there's no action for another five or six hours, there's always the chance of a leak, with around twenty people in the know."

"And if there's a leak," Quillan agreed, "we've probably had it. No, you'd better wait with that! If I'm not out, and you haven't heard from me before the *Camelot's* actually due to dock, Heraga can still take the group— everyone but yourself—in as scheduled."

"Why everyone but me?" Reetal asked.

"If nothing else works, you might find some way of getting a warning to the liner's security force after they've docked. It isn't much of a possibility, but we can't afford to throw it away."

"Yes, I see." Reetal looked reflective. "What do you think, Heraga?"

The little man shrugged. "You told me that Mr. Quillan is not inexperienced in dealing with, ah, his enemies. If he feels he might accomplish something in the Executive Block, I'm in favor of the plan. The situation certainly could hardly become worse."

"That's the spirit!" Quillan approved. "The positive outlook—that's what a thing like this mainly takes. Can you arrange for the diner and the uniform?"

"Oh, yes," Heraga said. "I've had myself put in charge of that detail, naturally."

"Then what can you tell me about the Executive Block's layout?"

Reetal stood up. "Come over to the desk," she said. "We've got diagrams."

"The five levels, as you see," Heraga was explaining a few moments later, "are built directly into the curve of the Star's shells. Level Five, on the top, is therefore quite small. The other levels are fairly extensive. Two, Three, and Four could each accommodate a hundred men comfortably. These levels contain mainly living quarters, private offices, and the like. The Brotherhood men appear to be occupying the fourth level; Velladon's group the second. The third may be reserved for meetings between representatives of the two groups. All three of these levels are connected by single-exit portals to the large entrance area on the ground level.

"The portals stood open when I went in earlier today, and there were about twenty armed men lounging about the entrance hall. I recognized approximately half of them as being members of the Star's security force. The others were unfamiliar." Heraga cleared his throat. "There is a possibility that the two groups do not entirely trust each other."

Quillan nodded. "If they're playing around with something like sixty million CR, anybody would have to be crazy to trust the Brotherhood of Beldon. The transmitter room and the control offices are guarded, too?"

"Yes, but not heavily," Heraga said. "There seem to be only a few men stationed at each of those points. Ostensibly, they're there as a safeguard—in case the imaginary raiders attempt to break out of the subspace section."

"What's the arrangement of the ordinary walk-in tube portals in the Executive Block?"

"There is one which interconnects the five levels. On each of the lower levels there are, in addition, several portals which lead out to various points in the Seventh Star Hotel. On the fifth level, there is only one portal of this kind. Except for the portal which operates between the different levels in the Executive Block, all of them have been rendered unusable at present."

"Unusable in what way?"

"They have been sealed off on the Executive Block side."

"Can you get me a diagram of the entry and exit systems those outgoing portals connect with?" Quillan asked. "I might turn one of them usable again."

"Yes, I can do that."

"How about the communication possibilities?"

"The ComWeb system is functioning normally on the second, third, and fourth levels. It has been shut off on the first level—to avoid the spread of 'alarming rumors' by office personnel. There is no ComWeb on the fifth level."

Reetal said, "We'll shift our operating headquarters back to my registered suite then. The ComWebs are turned off in these vacant sections. I'll stay in the other suite in case you find a chance to signal in."

Heraga left a few minutes later to make his arrangements. Reetal smiled at Quillan, a little dubiously.

"Good luck, guy," she said. "Anything else to settle before you start off?"

Quillan nodded. "Couple of details. If you're going to be in your regular suite, and Fluel finds himself with some idle time on hand, he might show up for the dalliance you mentioned."

Reetal's smile changed slightly. Her left hand fluffed the hair at the back of her head, flicked down again. There was a tiny click, and Quillan looked at a small jeweled hair-clasp in her palm, its needle beak pointing at him.

"It hasn't got much range," Reetal said, "but within ten feet it will scramble the Duke's brains just as thoroughly as they need to be scrambled."

"Good enough," Quillan said. "Just don't give that boy the ghost of a chance, doll. He has a rep for playing very un-nice games with the ladies."

"I know his reputation." Reetal replaced the tiny gun in her hair. "Anything else?"

"Yes. Let's look in on the Kinmarten girl for a moment. If she's awake, she may have remembered something or other by now that she didn't think to tell you."

They found Solvey Kinmarten awake, and tearfully glad to see Reetal. Quillan was introduced as a member of the legal profession who would do what he could for Solvey and her husband. Solvey frowned prettily, trying very hard to remember anything that might be of use. But it appeared that she had told Reetal all she knew.

2

The blue and white Phalagon House diner, driven by Heraga, was admitted without comment into the

Executive Block. It floated on unchallenged through the big entry hall and into a corridor. Immediately behind the first turn of the corridor, the diner paused a few seconds. Its side door opened and closed. The diner moved on.

Quillan, coatless and with the well-worn butt of a big Miam Devil Special protruding from the holster on his right hip, came briskly back along the corridor. Between fifteen and twenty men, their guns also conspicuously in evidence, were scattered about the entrance hall, expressions and attitudes indicating a curious mixture of boredom and uneasy tension. The eyes of about half of them swiveled around to Quillan when he came into the hall; then, with one exception, they looked indifferently away again.

The exception, leaning against the wall near the three open portals to the upper levels, continued to stare as Quillan came toward him, forehead creased in a deep scowl as if he were painfully ransacking his mind for something. Quillan stopped in front of him.

"Chum," he asked, "any idea where Movaine is at the moment? They just give me this message for him—"

Still scowling, the other scratched his chin and blinked. "Uh . . . dunno for sure," he said after a moment. "He oughta be in the third level conference room with the rest of 'em. Uh . . . dunno you oughta barge in there right now, pal! The commodore's *reeelly* hot about somethin'!"

Quillan looked worried. "Gotta chance it, I guess! Message is pretty important, they say—" He turned, went through the center portal of the three, abruptly found himself walking along a wide, well-lit hall.

Nobody in sight here, or in the first intersecting passage he came to. When he reached the next passage he heard voices on the right, turned toward them, went by a string of closed doors on both sides until, forty feet on, the passage angled again and opened into a long, high-ceilinged room. The voices came through an open door on the right side of the room. Standing against the wall beside the door were two men whose heads turned sharply toward Quillan as he appeared in the passage. The short, chunky one scowled. The big man next to him, the top of whose head had been permanently seared clear of hair years before by a near miss from a blaster, dropped his jaw slowly. His eyes popped.

"My God!" he said.

"Movaine in there, Baldy?" Quillan inquired, coming up.

"Movaine! He . . . you . . . how—"

The chunky man took out his gun, waved it negligently at Quillan. "Tell the ape to blow, Perk. He isn't wanted here."

"Ape?" Quillan asked softly. His right hand moved, had the gun by the barrel, twisted, reversed the gun, jammed it back with some violence into the chunky man's stomach. "Ape?" he repeated. The chunky man went white.

"Bad News—" Baldy Perk breathed. "Take it easy! That's Orca. He's the commodore's torpedo. How—"

"Where's Movaine?"

"Movaine . . . he . . . uh—"

"All right, he's not here. And Lancion can't have arrived yet. Is Cooms in there?"

"Yeah," Baldy Perk said weakly. "Cooms is in there, Quillan."

"Let's go in." Quillan withdrew the gun, slid it into a pocket, smiled down at Orca. "Get it back from your boss, slob. Be seeing you!"

Orca's voice was a husky whisper.

"You will, friend! You will!"

The conference room was big and sparsely furnished. Four men sat at the long table in its center. Quillan knew two of them—Marras Cooms, second in command of the Beldon Brotherhood's detachment here, and the Duke of Fluel, Movaine's personal gun. Going by Heraga's descriptions, the big, florid-faced man with white hair and flowing white mustaches who was doing the talking was Velladon, the commodore; while the fourth man, younger, wiry, with thinning black hair plastered back across his skull, would be Ryter, chief of the Star's security force.

"What I object to primarily is that the attempt was made without obtaining my consent, and secretly," Velladon was saying, with a toothy grin but in a voice that shook with open fury. "And now it's been made and bungled, you have a damn nerve asking for our help. The problem is yours—and you better take care of it fast! I can't spare Ryter. If—"

"Cooms," Baldy Perk broke in desperately from the door, "Bad News Quillan's here an'—"

The heads of the four men at the table came around simultaneously. The eyes of two of them widened for an instant. Then Marras Cooms began laughing softly.

"Now everything's happened!" he said.

"Cooms," the commodore said testily, "I prefer not to be interrupted. Now—"

"Can't be helped, commodore," Quillan said, moving forward, Perk shuffling along unhappily beside him. "I've got news for Movaine, and the news can't wait."

"Movaine?" the commodore repeated, blue eyes bulging at Quillan. "Movaine! Cooms, who *is* this man?"

"You're looking at Bad News Quillan," Cooms said. "A hijacking specialist, with somewhat numerous sidelines. But the point right now is that he isn't a member of the Brotherhood."

"*What!*" Velladon's big fist smashed down on the table. "*Now* what kind of a game . . . how did he get *in* here?"

"Well," Quillan said mildly, "I oozed in through the north wall about a minute ago. I—"

He checked, conscious of having created some kind of sensation. The four men at the table were staring up at him without moving. Baldy Perk appeared to be holding his breath. Then the commodore coughed, cleared his throat, drummed his fingers on the table.

He said reflectively: "He could have news—good or bad—at that! For all of us." He chewed on one of his mustache tips, grinned suddenly up at Quillan. "Well, sit down, friend! Let's talk. You can't talk to Movaine, you see. Movaine's, um, had an accident. Passed away suddenly half an hour ago."

"Sorry to hear it," Quillan said. "That's the sort of thing that happens so often in the Brotherhood." He swung a chair around, sat down facing the table. "You're looking well tonight, Fluel," he observed.

The Duke of Fluel, lean and dapper in silver jacket and tight-fitting silver trousers, gave him a wintry smile, said nothing.

"Now, then, friend," Velladon inquired confidentially, "just what was your business with Movaine?"

"Well, it will come to around twenty per cent of the take," Quillan informed him. "We won't argue about a half-million CR more or less. But around twenty per."

The faces turned thoughtful. After some seconds, the commodore asked, "And who's we?"

"A number of citizens," Quillan said, "who have been rather unhappy since discovering that you, too, are interested in Lady Pendrake and her pals. We'd gone to considerable expense and trouble to . . . well, her ladyship was scheduled to show up in Mezmiali, you know. And now she isn't going to show up there. All right, that's business. Twenty per—no hard feelings. Otherwise, it won't do you a bit of good to blow up the Star and the liner. There'd still be loose talk—maybe other complications, too. You know how it goes. You wouldn't be happy, and neither would Yaco. Right?"

The commodore's massive head turned back to Cooms. "How well do you know this man, Marras?"

Cooms grinned dryly. "Well enough."

"Is he leveling?"

"He'd be nuts to be here if he wasn't. And he isn't nuts—at least, not that way."

"There might be a question about that," Fluel observed. He looked at the commodore. "Why not ask him for a couple of the names that are in it with him?"

"Hagready and Boltan," Quillan said.

Velladon chewed the other mustache tip. "I know Hagready. If he—"

"I know both of them," Cooms said. "Boltan works hijacking crews out of Orado. Quillan operates there occasionally."

"Pappy Boltan's an old business associate," Quillan agreed. "Reliable sort of a guy. Doesn't mind taking a few chances either."

Velladon's protruding blue eyes measured him a moment. "We can check on those two, you know—"

"Check away," Quillan said.

Velladon nodded. "We will." He was silent for a second or two, then glanced over at Cooms. "There've been no leaks on our side," he remarked. "And they must have known about this for weeks! Of all the inept, bungling—"

"Ah, don't be too hard on the Brotherhood, commodore," Quillan said. "Leaks happen. You ought to know."

"What do you mean?" Velladon snapped.

"From what we heard, the Brotherhood's pulling you out of a hole here. You should feel rather kindly toward them."

The commodore stared at him reflectively. Then he grinned. "Could be I should," he said. "Did you come here alone?"

"Yes."

The commodore nodded. "If you're bluffing, God help you. If you're not, your group's in. Twenty per. No time for haggling—we can raise Yaco's price to cover it." He stood up, and Ryter stood up with him. "Marras," the commodore went on, "tell him what's happened. If he's half as hot as he sounds, he's the boy to put on that job. Let him get in on a little of the work for the twenty per cent. Ryter, come on. We—"

"One moment, sir," Quillan interrupted. He took Orca's gun by the muzzle from his pocket, held it out to Velladon. "One of your men lost this thing. The one outside the door. If you don't mind—he might pout if he doesn't get it back."

The fifth level of the Executive Block appeared to be, as Heraga had said, quite small. The tiny entry hall, on which two walk-in portals opened, led directly into the large room where the two Pendrake rest cubicles had been placed. One of the cubicles now stood open. To right and left, a narrow passage stretched away from the room, ending apparently in smaller rooms.

Baldy Perk was perspiring profusely.

"Now right here," he said in a low voice, "was where I was standing. Movaine was over there, on the right of the cubicle, and Cooms was beside him. Rubero was a little behind me, hanging on to the punk—that Kinmarten. An' the Duke"—he nodded back at the wide doorspace to the hall—"was standing back there."

"All right. The punk's opened the cubicle a crack, looking like he's about to pass out while he's doin' it. This bearded guy, Eltak, stands in front of the cubicle, holding the gadget he controls the thing with—"

"Where's the gadget now?" Quillan asked.

"Marras Cooms' got it."

"How does it work?"

Baldy shook his head. "We can't figure it out. It's got all kinds of little knobs and dials on it. Push this one an' it squeaks, turn that one an' it buzzes. Like that."

Quillan nodded. "All right. What happened?"

"Well, Movaine tells the old guy to go ahead an' do the demonstrating. The old guy sort of grins and fiddles with the gadget. The cubicle door pops open an' this thing comes pouring out. I never seen nothin' like it! It's like a barn door with dirty fur on it! It swirls up an' around an'—it wraps its upper end clean around poor Movaine. He never even screeches."

"Then everything pops at once. The old guy is laughing like crazy, an' that half-smart Rubero drills him right through the head. I take one shot at the thing, low so's not to hit Movaine, an' then we're all running. I'm half-way to the hall when Cooms tears past me like a rocket. The Duke an' the others are already piling out through the portal. I get to the hall, and there's this terrific smack of sound in the room. I look back . . . an' . . . an'—" Baldy paused and gulped.

"And what?" Quillan asked.

"There, behind the cubicles, I see poor Movaine stickin' halfway out o' the wall!" Baldy reported in a hushed whisper.

"*Half*way out of the wall?"

"From the waist up he's in it! From the waist down he's dangling into the room! I tell you, I never seen nothin' like it."

"And this Hlat creature—"

"That's gone. I figure the smack I heard was when it hit the wall flat, carrying Movaine. It went on into it. Movaine didn't—at least, the last half of him didn't."

"Well," Quillan said after a pause, "in a way, Movaine got his demonstration. The Hlats can move through solid matter and carry other objects along with them, as advertised. If Yaco can work out how it's done and build a gadget that does the same thing, they're getting the Hlats cheap. What happened then?"

"I told Marras Cooms about Movaine, and he sent me and a half dozen other boys back up here with riot guns to see what we could do for him. Which was nothin', of course." Baldy gulped again. "We finally cut this end of him off with a beam and took it back down."

"The thing didn't show up while you were here?"

Baldy shuddered and said, "Naw."

"And the technician . . . was dead?"

"Sure. Hole in his head you could shove your fist through."

"Somebody," Quillan observed, "ought to drill Rubero for that stupid trick!"

"The Duke did—first thing after we got back to the fourth level."

"So the Hlat's on the loose, and all we really have at the moment are the cubicles . . . and Rest Warden Kinmarten. Where's he, by the way?"

"He tried to take off when we got down to Level Four, an' somebody cold-cocked him. The doc says he ought to be coming around again pretty soon."

Quillan grunted, shoved the Miam Devil Special into its holster, said, "O.K., you stay here where you can watch the room and those passages and the hall. If you feel the floor start moving under you, scream. I'll take a look at the cubicle."

Lady Pendrake's cubicle was about half as big again as a standard one; but, aside from one detail, its outer settings, instruments, and operating devices appeared normal. The modification was a recess almost six feet long and a foot wide and deep, in one side, which could be opened either to the room or to the interior of the rest cubicle, but not simultaneously to both. Quillan already knew its purpose; the supposed other cubicle was a camouflaged food locker, containing fifty-pound slabs of sea beef, each of which represented a meal for the Hlat. The recess made it possible to feed it without allowing it to be seen, or, possibly, attempting to emerge. Kinmarten's nervousness, as reported by his wife, seemed understandable. Any rest warden might get disturbed over such a charge.

Quillan asked over his shoulder, "Anyone find out yet why the things can't get out of a closed rest cubicle?"

"Yeah," Baldy Perk said. "Kinmarten says it's the cubicle's defense fields. They could get through the material. They can't get through the field."

"Someone think to energize the Executive Block's battle fields?" Quillan inquired.

"Yeah. Velladon took care of that before he came screaming up to the third level to argue with Cooms and Fluel."

"So it can't slip out of the Block unless it shows itself down on the ground level when the entry lock's open."

"Yeah," Baldy muttered. "But I dunno. Is that good?"

Quillan looked at him. "Well, we *would* like it back."

"Why? There's fifty more coming in on the liner tonight"

"We don't have the fifty yet. If someone louses up that detail—"

"Yawk!" Baldy said faintly. There was a crash of sound as his riot gun went off. Quillan spun about, hair bristling, gun out. "What happened?"

"I'll swear," Baldy said, white-faced, "I saw something moving along that passage!"

Quillan looked, saw nothing, slowly replaced the gun. "Baldy," he said, "if you think you see it again, just say so. That's an order! If it comes at us, we get out of this level fast. But we don't shoot before we have to. If we kill it, it's no good to us. Got that?"

"Yeah," Baldy said. "But I got an idea now, Bad News." He nodded at the other cubicle. "Let's leave that meat box open."

"Why?"

"If it's hungry," Baldy explained simply, "I'd sooner it wrapped itself around a few chunks of sea beef, an' not around me."

Quillan punched him encouragingly in the shoulder. "Baldy," he said, "in your own way, you *have* had an idea! But we won't leave the meat box open. When Kinmarten wakes up, I want him to show me how to bait this cubicle with a piece of sea beef, so it'll snap shut if the Hlat goes inside. Meanwhile it won't hurt if it gets a little hungry."

"That," said Baldy, "isn't the way I feel about it."

"There must be around a hundred and fifty people in the Executive Block at present," Quillan said. "Look at it that way! Even if the thing keeps stuffing away, your odds are pretty good, Baldy."

Baldy shuddered.

Aside from a dark bruise high on his forehead, Brock Kinmarten showed no direct effects of having been knocked out. However, his face was strained and his voice not entirely steady. It was obvious that the young rest warden had never been in a similarly unnerving situation before. But he was making a valiant effort not to appear frightened and, at the same time, to indicate that he would co-operate to the best of his ability with his captors.

He'd regained consciousness by the time Quillan and Perk returned to the fourth level, and Quillan suggested bringing him to Marras Cooms' private quarters for questioning. The Brotherhood chief agreed; he was primarily interested in finding out how the Hlat-control device functioned.

Kinmarten shook his head. He knew nothing about the instrument, he said, except that it was called a Hlat-talker. It was very unfortunate that Eltak had been shot, because Eltak undoubtedly could have told them all they wanted to know about it. If what he had told Kinmarten was true, Eltak had been directly involved in the development of the device.

"Was he some Federation scientist?" Cooms asked, fiddling absently with the mysterious cylindrical object.

"No, sir," the young man said. "But—again if what he told me was the truth—he was the man who actually discovered these Hlats. At least, he was the first man to discover them who wasn't immediately killed by them."

Cooms glanced thoughtfully at Quillan, then asked, "And where was that?"

Kinmarten shook his head again. "He didn't tell me. And I didn't really want to know. I was anxious to get our convoy to its destination, and then to be relieved of the assignment. I . . . well, I've been trained to act as Rest Warden to human beings, after all, not to monstrosities!" He produced an uncertain smile, glancing from one to the other of his interrogators. The smile promptly faded out again.

"You've no idea at all then about the place they came from?" Cooms asked expressionlessly.

"Oh, yes," Kinmarten said hastily. "Eltak talked a great deal about the Hlats, and actually—except for its location—gave me a fairly good picture of what the planet must be like. For one thing, it's an uncolonized world, of course. It must be terratype or very nearly so, because Eltak lived there for fifteen years with apparently only a minimum of equipment. The Hlats are confined to a single large island. He discovered them by accident and—"

"What was he doing there?"

"Well, sir, he came from Hyles-Frisian. He was a crim . . . he'd been engaged in some form of piracy, and when the authorities began looking for him, he decided it would be best to get clean out of the Hub. He cracked up his ship on this world and couldn't leave again. When he discovered the Hlats and realized their peculiar ability, he kept out of their way and observed them. He found out they had a means of communicating with each other, and that he could duplicate it. That stopped them from harming him, and eventually, he said, he was using them like hunting dogs. They were accustomed to co-operating with one another, because when there was some animal around that was too large for one of them to handle, they would attack it in a group . . ."

He went on for another minute or two on the subject.

The Hlats—the word meant "rock lion" in one of the Hyles-Frisian dialects, describing a carnivorous animal which had some superficial resemblance to the creatures Eltak had happened on—frequented the seacoast and submerged themselves in sand, rocks and debris, whipping up out of it to seize some food animal, and taking it down with them again to devour it at leisure.

Quillan interrupted, "You heard what happened to the man it attacked on the fifth level?"

"Yes, sir."

"Why would the thing have left him half outside the wall as it did?"

Kinmarten said that it must simply have been moving too fast. It could slip into and out of solid substances without a pause itself, but it needed a little time to restructure an object it was carrying in the same manner. No more time, however, than two or three seconds—depending more on the nature of the object than on its size, according to Eltak.

"It can restructure *anything* in that manner?" Quillan asked.

Kinmarten hesitated. "Well, sir, I don't know. I suppose there might be limitations on its ability. Eltak told me the one we were escorting had been the subject of extensive experimentation during the past year, and that the results are very satisfactory."

"Suppose it carries a living man through a wall. Will the man still be alive when he comes out on the other side, assuming the Hlat doesn't kill him deliberately?"

"Yes, sir. The process itself wouldn't hurt him."

Quillan glanced at Cooms. "You know," he said, "we might be letting Yaco off too cheaply!"

Cooms raised an eyebrow warningly, and Quillan grinned. "Our friend will be learning about Yaco soon enough. Why did Eltak tell the creature to attack, Kinmarten?"

"Sir, I don't know," Kinmarten said. "He was a man of rather violent habits. My impression, however, was that he was simply attempting to obtain a hostage."

"How did he get off that island with the Hlat?"

"A University League explorer was investigating the planet. Eltak contacted them and obtained the guarantee of a full pardon and a large cash settlement in return for what he could tell them about the Hlats. They took him and this one specimen along for experimentation."

"What about the Hlats on the *Camelot*?"

"Eltak said those had been quite recently trapped on the island."

Cooms ran his fingers over the cylinder, producing a rapid series of squeaks and whistles. "That's one thing Yaco may not like," he observed. "They won't have a monopoly on the thing."

Quillan shook his head. "Their scientists don't have to work through red tape like the U-League. By the time the news breaks—if the Federation ever intends to break it—Yaco will have at least a five-year start on everyone else. That's all an outfit like that needs." He looked at Kinmarten. "Any little thing you haven't thought to tell us, friend?" he inquired pleasantly.

A thin film of sweat showed suddenly on Kinmarten's forehead.

"No, sir," he said. "I've really told you everything I know. I—"

"Might try him under dope," Cooms said absently.

"Uh-uh!" Quillan said. "I want him wide awake to help me bait the cubicle for the thing. Has Velladon shown any indication of becoming willing to co-operate in hunting it?"

Cooms gestured with his head. "Ask Fluel! I sent him down to try to patch things up with the commodore. He just showed up again."

Quillan glanced around. The Duke was lounging in the

doorway. He grinned slightly, said, "Velladon's still sore at us. But he'll talk to Quillan. Kinmarten here . . . did he tell you his wife's on the Star?"

Brock Kinmarten went utterly white. Cooms looked at him, said softly, "No, that must have slipped his mind."

Fluel said, "Yeah. Well, she is. And Ryter says they'll have her picked up inside half an hour. When they bring her in, we really should check on how candid Kinmarten's been about everything."

The rest warden said in a voice that shook uncontrollably, "Gentlemen, my wife knows absolutely nothing about these matters! I swear it! She—"

Quillan stood up. "Well, I'll go see if I can't get Velladon in a better mood. Are you keeping that Hlattalker, Cooms?"

Cooms smiled. "I am."

"Marras figures," the Duke's flat voice explained, "that if the thing comes into the room and he squeaks at it a few times, he won't get hurt."

"That's possible," Cooms said, un-ruffled. "At any rate, I intend to hang on to it."

"Well, I wouldn't play around with those buttons too much," Quillan observed.

"Why not?"

"You might get lucky and tap out some pattern that spells 'Come to chow' in the Hlat's vocabulary."

3

There were considerably more men in evidence on Level Two than on the fourth, and fewer signs of nervousness. The Star men had been told of the Hlat's escape from its cubicle, but weren't taking it too seriously. Quillan was conducted to the commodore and favored with an alarmingly toothy grin. Ryter, the security chief, joined them a few seconds later. Apparently, Velladon had summoned him.

Velladon said, "Ryter here's made a few transmitter calls. We hear Pappy Boltan pulled his outfit out of the Orado area about a month ago. Present whereabouts unknown. Hagready went off on some hush-hush job at around the same time."

Quillan smiled. "Uh-huh! So he did."

"We also," said Ryter, "learned a number of things about you personally." He produced a thin smile. "You lead a busy and—apparently—profitable life."

"Business is fair," Quillan agreed. "But it can always be improved."

The commodore turned on the toothy grin. "So all right," he growled, "you're clear. We rather liked what we learned. Eh, Ryter?"

Ryter nodded.

"This Brotherhood of Beldon, now—" The commodore shook his head heavily.

Quillan was silent a moment. "They might be getting sloppy," he said. "I don't know. It's one possibility. They used to be a rather sharp outfit, you know."

"That's what I'd heard!" Velladon chewed savagely on his mustache, asked finally, "What's another possibility?"

Quillan leaned back in his chair. "Just a feeling, so far. But the business with the cubicle upstairs might have angles that weren't mentioned."

They looked at him thoughtfully. Ryter said, "Mind amplifying that?"

"Cooms told me," Quillan said, "that Nome Lancion had given Movaine instructions to make a test with Lady Pendrake on the quiet and find out if those creatures actually can do what they're supposed to do. I think he was telling the truth. Nome tends to be overcautious when it's a really big deal. Unless he's sure of the Hlats, he wouldn't want to be involved in a thing like blowing up the Star and the liner."

The commodore scowled absently. "Uh-huh," he said. "He knows we can't back out of it—"

"All right. The Brotherhood's full of ambitious men. Behind Lancion, Movaine was top man. Cooms behind him; Fluel behind Cooms. Suppose that Hlat-control device Cooms is hanging on to so tightly isn't as entirely incomprehensible as they make it out to be. Suppose Cooms makes a deal with Eltak. Eltak tickles the gadget, and the Hlat kills Movaine. Rubero immediately guns down Eltak—and is killed by Fluel a couple of minutes later, supposedly for blowing his top and killing the man who knew how to control the Hlat."

Ryter cleared his throat. "Fluel was Movaine's gun," he observed.

"So he was," Quillan said. "Would you like the Duke to be yours?"

Ryter grinned, shook his head. "No, thanks!"

Quillan looked back at Velladon. "How well are you actually covered against the Brotherhood?"

"Well, *that's* air-tight," the commodore said. "We've got 'em outgunned here. When the liner lands, we'll be about even. But Lancion won't start anything. We're *too* even. Once we're clear of the Star, we don't meet again. We deal with Yaco individually. The Brotherhood has the Hlats, and we have the trained Federation technicians accompanying them, who . . . who—"

"Who alone are supposed to be able to inform Yaco how to control the Hlats," Ryter finished for him. The security chief's face was expressionless.

"By God!" the commodore said softly.

"Well, it's only a possibility that somebody's playing dirty," Quillan remarked. "We'd want to be sure of it. But if anyone can handle a Hlat with that control instrument, the Brotherhood has an advantage now that it isn't talking about—it can offer Yaco everything Yaco needs in one package. Of course, Yaco might still be willing to pay for the Hlat technicians. If it didn't, you and Ryter could make the same kind of trouble for it that my friends can."

The color was draining slowly from Velladon's face. "There's a difference," he said. "If we threaten to make trouble for Yaco, they'd see to it that our present employers learn that Ryter and I are still alive."

"That's the Mooleys, eh?"

"Yes."

"Tough." Quillan knuckled his chin thoughtfully. "Well, let's put it this way then," he said. "My group doesn't have *that* kind of problem, but if things worked out so that we'd have something more substantial than nuisance value to offer Yaco, we'd prefer it, of course."

Velladon nodded. "Very understandable! Under the circumstances co-operation appears to be indicated, eh?"

"That's what I had in mind."

"You've made a deal," Velladon said. "Any immediate suggestions?"

Quillan looked at his watch. "A couple. We don't want to make any mistake about this. It's still almost five hours before the *Camelot* pulls in, and until she does you're way ahead on firepower. I wouldn't make any accusations just now. But you might mention to Cooms you'd like to borrow the Hlat gadget to have it examined by some of your technical experts. The way he reacts might tell us something. If he balks, the matter shouldn't be pushed too hard at the moment—it's a tossup whether you or the Brotherhood has a better claim to the thing.

"But then there's Kinmarten, the rest warden in charge of the cubicle. I talked with him while Cooms and Fluel were around, but he may have been briefed on what to say. Cooms mentioned doping him, which could be a convenient way of keeping him shut up, assuming he knows more than he's told. He's one of the personnel you're to offer Yaco. I think you can insist on having Kinmarten handed over to you immediately. It should be interesting again to see how Cooms reacts."

Velladon's big head nodded vigorously. "Good idea!"

"By the way," Quillan said, "Fluel mentioned you've been looking for Kinmarten's wife, the second rest warden on the Pendrake convoy. Found her yet?"

"Not a trace, so far," Ryter said.

"That's a little surprising, too, isn't it?"

"Under the circumstances," the commodore said, "it might not be surprising at all!" He had regained his color, was beginning to look angry. "If they—"

"Well," Quillan said soothingly, "we don't *know*. It's just that things do seem to be adding up a little. Now, there's one other point. We should do something immediately about catching that Hlat."

Velladon grunted and picked at his teeth with his thumbnail. "It would be best to get it back in its cubicle, of course. But I'm not worrying about it—just an animal, after all. Even the light hardware those Beldon fancy Dans carry should handle it. You use a man-sized gun, I see. So do I. If it shows up around here, it gets smeared, that's all. There're fifty more of the beasts on the *Camelot*."

Quillan nodded. "You're right on that. But there's the possibility that it is being controlled by the Brotherhood at present. If it is, it isn't just an animal any more. It could be turned into a thoroughly dangerous nuisance."

The commodore thought a moment, nodded. "You're right, I suppose. What do you want to do about it?"

"Baiting the cubicle on the fifth level might work. Then there should be life-detectors in the Star's security supplies—"

Ryter nodded. "We have a couple of dozen of them, but not in the Executive Block. They were left in the security building."

The commodore stood up. "You stay here with Ryter," he told Quillan. "There're a couple of other things I want to go over with you two. I'll order the life-detectors from the office here—second passage down, isn't it, Ryter? . . . And, Ryter, I have another idea. I'm pulling the man in space-armor off the subspace portal and detailing him to Level Five." He grinned at Quillan. "That boy's got a brace of grenades and built-in spray guns! If Cooms is thinking of pulling any funny stunts up there, he'll think again."

The commodore headed briskly down the narrow passageway, his big holstered gun slapping his thigh with every step. The two security guards stationed at the door to the second level office came to attention as he approached, saluted smartly. He grunted, went in without returning the salutes, and started over toward the ComWeb on a desk at the far end of the big room, skirting the long, dusty-looking black rug beside one wall.

Velladon unbuckled his gun belt, placed the gun on the desk, sat down and switched on the ComWeb.

Behind him, the black rug stirred silently and rose up.

"You called that one," Ryter was saying seven or eight minutes later, "almost too well!"

Quillan shook his head, poked at the commodore's gun on the desk with his finger, looked about the silent office and back at the door where a small group of security men stood staring in at them.

"Three men gone without a sound!" he said. He indicated the glowing disk of the ComWeb. "He had time enough to turn it on, not time enough to make his call. Any chance of camouflaged portals in this section?"

"No," Ryter said. "I know the location of every portal in the Executive Block. No number of men could have taken Velladon and the two guards without a fight anyway. We'd have heard it. It didn't happen that way."

"Which leaves," Quillan said, "one way it could have

happened." He jerked his head toward the door. "Will those men keep quiet?"

"If I tell them to."

"Then play it like this. Two guards have vanished. The Hlat obviously did it. The thing's deadly. That'll keep every man in the group on the alert every instant from now on. But we don't say Velladon has vanished. He's outside in the Star at the moment, taking care of something."

Ryter licked his lips. "What does that buy us?"

"If the Brotherhood's responsible for this—"

"I don't take much stock in coincidences," Ryter said.

"Neither do I. But the Hlat's an animal; it can't tell them it's carried out the job. If they don't realize we suspect them, it gives us some advantage. For the moment, we just carry on as planned, and get rid of the Hlat in one way or another as the first step. The thing's three times as dangerous as anyone suspected—except, apparently, the Brotherhood. Get the life-detectors over here as soon as you can, and slap a space-armor guard on the fifth level."

Ryter hesitated, nodded. "All right."

"Another thing," Quillan said, "Cooms may have the old trick in mind of working from the top down. If he can take you out along with a few other key men, he might have this outfit demoralized to the point of making up for the difference in the number of guns— especially if the Hlat's still on his team. You'd better keep a handful of the best boys you have around here glued to your back from now on."

Ryter smiled bleakly. "Don't worry. I intend to. What about you?"

"I don't think they're planning on giving me any personal attention at the moment. My organization is outside, not here. And it would look odd to the Brotherhood if I started dragging a few Star guards around with me at this point."

Ryter shrugged. "Suit yourself. It's your funeral if you've guessed wrong."

"There was nothing," Quillan told Marras Cooms, "that you could actually put a finger on. It was just that I got a very definite impression that the commodore and Ryter may have something up their sleeves. Velladon's looking too self-satisfied to suit me."

The Brotherhood chief gnawed his lower lip reflectively. He seemed thoughtful, not too disturbed. Cooms might be thoroughly afraid of the escaped Hlat, but he wouldn't have reached his present position in Nome Lancion's organization if he had been easily frightened by what other men were planning.

He said, "I warned Movaine that if Velladon learned we'd checked out the Hlat, he wasn't going to like it."

"He doesn't," Quillan said. "He regards it as something pretty close to an attempted double cross."

Cooms grinned briefly. "It was."

"Of course. The question is, what can he do about it? He's got you outgunned two to one, but if he's thinking of jumping you before Lancion gets here, he stands to lose more men than he can afford to without endangering the entire operation for himself."

Cooms was silent a few seconds. "There's an unpleasant possibility which didn't occur to me until a short while ago," he said then. "The fact is that Velladon actually may have us outgunned here by something like four to one. If that's the case, he can afford to lose quite a few men. In fact, he'd prefer to."

Quillan frowned. "*Four* to one? How's that?"

Cooms said, "The commodore told us he intended to let only around half of the Seventh Star's security force in on the Hlat deal. The other half was supposed to have been dumped out of one of the subspace section's locks early today, without benefit of suits. We had no reason to disbelieve him. Velladon naturally would want to cut down the number of men who got in on the split with him to as many as he actually needed. But if he's been thinking about eliminating us from the game, those other men may still be alive and armed."

Quillan grunted. "I see. You know, that could explain something that looked a little odd to me."

"What was that?" Cooms asked.

Quillan said, "After they discovered down there that two of their guards were missing and decided the Hlat must have been on their level, I tried to get hold of the commodore again. Ryter told me Velladon won't be available for a while, that he's outside in the Star, taking care of something there. I wondered what could be important enough to get Velladon to leave the Executive Block at present, but—"

"Brother, I'm way ahead of you!" Cooms said. His expression hardened. "That doesn't look good. But at least he can't bring in reinforcements without tipping us off. We've got our own guards down with theirs at the entrance."

Quillan gave him a glance, then nodded at the wall beyond them. "That's a portal over there, Marras. How many of them on this level?"

"Three or four. Why? The outportals have been plugged, man! Sealed off. Fluel checked them over when we moved in."

"Sure they're sealed." Quillan stood up, went to the portal, stood looking at the panel beside it a moment, then pressed on it here and there, and removed it. "Come over here, friend. I suppose portal work's been out of your line. I'll show you how fast a thing like that can get *un*-plugged!"

He slid a pocketbook-sized tool kit out of his belt, snapped it open. About a minute later, the lifeless VACANT sign above the portal flickered twice, then acquired a steady white glow.

"Portal in operation," Quillan announced. "I'll seal it
off again now. But that should give you the idea."

Cooms' tongue flicked over his lips. "Could somebody
portal through to this level from the Star while the exits
are sealed here?"

"If the mechanisms have been set for that purpose,
the portals can be opened again at any time from the
Star side. The Duke's an engineer of sorts, isn't he?
Let him check on it. He should have been thinking
of the point himself, as far as that goes. Anyway,
Velladon can bring in as many men as he likes to his
own level without using the main entrance." He considered. "I didn't see anything to indicate that he's
started doing it—"

Marras Cooms shrugged irritably. "That means nothing! It would be easy enough to keep half a hundred men
hidden away on any of the lower levels."

"I suppose that's right. Well, if the commodore intends
to play rough, you should have some warning anyway."

"What kind of warning?"

"There's Kinmarten and that Hlat-talking gadget, for
example," Quillan pointed out. "Velladon would want both
of those in his possession and out of the way where they
can't get hurt before he starts any shooting."

Cooms looked at him for a few seconds. "Ryter," he
said then, "sent half a dozen men up here for Kinmarten
just after you got back! Velladon's supposed to deliver the
Hlats' attendants to Yaco, so I let them have Kinmarten."
He paused. "They asked for the Hlat-talker, too."

Quillan grunted. "Did you give them that?"

"No."

"Well," Quillan said after a moment, "that doesn't
necessarily mean that we're in for trouble with the Star
group. But it does mean, I think, that we'd better stay
ready for it!" He stood up. "I'll get back down there and
go on with the motions of getting the hunt for the Hlat
organized. Velladon would sooner see the thing get

caught, too, of course, so he shouldn't try to interfere with that. If I spot anything that looks suspicious, I'll get the word to you."

"I never," said Orca, unconsciously echoing Baldy Perk, "saw anything like it!" The commodore's chunky little gunman was ashen-faced. The circle of Star men standing around him hardly looked happier. Most of them were staring down at the empty lower section of a suit of space armor which appeared to have been separated with a neat diagonal slice from its upper part.

"Let's get it straight," Ryter said, a little unsteadily. "You say this half of the suit was lying against the wall like *that?*"

"Not exactly," Quillan told him. "When we got up to the fifth level the suit was stuck against the wall—like that—about eight feet above the floor. That was in the big room where the cubicles are. When Kinmarten and Orca and I finally got the suit worked away from the wall, I expected frankly that we'd find half the body of the guard still inside. But he'd vanished."

Ryter cleared his throat. "Apparently," he said, "the creature drew the upper section of the suit into the wall by whatever means it uses, then stopped applying the transforming process to the metal, and simply moved on with the upper part of the suit and the man."

Quillan nodded. "That's what it looks like."

"But he had *two grenades!*" Orca burst out. "He had sprayguns! How could it get him that way?"

"Brother," Quillan said, "grenades won't help you much if you don't spot what's moving up behind you!"

Orca glared speechlessly at him. Ryter said, "All right! We've lost another man. We're not going to lose any more. We'll station no more guards on the fifth level. Now, get everyone who isn't on essential guard duty to the main room, and split 'em up into life-detector units. Five men to each detail, one to handle the detector, four to stay with him, guns out. If the thing comes back to this level, we want to have it spotted the instant it arrives. Orca, you stay here—and keep *your* gun out!"

The men filed out hurriedly. Ryter turned to Quillan. "Were you able to get the cubicle baited?"

Quillan nodded. "Kinmarten figured out how the thing should be set for the purpose. If the Hlat goes in after the sea beef, it's trapped. Of course, if the hunting it's been doing was for food, it mightn't be interested in the beef."

"We don't know," Ryter said, "that the hunting it's been doing was for food."

"No. Did you manage to get the control device from Cooms?"

Ryter shook his head. "He's refused to hand it over."

"If you tried to take it from him," Quillan said, "you might have a showdown on your hands."

"And if this keeps on," Ryter said, "I may prefer a showdown! Another few rounds of trouble with the Hlat, and the entire operation could blow up in our faces! The men aren't used to that kind of thing. It's shaken them up. If we've got to take care of the Brotherhood, I'd rather do it while I still have an organized group. Where did you leave Kinmarten, by the way?"

"He's back in that little room with his two guards," Quillan said.

"Well, he should be all right there. We can't spare—" Ryter's body jerked violently. *"What's that?"*

There had been a single thudding crash somewhere in the level. Then shouts and cursing.

"Main hall!" Quillan said. "Come on!"

The main hall was a jumble of excitedly jabbering Star men when they arrived there. Guns waved about, and the various groups were showing a marked tendency to stand with their backs toward one another and their faces toward the walls.

Ryter's voice rose in a shout that momentarily shut off the hubbub. *"What's going on here?"*

Men turned, hands pointed, voices babbled again. Someone nearby said sharply and distinctly, " . . . Saw it drop right out of the ceiling!" Farther down the hall, another group shifted aside enough to disclose it had been clustered about something which looked a little like the empty shell of a gigantic black beetle.

The missing section of the suit of space armor had been returned. But not its occupant.

Quillan moved back a step, turned, went back down the passage from which they had emerged, pulling the Miam Devil from its holster. Behind him the commotion continued; Ryter was shouting something about getting the life-detector units over there. Quillan went left down the first intersecting corridor, right again on the following one, keeping the gun slightly raised before him. Around the next corner, he saw the man on guard over the portal connecting the building levels facing him, gun pointed.

"What happened?" the guard asked shakily.

Quillan shook his head, coming up. "That thing got another one!"

The guard breathed, "By God!" and lowered his gun a little. Quillan raised his a little, the Miam Devil grunted, and the guard sighed and went down. Quillan went past him along the hall, stopped two doors beyond the portal and rapped on the locked door.

"Quillan here. Open up!"

The door opened a crack, and one of Kinmarten's guards looked out questioningly. Quillan shot him through the head, slammed on into the room across the collapsing body, saw the second guard wheeling toward him, shot again, and slid the gun back into the holster. Kinmarten, standing beside a table six feet away, right hand gripping a heavy marble ashtray, was staring at him in white-faced shock.

"Take it easy, chum!" Quillan said, turning toward him. "I—"

He ducked hurriedly as the ashtray came whirling through the air toward his head. An instant later, a large fist smacked the side of Kinmarten's jaw. The rest warden settled limply to the floor.

"Sorry to do that, pal," Quillan muttered, stooping over him. "Things are rough all over right now." He hauled Kinmarten upright, bent, and had the unconscious young man across his shoulder. The hall was still empty except for the body of the portal guard. Quillan laid Kinmarten on the carpet before the portal, hauled the guard off into the room, and pulled the door to the room shut behind him as he came out. Picking up Kinmarten, he stepped into the portal with him and jabbed the fifth level button. A moment later, he moved out into the small dim entry hall on the fifth level, the gun in his right hand again.

He stood there silently for some seconds, looking about him listening. The baited cubicle yawned widely at him from the center of the big room. Nothing seemed to be stirring. Kinmarten went back to the floor. Quillan moved over to the panel which concealed the other portal's mechanisms.

He had the outportal unsealed in considerably less than a minute this time, and slapped the panel gently back in place. He turned back to Kinmarten and started to bend down for him, then straightened quietly again, turning his head.

Had there been a flicker of shadowy motion just then at the edge of his vision, behind the big black cube of the Hlat's food locker? Quillan remained perfectly still, the Miam Devil ready and every sense straining for an indication that the thing was there—or approaching stealthily now, gliding behind the surfaces of floor or ceiling or walls like an underwater swimmer.

But half a minute passed and nothing else happened.

He went down on one knee beside Kinmarten, the gun still in his right hand. With his left, he carefully wrestled the rest warden back up across his shoulder, came upright, moved three steps to the side, and disappeared in the outportal.

4

Reetal Destone unlocked the entry door to her suite and stepped hurriedly inside, letting the door slide shut behind her. She crossed the room to the ComWeb stand and switched on the playback. There was the succession of tinkling tones which indicated nothing had been recorded.

She shut the instrument off again, passing her tongue lightly over her lips. No further messages from Heraga . . .

And none from Quillan.

She shook her head, feeling a surge of sharp anxiety, glanced at her watch and told herself that, after all, less than two hours had passed since Quillan had gone into the Executive Block. Heraga reported there had been no indications of disturbance or excitement when he passed through the big entrance hall on his way out. So Quillan, at any rate, had succeeded in bluffing his way into the upper levels.

It remained a desperate play, at best.

Reetal went down the short passage to her bedroom. As she came into the room, her arms were caught from the side at the elbows, pulled suddenly and painfully together behind her. She stood still, frozen with shock.

"In a hurry, sweetheart?" Fluel's flat voice said.

Reetal managed a breathless giggle. "Duke! You startled me! How did you get in?"

She felt one hand move up her arm to her shoulder.

Then she was swung about deftly and irresistibly, held pinned back against the wall, still unable to move her arms.

He looked at her a moment, asked, "Where are you hiding it this time?"

"Hiding what, Duke?"

"I've been told sweet little Reetal always carries a sweet little gun around with her in some shape or form or other."

Reetal shook her head, her eyes widening. "Duke, what's the matter? I . . ."

He let go of her suddenly, and his slap exploded against the side of her face. Reetal cried out, dropping her head between her hands. Immediately he had her wrists again, and her fingers were jerked away from the jeweled ornament in her hair.

"So that's where it is!" Fluel said. "Thought it might be. Don't get funny again now, sweetheart. Just stay quiet."

She stayed quiet, wincing a little as he plucked the glittering little device out of her hair. He turned it around in his fingers, examining it, smiled and slid it into an inside pocket, and took her arm again. "Let's go to the front room, Reetal," he said almost pleasantly. "We've got a few things to do."

A minute later, she was seated sideways on a lounger, her wrists fastened right and left to its armrests. The Duke placed a pocket recorder on the floor beside her. "This is a crowded evening, sweetheart," he remarked, "which is lucky for you in a way. We'll have to rush things along a little. I'll snap the recorder on in a minute so you can answer questions—No, keep quiet. Just listen very closely now, so you'll know what the right answers are. If you get rattled and gum things up, the Duke's going to get annoyed with you."

He sat down a few feet away from her, hitched his

shoulders to straighten out the silver jacket, and lit a cigarette. "A little while after Bad News Quillan turned up just now," he went on, "a few things occurred to me. One of them was that a couple of years ago you and he were operating around Beldon at about the same time. I thought, well, maybe you knew each other; maybe not. And then—"

"Duke," Reetal said uncertainly, "just what are you talking about? I don't know—"

"Shut up." He reached over, tapped her knee lightly with his fingertips. "Of course, if you want to get slapped around, all right. Otherwise, don't interrupt again. Like I said, you're in luck; I don't have much time to spend here. You're getting off very easy. Now just listen.

"Bad News knew a lot about our operation and had a story to explain that. If the story was straight, we couldn't touch him. But I was wondering about the two of you happening to be here on the Star again at the same time. A team maybe, eh? But he didn't mention you as being in on the deal. So what was the idea?

"And then, sweetheart, I remembered something else—and that tied it in. Know that little jolt people sometimes get when they're dropping off to sleep? Of course. Know another time they sometimes get it? When they're snapping back out of a Moment of Truth, eh? I remembered suddenly I'd felt a little jump like that while we were talking today. Might have been a reflex of some kind. Of course, it didn't occur to me at the time you could be pulling a lousy stunt like that on old Duke. Why take a chance on getting your neck broken?

"But, sweetheart, that's the tie-in! Quillan hasn't told it straight. He's got no backing. He's on his own. There's no gang outside somewhere that knows all about our little deal. He got his information right here, from you. And you got it from dumb old Duke, eh?"

"Duke," Reetal said quite calmly. "can I ask just one question?"

He stared bleakly at her a moment, then grinned. "It's my night to be big-hearted, I guess. Go ahead."

"I'm not trying to argue. But it simply doesn't make sense. If I learned about this operation you're speaking of from you, what reason could I have to feed you Truth in the first place? There'd be almost a fifty-fifty chance that you'd spot it immediately. Why should I take such a risk? Don't you see?"

Fluel shrugged, dropped his cigarette and ground it carefully into the carpet with the tip of his shoe.

"You'll start answering those questions yourself almost immediately, sweetheart! Let's not worry about that now. Let me finish. Something happened to Movaine couple of hours ago. Nobody's fault. And something else happened to Marras Cooms just now. That puts me in charge of the operation here. Nice! isn't it? When we found Cooms lying in the hall with a hole through his stupid head, I told Baldy Perk it looked like Bad News had thrown in with the Star boys and done it. Know Baldy? He's Cooms' personal gun. Not what you'd call bright, and he's mighty hot now about Cooms. I left him in charge on our level, with orders to get Quillan the next time he shows up there. Well and good. The boys know Bad News' rep too well to try asking him questions. They won't take chances with him. They'll just gun him down together the instant they see him."

He paused to scuff his shoe over the mark the cigarette had left on the carpet, went on, "But there's Nome Lancion now. He kind of liked Cooms, and he might get suspicious. When there's a sudden vacancy in the organization like that, Nome takes a good look first at the man next in line. He likes to be sure the facts are as stated.

"So now you know the kind of answers from you I want to hear go down on the recorder, sweetheart. And be sure they sound right. I don't want to waste time on replays. You and Quillan were here on the Star. You got some idea of what was happening, realized you were due to be vaporized along with the rest of them after we left. There was no way out of the jam for you unless you could keep the operation from being carried out. You don't, by the way, mention getting any of that information from me. I don't want Lancion to think I'm beginning to get dopey. You and Quillan just cooked up this story, and he managed to get into the Executive Block. The idea being to knock off as many of the leaders as he could, and mess things up."

Fluel picked up the recorder, stood up, and placed it on the chair. "That's all you have to remember. You're a smart girl; you can fill in the detail any way you like. Now let's get started—"

She stared at him silently for instant, a muscle beginning to twitch in her cheek. "If I do that," she said, "if I give you a story Nome will like, what happens next?"

Fluel shrugged. "Just what you're thinking happens next. You're a dead little girl right now, Reetal. Might as well get used to the idea. You'd be dead anyhow four, five hours from now, so that shouldn't make too much difference. What makes a lot of difference is just how unpleasant the thing can get."

She drew a long breath. "Duke, I—"

"You're stalling, sweetheart."

"Duke, give me a break. I really didn't know a thing about this. I—"

He looked down at her for a moment. "I gave you a break," he said. "You've wasted it. Now we'll try it the other way. If we work a few squeals into the recording, that'll make it more convincing to Lancion. He'll figure little Reetal's the type who wouldn't spill a thing like that without a little pressure." He checked himself, grinned. "And that reminds me. When you're talking for the record, use your own voice."

"My own voice?" she half whispered.

"Nome will remember what you sound like—and I've heard that voice imitations are part of your stock in trade. You might think it was cute if Nome got to wondering after you were dead whether that really had been you talking. Don't try it, sweetheart."

He brought a glove out of his jacket pocket, slipped it over his left hand, flexing his fingers to work it into position. Reetal's eyes fastened on the rounded metal tips capping thumb, forefinger and middle finger of the glove. Her face went gray.

"Duke," she said. "No—"

"Shut up." He brought out a strip of transparent plastic, moved over to her. The gloved hand went into her hair, gripped it, turned her face up. He laid the plastic gag lengthwise over her mouth, pressed it down and released it. Reetal closed her eyes.

"That'll keep it shut," he said. "Now—" His right hand clamped about the back of her neck, forcing her head down and forward almost to her knees. The gloved left hand brushed her hair forwards, then its middle finger touched the skin at a point just above her shoulder blades.

"Right there," Fluel said. The finger stiffened, drove down.

Reetal jerked violently, twisted, squirmed sideways, wrists straining against the grip of the armrests. Her breath burst out of her nostrils, followed by squeezed, whining noises. The metal-capped finger continued to grind savagely against the nerve center it had found.

"Thirty," Fluel said finally. He drew his hand back, pulled her upright again, peeled the gag away from her lips. "Only thirty seconds, sweetheart. Think you'd sooner play along now?"

Reetal's head nodded.

"Fine. Give you a minute to steady up. This doesn't really waste much time, you see—" He took up the recorder, sat down on the chair again, watching her. She was breathing raggedly and shallowly, eyes wide and incredulous. She didn't look at him.

The Duke lit another cigarette.

"Incidentally," he observed, "if you were stalling because you hoped old Bad News might show up, forget it. If the boys haven't gunned him down by now, he's tied up on a job the commodore gave him to do. He'll be busy another hour or two on that. He—"

He checked himself. A central section of the wall paneling across the room from him had just dilated open. Old Bad News stood in the concealed suite portal, Rest Warden Kinmarten slung across his shoulder.

Both men moved instantly. Fluel's long legs bounced him sideways out of the chair, right hand darting under his coat, coming out with a gun. Quillan turned to the left to get Kinmarten out of the way. The big Miam Devil seemed to jump into his hand. Both guns spoke together.

Fluel's gun thudded to the carpet. The Duke said, "Ah-aa-ah!" in a surprised voice, rolled up his eyes, and followed the gun down.

Quillan said, stunned, "He was fast! I felt that one parting my hair."

He became very solicitous then—after first ascertaining that Fluel had left the Executive Block unaccompanied, on personal business. He located a pain killer spray in Reetal's bedroom and applied it to the bruised point below the back of her neck. She was just beginning to relax gratefully, as the warm glow of the spray washed out the pain and the feeling of paralysis, when Kinmarten, lying on the carpet nearby, began to stir and mutter.

Quillan hastily put down the spray.

"Watch him!" he cautioned. "I'll be right back. If he sits up, yell. He's a bit wild at the moment. If he wakes up and sees the Duke lying there, he'll start climbing the walls."

"What—" Reetal began. But he was gone down the hall.

He returned immediately with a glass of water, went down on one knee beside Kinmarten, slid an arm under the rest warden's shoulder, and lifted him to a sitting position.

"Wake up, old pal!" he said loudly. "Come on, wake up! Got something good for you here—"

"What are you giving him?" Reetal asked, cautiously massaging the back of her neck.

"Knockout drops. I already had to lay him out once. We want to lock him up with his wife now, and if he comes to and tells her what's happened, they'll both be out of their minds by the time we come to let them out—"

He interrupted himself. Kinmarten's eyelids were fluttering. Quillan raised the glass to his lips. "Here you are, pal," he said in a deep, soothing voice. "Drink it! It'll make you feel a lot better."

Kinmarten swallowed obediently, swallowed again. His eyelids stopped fluttering. Quillan lowered him back to the floor.

"That ought to do it," he said.

"What," Reetal asked, "did happen? The Duke—"

"Tell you as much as I can after we get Kinmarten out of the way. I have to get back to the Executive Block. Things are sort of teetering on the edge there." He jerked his head at Fluel's body. "I want to know about him, too, of course. Think you can walk now?"

Reetal groaned. "I can try," she said.

They found Solvey Kinmarten dissolved in tears once more. She flung herself on her husband's body when Quillan placed him on the bed. "What have those *beasts* done to Brock?" she demanded fiercely.

"Nothing very bad," Quillan said soothingly. "He's, um, under sedation at the moment, that's all. We've got him away from them now, and he's safe . . . look at it that way. You stay here and take care of him. We'll have the whole deal cleared up before morning, doll. Then you can both come out of hiding again." He gave her an encouraging wink.

"I'm so very grateful to both of you—"

"No trouble, really. But we'd better get back to work on the thing."

"Heck," Quillan said a few seconds later, as he and Reetal came out on the other side of the portal, "I feel like hell about those two. Nice little characters! Well, if the works blow up, they'll never know it."

"*We'll* know it," Reetal said meaningly. "Start talking."

He rattled through a brief account of events in the Executive Block, listened to her report on the Duke's visit, scratched his jaw reflectively.

"That might help!" he observed. "They're about ready to jump down each other's throats over there right now. A couple more pushes—" He stood staring down at the Duke's body for a moment. Blood soiled the back of the silver jacket, seeping out from a tear above the heart area. Quillan bent down, got his hands under Fluel's armpits, hauled the body upright.

Reetal asked, startled, "What are you going to do with it?"

"Something useful, I think. And wouldn't that shock the Duke . . . the first time he's been of any use to anybody. Zip through the Star's ComWeb directory, doll, and get me the call symbol for Level Four of the Executive Block!"

Solvey Kinmarten dimmed the lights a trifle in the bedroom, went back to Brock, rearranged the pillows under his head, and bent down to place her lips tenderly to the large bruises on his forehead and the side of his jaw. Then she brought a chair up beside the bed, and sat down to watch him.

Perhaps a minute later, there was a slight noise behind her. Startled, she glanced around, saw something huge, black and shapeless moving swiftly across the carpet of the room toward her.

Solvey quietly fainted.

"Sure you know what to say?" Quillan asked.

Reetal moistened her lips. "Just let me go over it in my mind once more." She was sitting on the floor, on the right side of the ComWeb stand, her face pale and intent. "You know," she said, "this makes me feel a little queasy somehow, Quillan! And suppose they don't fall for it?"

"They'll fall for it!" Quillan was on his knees in front of the stand, supporting Fluel's body, which was sprawled half across it, directly before the lit vision screen. An outflung arm hid the Duke's face from the screen. "You almost had *me* thinking I was listening to Fluel when you did the take-off on him this evening. A dying man can be expected to sound a little odd, anyway." He smiled at her encouragingly. "Ready now?"

Reetal nodded nervously, cleared her throat.

Quillan reached across Fluel, tapped out Level Four's call symbol on the instrument, ducked back down below the stand. After a moment, there was a click.

Reetal produced a quavering, agonized groan. Somebody else gasped.

"*Duke!*" Baldy Perk's voice shouted. "What's happened?"

"Baldy Perk!" Quillan whispered quickly.

Reetal stammered hoarsely, "The c-c-commodore, Baldy! Shot me . . . shot Marras! They're after . . . Quillan . . . now!"

"I thought Bad News . . ." Baldy sounded stunned.

"Was w-wrong, Baldy," Reetal croaked. "Bad News . . . with us! Bad News . . . pal! The c-c-comm—"

Beneath the ComWeb stand the palm of Quillan's right hand thrust sharply up and forward. The stand tilted, went crashing back to the floor. Fluel's body lurched over with it. The vision screen shattered. Baldy's roaring question was cut off abruptly.

"Great stuff, doll!" Quillan beamed, helping Reetal to her feet. "You sent shudders down my back!"

"Down mine, too!"

"I'll get him out of here now. Ditch him in one of the shut-off sections. Then I'll get back to the Executive Block. If Ryter's thought to look into Kinmarten's room, they'll really be raving on both sides there now!"

"Is that necessary?" Reetal asked. "For you to go back, I mean. Somebody besides Fluel might have become suspicious of you by now."

"Ryter might," Quillan agreed "He's looked like the sharpest of the lot right from the start. But we'll have to risk that. We've got all the makings of a shooting war there now but we've got to make sure it gets set off before somebody thinks of comparing notes. If I'm around, I'll keep jolting at their nerves."

"I suppose you're right. Now, our group—"

Quillan nodded. "No need to hold off on that any longer, the way things are moving. Get on another ComWeb and start putting out those Mayday messages right now! As soon as you've rounded the boys up—"

"That might," Reetal said, "take a little less than an hour."

"Fine. Then move them right into the Executive Block. With just a bit of luck, one hour from now should land them in the final stages of a beautiful battle on the upper levels. Give them my description and Ryter's, so we don't have accidents."

"Why Ryter's?"

"Found out he was the boy who took care of the bomb-planting detail. We want him alive. The others mightn't know where it's been tucked away. Heraga says the clerical staff and technicians in there are all wearing the white Star uniforms. Anyone else who isn't in one of those uniforms is fair game—" He paused. "Oh, and tip them off about the Hlat. God only knows what that thing will be doing when the ruckus starts."

"What about sending a few men in through the fifth level portal, the one you've unplugged?"

Quillan considered, shook his head. "No. Down on the ground level is where we want them. They'd have to portal there again from the fifth, and a portal is too easy to seal off and defend. Now let's get a blanket or something to tuck Fluel into. I don't want to feel conspicuous if I run into somebody on the way."

5

Quillan emerged cautiously from the fifth portal in the Executive Block a short while later, came to a sudden stop just outside it. In the big room beyond the entry hall, the door of the baited cubicle was closed and the life-indicator on the door showed a bright steady green glow.

Quillan stared at it a moment, looking somewhat surprised, then went quietly into the room and bent to study the cubicle's instruments. A grin spread slowly over his face. The trap had been sprung. He glanced at the deep-rest setting and turned it several notches farther down.

"Happy dreams, Lady Pendrake!" he murmured. "That takes care of you. What an appetite! And now—"

As the Level Four portal dilated open before him, a gun blazed from across the hall. Quillan flung himself out and down, rolled to the side, briefly aware of a litter of bodies and tumbled furniture farther up the hall. Then he was flat on the carpet, gun out before him, pointing back at the overturned, ripped couch against the far wall from which the fire had come.

A hoarse voice bawled, "Bad News—hold it!"

Quillan hesitated, darting a glance right and left. Men lying about everywhere, the furnishings a shambles. "That you, Baldy?" he asked.

"Yeah," Baldy Perk half sobbed. "I'm hurt—"

"What happened?"

"*Star* gang jumped us. Portaled in here—spitballs and riot guns! Bad News, we're clean wiped out! Everyone that was on this level—"

Quillan stood up, holstering the gun, went over to the couch and moved it carefully away from the wall. Baldy was crouched behind it, kneeling on the blood-soaked carpet, gun in his right hand. He lifted a white face, staring eyes, to Quillan.

"Waitin' for 'em to come back," he muttered. "Man, I'm not for long! Got hit twice. Near passed out a couple of times already."

"What about your boys on guard downstairs?"

"Same thing there, I guess . . . or they'd have showed up. They got Cooms and the Duke, too! Man, it all happened fast!"

"And the crew on the freighter?"

"Dunno about them."

"You know the freighter's call number?"

"Huh? Oh, yeah. Sure. Never thought of that," Baldy said wearily. He seemed dazed now.

"Let's see if you can stand."

Quillan helped the big man to his feet. Baldy hadn't bled too much outwardly, but he seemed to have estimated his own condition correctly. He wasn't for long. Quillan slid an arm under his shoulders.

"Where's a ComWeb?" he asked.

Baldy blinked about. "Passage there—" His voice was beginning to thicken.

The ComWeb was in the second room up the passage. Quillan eased Perk into the seat before it. Baldy's head lolled heavily forward, like a drunken man's. "What's the number?" Quillan asked.

Baldy reflected a few seconds. blinking owlishly at the instrument, then told him. Quillan tapped out the number, flicked on the vision screen, then stood aside and back, beyond the screen's range.

"Yeah, Perk?" a voice said some seconds later. "Hey, *Perk* . . . Perk, what's with ya?"

Baldy spat blood, grinned. "Shot—" he said.

"*What?*"

"Yeah." Baldy scowled, blinking. "Now, lessee—Oh, yeah. Star gang's gonna jump ya! Watch it!"

"What?"

"Yeah, watch—" Baldy coughed, laid his big head slowly down face forward on the ComWeb stand, and stopped moving.

"Perk! Man, wake up! Perk!"

Quillan quietly took out the gun, reached behind the stand and blew the ComWeb apart. He wasn't certain what the freighter's crew would make of the sudden break in the connection, but they could hardly regard it as reassuring. He made a brief prowl then through the main sections of the level. Evidence everywhere of a short and furious struggle, a struggle between men panicked and enraged almost beyond any regard for self-preservation. It must have been over in minutes. He found that the big hall portal to the ground level had been sealed, whether before or after the shooting he couldn't know. There would have been around twenty members of the Brotherhood on the level. None of them had lived as long as Baldy Peak, but they seemed to have accounted for approximately an equal number of the Star's security force first.

Five Star men came piling out of the fifth level portal behind him a minute or two later, Ryter in the lead. Orca behind Ryter. All five held leveled guns.

"You won't need the hardware," Quillan assured them. "It's harmless enough now. Come on in."

They followed him silently up to the cubicle, stared comprehendingly at dials and indicators. "The thing's back inside there, all right!" Ryter said. He looked at Quillan. "Is this where you've been all the time?"

"Sure. Where else?" The others were forming a half-circle about him, a few paces back.

"Taking quite a chance with that Hlat, weren't you?" Ryter remarked.

"Not too much. I thought of something." Quillan indicated the outportal in the hall. "I had my back against that. A portal's space-break, not solid matter. It couldn't come at me from behind. And if it attacked from any other angle"—he tapped the holstered Miam Devil lightly, and the gun in Orca's hand jerked upward a fraction of an inch—"There aren't many animals that can swallow more than a bolt or two from that baby and keep coming."

There was a moment's silence. Then Orca said thoughtfully, "That would work!"

"Did it see you?" Ryter asked.

"It couldn't have. First I saw of it, it was sailing out from that corner over there. It slammed in after that chunk of sea beef so fast, it shook the cubicle. And that was that." He grinned. "Well, most of our troubles should be over now!"

One of the men gave a brief, nervous laugh. Quillan looked at him curiously. "Something, chum?"

Ryter shook his head. "Something is right! Come on downstairs again, Bad News. This time we have news for you—"

The Brotherhood guards on the ground level had been taken by surprise and shot down almost without losses for the Star men. But the battle on the fourth level had cost more than the dead left up there. An additional number had returned with injuries that were serious enough to make them useless for further work.

"It's been expensive," Ryter admitted. "But one more attack by the Hlat would have left me with a panicked mob on my hands. If we'd realized it was going to trap itself—"

"I wasn't so sure that would work either," Quillan said. "Did you get Kinmarten back?"

"Not yet. The chances are he's locked up somewhere on the fourth level. Now the Hlat's out of the way, some of the men have gone back up there to look for him. If Cooms thought he was important enough to start a fight over, I want him back."

"How about the crew on the Beldon ship?" Quillan asked. "Have they been cleaned up?"

"No," Ryter said. "We'll have to do that now, of course."

"How many of them?"

"Supposedly twelve. And that's probably what it is."

"If they know or suspect what's happened," Quillan said, "twelve men can give a boarding party in a lock a remarkable amount of trouble."

Ryter shrugged irritably. "I know, but there isn't much choice. Lancion's bringing in the other group on the *Camelot*. We don't want to have to handle both of them at the same time."

"How are you planning to take the freighter?"

"When the search party comes back down, we'll put every man we can spare from guard duty here on the job. They'll be instructed to be careful about it . . . if they can wind up the matter within the next several hours, that will be early enough. We can't afford too many additional losses now. But we should come out with enough men to take care of Lancion and handle the shipment of Hlats. And that's what counts."

"Like me to take charge of the boarding party?" Quillan inquired. "That sort of thing's been a kind of specialty of mine."

Ryter looked at him without much expression on his face. "I understand that," he said. "But perhaps it would be better if you stayed up here with us."

✧   ✧   ✧

The search party came back down ten minutes later. They'd looked through every corner of the fourth level. Kinmarten wasn't there, either dead or alive. But one observant member of the group had discovered, first, that the Duke of Fluel was also not among those present, and, next, that one of the four outportals on the level had been unsealed. The exit on which the portal was found to be set was in a currently unused hall in the General Offices building on the other side of the Star. From that hall, almost every other section of the Star was within convenient portal range.

None of the forty-odd people working in the main control office on the ground level had actually witnessed any shooting; but it was apparent that a number of them were uncomfortably aware that something quite extraordinary must be going on. They were a well-disciplined group, however. An occasional uneasy glance toward one of the armed men lounging along the walls, some anxious faces, were the only noticeable indications of tension. Now and then, there was a brief, low-pitched conversation at one of the desks.

Quillan stood near the center of the office, Ryter and Orca a dozen feet from him on either side. Four Star guards were stationed along the walls. From the office one could see through a large doorspace cut through both sides of a hall directly into the adjoining transmitter room. Four more guards were in there. Aside from the men in the entrance hall and at the subspace portal, what was available at the moment of Ryter's security force was concentrated at this point.

The arrangement made considerable sense; and Quillan gave no sign of being aware that the eyes of the guards shifted to him a little more frequently than to any other point in the office, or that none of them had moved his hand very far away from his gun since they had come in here. But that also made sense. In the general tension area of the Executive Block's ground level, a specific point of tension—highly charged though undetected by the noninvolved personnel—was the one provided by the presence of Bad News Quillan here. Ryter was more than suspicious by now; the opened portal on the fourth level, the disappearance of Kinmarten and the Duke, left room for a wide variety of speculations. Few of those speculations could be very favorable to Bad News. Ryter obviously preferred to let things stand as they were until the Beldon freighter was taken and the major part of his group had returned from the subspace sections of the Star. At that time, Bad News could expect to come in for some very direct questioning by the security chief.

The minutes dragged on. Under the circumstances, a glance at his watch could be enough to bring Ryter's uncertainties up to the explosion point, and Quillan also preferred to let things stand as they were for the moment. But he felt reasonably certain that over an hour had passed since he'd left Reetal; and so far there had been no hint of anything unusual occurring in the front part of the building. The murmur of voices in the main control office continued to eddy about him. There were indications that in the transmitter room across the hall messages had begun to be exchanged between the Star and the approaching liner.

A man sitting at a desk near Quillan stood up presently, went out into the hall and disappeared. A short while later, the white-suited figure returned and picked up the interrupted work. Quillan's glance went over the clerk, shifted on. He felt something tighten up swiftly inside him. There was a considerable overall resemblance, but *that* wasn't the man who had left the office.

Another minute or two went by. Then two other uniformed figures appeared at the opening to the hall, a sparse elderly man, a blond girl. They stood there talking earnestly together for some seconds, then came slowly down the aisle toward Quillan. It appeared to be an argument about some detail of her work. The girl frowned, stubbornly shaking her head. Near Quillan they separated, started off into different sections of the office. The girl, glancing back, still frowning, brushed against Ryter. She looked up at him, startled.

"I'm sorry," she said.

Ryter scowled irritably, started to say something, suddenly appeared surprised. Then his eyes went blank and his knees buckled under him.

The clerk sitting at the nearby desk whistled shrilly.

Quillan wheeled, gun out and up, toward the wall behind him. The two guards there were still lifting their guns. The Miam Devil grunted disapprovingly twice, and the guards went down. Noise crashed from the hall . . . heavy sporting rifles. He turned again, saw the two other guards stumbling backward along the far wall. Feminine screaming erupted around the office as the staff dove out of sight behind desks, instrument stands and filing cabinets. The elderly man stood above Orca, a sap in his hand and a pleased smile on his face.

In the hallway, four white-uniformed men had swung about and were pointing blazing rifles into the transmitter room. The racketing of the gunfire ended abruptly and the rifles were lowered again. The human din in the office began to diminish, turned suddenly into a shocked, strained silence. Quillan realized the blond girl was standing at his elbow.

"Did you get the rest of them?" he asked quickly, in a low voice.

"Everyone who was on this level," Reetal told him. "There weren't many of them."

"I know. But there's a sizable batch still in the subspace section. If we can get the bomb disarmed, we'll just leave them sealed up there. How long before you can bring Ryter around?"

"He'll be able to talk in five minutes."

6

Quillan had been sitting for some little while in a very comfortable chair in what had been the commodore's personal suite on the Seventh Star, broodingly regarding the image of the *Camelot* in a huge wall screen. The liner was still over two hours' flight away but would arrive on schedule. On the Star, at least in the normspace section, everything was quiet; and in the main control offices and in the transmitter room normal working conditions had been restored.

A room portal twenty feet away opened suddenly, and Reetal Destone stepped out.

"So there you are!" she observed.

Quillan looked mildly surprised then grinned. "I'd hate to have to try to hide from you!" he said.

"Hm-m-m!" said Reetal. She smiled. "What are you drinking?"

He nodded at an open liquor cabinet near the screen. "Velladon was leaving some excellent stuff behind. Join me?"

"Hm-m-m." She went to the cabinet, looked over the bottles, made her selection and filled a glass. "One has the impression," she remarked, "that you *were* hiding from me."

"One does? I'd have to be losing my cotton-picking mind—"

"Not necessarily." Reetal brought the drink over to his chair, sat down on the armrest with it. "You might just have a rather embarrassing problem to get worked out before you give little Reetal a chance to start asking questions about it."

Quillan looked surprised. "What gave you that notion?"

"Oh," Reetal said, "adding things up gave me that notion . . . Care to hear what the things were?"

"Go ahead, doll."

"First," said Reetal, "I understand that a while ago, after you'd first sent me off to do some little job for you, you were in the transmitter room having a highly private—shielded and scrambled—conversation with somebody on board the *Camelot*."

"Why, yes," Quillan said. "I was talking to the ship's security office. They're arranging to have a Federation police boat pick up what's left of the commodore's boys and the Brotherhood in the subspace section."

"And that," said Reetal, "is where that embarrassing little problem begins. Next, I noticed, as I say, that you were showing this tendency to avoid a chance for a private talk between us. And after thinking about that for a little, and also about a few other things which came to mind at around that time, I went to see Ryter."

"Now why—?"

Reetal ran her fingers soothingly through his hair. "Let me finish, big boy. I found Ryter and Orca in a highly nervous condition. And do you know why they're nervous? They're convinced that some time before the *Camelot* gets here, you're going to do them both in."

"Hm-m-m," said Quillan.

"Ryter," she went on, "besides being nervous, is also very bitter. In retrospect, he says, it's all very plain what you've done here. You and your associates—a couple of tough boys named Hagready and Boltan, and others not identified—are also after these Hlats. The Duke made some mention of that, too, you remember. The commodore and Ryter bought the story you told them because a transmitter check produced the information that Hagready and Boltan had, in fact, left their usual work areas and gone off on some highly secret business about a month ago.

"Ryter feels that your proposition—to let your gang in on the deal for twenty per cent, or else—was made in something less than good faith. He's concluded that when you learned of the operation being planned by Velladon and the Brotherhood, you and your pals decided to obstruct them and take the Hlats for delivery to Yaco yourselves, without cutting anybody in. He figures that someone like Hagready or Boltan is coming in on the *Camelot* with a flock of sturdy henchmen to do just that. You, personally, rushed to the Seventh Star to interfere as much as you could here. Ryter admits reluctantly that you did an extremely good job of interfering. He says it's now obvious that every move you made since you showed up had the one purpose of setting the Star group and the Brotherhood at each other's throats. And now that they've practically wiped each other out, you and your associates can go on happily with your original plans.

"But, of course, you can't do that if Ryter and Orca are picked up alive by the Federation cops. The boys down in the subspace section don't matter; they're ordinary gunhands and all they know is that you were somebody who showed up on the scene. But Ryter could, and certainly would, talk—"

"Ah, he's too imaginative," Quillan said, taking a swallow of his drink. "I never heard of the Hlats before I got here. As I told you, I'm on an entirely different kind of job at the moment. I had to make up some kind of story to get an in with the boys, that's all."

"So you're not going to knock those two weasels off?"

"No such intentions. I don't mind them sweating about it till the Feds arrive, but that's it."

"What about Boltan and Hagready?"

"What about them? I did happen to know that if anyone started asking questions about those two, he'd learn that neither had been near his regular beat for close to a month."

"I'll bet!" Reetal said cryptically.

"What do you mean by that?"

"Hm-m-m," she said. "Bad News Quillan! A really tough boy, for sure. You know, I didn't believe for an instant that you were after the Hlats—"

"Why not?"

Reetal said, "I've been on a couple of operations with you, and you'd be surprised how much I've picked up about you from time to time on the side. Swiping a shipment of odd animals and selling them to Yaco, that could be Bad News, in character. Selling a couple of hundred human beings—like Brock and Solvey Kinmarten—to go along with the animals to an outfit like Yaco would not be in character."

"So I have a heart of gold," Quillan said.

"So you fell all over your own big feet about half a minute ago!" Reetal told him. "Bad News Quillan—with no interest whatsoever in the Hlats—still couldn't afford to let Ryter live to talk about him to the Feds, big boy!"

Quillan looked reflective for a moment. "Dirty trick!" he observed. "For that, you might freshen up my glass."

Reetal took both glasses over to the liquor cabinet, freshened them up, and settled down on the armrest of the chair again. "So there we're back to the embarrassing little problem," she said.

"Ryter?"

"No, idiot. We both know that Ryter is headed for Rehabilitation. Fifteen years or so of it, at a guess. The problem is little Reetal who has now learned a good deal more than she was ever intended to learn. Does she head for Rehabilitation, too?"

Quillan took a swallow of his drink and set the glass down again. "Are you suggesting," he inquired, "that I might be, excuse the expression, a cop?"

Reetal patted his head. "Bad News Quillan! Let's look back at his record. What do we find? A shambles, mainly. Smashed-up organizations, outfits, gangs. Top-level crooks with suddenly vacant expressions and unexplained holes in their heads. Why go on? The name is awfully well earned! And nobody realizing anything because the ones who do realize it suddenly . . . well, where *are* Boltan and Hagready at the moment?"

Quillan sighed. "Since you keep bringing it up—Hagready played it smart, so he's in Rehabilitation. Be cute if Ryter ran into him there some day. Pappy Boltan didn't want to play it smart. I'm not enough of a philosopher to make a guess at where he might be at present. But I knew he wouldn't be talking."

"All right," Reetal said, "we've got that straight. Bad News is Intelligence of some kind. Federation maybe, or maybe one of the services. It doesn't matter, really, I suppose. Now, what about me?"

He reached out and tapped his glass with a fingertip. "That about you, doll. You filled it. I'm drinking it. I may not think quite as fast as you do, but I still think. Would I take a drink from a somewhat lawless and very clever lady who really believed I had her lined up for Rehabilitation? Or who'd be at all likely to blab out something that would ruin an old pal's reputation?"

Reetal ran her fingers through his hair again. "I noticed the deal with the drink," she said. "I guess I just wanted to hear you say it. You don't tell on me, I don't tell on you. Is that it?"

"That's it," Quillan said. "What Ryter and Orca want to tell the Feds doesn't matter. It stops there; the Feds will have the word on me before they arrive. By the way, did you go wake up the Kinmartens yet?"

"Not yet," Reetal said. "Too busy getting the office help soothed down and back to work."

"Well, let's finish these drinks and go do that, then. The little doll's almost bound to be asleep by now, but she might still be sitting there biting nervously at her pretty knuckles."

Major Heslet Quillan, of Space Scout Intelligence, was looking unhappy. "We're still searching for them everywhere," he explained to Klayung, "but it's a virtual certainty that the Hlat got them shortly before it was trapped."

Klayung, a stringy, white-haired old gentleman, was an operator of the Psychology Service, in charge of the shipment of Hlats the *Camelot* had brought in. He and Quillan were waiting in the vestibule of the Seventh Star's rest cubicle vaults for Lady Pendrake's cubicle to be brought over from the Executive Block.

Klayung said reflectively, "Couldn't the criminals with whom you were dealing here have hidden the couple away somewhere?"

Quillan shook his head. "There's no way they could have located them so quickly. I made half a dozen portal switches when I was taking Kinmarten to the suite. It would take something with a Hlat's abilities to follow me over that route and stay undetected. And it must be an unusually cunning animal to decide to stay out of sight until I'd led it where it wanted to go."

"Oh, they're intelligent enough," Klayung agreed absently. "Their average basic I.Q. is probably higher than that of human beings. A somewhat different type of mentality, of course. Well, when the cubicle arrives, I'll question the Hlat and we'll find out."

Quillan looked at him. "Those control devices make it possible to hold two-way conversations with the things?"

"Not exactly," Klayung said. "You see, major, the government authorities who were concerned with the discovery of the Hlats realized it would be almost impossible to keep some information about them from getting out. The specimen which was here on the Star has been stationed at various scientific institutions for the past year; a rather large number of people were involved in investigating it and experimenting with it. In consequence, several little legends about them have been deliberately built up. The legends aren't entirely truthful, so they help to keep the actual facts about the Hlats satisfactorily vague."

"The Hlat-talker is such a legend. Actually, the device does nothing. The Hlats respond to telepathic stimuli, both among themselves and from other beings, eventually begin to correlate such stimuli with the meanings of human speech."

"Then you—" Quillan began.

"Yes. Eltak, their discoverer, was a fairly good natural telepath. If he hadn't been abysmally lazy, he might have been very good at it. I carry a variety of the Service's psionic knickknacks about with me, which gets me somewhat comparable results."

He broke off as the vestibule portal dilated widely. Lady Pendrake's cubicle floated through, directed by two gravity crane operators behind it. Klayung stood up.

"Set it there for the present, please," he directed the operators. "We may call for you later if it needs to be moved again."

He waited until the portal had closed behind the men before walking over to the cubicle. He examined the settings and readings at some length.

"Hm-m-m, yes," he said, straightening finally. His expression became absent for a few seconds; then he went on. "I'm beginning to grasp the situation, I believe. Let me tell you a few things about the Hlats, major. For one, they form quite pronounced likes and dislikes. Eltak, for example, would have been described by most of his fellow men as a rather offensive person. But the Hlats actually became rather fond of him during the fifteen or so years he lived on their island.

"That's one point. The other has to do with their level of intelligence. We discovered on the way out here that our charges had gained quite as comprehensive an understanding of the functioning of the cubicles that had been constructed for them as any human who was not a technical specialist might do. And—"

He interrupted himself, stood rubbing his chin for a moment.

"Well, actually," he said, "that should be enough to prepare you for a look inside the Hlat's cubicle."

Quillan gave him a somewhat surprised glance. "I've been told it's ugly as sin," he remarked. "But I've seen some fairly revolting looking monsters before this."

Klayung coughed. "That's not exactly what I meant," he said. "I . . . well, let's just open the thing up. Would you mind, major?"

"Not at all." Quillan stepped over to the side of the cubicle, unlocked the door switch and pulled it over. They both moved back a few feet before the front of the cubicle. A soft humming came for some seconds from the door's mechanisms; then it suddenly swung open. Quillan stooped to glance inside, straightened instantly again, hair bristling.

"*Where is it?*" he demanded, the Miam Devil out in his hand.

Klayung looked at him thoughtfully. "Not very far away, I believe. But I can assure you, major, that it hasn't the slightest intention of attacking us—or anybody else—at present."

Quillan grunted, looked back into the cubicle. At the far end, the Kinmartens lay side by side, their faces composed. They appeared to be breathing regularly.

"Yes," Klayung said, "they're alive and unharmed." He rubbed his chin again. "And I think it would be best if we simply closed the cubicle now. Later we can call a doctor over from the hospital to put them under sedation before they're taken out. They've both had thoroughly unnerving experiences, and it would be advisable to awaken them gradually to avoid emotional shock."

He moved over to the side of the cubicle, turned the door switch back again. "And now for the rest of it," he said. "We may as well sit down again, major. This may take a little time."

"Let's look at the thing for a moment from the viewpoint of the Hlat," he resumed when he was once more comfortably seated. "Eltak's death took it by surprise. It hadn't at that point grasped what the situation in the Executive Block was like. It took itself out of sight for the moment, killing one of the gang leaders in the process, then began prowling about the various levels of the building, picking up information from the minds and conversation of the men it encountered. In a fairly short time, it learned enough to understand what was planned by the criminals; and it arrived at precisely your own conclusion . . . that it might be possible to reduce and demoralize the gangs to the extent that they would no longer be able to carry out their plan. It began a systematic series of attacks on them with that end in mind.

"But meanwhile you had come into the picture. The Hlat was rather puzzled by your motive at first because there appeared to be an extraordinary degree of discrepancy between what you were saying and what you were thinking. But after observing your activities for a while, it began to comprehend what you were trying to do. It realized that your approach was more likely to succeed than its own, and that further action on its side might interfere with your plans. But there remained one thing for it to do.

"I may tell you in confidence, major, that another legend which has been spread about these Hlats is their supposed inability to escape from the cubicles. Even their attendants are supplied with this particular bit of misinformation. Actually, the various force fields in the cubicles don't hamper them in the least. The cubicles are designed simply to protect the Hlats and keep them from being seen; and rest cubicles, of course, can be taken anywhere without arousing undue curiosity.

"You mentioned that the Kinmartens are very likable young people. The Hlat had the same feeling about them; they were the only human beings aside from Eltak with whose minds it had become quite familiar. There was no assurance at this point that the plans to prevent a bomb from being exploded in the Star would be successful, and the one place where human beings could hope to survive such an explosion was precisely the interior of the Hlat's cubicle, which had been constructed to safeguard its occupant against any kind of foreseeable accident.

"So the Hlat sprang your cubicle trap, removed the bait, carried the Kinmartens inside, and whipped out of the cubicle again before the rest current could take effect on it. It concluded correctly that everyone would decide it had been recaptured. After that, it moved about the Executive Block, observing events there and prepared to take action again if that appeared to be advisable. When you had concluded your operation successfully, it remained near the cubicle, waiting for me to arrive."

Quillan shook his head. "That's quite an animal!" he observed after some seconds. "You say it's in our general vicinity now?"

"Yes," Klayung said. "It followed the cubicle down here, and has been drifting about the walls of the vestibule while we . . . well, while I talked."

"Why doesn't it show itself?"

Klayung cleared his throat. "For two reasons," he said. "One is that rather large gun you're holding on your knees. It saw you use it several times, and after all the shooting in the Executive Block, you see—"

Quillan slid the Miam Devil into its holster. "Sorry," he said. "Force of habit, I guess. Actually, of course, I've understood for some minutes now that I wasn't . . . well, what's the other reason?"

"I'm afraid," Klayung said, "that you offended it with your remark about its appearance. Hlats may have their share of vanity. At any rate, it seems to be sulking."

"Oh," said Quillan. "Well, I'm sure," he went on rather loudly, "that it understands I received the description from a prejudiced source. I'm quite willing to believe it was highly inaccurate."

"Hm-m-m," said Klayung. "That seems to have done it, major. The wall directly across from us—"

Something like a ripple passed along the sidewall of the vestibule. Then the wall darkened suddenly, turned black. Quillan blinked, and the Hlat came into view. It hung, spread out like a spider, along half the length of the vestibule wall. Something like a huge, hairy amoeba in overall appearance, though the physical structures under the coarse, black pelt must be of very unamoebalike complexity. No eyes were in sight, but Quillan had the impression of being regarded steadily. Here and there, along the edges and over the surface of the body, were a variety of flexible extensions.

Quillan stood up, hitched his gun belt into position, and started over toward the wall.

"Lady Pendrake," he said, "honored to meet you. Could we shake hands?"

Aura of Immortality

Commissioner Holati Tate had been known to state on occasion that whenever there was a way for Professor Mantelish to get himself into a mess of trouble, Mantelish would find it.

When, therefore, the Commissioner, while flicking through a series of newscasts, caught a momentary view of Mantelish chatting animatedly with a smiling young woman he stopped the instrument instantly, and with a touch of apprehension went back to locate the program in question. The last he had heard of Mantelish, the professor had been on a government-sponsored expedition to a far-off world, from which, the Commissioner had understood, he would not be returning for some time. However, Commissioner Tate had just got back to Maccadon from an assignment himself, for all he knew Mantelish might have changed his plans. Indeed, it would seem he had.

He caught the program again, clicked it in. One good look at the great, bear-like figure and the mane of thick white hair told him it was indeed his old friend Mantelish. The dainty lady sitting across the table from Mantelish was a professional newscaster. The background was the Ceyce spaceport on Maccadon. The professor evidently had just come off his ship.

His sense of apprehension deepening, Commissioner Tate began to listen sharply to what was being said.

Professor Mantelish ordinarily was allergic in the extreme to newscasters and rebuffed their efforts to pump him about his projects with such heavy sarcasm that even the brashest did not often attempt to interview him on a live show. On the other hand he was highly susceptible to pretty women. When a gorgeous little reporter spotted him among the passengers coming off a spaceliner at Ceyce Port and inquired timidly whether he would answer a few questions for her viewers, the great scientist surprised her no end by settling down for a friendly fifteen-minute chat during which he reported on his visit to the little-known planet of the Tang from which he had just returned.

It was a fine scoop for the newscaster. Professor Mantelish's exploits and adventures were a legend in the Hub and he was always good copy—when he could be persuaded to talk. On this occasion, furthermore, he had something to tell which was in itself of more than a little interest. The Tang—who could be called a humanoid species only if one were willing to stretch a number of points—had been contacted by human explorers some decades before. They tended to be ferociously hostile to strangers and had a number of other highly unpleasant characteristics; so far little had become known of them beyond the fact that they were rather primitive creatures living in small, footloose tribes on a cold and savage planet.

Professor Mantelish, however, had spent several months among them, accompanied by a team of specialists with whose help he had cracked the language barrier which previously had prevented free communication with the

Tang. He had made copious recordings of their habits and customs, had even been permitted to bring back a dead Tang embalmed by freezing as was their practice. From the scientific viewpoint this was a very valuable specimen, since the Tang appeared to die only as a result of accident, murder, or in encounters with ferocious beasts. They did not suffer from diseases and had developed a means of extending their natural life span almost indefinitely . . .

The young newscaster latched on to that statement like a veteran. Wide-eyed and innocent, she slipped in a few leading questions and Mantelish launched into a detailed explanation.

It had taken some months before he gained the confidence of the Tang sufficiently to induce them to reveal their secret: they distilled the juice of a carefully tended and guarded plant through an involved procedure. The drug they obtained in this way brought about a reversal of the normal aging process so that they retained their youthful health and vigor for a length of time which, though it had not been precisely determined, the Tang regarded as "forever."

Could this drug, the little reporter asked, perhaps be adapted for human use?

Mantelish said he could not be definite about that, but it seemed quite possible. While the Tang had not let the members of his expedition know what plant they cultivated for the purpose, they had obligingly presented him with several liters of the distilled drug for experimentation which he had brought back with him. Analysis of the drug while still on the Tang planet had revealed the presence of several heretofore unknown forms of protein with rather puzzling characteristics; the question was whether or not these could be reproduced in the laboratory. To settle the question might well take a number of years—it could not of course be stated at present what the long-term effect of the drug on human beings would be. It was, however, apparently harmless. He and several other members of his group had been injected with significant quantities of the drug while on the planet, and had suffered no ill effects.

Big-eyed again, the newscaster inquired whether this meant that he, Professor Mantelish, was now immortal?

No, no, Mantelish said hastily. In humans, as in the Tang, the effects of a single dose wore off in approximately four months. To retain youth, or to bring about the gradual rejuvenation of an older body, it was necessary to repeat the dosage regularly at about this interval. The practice of the Tang was to alternately permit themselves to age naturally for about ten years, then to use the drug for roughly the same length of time or until youthfulness was restored.

To protect both the Tang and their miracle plant from illegal exploitation, the Federation, following his initial report on the matter, was having the space about the planet patrolled. What the final benefits of the discovery to humanity would be was still open to question. It was, however, his personal opinion that the Tang drug eventually would take its place as a very valuable addition to the various rejuvenation processes currently being employed in the Hub . . .

"The old idiot!" Commissioner Holati Tate muttered to himself. He swung around, found a redheaded young woman standing behind him, large, gray eyes intently watching the screen. "Did you hear all that, Trigger?" he demanded.

"Enough to get the idea," Trigger said. "I came in as soon as I recognized the prof's voice . . . After those remarks, he'd be safer back among the Tang! He doesn't even seem to have a bodyguard around."

Commissioner Tate was dialing a ComWeb number. "I'll call the spaceport police! They'll give him an escort. Hop on the other ComWeb and see his home and lab are under guard by the time he gets there."

"I just did that," Trigger said.

"Then see if you can make an emergency contact with that newscaster female before Mantelish strays off . . ."

Trigger shook her head. "I tried it. No luck! It's a floating program."

She watched the final minute and a half of the newscast, biting her lip uneasily, while the Commissioner made hasty arrangements with the spaceport police. To hear Professor Mantelish blabbing out the fact that he might have the answer to man's search for immortality in his possession was disconcerting. It was an open invitation to all the criminal elements currently on Maccadon to try to get it from him. The prof simply shouldn't be allowed to wander around without tactful but efficient nursemaiding! Usually, she or Holati or somebody else made sure he got it, but they'd assumed that on a Federation expedition he'd be kept out of jams . . .

When the Commissioner had finished, she switched off the newscast, said glumly, "You missed something, Holati. Mantelish just showed everybody watching on umpteen worlds the container he's got that drug in!"

"The Tang stuff?"

"Yes. It's in that round sort of suitcase he had standing beside his chair."

The Commissioner swore.

"Come along!" he said. "We'll take my car and head for the spaceport. The police weren't sure from exactly where that newscast was coming but if they catch up with Mantelish before he leaves they'll wait for us and we'll ride in to his lab with him."

"And if they don't?"

"They'll call the car. Then we'll go to the lab and wait for him to show up."

Almost as soon as he'd bid the charming little newscaster goodbye, Professor Mantelish himself began to feel some qualms about the revelations he'd allowed to escape.

He began to realize he might have been a trifle indiscreet. Walking on with the crowds moving towards the spaceport exit hall, he found himself growing acutely conscious of the Tang drug container in the suitcase he carried. Normally preoccupied with a variety of matters of compelling scientific interest, it was almost impossible for him to conceive of himself as being in personal danger. Nevertheless, now that his attention was turned on the situation he had created it became clear that many people who had watched the newscast might feel tempted to bring the drug into their possession, either for selfish reasons or out of perhaps excessive zeal for private research . . .

The average citizen at this point might have started looking around for the nearest police officer. Professor Mantelish, however, was of independent nature; such a solution simply did not occur to him. He had advertised the fact that he was headed for his laboratory. That had been a mistake. Therefore he would not go there—which should foil anyone who was presently entertaining illegal notions about the Tang drug. Instead, he would take himself and the drug immediately to a little seaside hideout he maintained which was known only to his closest associates. Once there he could take steps to have the drug safeguarded.

Satisfied with this decision Mantelish lengthened his stride. About a hundred yards ahead was the entry to an automatic aircar rental station. As he came up half a dozen people turned into it in a group, obviously harmless citizens. Mantelish followed them in, moved over to the wall just inside the entry, turned and stood waiting, prepared, if required, to swing the weighted suitcase he held under his flowing robe like an oversized club. But half a minute passed and no one else came in. Satisfied, he hurried after the little group, catching up with them just as they reached the line of waiting cars and climbed into a car together, laughing and joking. Mantelish got into the car behind them, deposited a five-credit piece. The cars began to move forwards, rose toward the exit. He glanced back to make sure again that no one was following, placed the Tang container on the floorboards beside him, snapped the car's canopy shut and put his hands on the controls.

The aircars emerged from the fifteenth floor of the spaceport exit building, the lights of Ceyce glittering under its night-screen before them. Mantelish turned immediately to the left, directed the car up to one of the main traffic lines, moved along it for a minute, then shifted abruptly to one of the upper high-speed lanes.

He reached his hideaway a scant fifteen minutes later. It was in a residential shore area, featuring quiet and privacy. The house, overlooking a shallow, sheltered ocean bay, was built on sloping ground thirty feet above tide level. It was a pleasant place, fit for an elderly retired man of remarkable habits. None of Mantelish's neighbors knew him by name or suspected he maintained a laboratory within his walls—an installation in absolute violation of the local zoning regulations.

He locked the entry door behind him, crossed a hall, opened the door to the laboratory. He stood motionless a moment, looking around. Everything was as he had left it months before, kept spotlessly clean by automatic maintenance machinery. He went over to a table on which lay a variety of items, the results of projects he had hastily completed or left incomplete before setting out on the expedition to the Tang world. He put the Tang container on the table between a chemical gun and a packaged device which, according to the instructions attached to it, was a mental accelerator with a ratio of two hundred and eighty to one, instantly lethal if used under conditions other than those specified in the instructions. He looked about once more, went out by another door to the kitchen of the house.

A minute or two later, he heard the laboratory ComWeb buzzing shrilly. Mantelish glanced around from the elaborate open-face sandwiches he was preparing. He frowned. Among the very few people who knew the number of that ComWeb, only two were at all likely to be calling him at this moment. One was Commissioner Tate, the other was Trigger Argee. If either of them— Trigger, in particular—had caught the newscast at the spaceport just now they were going to give him hell.

His frown deepened. Should he ignore the call? No, he decided; however unnecessarily, the caller was no doubt concerned about his safety. He must let them know he was all right.

Mantelish lumbered hurriedly back into the laboratory, came to a sudden stop just beyond the door. There were two men there. One was seated at the table where he had put down the Tang container; the other leaned against the wall beside the hall door. Both held guns, which at the moment were pointed at him.

Mantelish looked from one to the other, lifting his eyebrows. This, he told himself, was a most unfortunate situation. He knew the pair from a previous meeting, the conclusion of which had been marked by a certain amount of physical violence. He didn't like the look of the guns but perhaps he could bluff it out.

"Fiam," he said with stern dignity to the man at the table, "I am not at all pleased by your intrusion. I thought I had made it clear to you last year when I threw you out of my laboratory that there was no possibility of our doing business. If I failed, I shall make the point very clear indeed immediately after I have answered this call!"

He turned toward the clamoring ComWeb. Suddenly he felt an excruciating pain in his left leg, centered on the kneecap. He grunted, stopped.

"That's enough for now, Welk," Paes Fiam said lazily from the table. "He's got the idea . . ."

The pain faded away. The man standing by the door

grinned and lowered his gun. Fiam went on, "Sit down over there, professor—across from me. Forget the ComWeb. This shouldn't take long. These guns of ours, as you've noticed, can be very painful. They can also kill very quickly. So let's not have any unpleasantness."

Mantelish scowled at him but sat down. "Why have you come here?" he demanded.

Fiam smiled. "To ask you for a small favor. And a little information." He picked up the chemical gun lying on the table beside the Tang container, looked at it a moment. "This device," he said, "appears to be something you've developed. "

"It is," Mantelish said.

"What is so remarkable about it?"

Mantelish snorted. "It kills the intended victim immediately on spray contact while placing the user in no danger whatsoever, even when carelessly handled."

"So the label says," Paes Fiam agreed. "A one to four foot range. Very interesting!" He laid the gun back on the table. "I find it a little strange, professor, that a man holding the high ethical principles you outlined to me in our previous conversation should devote his time to creating such a murderous little weapon!"

Mantelish snorted again. "What I am willing to create depends on the clients with whom I am dealing. I would not place such weapons in the hands of common crooks like yourselves."

The ComWeb's noise stopped. Fiam smiled briefly, said, "Not common crooks, Professor Mantelish. We happen to be exceptionally talented and efficient crooks. As the present situation demonstrates."

"What do you mean?" Mantelish asked coldly.

"I happened to be at the Ceyce spaceport," Fiam said, "while you were bragging about your Tang immortality drug on the newscast. I took steps immediately to make sure I knew where you went. Welk and I followed you here without very much trouble. We made sure in the process that nobody else was tailing you." He patted the Tang container. "This is what we're after, professor! And we've got it."

"You are being very foolish," Mantelish said. "As I indicated during the newscast, it remains questionable whether the Tang drug can be produced under laboratory conditions. If it is possible, it will involve years of research at the highest level. I—"

"Hold it, professor!" Fiam raised his hand, nodded at Welk. "Your statements are very interesting, but let's make sure you're not attempting to mislead us."

"Mislead you?" Mantelish rumbled indignantly.

"You might, you know. But Welk will now place the pickup of a lie detector at your feet. Sit very still while he's doing it—you know I can't miss at this range." Fiam brought a small instrument out of his pocket, placed it on the table before him. "This is the detector's indicator," he went on. "A very dependable device, every time it shows me you're being less than truthful you'll get an admonishing jolt from Welk's gun. Welk's never really forgiven you for not opening the lab door before you ejected him last year. Better stick to the truth, professor!"

"I have no intention of lying," Mantelish said with dignity.

Paes Fiam waited until Welk had positioned the pickup and stepped back, went on. "Now, professor, you were suggesting that at present the Tang drug has no commercial value . . ."

Mantelish nodded. "Exactly! The quantity on the table here—and it's every drop of the drug to be found off the Tang world now—is not nearly enough to be worth the risk you'd be taking in stealing and trying to market it. It might extend the life of one human being by a very considerable extent, and that is all. And what potential client would take your word for it that it would do that— or that it wouldn't, for that matter, harm him instead, perhaps kill him within a few months?"

"A large number of potential clients would, if they were desperate enough for life," Fiam said, watching the detector indicator. "You were skirting the fringes of deception with that question, professor. But that's not the point. *Does* the drug have harmful physical or mental effects?"

Mantelish said, "A calculated quantity was given to six members of our expedition, including myself. During the past four months, no harmful physical or mental effects have been observed, and the overall effect has worn off again. That's all I can say."

"And the Tang drug did have a rejuvenating effect on these human subjects?"

Mantelish hesitated, admitted, "A slight but measurable one. That was in accordance with our expectations."

Fiam smiled. "I see. What other expectations did you have in connection with the use of the drug on human beings?"

Mantelish said reluctantly, "That the dosage given human subjects would wear out of the system in about four months—as it did. And that if the rejuvenation effect were to continue the treatment would therefore have to be repeated regularly at four-month intervals."

"What do you believe will happen if that is done?"

"Within a ten-year period," Mantelish said, "the subject should find that his biological age has not advanced but has been reduced by about five years. The Tang rejuvenation process is a slow, steady one. The Tang themselves select the biological age they prefer, and remain within a few years of it by a judicious use of the drug. It is, of course, impossible to reduce the biological age beyond late adolescence."

"I understand," Fiam said. "And how is the drug administered?"

"The Tang drink the extract," Mantelish said. "On human beings it has a violently nauseating effect when administered in that form. We found it more practical to administer a subcutaneous injection."

"There's nothing essentially different between that and any other subcutaneous injection?"

"No, none at all."

Paes Fiam patted the container again, smiled, said, "The drug extract in here is ready to be used exactly as it is?"

"Yes."

"Are there any special measures required to preserve its usefulness and harmlessness indefinitely?"

"It's self-preserving," Mantelish said. "There should be no significant difference in its properties whether it's used today or after a century. But as I have pointed out, I cannot and will not say that it is harmless. A test on six subjects is by no means definitive. The seventh one might show very undesirable physical reactions. Or undesirable reactions might develop in the six who have been tested five, or ten, or fifteen years from now . . ."

"No doubt," Fiam said. He smacked his lips lightly. "Be careful how you answer my next question. You said the drug in this container should extend the life of one human being very considerably. What does that mean in standard years?"

Mantelish hesitated, said grudgingly, "My estimate would be about three hundred years. That is an approximation."

Fiam grinned happily at Welk. "Three hundred years, eh? That's good enough for us, professor! As you may have begun to surmise, we're the clients for whom the drug is intended. We have no intention of trying to sell it. And we'll take a chance on undesirable reactions showing up in five or ten years against the probability of another hundred and fifty years of interesting and profitable living!"

He stood up, moved back from the table. "Now then, you've got the equipment to administer a subcutaneous injection somewhere around the lab. You'll get it out while I keep this gun on you. You'll show Welk exactly what you're doing, describe the exact amount of drug that is required for each injection. And you'll do all that while you're within range of the lie detector. So don't make any mistakes at this stage or, believe me, you'll get hurt abominably!

"Finally, you'll give me the initial four-month injection. I shall then give Welk an identical injection under your supervision. After that, we'll just wrap up the container with the rest of the drug and be on our way . . ."

Ten minutes later Mantelish sat at the table, gloomily watching Fiam store the container, along with several other of the finished products on the table which had caught his fancy, into the suitcase. Welk stood behind the professor's chair, gun pointed at Mantelish's neck.

"Now let me give you the rest of the story on this, professor," Fiam said. He picked up Mantelish's chemical gun, looked at it and placed it on top of the suitcase. "You've mentioned several times that I can't expect to get away with this. Let me reassure you on the point.

"For one thing, we set up a temporal scrambler in this room as soon as we came in. It's on one of those shelves over there. It will remain there and continue in action for thirty minutes after we've left, so no one will be able to restructure the events of the past few hours and identify us in that way. We're wearing plastiskin gloves, of course, and we haven't made any foolish mistakes to give investigators other leads to who might have been here.

"Also we enjoy—under other names—an excellent reputation on this planet as legitimate businessmen from Evalee. Should foul play be suspected, we, even if somebody should think of us, certainly will not be suspected of being involved in it. As a matter of fact"—Fiam checked his watch—"twenty minutes from now, we shall be attending a gay social function in Ceyce to which we have been invited. As far as anybody could prove, we'll have spent all evening there."

He smiled at Mantelish. "One more thing; you will be found dead of course; but there will be some question about the exact manner in which you died. We shall leave an interesting little mystery behind us. The Tang container will be missing. But why is it missing? Did you discover, or fancy you had discovered, some gruesome reaction to the drug in yourself, and drop it out over the sea so no one else would be endangered by it? Did you then perhaps commit suicide in preference to waiting around for the inevitable end?"

"Suicide—pfah!" growled Mantelish. "No one is lunatic enough to commit suicide with a pain-stimulant gun!"

"Quite right," Fiam agreed. He took up the professor's chemical gun from the suitcase again. "I've been studying this little device of yours. It functions in a quite simple and obvious manner. This sets the triggering mechanism—correct? It is now ready to fire." He pointed the gun at Mantelish, added, "Stand aside, Welk."

Welk moved swiftly four feet to one side. Mantelish's eyes widened. "You wouldn't—"

"But I would," Fiam said. And as the professor started up with a furious bellow, he pulled the trigger.

Mantelish's body went rigid, his face contorting into a grisly grin. He thumped sideways down on the table, rolled off it on the side away from Fiam, went crashing down to the floor.

"Ugh!" Welk said, staring down in fascinating incredulity. "His whole face has turned blue!"

"Is he dead?" Fiam inquired, peering over the table.

"I never saw anyone look deader! Or bluer!" Welk reported shakenly.

"Well, don't touch him! The stuff might hit you even through the gloves." Fiam came around the table, laid the gun gingerly on the floor, said, "Shove it over by his hand with something. Then we'll get ourselves lost . . ."

The ComWeb was shrilling again as they went out into the hall, closed the door behind them. After it stopped the laboratory and the rest of Mantelish's house was quiet as a tomb.

"It's a miracle," Trigger said, "that you're still alive!" She looked pale under her tan. The professor had lost the bright cerulean tint Welk had commented on by the time she and Commissioner Tate came rushing into the house a minute or two ago. The skin of his face was now a nasty green through which patches of his normal weathered-brick complexion were just beginning to show.

"No miracle at all, my dear," Mantelish said coolly. "Paes Fiam has encountered the kind of misfortune the uninformed layman may expect when he ventures to challenge the scientist on his own ground. He had lost the game, literally, at the moment he stepped into this laboratory! I had half a dozen means at my disposal here to foil his criminal plans. Since I was also in the laboratory at the time, most of them might have been harmful— or at least extremely disagreeable—to me. So as soon as I saw he intended to use the chemical gun, I decided to employ that method to rid myself of his presence."

Commissioner Tate had been studying the gun's label. "*This* says the gun kills instantly," he observed.

"It does kill instantly," Mantelish said, "if aimed at an attacking Rumlian fire roach. I designed it to aid in the eradication of that noisome species. On the human organism it has only a brief paralyzing effect."

"It makes you look revolting, too!" Trigger said, studying him fascinatedly.

"A minor matter, my dear. Within an hour or two I shall have regained my normal appearance."

Holati Tate sighed, placed the gun back on the table. "Well, we should be able to pick up your friends since we know who they are," he said. "I'll alert the spaceports immediately and get Scout Intelligence on the job. We're lucky though that they didn't get more of a head start."

Mantelish held up his hand. "Please don't concern

yourself about the Tang drug, Holati," he said. "I've notified the police and Fiam and Welk will be arrested very shortly."

The Commissioner said doubtfully, "Well, our Maccadon police—"

"The matter will require no brilliance on their part, Holati. Fiam informed me he and Welk intended to be enjoying themselves innocently at a social function within twenty minutes after leaving this laboratory. That was approximately half an hour ago . . ." Professor Mantelish nodded at the ComWeb. "I expect the police to call at any moment, to advise me they have been picked up."

"Better not take a chance on that, Professor," Trigger warned. "They might change their plans now they have the stuff, and decide to get off the planet immediately."

"It would make very little difference, Trigger. If Paes Fiam had waited until the official report on the Tang planet was out he would have known better than to force me to inject him with the immortality drug. Aside from their savage ways the Tang are literally an unapproachable people while under its influence. I and the various members of our expedition who experimented with it on ourselves had to wait several months for its effect to wear off again before we were able to return to civilization. We would not have been able to live among the Tang at all if we had not had our olfactory centers temporarily shut off."

"Olfactory centers?" said Trigger.

"Yes. It was absolutely necessary. Within half an hour after being administered to an animal organism, the Tang drug produces the most offensive and hideously penetrating stench I have ever encountered. Wherever Paes Fiam and Welk may be on the planet, they have by now been prostrated by it and are unmistakably advertising their presence to anyone within half a mile of them. I have advised the police that space helmets will be needed by the men sent to arrest them, and—"

He broke off as the ComWeb began shrilling its summons, added, "Ah, there is the call I have been expecting! Perhaps you'll take it, Trigger? Say I'm indisposed; I'm afraid the authorities may be feeling rather irritable with me at the moment."

Forget It

⚬◦⚬

1

At best, Major Heslet Quillan decided, giving his mud-caked boot tips a brooding scowl, amnesia would be an annoying experience. But to find oneself, as he had just done, sitting on the rocky hillside of an unfamiliar world which showed no sign of human habitation, with one's think-tank seemingly in good general working order but with no idea of how one had got there, was more than annoying. It could be fatal.

The immediate situation didn't look too dangerous. He might have picked up some appalling local disease which would presently manifest itself, but it wasn't likely. An agent of Space Scout Intelligence for the Federation of the Hub's Overgovernment was immunized early in his career against almost every possible form of infection.

Otherwise, there was a variety of strange lifeforms in sight, each going about its business. Some looked big enough to make a meal of a human being—and might, if they noticed him. But the gun on Quillan's hip should be adequate to knock such ideas out of predators who came too close.

He'd checked the gun over automatically on discovering a few minutes before that he had one. It was a standard military type, manufactured by upward of a dozen Hub worlds. There were no markings to indicate its origin; but more important at the moment was the fact that the ammocounter indicated that it contained a full charge.

What could have happened to get him into this position?

The amnesia, however he'd acquired it, took a peculiar form. He had no questions about his identity. He knew who he was. Further, up to a point—in fact, practically up to a specific second of his life—his memory seemed normal. He'd been on Orado. And he was walking along a hall on the eighteenth floor of the headquarters building, not more than thirty feet from the door of his office, when his memory simply stopped. He couldn't recall a thing between that moment and the one when he'd found himself sitting there.

Presumably he'd had an assignment, and presumably he'd been briefed on it and had set off. If he could extend his memory even thirty minutes beyond the instant of approaching the door, he might have a whole fistful of clues to what had gone on during the interval. But not a thing would come to mind. It wasn't a matter of many years being wiped out; if he'd aged at all, he couldn't detect it. Some months, however, might easily have vanished, or even as much as two or three years . . . .

Had somebody given him a partially effective memory wipeout and left him marooned here? Not at all likely. A rather large number of people unquestionably would be glad to see Intelligence deprived of his talents, but they wouldn't resort to such roundabout methods. An energy bolt through his head, and the job would have been done.

The thought that he'd been on a spaceship which had cracked up in attempting a landing on this planet, knocking him out in the process, seemed more probable. He might have been the only survivor and staggered away from the wreck, his wits somewhat scrambled. If that was it, it had happened very recently.

He was thirsty, hungry, dirty, and needed a shave. But neither he nor his clothing suggested he had been an addled castaway on a wild planet for any significant length of time. The clothes were stained with mud and vegetable matter but in good general condition. He might have stumbled into a mud hole in the swamps which began at the foot of the hills below him and stretched away to the right, then climbed up here and sat down until he dried off. There was, in fact, a blurred impression that he'd been sitting in this spot an hour or so, blinking foggily at the landscape, before he'd suddenly grown aware of himself and his surroundings.

Quillan's gaze shifted slowly about the panorama before him, searching for the glitter of a downed ship or any signs of human activity. There was no immediate point in moving until he could decide in which direction he should go. It was a remarkable view of a rather unremarkable world. The yellow sun disk was somewhat larger than he was used to. Glancing at it, he had a feeling it had been higher above the horizon when he'd noticed it first, which would make it afternoon in this area. It was warm but not disagreeably so; and, now that he thought of it, his body was making no complaints about atmospheric conditions and gravity.

He saw nothing that was of direct interest to him. Ahead and to the left a parched plain extended from the base of the hills to the horizon. In the low marshland on the right, pools of dark, stagnant water showed occasionally through thick vegetation. Higher up, lichen-gray trees formed a dense forest sweeping along the crests of the hills to within a quarter-mile of where Quillan sat.

The rock-clustered hillside about him bore only patches
of bushy growth.

The fairly abundant animal life in view was of assorted
sizes and shapes and, to Quillan's eyes, rather ungainly
in appearance. Down at the edge of the marshes, herds
of several species mingled peacefully, devoting themselves
to chomping up the vegetation. An odd, green, bulky
creature, something like a walking vegetable and about
the height of a man, moved about slowly on stubby hind
legs. It was using paired upper limbs to stuff leaves and
whole plants into its lump of a head. Most of the other
animals were quadrupeds. Only one of the carnivorous
types was active . . . a dog-sized beast with a narrow rod
for a body and a long, weaving neck tipped by a round
cat-head. A pack of them quartered the tall grass between
marsh and plain in a purposeful manner, evidently intent
on small game.

The other predators Quillan could see might be waiting
for nightfall before they did something about dinner. Half
a dozen heavy leonine brutes lay about companionably
on the open plain, evidently taking a sunbath. Something
much larger and darker squatted in the shade of a tree
on the far side of the marsh, watching the browsing herds
but making no move to approach them.

The only lifeforms above the size of a lizard on the
slopes near Quillan were a smallish gray hopper, which
moved with nervous jerkiness from one clump of shrubs
to another. They seemed to be young specimens of the
green biped in the marsh. There was a fair number of
those downhill on the slopes, ranging between one and
three feet in height. They were more active than their
elders; now and then about two or three would go gam-
boling clumsily around a bush together, like fat puppies
at play. After returning to the business of stripping clumps
of leaves from the shrubbery they would stuff them into
the mouth-slits of their otherwise featureless heads. One
of them, eating steadily away, was about twenty feet below

him. It showed no interest whatever in the visitor from space.

However he considered the matter, he couldn't have been stumbling around by himself on this world for more than fifteen hours. And he could imagine no circumstances under which he might have been abandoned here deliberately. Therefore there should be, within a fifteen-hour hike at the outside, something—ship, camp, Intelligence post, settlement—from which he had started out.

If it was a ship, it might be a broken wreck. But even a wreck would provide shelter, food, perhaps a means of sending an SOS call to the Hub. There might be somebody else still alive on it. If there wasn't, studying the ship itself should give him many indications of what had occurred, and why he was here.

Whatever he would find, he had to get back to his starting point—

Quillan stiffened. Then he swore, relaxed slightly, sat still. There was a look of intense concentration on his face.

Quietly, unnoticed, while his attention had been fixed on the immediate problem, a part of his lost memories had returned. They picked up at the instant he was walking along the hall toward his office, ran on for a number of weeks, ended again in the same complete, uncompromising manner as before.

He still didn't know why he was on this world. But he felt he was close to the answer now—perhaps very close indeed.

2

The Lorn Worlds, Imperial Rala—the Sigma File— Imperial Rala, the trouble maker, was one of the Hub's two hundred and fourteen Restricted Planets. It had emerged from the War Centuries in rather good shape—a local power with quite a high level of technology, with ambitions to become a major force in interstellar politics. It had absorbed a number of other systems of minor status, turned its attention then on the nearby Lorn Worlds as its first important target of conquest.

Quillan had been assigned to the Lorn Worlds some years previously. At that time the Lornese had been attempting to placate Rala and had refused all assistance to Intelligence.

Holati had called him to the office that day to inform him there had been a basic shift in Lornese policies. He was being sent back. A full-scale invasion by Imperial Rala was in the making, and the Lorn Worlds had called for Federation support. This time he would be given their full cooperation.

Quillan worked closely with Lornese intelligence men, setting up the Sigma File. It contained in code every scrap of previously withheld information they could give against Rala. For years, the Lornese had been concerned almost exclusively with the activities of their menacing neighbor and with their own defensive plans. The file would be of immense importance in determining the Federation's immediate strategy. For Rala, its possession would be of equal importance.

Quillan set off with it finally in a Lornese naval courier to make the return run to Orado. The courier was a very fast small ship which could rely on its speed alone to avoid interception. As an additional precaution, it would follow a route designed to keep it well beyond the established range of Ralan patrols. This would actually take it outside the Hub before re-entering a good distance from Rala.

A week later, something happened to it. Just what, Quillan didn't yet know.

Besides himself there had been three men on board: the two pilot-navigators and an engineering officer. They were picked men and Quillan had no doubt of their competence. He didn't know whether they had been told the nature of his mission; the matter was not brought up. It should have been an uneventful, speedy voyage home.

When one of the Lornese pilots summoned Quillan to the control room to tell him the courier was being tracked by another ship, the man showed no serious concern. Their pursuer could be identified on the screen. It was a Ralan raider of the *Talada* class, ten times the courier's tonnage but still a rather small ship. More importantly, a *Talada* could produce nothing like the courier's speed.

Nevertheless, Quillan didn't like the situation in the least. He had been assured that the odds against encountering Ralan vessels in this area of space were improbably high. By nature and training he distrusted coincidences. However, the matter was out of his hands. The pilots already were preparing to shift to emergency speed and, plainly, there was nothing to be done at the moment.

He settled down to watch the operation. One of the pilots was speaking to the engineering officer over the intercom; the other handled the controls.

It was this second man who suddenly gave a startled shout.

In almost the same instant, the ship seemed to be wrenched violently to the left. Quillan was hurled out of his seat, realized there was nothing he could do to keep from smashing into the bulkhead on his right . . .

At that precise point, his memories shut off again.

"Fleegle!" something was crying shrilly. "Fleegle! Fleegle! Fleegle!"

Quillan started, looked around. The small green biped nearest him downhill was uttering the cries. It had turned and was facing him frontside. Presumably it had just become aware of him and was expressing alarm. It waved its stubby forelimbs excitedly up and down. Farther down the slope several of its companions joined in with "Fleegle!" pipings of their own. Others stood watchfully still. They probably had eyes of a sort somewhere in the wrinkled balls of their heads, at any rate, they all seemed to be staring up at him.

"Fleegle! Fleegle! Fleegle!"

The whole hillside below suddenly seemed alive with the shrilling voices and waving green forelimbs. Quillan twisted half around, glanced up the slope behind him.

He was sliding the gun out of its holster as he came quietly to his feet, completing the turn. The thing that had been coming down toward him stopped in midstride, not much more than forty feet away.

It was also a biped, of a very different kind, splotchy gray-black in color and of singularly unpleasant appearance. About eight feet tall, it had long, lean talon-tipped limbs and a comparatively small body like a bloated sack. The round, black head above the body looked almost fleshless, sharp bone-white teeth as completely exposed as those of a skull. Two circular yellow eyes a few inches above the teeth stared steadily at Quillan.

He felt a shiver of distaste. The creature obviously was a carnivore and could have become dangerous to him if he hadn't been alerted by the clamor of the fleegle pack. In spite of its scrawny, gangling look, it should weigh around two hundred and fifty pounds, and the teeth and talons would make it a formidable attacker. Perhaps it had come skulking down from the forest to pick up one of the browsing fleegles and hadn't noticed Quillan until he arose. But he had its full attention now.

He waited, unmoving, gun in hand, not too seriously concerned—a couple of blasts should be enough to rip that pulpy body to shreds—but hoping it would decide to leave him alone. The creature was a walking nightmare, and tangling with unknown lifeforms always involved a certain amount of risk. He would prefer to have nothing to do with it.

The fleegle racket had abated somewhat. But now the toothy biped took a long, gliding step forward and the din immediately set up again. Perhaps it didn't like the noise, or else it was interested primarily in Quillan; at any rate, it opened its mouth as if it were snarling annoyedly and drew off to the right, moving horizontally along the slope with long, unhurried spider strides, round yellow eyes still fixed on Quillan. The fleegle cries tapered off again as the enemy withdrew. By the time it had reached a point around sixty feet away, the slopes were quiet.

Now the biped started downhill, threading its way deliberately among the boulders like a long-legged, ungainly bird. But Quillan knew by then it was after him, and those long legs might hurl it forward with startling speed when it decided to attack. He thumbed the safety off the gun.

With the fleegles silent, he could hear the rasping sounds the thing made when it opened its mouth in what seemed to be its version of a snarl . . . working up its courage, Quillan thought, to tackle the unfamiliar creature it had chanced upon.

As it came level with him on the hillside, it was snarling almost incessantly. It turned to face him then, lifted its clawed forelegs into a position oddly like that of a human boxer, hesitated an instant and came on swiftly.

A shrill storm of fleegle pipings burst out along the slope behind Quillan as he raised the gun. He'd let the thing cut the distance between them in half, he decided, then blow it apart. . . .

Almost with the thought, he saw the big biped stumble awkwardly across a rock. It made a startled, bawling noise, its forelimbs flinging out to help it catch its balance; then it went flat on its face with a thump.

There was instant stillness on the hillside. The fleegles

apparently were watching as intently as Quillan was. The biped sat up slowly. It seemed dazed. It shook its ugly head and whimpered complainingly, glancing this way and that about the slope. Then the yellow eyes found Quillan.

Instantly, the biped leaped to its feet, and Quillan hurriedly brought the gun up again. But the thing wasn't resuming its charge. It wheeled, went plunging away up the slope, now and then uttering the bawling sound it had made as it stumbled. It appeared completely panicked.

Staring after it, Quillan scratched his chin reflectively with his free hand. "Wonder what got into him?" he muttered. After a moment, he re-safetied the gun, shoved it back into the holster. He felt relieved but puzzled.

The biped, plainly, was not a timid sort of brute. It must possess a certain amount of innate ferocity to have felt impelled to attack a creature of whose fighting ability it knew nothing. Then why this sudden, almost ludicrous flight? It might be convinced he had knocked it down in some manner as it had come at him, but still—

Quillan shrugged. It was unimportant, after all. The biped had almost reached the top of the slope by now, was angling to the left to reach the lichen-gray forest a few hundred yards away. Its pace hadn't lessened noticeably. He was rid of it.

Then, as Quillan's gaze shifted along the boulder-studded top of the hill, something like a half-remembered fact seemed to nudge his mind. He stared, scowling abstractedly. Was there something familiar about that skyline? Something he should . . . He made a shocked sound.

An instant later, he was climbing hurriedly, in something like a panic of his own, up the rocky slope.

Beyond that crest, he remembered now, the ground dropped away into a shallow valley. And in that valley— how many hours ago?—he had landed the *Talada*'s lifeboat, with the Sigma File on board. Every minute he had spent wandering dazedly about the area since then had brought him closer to certain recapture—

3

He had been slammed against the bulkhead on the Lornese courier with enough violence to stun him. When he awoke, he was a prisoner under guard on the *Talada*, lying on a bunk to which he was secured in a manner designed to make him as comfortable as possible. The cabin's furnishings indicated it belonged to one of the ship's officers.

It told Quillan among other things that they knew who he was. Raiders of the *Talada* class had a liquid-filled compartment in their holds into which several hundred human beings could be packed at a time, layered like so many sardines, and kept alive and semiconscious until the ship returned to port. An ordinary prisoner would simply have been dumped into that vat.

His suspicions were soon confirmed. A swarthy gentleman in the uniform of a Ralan intelligence officer came into the cabin. He waved out the attendant and turned to face Quillan.

"I'm Colonel Ajoran," he said. "As I'm sure you've figured out, you are now in Ralan custody. We've known about your mission on the Lorn Worlds for some time, and made arrangements to have the courier which would take you back to Orado intercepted along any of the alternate routes it might take. The courier's engineering officer was a Ralan agent who jammed the emergency drive to prevent your escape—"

"And then," said Quillan, nodding, "released a paralysis gas to keep me and the pilots helpless until the courier could be boarded. Waste of effort, in my case, since I'd already been knocked out by the jolt given the ship by the jammed drive. All around, a well-planned and executed operation. My congratulations, Colonel."

"I apologize for the inconvenience," said Ajoran. His smile was smooth and easy, and very cold. "But we do intend to get our hands on the Sigma File."

Quillan didn't bother to deny knowledge of the File. "What happened to the pilots?" he demanded.

Ajoran shrugged. "One of them shot himself in preference to becoming our prisoner. The other shot the engineering officer. He is now being tortured to death in retribution for his ill-considered slaying of a Ralan agent." The callousness of the statement itself, combined with the shrug, made it quite clear than Ajoran's politeness was a surface veneer which could be stripped off in an instant.

"Our proposition is simple, Major Quillan: we want your help in decoding and transcribing the Sigma File. In return, when we reach Rala, you will be treated as a reasonable man who understands that your best course is henceforth to serve Ralan interests as effectively as you have previously done those of the Federation. And you have my assurances that you will find Rala is generous to those who serve it well."

Quillan saw no point in expressing his opinion on the worth of the good Colonel's "assurances." He satisfied himself with a scowl which might as easily be taken for a man deep in thought. "And the alternative?" he asked abruptly.

The cold, smooth smile was back. "No need to go into that, is there? I'm quite sure, after all, that you *are* a reasonable man."

Ajoran turned away, headed for the door. "We will discuss the matter further after dinner." A moment later he was gone and the guard was re-entering the cabin.

"Depends how you define 'reasonable,'" murmured Quillan. But he turned away as he said it, partly so the guard wouldn't hear. But mostly so the guard wouldn't see the cold smile spreading across his own face.

During the next hour Quillan put in some heavy thinking. He had made one observation which presently might be of use to him. At the moment, of course, he could do nothing but wait. Colonel Ajoran's plan was a bold one, but it made sense. Evidently Ajoran held a position fairly high up in the echelons of Ralan intelligence. Knowing the contents of the Sigma File in detail, he immediately would become an important man to rival government groups to whom the information otherwise would not be readily available. He could improve his standing by many degrees at one stroke.

At the end of the hour, dinner was served to Quillan in his cabin by a woman who was perhaps as beautiful, in an unusual way, as any he had seen. She was very slender. Her skin seemed almost as pure a white as her close-cropped hair, and her eyes were so light a blue that in any other type they would have appeared completely colorless. She gave, nevertheless, an immediate impression of vitality and contained energy. She told Quillan her name was Hace, that she was Ajoran's lady, and that she had been instructed to see to it that he was provided with every reasonable comfort while he considered Ajoran's proposal.

She went on chatting agreeably until Quillan had finished his dinner in the bunk. The colonel then joined them for coffee. The discussion remained a very indirect one, but Quillan presently had the impression that he was being offered an alliance by Ajoran. He possessed unique information which the ambitious colonel could put to extremely good use in the future. Quillan would, in effect, remain on Ajoran's staff and receive every consideration due a valuable associate. He gathered that one of the immediate shipboard considerations being proffered for his cooperation was the colonel's lady.

When the pair left him, Ajoran observing that the *Talada*'s sleep period had begun, the thing had been made clear enough. Neither of the two guards assigned to Quillan reappeared in the cabin—which he had learned was a section of Ajoran's own shipboard suite—and the door remained closed. Presumably he was to be left undisturbed to his reflections for the next seven hours.

Quillan did not stay awake long. He had a professional's appreciation of the value of rest when under stress; and he already had appraised his situation here as thoroughly as was necessary.

He had a minimum goal—the destruction of the Sigma File—and he had observed something which indicated the goal might be achieved if he waited for circumstances to favor him. Beyond that, he had an ascending series of goals with an ascending level of improbability. They also had been sufficiently considered. There was nothing else he cared to think about at the moment. He stretched out and fell asleep almost at once.

When he awoke some time later with the hairs prickling at the base of his skull, he believed for a moment he was dreaming of the thing he had not cared to think about. There was light on his right and the shreds of a voice . . . ghastly whispered exhalations from a throat which had lost the strength to scream. Quillan turned his head to the right, knowing what he would see.

Part of the wall to one side of the door showed now as a vision screen; the light and the whispers came from there. Quillan told himself he was seeing a recording, that the Lornese pilot captured with him had been dead for hours. Colonel Ajoran was a practical man who would have brought this part of the matter to an end without unreasonable delay so that he could devote himself fully to his far more important dealings with Quillan, and the details shown in the screen indicated the pilot could not be many minutes from death.

The screen slowly went dark again and the whispers

ended. Quillan turned on his side. There was nothing at all he could have done for the pilot. He had simply been shown the other side of Ajoran's proposition.

A few minutes later, he was asleep again.

When he awoke the next time, the cabin was lit. His two guards were there, one of them arranging Quillan's breakfast on a wall table across from the bunk. The other simply stood with his back to the door, a nerve gun in his hand, his eyes on Quillan. Fresh clothes, which Quillan recognized as his own, brought over from the courier, had been placed on a chair. The section of wall which ordinarily covered the small adjoining bathroom was withdrawn.

The first guard completed his arrangements and addressed Quillan with an air of surly deference. Colonel Ajoran extended his compliments, was waiting in the other section of the suite and would like to see Major Quillan there after he had dressed and eaten. Having delivered the message, the guard came over to unfasten Quillan from the bunk, his companion shifting to a position from which he could watch the prisoner during the process. That done, the two withdrew from the room, Quillan's eyes following them reflectively.

He showered, shaved, dressed, and had an unhurried breakfast. He could assume that Ajoran felt the time for indirect promises and threats was over, and that they would get down immediately now to the business on hand.

When Quillan came out of the cabin, some thirty minutes after being released, he found his assumption confirmed. This section of the suite was considerably larger than the sleep cabin. The colonel and Hace were seated at the far right across the room, and a guard stood before a closed door a little left of the section's centerline. The door presumably opened on one of the *Talada's* passages. The guard was again holding a nerve gun, and a second gun of the same kind lay on a small table beside

Ajoran. Hace sat at a recording apparatus just beyond the colonel. Evidently she doubled as his secretary when the occasion arose.

At the center of the room, on a table large enough to serve as a work desk, was writing material, a chip reader and, near the left side of the table, the unopened Sigma File.

Quillan absorbed the implications of the situation as he came into the room. The three of them there were on edge, and the nerve guns showed his present status—they wouldn't injure him but could knot him up painfully in an instant and leave him helpless for minutes. He was being told his actions would have to demonstrate that he deserved Ajoran's confidence.

Almost simultaneously, the realization came to him that the favorable circumstances for which he had decided to wait were at hand.

He went up to the table, looked curiously down at the Sigma File. It was about the size and shape of a briefcase set upright. Quillan, glancing over at Ajoran, said, "I'm taking it for granted you've had the destruct charge removed."

Ajoran produced a thin smile.

"Since it could have no useful purpose now," he said, "I did, of course, have it removed."

Quillan gave him an ironic bow. His left hand, brushing back, struck the Sigma File, sent it toppling toward the edge of the table.

He might as well have stuck a knifepoint into all three of them. A drop to the floor could not damage the file, but they were too keyed up to check their reactions. Ajoran started to his feet with a sharp exclamation; even Hace came half out of her chair. The guard moved more effectively. He leaped forward from the wall, bending down, still holding the nerve gun, caught the file with his wrist and free hand as it went off the table, turned to place it back on the table.

Quillan stepped behind him. In the back of the jackets of both guards he had seen a lumpy bulge near the hip, indicating each carried a second gun, which could be assumed to be a standard energy type. His left hand caught the man by the shoulder; his right found the holstered gun under the jacket, twisted it upward and fired as he bent the guard over it. His left arm tingled—Ajoran had cut loose with the nerve gun, trying to reach him through the guard's body. Then Quillan had the gun clear, saw Ajoran coming around on his right and snapped off two hissing shots, letting the guard slide to the floor. Ajoran stopped short, hauled open the sleep cabin door and was through it in an instant, slamming it shut behind him.

Across the room, Hace, almost at the other door, stopped, too, as Quillan turned toward her. They looked at each other a moment, then Quillan stepped around the guard and walked up to her, gun pointed. When he was three steps away, Hace closed her eyes and stood waiting, arms limp at her sides. His left fist smashed against the side of her jaw and she dropped like a rag doll.

"Sorry, doll, but I had no choice," he said softly. Quillan looked back. The guard was twisting contortedly about on the floor. His face showed he was dead, but it would be a minute or two before the nerve charge worked itself out of his body. The colonel's lady wouldn't stir for a while. Ajoran himself . . . Quillan stared thoughtfully at the door of the sleep cabin.

Ajoran might be alerting the ship from in there at the moment, although there hadn't been any communication device in view. Or he could have picked up some weapon he fancied more than a nerve gun and was ready to come out again. The chances were good, however, that he'd stay locked in where he was until somebody came to inform him the berserk prisoner had been dealt with. It wasn't considered good form in Rala's upper echelons to take personal risks which could be delegated to subordinates.

Whatever happened, Quillan told himself he could achieve his minimum goal any time he liked now. A single energy bolt through the Sigma File would ignite it explosively. And its destruction, getting it out of Ralan hands, had been as much as he reasonably could expect to accomplish in the situation.

He glanced contemptuously at the closed door to the sleep cabin, then at the door which should open on one of the *Talada*'s passages. Quillan smiled, and decided he didn't feel reasonable.

He took the Sigma File from the table, carried it over to the passage door and set it down against the wall. He'd expected to see the second guard come bouncing in through the door as soon as the commotion began in here. The fact that he hadn't indicated either that he'd been sent away or that Ajoran's suite was soundproofed. Probably the latter . . .

Quillan raised the gun, grasped the door handle with his left hand, turned it suddenly, hauled the door open.

The second guard stood outside, but he wasn't given time to do much more than bulge his eyes at Quillan.

Quillan went quickly along the passage, the Sigma File in his left hand, the gun ready again in his right. By the rules he should, in such circumstances, have been satisfied with his minimum goal and destroyed the file before he risked another encounter with an armed man. If he'd been killed just now, it would have been there intact for Rala to decode.

But the other goals looked at least possible now, and he couldn't quite bring himself to put a bolt through the file before it became clear that he'd done as much as he could. "Reasonable," after all, was a flexible term.

He moved more cautiously as he approached the corner of the passage. This was officer's country, and his plans were based on a remembered general impression of the manner in which the *Talada* raiders were constructed. The passageway beyond the corner was three times the width of this one . . . it might be the main passage he was looking for.

He glanced around the corner, drew back quickly. About thirty feet away in the other side of the passage was a wide doorspace, and two men in officer's uniform had been walking in through it at the moment he looked. Quillan took a long, slow breath. His next goal suddenly seemed not at all far away.

He waited a few seconds, looked again. Now the passage was clear. Instantly he was around the corner, running down to the doorspace. As he stepped out before it, he saw his guess had been good. He was looking down a short flight of steps into the *Talada's* control room.

Looking and firing . . . . The gun in his hand hissed like an angry cat, but several seconds passed before any of the half-dozen men down there realized he was around. By then two of them were dead. They had happened to be in the gun's way. The subspace drive control panels, the gun's target, were shattering from end to end. Quillan swung the gun toward a big communicator in a corner. At that moment, somebody discovered him.

The man did the sensible thing. His hand darted out, throwing one of the switches before him.

A slab of battle-steel slid down across the doorspace, sealing the control room away from the passage.

Quillan sprinted on down the passage. The emergency siren came on.

The *Talada* howled monstrously, like a wounded beast, as it rolled and bucked, dropping out of subspace. Suddenly he was in another passage, heard shouts ahead, turned back, stumbled around a corner, went scrambling breathlessly up a steep, narrow stairway.

At its top, he saw ahead of him, like a wish-dream scene, the lit lock, two white-faced crewmen staggering on the heaving deck as they tried to lift a heavy oxygen tank into it.

Quillan came roaring toward them, wild-eyed, waving

the gun. They looked around at him, turned and ran as he leaped past them into the lock.

The man at the controls of the *Talada*'s lifeboat died before he realized somebody was running up behind him. Quillan dropped the Sigma File, hauled the body out of the seat, slid into it . . . .

He was several minutes' flight away from the disabled raider before he realized he was laughing like a lunatic.

He was clear. And now the odds, shifting all the way over, were decidedly in his favor. The question was how long it would take them to repair the damage and come after him. With enough of a start, they couldn't know which way he'd headed and the chance of being picked up before he got back to the Hub became negligible.

First things first. He checked the ship's fuel status— plenty there. Next he checked the environmental controls and got a shock. The ship had no oxygen stores. None! He had only as much air to breathe as filled the cabin space. Quillan made a grumbling mental note to steal a better quality lifeboat next time.

Still, it wasn't too bad. It would have been nicer if he could have given the two crewmen time to dump another few tanks of compressed oxygen on board before he had taken off. The ship's recyclers needed *something* to work with. But a scan of the stellar neighborhood showed two planets respectively seven and eight hours away indicating conditions which should allow a man to stay a short time without serious damage or discomfort. The lifeboat had the standard recharging equipment on board. A few hours on either of those worlds, and he'd be ready.

After dropping the body of the Ralan pilot into space, he decided the seven-hour run gave him a slight advantage. Once the *Talada* got moving, it had speed enough to check over both worlds without losing a significant amount of time. They could figure out his air requirements as well as he. If they arrived before he was finished and gone, the raider's scanning devices were almost certain to spot the lifeboat wherever he tried to hide it.

The chances seemed very good that they simply wouldn't get there soon enough. But the minimum goal remained a factor. Quillan decided to cache the Sigma File in some easily identifiable spot as soon as he touched ground, take the boat to another section of the planet to do his recharging, come back for the file when he was prepared to leave. It would cut the risk of being surprised with it to almost nothing. . . .

4

How many hours had passed since then? Clawing his way up through the boulders and shrubbery, slipping in loose soil, Quillan glanced back for a moment at the sun. It was noticeably lower in the sky again, appeared to be dropping almost visibly toward the horizon. But that told him nothing. He remembered the landing now; it had been daylight and he had come down to hide the Sigma File . . . *had* hidden it, his memory corrected him suddenly. And then, for the next six or ten or fourteen hours, he appeared to have simply waited around here, in some mental fog, for the *Talada* to come riding its fiery braking jets down from the sky.

The raider might arrive at any moment. Unless . . .

Quillan blocked off the rest of that thought. The slope had begun to level off as he approached the top; he covered the last stretch in a rush, lungs sobbing for breath. He clambered on hastily through a jagged crack in the back of the ridge. For an instant, he saw the shallow dip of the valley beyond.

He dropped flat immediately. *They were already here.*

It was a shock, but one he realized he had half expected. After a few seconds, he crept up to the shelter of a rock from where he could look into the valley without exposing himself.

The *Talada* had set down about a hundred yards back of the lifeboat, perhaps no more than half an hour ago. The smaller vessel's lock stood open; a man came climbing out of it, followed by two others. The last of the three closed the lock and they started back toward the raider, from which other men were emerging. Ajoran had ordered the lifeboat searched first, to make sure the Sigma File wasn't concealed on it. Without that delay they should have caught him while he was still climbing up the slope. . . . The group coming out of the *Talada* now was a hunting party; most of them had quick-firing energy rifles slung across their backs.

They lined up beside the ship while a wedge-shaped device was maneuvered out of the lock. It remained floating a little above the ground near the head of the line, about twenty feet long, perhaps a dozen feet across at its point of greatest width. Quillan had seen such devices before.

It was a man-tracker, a type used regularly in Ralan expeditions against settlements on other planets. Its power unit and instruments were packed into the narrow tip; most of its space was simply a container, enclosed and filled with the same kind of numbing liquid preservative as that in the prisoner vats in the *Talada* ships. It could be set either to hunt down specific individuals or any and all human beings within its range, and to either kill them as they were overtaken or pick them up with its grapplers and deposit them unharmed in the container. They could use it to follow him now, the clothing he had left on the ship would give it all the indications it needed to recognize and follow his trail.

More men had come out behind the machine, including one in a grav-suit. Colonel Ajoran apparently was assigning almost the entire complement of the *Talada* to the search for Quillan and the Sigma File.

Quillan decided he'd seen enough. If he had been observed on the hillside as the *Talada* was descending, they would have gone after him immediately. Instead, they would now follow their man-tracker over the ridge and down to the swamp where the herds of native animals were feeding. It gave him a little time.

He crawled backward a dozen feet into the narrow crevasse, rose and retraced his way through it to the other side of the ridge. Beyond the plain, the sun was almost touching the horizon. The gray forest into which the aggressive biped had retreated began a few hundred yards to his right. He'd have better shelter there than among the tumbled rocks of the ridge.

He went loping toward it, keeping below the crestline. His eyes shifted once toward the swamp. One great tree stood there, towering a good hundred feet above the vegetation about it. The Sigma File was wedged deep among the giant's root, a few feet below the water. He'd seen the tree from the air, put the lifeboat down in the little valley, hurried down to the swamp on foot. Twenty minutes later the file had been buried and he'd started wading back out of the swamp. What had happened between that moment and the one when he found himself sitting on the hillside he still didn't know. . . .

He reached the forest, came back among the trees over the top of the ridge until he saw the valley again. During the few minutes that had passed, the ridge's evening shadow had spread across half the lower ground. It had seemed possible that when they realized how close it was to nightfall here, the hunt for him would be put off till morning. But Ajoran evidently wanted no delay. The man in the grav-suit still stood near the open lock of the ship, but the search party was coming across the valley behind their tracking machine. They headed for a point of the open ridge about a quarter-mile away from Quillan. They'd have lights to continue on through the night if necessary.

The chase plan was simple but effective. If the man-tracker hadn't flushed him into view before morning, the *Talada* could take the lifeboat aboard, move after the search party and put down again. They could work on in relays throughout the following day, half of them resting at a time on the ship, until he was run down.

The Sigma File was safest where he'd left it. The tracker's scent perceptors were acute enough to follow his trail through the stagnant swamp, getting signs from the vegetation he'd brushed against or grasped in passing, even from lingering traces in the water itself. And it might very well detect the file beneath the surface. But—ironically, considering Ajoran's purpose—the discovery would be meaningless to the machine except as another indication that the man it was pursuing had been there. It would simply move on after him.

The worst thing he could attempt at the moment would be to get down to the swamp ahead of the searchers and destroy the file. He would almost certainly be sighted on the open slopes below the forest; and either the tracker or the man in the grav-suit could be overhead instants later.

Quillan's gaze shifted back to the grav-suited figure. He would have to watch out for that one. His immediate role presumably was to act as liaison man between the ship and the hunters, supplementing the communicator reports Ajoran would be getting on the progress of the search. But he was armed with a rifle; and if Quillan was seen, he could spatter the area around the fugitive with stun-gas pellets while remaining beyond range of a hand weapon. He had floated back up to the *Talada*'s lock for a moment, was now heading out to the ridge, drifting about fifty feet above the ground.

It wasn't a graceful operation. Maneuvering a grav-suit designed for weightless service on the surface of airless planets never was. But the fellow was handling himself fairly well, Quillan thought. He came up to the ridge as the troop began filing across it, hovered above the line a few seconds, then swung to the left and moved off in a series of slow, awkward bounces above the hillside. He seemed to be holding something up to his helmet, and Quillan guessed he was scanning the area with a pair of powerful glasses. After some minutes, he came back.

Quillan had crossed over to the other side of the ridge to follow the progress of the column. It had swung to the right as it started down, was angling straight toward the swamp along the route he had taken with the file. He watched, chewing his lip. If the man-tracker happened to cross his return trail on the way, he might be in trouble almost immediately. . . .

The man in the grav-suit drifted after the search party, passed above them some two hundred feet in the air, then remained suspended and almost unmoving. Quillan glanced over at the horizon. The sun was nearly out of sight; its thin golden rim shrank and disappeared as he looked at it. Without the starblaze of the Hub, night should follow quickly here, but as yet he couldn't see any advantage the darkness would bring him.

The man in the grav-suit was coming back to the ridge. He hovered above it a moment, settled uncertainly toward the flat top of a boulder, made a stumbling landing and righted himself. He turned toward the plain and the swamp, lifting the object that seemed to be a pair of glasses to the front of his helmet again. Evidently he'd had enough of the suit's airborne eccentricities for a while.

Quillan's throat worked. The man was less than two hundred yards away. . . .

His eyes shifted toward a tuft of shrubs twenty feet beyond the edge of the forest growth.

Some seconds later, he was there, studying the stretch of ground ahead. Other shrubs and rocks big enough to crouch behind . . . but they would give him no cover at all if for some reason the fellow decided to lift back into the air. The fading light wouldn't help then. Those were space glasses he was using, part of the suit, designed to provide clear vision even when only the gleam of distant stars was there for them to absorb.

But perhaps, Quillan told himself, Grav-suit would not decide to lift back into the air. In any case, no other approach was possible. The far side of the ridge was controlled by the *Talada*'s night-scanners, and they would be in use by now.

He moved, waited, gathered himself and moved again. Grav-suit was directing most of his attention downhill, but now and then he turned for a look along the ridge in both directions. Perhaps, as the air darkened, the closeness of the forest was getting on his nerves. Native sounds were drifting up from the plain, guttural bellowing and long-drawn ululations. The meat eaters were coming awake. Presently there was a series of short, savage roars from the general direction of the swamp; and Quillan guessed the search party had run into some big carnivore who had never heard about energy rifles. When the roaring stopped with a monstrous scream, he was sure of it.

He had reduced the distance between them by almost half when the grav-suit soared jerkily up from the boulder. Quillan had a very bad moment. But it lifted no more than a dozen feet, then descended again at a slant which carried it behind the boulder. The man had merely changed his position. And the new position he had selected took them out of each other's sight.

Quillan was instantly on his feet, running forward. Here the surface was rutted with weather fissures. He slipped into one of them, drawing out his gun, moved forward at a crouch. A moment later, he had reached the near side of the boulder on which Grav-suit had stood.

Where was he now? Quillan listened, heard a burst of thin, crackling noises. They stopped for some seconds, came briefly again, stopped again. The suit communicator . . . the man must have taken off the helmet, or the sound wouldn't have been audible. He couldn't be far away.

Quillan went down on hands and knees and edged along the side of the boulder to the right. From here he could see down the hillside. On the plain, the night was gathering; the boundaries between the open land and the swamp had blurred. But the bobbing string of tiny light beams down there, switching nervously this way and that, must already be moving through the marsh.

The communicator noises came again, now from a point apparently no more than fifteen feet beyond the edge of the boulder ahead of Quillan. It was as close as he could get. It was important that the man in the grav-suit should die instantly, which meant a head shot. Quillan rose up, stepped out quietly around the boulder, gun pointed.

The man stood faced half away, the helmet tipped back on his shoulders. In the last instant, as Quillan squeezed down on the trigger, sighting along the barrel, the head turned and he saw with considerable surprise that it was Colonel Ajoran.

Then the gun made its spiteful hissing sound.

Ajoran's head jerked slightly to the side and his eyes closed. The grav-suit held him upright for the second or two before he toppled. Quillan already was there, reaching under the collar for one of the communicator's leads. He found it, gave it a sharp twist, felt it snap.

5

In the *Talada*, the man watching the night-scanners saw Colonel Ajoran's grav-suit appear above the ridge and start back to the ship. He informed the control room and the lock attendant.

The outer lock door opened as the suit came to it.

Quillan made a skidding landing inside. His performance in the suit had been no improvement on Ajoran's. He shut off the suit drive, clumped up to the inner door, left arm raised across the front of the helmet, hand fumbling with the oxygen hose. It would hide his face for a moment from whoever was on the other side of the door. His right hand rested on his gun.

The door opened. The attendant stood at rigid attention before the control panel six feet away, rifle grounded, eyes front. Mentally blessing Ralan discipline, Quillan stepped up beside him, drew out the gun and gave the back of the man's skull a solid thump with the barrel.

When the attendant opened his eyes again a few minutes later, his head ached and there was a gag in his mouth. His hands were tied behind him, and Quillan was wearing his uniform.

Quillan hauled him to his feet, poked a gun muzzle against his back.

"Lead the way to the control room," he said.

The attendant led the way. Quillan followed, the uniform cap pulled down to conceal his face. Ajoran's handgun and a stunner he had taken from the attendant were stuck into his belt. The attendant's energy rifle and the one which had been strapped to the grav-suit were concealed in a closet near the lock. He had assembled quite an arsenal.

When they reached the wide main passage in the upper level of the ship, he halted the lock attendant. They retraced their steps to the last door they had passed. Quillan opened it. An office of some kind . . . he motioned the attendant in and followed him, closing the door.

He came out a few seconds later, shoved the stunner back under his belt, and stood listening. The *Talada* seemed almost eerily silent. Not very surprising, he thought. The number of men who had set out after him indicated that only those of the crew who were needed to coordinate the hunt and maintain the ship's planetary security measures had remained on board. That could be ten or twelve at most; and every one of them would be stationed at his post at the moment.

Quillan went out into the main passage, walked quietly along it. Now he could hear an intermittent murmur of voices from the control room. One of them seemed to be that of a woman, but he wasn't sure. They were being silent again before he came close enough to distinguish what was being said.

There was nothing to be gained by hesitating at this point. The control room was the nerve center of the ship, but there couldn't be more than four or five of them in it. Quillan had a gun in either hand as he reached the open doorspace. He turned through it, started unhurriedly down the carpeted stairs leading into the control room, eye and mind photographing the details of the scene below.

Ajoran's lady was nearest, seated at a small table, her attention on the man before the communicator set in a corner alcove on the left. This man's back was turned. A gun was belted to his waist. Farther down in the control room sat another man, facing the passage but bent over some instrument on the desk before him. The desk shielded him almost completely, which made him the most dangerous of the three at the moment. No one else was in view, but that didn't necessarily mean that no one else was here.

Hace became aware of him as he reached the foot of the stairs. Her head turned sharply; she seemed about to speak. Then her eyes went wide with shocked recognition.

He'd have to get the man at the desk the instant she screamed. But she didn't scream. Instead, her right hand went up, two fingers lifted and spread. She nodded fiercely at the communicator operator, next at the man behind the desk.

Only two of them? Well, that probably was true. But he'd better use the stunner on Hace before attempting to deal with the two armed men.

At that moment, the communicator operator looked around.

He was young and his reactions were as fast as Hace's. He threw himself sideways out of the chair with a shout of warning, hit the floor rolling over and clawing for his gun. The man behind the desk had no chance. As he jerked upright, startled, an energy bolt took him in the head. The operator had no real chance, either. Quillan swung the gun to the left, saw for an instant eyes fixed on him, bright with hatred, and the other gun coming up, and fired again.

He waited a number of seconds, then, alert for further motion. But the control room remained quiet. So Ajoran's lady hadn't lied. She stayed where she was, unstirring, until he turned toward her. Then she said quietly, her expression still incredulous, "It seemed like magic! How could you get into the ship?"

Quillan looked at the dark, ugly bruise his fist had printed along the side of her jaw, said, "In Ajoran's grav-suit, of course."

She hesitated. "He's dead?"

"Quite dead," Quillan said thoughtfully.

"I wanted," Hace said, "to kill him myself. I would have done it finally, I believe. . . ." She hesitated again. "It doesn't matter now. What can I do to help you? They're in trouble down in the swamp."

"What kind of trouble?"

"That isn't clear. It began two or three minutes ago, but we haven't been able to get an intelligible report from the two communicator men. They were excited, shouted, almost irrational."

Quillan scowled. After a moment, he shook his head. "Let's clean up the ship first. How many on board?"

"Nine besides those two . . . and myself."

"The man in the lock's taken care of," Quillan said. "Eight. On the lifeboat?"

"Nobody. Ajoran had a trap prepared for you there, in case you came back before they caught you. You could have got inside, but you couldn't have started the engines, and you would have been unable to get out again."

Quillan grunted. "Can you get the men in the ship to come individually to the control room?"

"I see. Yes, I think I can do that."

"I'll want to check you over for weapons first."

"Of course." Hace smiled slightly, stood up. "Why should you trust me?"

"I wouldn't know," Quillan said.

They came in, unsuspecting, one by one; and, one by one, the stunner brought them down from behind. Shortly afterwards, a freight carrier floated into the *Talada*'s vat room. Hace stood aside as Quillan unlocked the cover of the drop hole in the deck and hauled it back. A heavy stench surged up from the vat. Quillan looked down a moment at the oily black liquid eight feet below, then dragged the nine unconscious men in turn over from the carrier, dropped them in, and resealed the vat.

A man's voice babbled and sobbed. Another man screamed in sudden fright; then there was a sound of rapid, panicky breathing mingled with the sobs.

Quillan switched off the communicator, looked over at Hace. "Is this what it was like before?"

She moistened her lips. "No, this is insanity!" Her voice was unsteady. "They're both completely incapable of responding to us now. What could there be in that swamp at night to have terrified them to that extent? At least some of the others should have come back to the ship . . ." She paused. "Quillan, why do we stay here? You know what they're like—why bother with them? You don't need any of them to handle the ship. One person can take it to the Hub if necessary."

"I know," Quillan said. He studied her, added, "I'm wondering a little why you're willing to help me get back to the Hub."

Anger showed for an instant in the pale, beautiful face.

"I'm no Ralan! I was picked up in a raid on Beristeen when I was twelve. I've never wanted to do anything but get away from Rala since that day."

Quillan grunted, rubbed his chin. "I see. . . . Well, we can't leave immediately. For one thing, I left the Sigma File in that swamp."

Hace stared at him. "You haven't destroyed it?"

"No. It never quite came to that point."

She laughed shortly. "Quillan, you're rather wonderful! Ajoran was convinced the file was lost, and that his only chance of saving his own skin was to get you back alive so he could find out what you had learned on the Lorn Worlds. . . . No, you can't leave the file behind, of course! I understand that. But why don't we lift the ship out of atmosphere until it's morning here?" She nodded at the communicator. "*That* disturbance—whatever they've aroused down there—should have settled out by then. The swamp will be quiet again. Then you can work out a way to get the file back without too much danger."

Quillan shook his head, got to his feet. "No, that shouldn't be necessary. The man-tracker was being monitored from the ship, wasn't it? Where is the control set kept?"

Hace indicated the desk twenty feet behind her where the second man had sat when Quillan had come into the control room.

"It's lying over there. That's what he was doing."

Quillan said, "Let's take a look at it. I want the thing to return to the ship." He started toward the desk. Hace stood up, went over to the desk with him. "I'm afraid I can't tell you how to operate it."

"I should be able to do it," Quillan said. "I played around a few hours once with a captured man-tracker which had been shipped back to Lorn. This appears to be a very similar model." He looked down at the moving dark blurs in the screen which formed the center of the control set, twisted a knob to one side of it. "Let's see what it's doing now before I have it return to the ship."

The screen cleared suddenly. The scene was still dark, but in the machine's night-vision details were distinct. A rippling weed bed was gliding slowly past below; a taller leafy thicket ahead moved closer. Then the thicket closed about the tracker.

Hace said, "The operator was trying to discover through the tracker what was happening to the men down there, but it moved out of the range of their lights almost as soon as the disturbance began. Apparently the devices, once set, can't be turned around."

"Not unless you're riding them," Quillan agreed. "Tele-monitoring observes what they're doing, but has only limited control. They either go on and finish their business, or get their sensors switched off and return to their starting point. It's still following my trail. Now . . ."

"What's that light?" Hace asked uneasily. "It looks like the reflection of a fire."

The tracker had emerged from the thicket, swung to the left, and was gliding low over an expanse of open water, almost touching it. There were pale orange glitters on the surface ahead of it.

Quillan studied them, said, "At a guess, it simply means there's a moon in the sky." He pushed a stud on the set, and the scene vanished. "That wiped out the last instructions it was given. It will come back to the ship in a minute or two."

Hace looked at him. "What do you have in mind?"

"I'm riding it down to the swamp."

"Not now! In the morning you . . ."

"I don't think I'll be in any danger. Now let's find a place where I'm sure you'll stay locked up until I get

back. As you said, one person can do all that's needed
to lift this ship off the planet and head away. . . ."

6

Five hundred feet above the ground, the man-tracker's
open saddle was not the most reassuring place to be in.
But the machine was considerably easier to maneuver
than the grav-suit had been and the direct route by air
to the giant tree beneath which he'd concealed the Sigma
File was the shortest and fastest. Quillan was reasonably
certain nothing had happened to the file, but he wouldn't
know until he held it in his hands again.

The orange moon that had pushed above the horizon
was a big one, the apparent diameter of its disk twice
that of the vanished sun. Quillan was holding the tracker's
pace down. But no more than a few minutes passed
before he could make out the big tree in the vague light,
ahead and a little to his right. He guided the machine
over to it, circled its crown slowly twice, looking down,
then lowered the tracker down to a section of open water
near the base of the tree, turned it and went gliding in
toward the tangled root system of the giant. He turned
the control set off, remained in the saddle a few
moments, looking about and listening.

The swamp was full of sound, most of it of a minor
nature . . . chirps, twittering, soft hoots. Something whistled
piercingly three times in the tree overhead. Behind him,
not too far off, was a slow, heavy splashing which gradually moved away. At the very limit of his hearing was something else. It might have been human voices, faint with
distance, or simply his imagination at work.

Nearby, nothing moved. Quillan pulled the control set
out of its saddle frame, slid down from the saddle, clinging to it with one hand, finally dropped a few inches into

a layer of mud above the mass of tree roots. He climbed farther up on the roots, found a dry place under one of them where he shoved the control set out of sight. Then he went climbing cautiously on around the great trunk, slipping now and then on the slimy root tangle beneath the mud. . . .

And here was where he had concealed the Sigma File. A little bay of water extended almost to the trunk itself about five feet deep. Quillan slipped down into it. There was firm footing here. He moved forward to the tip of the bay, took a deep breath and crouched down. The warm water closed over his head. He groped about among the root shelves before him, touched the file, gripped it by its handle and drew it out.

He clambered up out of the water, started back around the tree . . .

And there the thing stood.

Quillan stopped short. This was almost an exact duplication of what happened after he'd brought the Sigma File down here and concealed it. It had been daylight then, and what he saw now as a bulky manlike shape in the shadow of the tree had been clearly visible. It was a green monstrosity, heavy as a gorilla, with a huge, round bobbing ball of a head which showed no features at all through its leafy appendages. It was bigger than it had looked at a distance from the hillside, standing almost eight feet tall.

The first time, it had been only a few yards away, moving toward him around the tree, when he had seen it. His instant reaction had been to haul out his gun. . . .

Now he stayed still, looking at it. His heartbeat had speeded up noticeably. This was, he told himself, an essentially vegetarian creature. And it was peaceable because it had a completely effective means of defense. It could sense the impulse to attack in an approaching carnivore, and it could make the carnivore forget its purpose.

As often as was necessary.

Quillan made himself start forward. He had no intention, his mind kept repeating, of harming this oversized fleegle, and it had no intention of harming him. It did not move out of his path as he came toward it, but turned slowly to keep facing him as he clambered past over the roots a few feet away.

Quillan didn't look back at it and heard no movement behind him. He saw the man-tracker floating motionless above the mud ahead, put the file down and pulled the tracker's control set out from under the root where he had left it. A minute or two later, he was back in the machine's saddle, out in the moonlight away from the big tree, the Sigma File fastened to his belt.

He tapped a pattern of instructions into the control set, checked them very carefully, slid the set into the saddle frame and switched it on.

The man-tracker swung about purposefully, went gliding away through the swamp. A hundred yards on, it encountered three fleegles, somewhat smaller than the one under the tree, wading slowly leg-deep through the mud. They stopped as the machine appeared, and Quillan thought friendly and admiring things about fleegles until they were well behind him again. Perhaps a minute later, the man-tracker stopped in the air above the first of the *Talada*'s lost crew.

He had crawled into a thicket and was blubbering noisily to himself. When two of the machine's grapplers flicked down into the thicket and locked about him, he bawled in horror. Quillan looked straight ahead, not particularly wanting to watch this. There was a click behind him as the preservative tank opened. For a moment, his nostrils were full of the stink of the liquid. Then there was a splash, and the bawling stopped abruptly. The tank clicked shut.

The man-tracker swung around on a new point, set off again. Its present instructions were to trail and collect every human being within the range of its sensory equipment, except its rider.

They'd been on edge to begin with here, Quillan told himself. Their rifles already had brought down one brute which had come roaring monstrously at them in the dusk; and presumably the rifles could handle anything else they might encounter. But they hadn't liked the look of the swamp the man-tracker was leading them into. Wading through pools, slipping in the mud, flashing their lights about at every menacing shadow, they followed the machine, mentally cursing the order that had sent them after the intelligence agent as night was closing in.

And then a great green ogre was standing in one of the light beams. . . .

Naturally, they tried to shoot it.

And as they made the decision, they began to forget.

Progressive waves of amnesia . . . first, perhaps, only a touch. The men lifting rifles forgot they were lifting them. Until they saw the fleegle again—

The past few hours might be wiped out next. They stood in a swamp at night, not knowing how they'd got there or why they were there. But they had rifles in their hands, and an ogrish shape was watching them.

Months forgotten now. The fleegle could keep it up.

About that point, they'd begun to stampede, scattered, ploughed this way and that through the swamp. But the fleegles were everywhere. And as often as a gun was lifted in panic, another chunk of memory would go. Until the last of the weapons was dropped.

The man-tracker wasn't rounding up men, but children in grown-up bodies, huddled in hiding on a wet, dark nightmare world, dazed and uncomprehending, unable to do more than wail wildly as the machine picked them up and placed them in its tank.

7

Quillan came out of the compartment where the man-tracker was housed, locked the door and turned off the control set.

"You haven't closed the vat yet," Hace said.

He nodded. "I know. Let's go back."

"I'm still not clear on just what did happen," she went on, walking beside him up the passage. "You say they lost their memories . . . ?"

"Yes. It's a temporary thing. I had the same experience when I first got here, though I don't seem to have been hit as hard as most of them were. If they weren't floating around in that slop now, they'd start remembering within hours."

He opened the door to the vat room, motioned her inside. Hace wrinkled her nose in automatic distaste at the odor of the preservative, said, "It's very strange. How could any creature affect a human mind in that manner?"

"I don't know," Quillan said. "But it isn't important now." He followed her in, closing the door behind him, went on, "Now this will be rather unpleasant, so let's get it over with."

She glanced back at him. "Get what over with, Quillan?"

"You're getting the ride to the Hub you said you wanted," Quillan told her, "but you're riding along with the crew down there."

Hace whirled to face him, her eyes wild with fear.

"Ah—no! Quillan . . . I . . . you couldn't . . ."

"I don't want you awake on the ship," he told her. "Though I might have thought of some other way of making sure you wouldn't be a problem if my pilot hadn't died as he did."

"What does that have to do with me?" Her voice was shrill. "Didn't I try to help you in the control room?"

"You played it smart in the control room," Quillan said. "But you would have gone into the vat with the first group if I hadn't thought you might be useful in some way."

"But *why*? Am I to blame for what Ajoran did?"

Quillan shrugged. "I'm not sorry for what happened to Ajoran. But I'm not stupid enough to think that a Ralan intelligence agent would go out in a grav-suit to help look for me, leaving the ship in charge of a couple of junior officers. Ajoran went out because he was ordered to do it. And there were a few other things. What they add up to, doll, is that you were the senior agent in this operation. And it would suit you just fine to get back to Rala with the Sigma File, and no one left alive to tell how you almost let it get away from you."

Hace wet her lips, her eyes darting wildly about his face.

"Quillan, I . . ." she started to plead.

A cold grin creased Quillan's face. "Forget it." He placed his hand flat against her chest, shoved hard. Hace went stumbling backward toward the open drop hole of the vat. There was a scream and a splash. He walked over and looked down. The oily surface was smooth again.

"Sweet dreams, doll." He slammed the cover down over the drop hole, sealed it and left the room.

Legacy

1

It was the time of sunrise in Ceyce, the White City, placidly beautiful capital of Maccadon, the University World of the Hub.

In the Colonial School's sprawling five-mile complex of buildings and tropical parks, the second student shift was headed for breakfast, while a large part of the fourth shift moved at a more leisurely rate toward their bunks. The school's organized activities were not much affected by the hour, but the big exercise quadrangle was almost deserted for once. Behind the railing of the firing range a young woman stood by herself, gun in hand, waiting for the automatic range monitor to select a new string of targets for release.

She was around twenty-four, slim and trim in the school's comfortable hiking outfit. Tan shirt and knee-length shorts, knee stockings, soft-soled shoes. Her sun hat hung on the railing, and the dawn wind whipped strands of shoulder-length, modishly white-silver hair along her cheeks. She held a small, beautifully worked handgun loosely beside her—the twin-barrelled sporting Denton which gunwise citizens of the Hub rated as a weapon for the precisionist and expert only. In institutions like the Colonial School it wasn't often seen.

At the exact instant the monitor released its new flight of targets, she became aware of the aircar gliding down toward her from the administration buildings on the right. Startled, she glanced sideways long enough to identify the car's two occupants, shifted her attention back to the cluster of targets speeding toward her, studied the flight pattern for another unhurried half-second, finally raised the Denton. The little gun spat its noiseless, invisible needle of destruction eight times. Six small puffs of crimson smoke hung in the air. The two remaining targets swerved up in a mocking curve and shot back to their discharge huts.

The girl bit her lip in moderate annoyance, safetied and holstered the gun and waved her hand left-right at the range attendant to indicate she was finished. Then she turned to face the aircar as it settled slowly to the ground twenty feet away. Her gray eyes studied its occupants critically.

"Fine example you set the students!" she remarked. "Flying right into a hot gun range!"

Doctor Plemponi, principal of the Colonial School, smiled soothingly. "Eight years ago, your father bawled me out for the very same thing, Trigger! Much more abusively, I must say. You know that was my first meeting with old Runser Argee, and I—"

"Plemp!" Mihul, Chief of Physical Conditioning, Women's Division, cautioned sharply from the seat behind him. "Watch what you're doing, you ass!"

Confused, Doctor Plemponi turned to look at her. The aircar dropped the last four feet to a jolting landing.

Mihul groaned. Plemponi apologized. Trigger walked over
to them.

"Does he do that often?" she asked interestedly.

"Every other time!" Mihul asserted. She was a tall, lean,
muscular slab of a woman, around forty. She gave Trigger a wink behind Plemponi's back. "We keep the chiro-
practors on stand-by duty when we go riding with Plemp."

"Now then! Now then!" Doctor Plemponi said. "You
distracted my attention for a moment, that's all. Now,
Trigger, the reason we're here is that Mihul told me at
our pre-breakfast conference you weren't entirely happy
at the good old Colonial School. So climb in, if you don't
have much else to do, and we'll run up to the office and
discuss it." He opened the door for her.

"Much else to do!" Trigger gave him a look. "All right,
Doctor. We'll run up and discuss it."

She went back for her sun hat, climbed in, closed the
door and sat down beside him, shoving the holstered
Denton forward on her thigh.

Plemponi eyed the gun dubiously. "Brushing up in case
there's another grabber raid?" he inquired. He reached
out for the guide stick.

Trigger shook her head. "Just working off hostility, I
guess." She waited till he had lifted the car off the ground
in a reckless swoop. "That business yesterday—it really
was a grabber raid?"

"We're almost sure it was," Mihul said behind her,
"though I did hear some talk they might have been after
those two top-secret plasmoids in your Project."

"*That's* not very likely," Trigger remarked. "The raiders were a half mile away from where they should have
come down if the plasmoids were what they wanted. And
from what I saw of them, they weren't nearly a big
enough gang for a job of that kind."

"I thought so, too," Mihul said. "They were topflight pro-
fessionals, in any case. I got a glimpse of some of their equipment. Knockout guns—foggers—and that was a fast car!"

"Very fast car," Trigger agreed. "It's what made me suspicious when I first saw them come in."

"They also," said Mihul, "had a high-speed interplanetary hopper waiting for them in the hills. Two more men in it. The cops caught them, too." She added, "They were grabbers, all right."

"Anything to indicate whom they were after?" Trigger asked.

"No," Mihul said. "Too many possibilities. Twenty or more of the students in that area at the time had important enough connections to class as grabber bait. The cops won't talk except to admit they were tipped off about the raid. Which was obvious. The way they popped up out of nowhere and closed in on those boys was a beautiful sight to see."

"I," Trigger admitted, "didn't see it. When that car homed in, I yelled a warning to the nearest bunch of students and dropped flat behind a rock. By the time I risked a look, the cops had them."

"You showed very good sense," Plemponi told her earnestly. "I hope they burn those thugs! Grabbing's a filthy business."

"That large object coming straight at you," Mihul observed calmly, "is another aircar. In this lane it has the right of way. You do not have the right of way. Got all that, Plemp?"

"Are you sure?" Doctor Plemponi asked her bewilderedly. "Confound it! I shall blow my siren."

He did. Trigger winced. "There!" Plemponi said triumphantly, as the other driver veered off in fright.

Trigger told herself to relax. Aircars were so nearly accident-proof that even Plemponi couldn't do more than snarl up traffic in one. "Have there been other raids in the school area since I left?" she asked, as he shot up out of the quadrangle and turned toward the balcony of his office.

"That was just under four years ago, wasn't it?" Mihul

said. "No, you were still with us when we had the last one . . . Six years back. Remember?"

Trigger did. Two students had been picked up on that occasion—sons of some Federation official. The grabbers had made a clean getaway, and it had been several months later before she heard the boys had been redeemed safely.

Plemponi descended to a teetery but gentle landing on the office balcony. He gave Trigger a self-satisfied look. "See?" he said tersely. "Let's go in, ladies. Had breakfast yet, Trigger?"

Trigger had finished breakfast a half-hour earlier, but she accepted a cup of coffee. Mihul, all athlete, declined. She went over to Plemponi's desk and stood leaning against it, arms folded across her chest, calm blue eyes fixed thoughtfully on Trigger. With her lithe length of body, Mihul sometimes reminded Trigger of a ferret, but the tanned face was a pleasant one and there was humor around the mouth. Even in Trigger's pregraduate days, she and Mihul had been good friends.

Doctor Plemponi removed a crammed breakfast tray from a wall chef, took a chair across from Trigger, sat down with the tray on his knees, excused himself, and began to eat and talk simultaneously.

"Before we go into that very reasonable complaint you made to Mihul yesterday," he said, "I wish you'd let me point out a few things."

Trigger nodded. "Please do."

"You, Trigger," Plemponi told her, "are an honored guest here at the Colonial School. You're the daughter of our late friend and colleague Runser Argee. You were one of our star pupils—not just as a smallarms medalist either. And now you're the secretary and assistant of the famous Precolonial Commissioner Holati Tate—which makes you almost a participant in what may well turn out to be the greatest scientific event of the century . . . I'm referring, of course," Plemponi added, "to Tate's discovery of the Old Galactic plasmoids."

"Of course," agreed Trigger. "And what is all this leading up to, Plemp?"

He waved a piece of toast at her. "No. Don't interrupt! I still have to point out that because of the exceptional managerial abilities you revealed under Tate, you've been sent here on detached duty for the Precolonial Department to aid the Commissioner and Professor Mantelish in the University League's Plasmoid Project. That means you're a pretty important person, Trigger! Mantelish, for all his idiosyncrasies, is undoubtedly the greatest living biologist in the League. And the Plasmoid Project here at the school is without question the League's most important current undertaking."

"So I've been told," said Trigger. "That's why I want to find out what's gone haywire with it."

"In a moment," Plemponi said. "In a moment." He located his napkin, wiped his lips carefully. "Now I've mentioned all this simply to make it very, very clear that we'll do anything we can to keep you satisfied. We're delighted to have you with us. We are honored!" He beamed at her. "Right?"

Trigger smiled. "If you say so. And thanks very much for all the lovely compliments, Doctor. But now let's get down to business."

Plemponi glanced over at Mihul and looked evasive. "That being?" he asked.

"You know," Trigger said. "But I'll put it into specific questions if you like. Where's Commissioner Tate?"

"I don't know."

"Where is Mantelish?"

He shook his head. "I don't know that either." He began to look unhappy.

"Oh?" said Trigger. "Who does know then?"

"I'm not allowed to tell you," Doctor Plemponi said firmly.

Trigger raised an eyebrow. "Why not?"

"Federation security," Plemponi said, frowning. He added, "I wasn't supposed to tell you that either, but what could I do?"

"Federation security? Because of the plasmoids?"

"Yes . . . Well . . . I'd—I don't know."

Trigger sighed. "Is it just me you're not supposed to tell these things to?"

"No, no, no," Plemponi said hastily. "Nobody. I'm not supposed to admit to anyone that I know anything of the whereabouts of Holati Tate or Professor Mantelish."

"Fibber!" Trigger said quietly. "So you know!"

Plemponi looked appealingly at Mihul. She was grinning. "My lips are sealed, Trigger! I can't help it. Please believe me."

"Let *me* sum it up then," Trigger said, tapping the arm of her chair with a fingertip. "Eight weeks ago I get pulled off my job in the Manon System and sent here to arrange the organizational details of this Plasmoid Project. The only reason I took on the job, as a temporary assignment, was that Commissioner Tate convinced me it was important to him to have me do it. I even let him talk me into doing it under the assumed name of Ruya Farn and"—she reached up and touched the side of her head—"and to dye my hair. For no sane reason that I could discover! He said the U-League had requested it."

Doctor Plemponi coughed. "Well, you know, Trigger, how sensitive the League is to personal notoriety."

The eyebrow went up again. "Notoriety?"

"Not in the wrong sense!" Plemponi said hastily. "But your name has become much more widely known than you may believe. The news viewers mentioned you regularly in their reports on *Harvest Moon* and the Commissioner. Didn't they, Mihul?"

Mihul nodded. "You made good copy, kid! We saw you in the solidopics any number of times."

"Well, maybe," Trigger said. "The cloak and dagger

touches still don't make much sense to me. But let's forget them and go on.

"When we get here, I manage to see Mantelish just once to try to find out what his requirements will be. He's pretty vague about them. Commissioner Tate is in and out of the Project—usually out. He's also turned pretty vague. About everything. Three weeks ago today I'm told he's gone. Nobody here can, or will, tell me where he's gone or how he can be contacted. Same thing at the Maccadon Precol office. Same thing at the Evalee home office. Same thing at the U-League—any office. Then I try to contact Mantelish. I'm informed he's with Tate! The two of them have left word I'm to carry on."

She spread her hands. "Carry on with what? I've done all I can do until I get further instructions from the people supposedly directing this supposedly very urgent and important project! Mantelish doesn't even seem to have a second in command . . ."

Plemponi nodded. "I was told he hadn't selected his Project assistants yet."

"Except," said Trigger, "for that little flock of junior scientists who keep themselves locked in with the plasmoids. They know less than nothing and would be too scared to tell me that if I asked them."

Plemponi looked confused for a moment. "That last sentence—" He checked himself. "Well, let's not quibble. Go on."

Trigger said, "That's it. Holati didn't need me on this job to begin with. There's nothing involved about the organizational aspects. Unless something begins to happen—and rather soon—there's no excuse for me to stay here."

"Couldn't you," Plemponi suggested, "regard this as a kind of well-earned little vacation?"

"I've tried to regard it as that. Holati impressed on me that one of us had to remain in the area of the

Project at all times, so I haven't even been able to leave the school grounds. I've caught up with my reading, and Mihul has put me through two of her tune-up commando courses. But the point is that I'm not on vacation. I don't believe Precol would feel that any of my present activities come under the heading of detached duty work!"

There was a short silence. Plemponi stared down at his empty tray, said, "Excuse me," got up and walked over to the wall chef with the tray.

"Wrong slot," Trigger told him.

He looked back. "Eh?"

"You want to put it in the disposal, don't you?"

"Thanks," Plemponi said absently. "Always doing that. Confusing them . . ." He dropped the tray where it belonged, shoved his hands into the chef's cleaning recess and waved them around, then came back, still looking absent-minded, and stopped before Trigger's chair. He studied her face for a moment.

"Commissioner Tate gave me a message for you," he said suddenly.

Trigger's eyes narrowed slightly. "When?"

"The day after he left." Plemponi lifted a hand. "Now wait! You'll see how it was. He called in and said, and I quote, 'Plemp, you don't stand much of a chance at keeping secrets from Trigger, so I'll give you no unnecessary secrets to keep. If this business we're on won't let us get back to the Project in the next couple of weeks, she'll get mighty restless. When she starts to complain—but no earlier—just tell her there are reasons why I can't contact her at present, or let her know what I'm doing, and that I will contact her as soon as I possibly can.' End of quote."

"That was all?" asked Trigger.

"Yes."

"He didn't say a thing about how long this situation might continue?"

"No. I've given you the message word for word. My memory is excellent, Trigger."

"So it could be more weeks? Or months?"

"Yes. Possibly. I imagine . . ." Plemponi had begun to perspire.

"Plemp," said Trigger, "will you give Holati a message from me?"

"Gladly!" said Plemponi. "What—oh, oh!" He flushed.

"Right," said Trigger. "You can contact him. I thought so."

Doctor Plemponi looked reproachful. "That was unfair, Trigger! You're quick-witted."

Trigger shrugged. "I can't see any justification for all this mystery, that's all." She stood up. "Anyway, here's the message. Tell him that unless somebody—rather promptly—gives me a good sane reason for hanging around here, I'll ask Precol to transfer me back to the Manon job."

Plemponi tut-tutted gloomily. "Trigger," he said, "I'll do my best about the message. But otherwise—"

She smiled nicely at him. "I know," she said, "your lips are sealed. Sorry if I've disturbed you, Plemp. But I'm just a Precol employee, after all. If I'm to waste their time, I'd like to know at least why it's necessary."

Plemponi watched her walk out of the room and off down the adjoining hall. In his face consternation struggled with approval.

"Lovely little figure, hasn't she?" he said to Mihul. He made vague curving motions in the air with one hand, more or less opposing ones with the other. "That sort of an up-and-sideways lilt when she walks."

"Uh-huh," said Mihul. "Old goats."

"Eh?" said Doctor Plemponi.

"I overheard you discussing Trigger's lilt with Mantelish."

Plemponi sat down at his desk. "You shouldn't eavesdrop, Mihul," he said severely. "I'd better get that message promptly to Tate, I suppose. She meant what she said, don't you think?"

"Every bit of it," said Mihul.

"Tate warned me she might get very difficult about this time. She's too conscientious, I feel."

"She also," said Mihul, "has a boy friend in the Manon System. They've been palsy ever since they went through the school here together."

"Ought to get married then," Plemponi said. He shuddered. "My blood runs cold every time I think of how close those grabbers got to her yesterday!"

Mihul shrugged. "Relax! They never had a chance. The characters Tate has guarding her are the fastest moving squad I ever saw go into action."

"That," Plemponi said reflectively, "doesn't sound much like our Maccadon police."

"I don't think they are. Imported talent of some kind, for my money. Anyway, if someone wants to pick up Trigger Argee here, he'd better come in with a battleship."

Plemponi glanced nervously across the balcony at the cloudless blue sky above the quadrangle.

"The impression I got from Holati Tate," he said, "is that somebody might."

2

There was a tube portal at the end of the hall outside Doctor Plemponi's office. Mihul stepped into the portal, punched the number of her personal quarters, waited till the overhead light flashed green a few seconds later, and stepped out into another hall seventeen floors below Plemponi's office and a little over a mile and a half away from it.

Mihul crossed the hall, went into her apartment, locked the door behind her and punched a shield button. In her bedroom, she opened a wall safe and swung out a high-powered transmitter. She switched the transmitter to active.

"Yes?" said a voice.

"Mihul here," said Mihul. "Quillan or the Commissioner . . ."

"Quillan here," the transmitter said a few seconds later in a different voice, a deep male one. "Go ahead, doll."

Mihul grunted. "I'm calling," she said, "because I feel strongly that you boys had better take some immediate action in the Argee matter."

"Oh?" said the voice. "What kind of action?"

"How the devil would I know? I'm just telling you I can't be responsible for her here much longer."

"Has something happened?" Quillan asked quickly.

"If you mean has somebody taken another swing at her, no. But she's all wound up to start swinging herself. She isn't going to do much waiting either."

Quillan said thoughtfully, "Hasn't she been that way for quite a while?"

"Not like she's been the last few days." Mihul hesitated. "Would it be against security if you told me whether something has happened to her?"

"Happened to her?" Quillan repeated cautiously.

"To her mind."

"What makes you think so?"

Mihul frowned at the transmitter.

"Trigger always had a temper," she said. "She was always obstinate. She was always an individualist and ready to fight for her own rights and anyone else's. But she used to show good sense. She's got one of the highest I.Q.s we ever processed through this place. The way she's acting now doesn't look too rational."

"How would she have acted earlier?" Quillan asked.

Mihul considered. "She would have been very annoyed with Commissioner Tate," she said. "I don't blame her for that—I'd be, too, in the circumstances. When he got back, she'd have wanted a reasonable explanation for what has been going on. If she didn't get one that satisfied her, she'd have quit. But she would have waited till he got back. Why not, after all?"

"You don't think she's going to wait now?"

"I do not," Mihul said. "She's forwarded him a kind of ultimatum through Plemponi. Communicate-or-else, in effect. Frankly I wouldn't care to guarantee she'll stay around to hear the answer."

"Hm . . . What do you expect she'll do?"

"Take off," Mihul said. "One way or the other."

"Ungh," Quillan said disgustedly. "You make it sound like the girl's got built-in space drives. You can stop her, can't you?"

"Certainly I can stop her," Mihul said. "If I can lock her in her room and sit on her to make sure she doesn't leave by the window. But 'unobtrusively?' You're the one who stressed she isn't to know she's being watched."

"True," Quillan said promptly. "I spoke like a loon, Mihul."

"True, Major Quillan, sir," said Mihul. "Now try again."

The transmitter was silent a few seconds. "Could you guarantee her for three days?" he asked.

"I could not," said Mihul. "I couldn't guarantee her another three hours."

"As bad as that?"

"Yes," said Mihul. "As bad as that. She was controlling herself with Plemponi. But I've been observing her in the physical workouts. I've fed it to her as heavy as I could, but there's a limit to what you can do that way. She's kept herself in very good shape."

"One of the best, I've been told," said Quillan.

"Condition, I meant," said Mihul. "Anyway, she's trained down fine right now. Any more of it would just make her edgier. You know how it goes."

"Uh-huh," he said. "Fighter nerves."

"Same deal," Mihul agreed.

There was a short pause. "How about slapping a guard on all Colonial School exits?" he suggested.

"Can you send me an army?"

"No."

"Then forget it. She was a student here, remember? Last year a bunch of our students smuggled the stuffed restructured mastodon out and left it in the back garden of the mayor of Ceyce, just for laughs. Too many exits. And Trigger was a trickier monkey than most that way, when she felt like it. She'll fade out of here whenever she wants to."

"It's those damn tube portal systems!" said Quillan, with feeling. "Most gruesome invention that ever hit the tailing profession." He sighed. "You win, Mihul! The Commissioner isn't in at the moment. But whether he gets in or not, I'll have someone over today to pick her up. Matter of fact, I'll come along myself."

"Good for you, boy!" Mihul said relievedly. "Did you get anything out of yesterday's grabbers?"

"A little. 'Get her, don't harm her' were their instructions. Otherwise it was like with those other slobs. A hole in the head where the real info should be. But at least we know for sure now that someone is specifically after Argee. The price was kind of interesting."

"What was it?"

"Flat half million credits."

Mihul whistled. "Poor Trigger!"

"Well, nobody's very likely to earn the money."

"I hope not. She's a good kid. All right, Major. Signing off now."

"Hold on a minute," said Quillan. "You asked a while ago if the girl had gone ta-ta."

"So I did," Mihul said, surprised. "You didn't say. I figured it was against security."

"It probably is," Quillan admitted. "Everything seems to be, right now. I've given up trying to keep up with that. Anyway—I don't know that she has. Neither does the Commissioner. But he's worried. And Argee has a date she doesn't know about with the Psychology Service, four days from now."

"The eggheads?" Mihul was startled. "What do they want with her?"

"You know," Quillan remarked reflectively, "that's odd! They didn't think to tell me."

"Why are you letting me know?" Mihul asked.

"You'll find out, doll," he said.

The U-League guard leaning against the wall opposite the portal snapped to attention as it opened. Trigger stepped out. He gave her a fine flourish of a salute.

"Good morning, Miss Farn."

"Morning," Trigger said. She flashed him a smile. "Did the mail get in?"

"Just twenty minutes ago."

She nodded, smiled again and walked past him to her office. She always got along fine with cops of almost any description, and these League boys were extraordinarily pleasant and polite. They were also, she'd noticed, a remarkably muscled group.

She locked the office door behind her—part of the Plasmoid Project's elaborate security precautions—went over to her mail file and found it empty. Which meant that whatever had come in was purely routine and already being handled by her skeleton office staff. Later in the day she might get a chance to scrawl Ruya Farn's signature on a few dozen letters and checks. Big job! Trigger sat down at her desk.

She brooded there a minute or two, tapping her teeth with her thumbnail. The Honorable Precolonial Commissioner Tate, whatever else might be said of him, undoubtedly was one of the brainiest little characters she'd ever come across. He probably saw some quite valid reason for keeping her here, isolated and uninformed. The question was what the reason could be.

Security . . . Trigger wrinkled her nose. Security didn't

mean a thing. Everybody and everything associated with the Old Galactic plasmoids had been wrapped up in Federation security measures since the day the plasmoid discovery was announced. And she'd been in the middle of the operations concerning them right along. Why should Holati Tate have turned secretive on her now? When even blabby old Plemponi could contact him.

It was more than a little annoying . . .

Trigger shrugged, reached into a desk drawer and took out a small solidopic. She set it on the desk and regarded it moodily.

The face of an almost improbably handsome young man looked back at her. Startling dark-blue eyes; a strong chin, curly brown hair. There was a gleam of white teeth behind the quick, warm smile which always awoke a responsive glow in her.

She and Brule Inger had been the nearest thing to engaged for the last two and a half years, ever since Precol sent them out together to its project on Manon Planet. They'd been dating before that, while they were both still attending the Colonial School. But now she was here, perhaps stuck here indefinitely—unless she did something about it—and Brule was on Manon Planet. By the very fastest subspace ships the Manon System was a good nine days away. For the standard Grand Commerce express freighter or the ordinary liner it was a solid two-months' run. Manon was a *long* way away!

It was almost a month since she'd even heard from Brule. She could make up another personal tape to him today if she felt like it. He would get it in fourteen days or so via a Federation packet. But she'd already sent him three without reply. Brule wasn't at all good at long distance lovemaking, and she didn't blame him much. She was a little awkward herself when it came to feeding her personal feelings into a tape. And—because of security again—there was very little else she could feed into it. She couldn't even let Brule know just where she was.

She put the solido back in its drawer, reached for one of the bank of buttons on the right side of the desk and pushed it down. A desk panel slid up vertically in front of her, disclosing a news viewer switched to the index of current headlines.

Trigger glanced over the headlines, while a few items dissolved slowly here and there and were replaced by more recent developments. Under the "Science" heading a great deal seemed to be going on, as usual, in connection with plasmoid experiments around the Hub.

She dialed in the heading, skimmed through the first item that appeared. Essentially it was a summary of reports on Hubwide rumors that nobody could claim any worthwhile progress in determining what made the Old Galactic plasmoids tick. Which, so far as Trigger knew, was quite true. Other rumors, rather unpleasant ones, were that the five hundred or so scientific groups to whom individual plasmoids had been issued by the Federation's University League actually had gained important information, but were keeping it to themselves.

The summary plowed through a few of the learned opinions and counter-opinions most recently obtained, then boiled them down to the statement that a plasmoid might be compared to an engine which appeared to lack nothing but an energy source. Or perhaps more correctly—assuming it might have an as yet unidentified energy source—a starter button. One group claimed to have virtually duplicated the plasmoid loaned to it by the Federation, producing a biochemical structure distinguishable from the Old Galactic model only by the fact that it had—quite predictably—fallen apart within hours. But plasmoids didn't fall apart. The specimens undergoing study had shown no signs of deterioration. A few still absorbed nourishment from time to time; some had been observed to move slightly. But none could be induced to operate. It was all very puzzling!

It was very puzzling, Trigger conceded. Back in the Manon System, when they had been discovered, the plasmoids were operating with high efficiency on the protein-collecting station which the mysterious Old Galactics appeared to have abandoned, or forgotten about, some hundreds of centuries ago. It was only when humans entered the base and switched off its mechanical operations that the plasmoids stopped working—and then, when the switches which appeared to have kept them going were expectantly closed again, they had stayed stopped.

The economic benefit, if they could be restarted, was obvious. On the *Harvest Moon* there had been a differently shaped plasmoid for every job. They could apparently take any form necessary for their function, and would sit and perform that function indefinitely. Personally, Trigger couldn't have cared less if they never did move again. It was nice that old Holati Tate had made an almost indecently vast fortune out of his first-discovery rights to the things, because she was really very fond of the Commissioner when he wasn't being irritating. But in some obscure way she found the plasmoids themselves and the idea of unlimitedly plastic life which they embodied rather appalling. However, she was in a minority there. Practically everybody else seemed to feel that plasmoids were the biggest improvement since the creation of Eve.

She switched the viewer presently to its local-news setting and dialed in the Manon System's reference number. Keeping tab on what was going on out there had become a private little ritual of late. Occasionally she even picked up references to Brule Inger, who functioned nowadays as Precol's official greeter and contact man in the system. He was very popular with the numerous important Hub citizens who made the long run out to

Manon—some bent on getting a firsthand view of the marvels of Old Galactic science, and a great many more bent on getting an early stake in the development of Manon Planet, which was rapidly approaching the point where its status would shift from Precol Project to Federation Territory, opening it to all qualified comers.

Today there was no news about Brule. Grand Commerce had opened its first business and recreation center on Manon, not ten miles from the Precol Headquarters dome where Trigger recently had been working. The subspace net which was being installed about the Old Galactic base was very nearly completed. The permanent Hub population on Manon Planet had just passed the forty-three thousand mark. There had been, Trigger recalled, a trifle nostalgically, barely eight hundred Precol employees, and not another human being, on that world in the days before Holati Tate announced his discovery.

She was just letting the viewer panel slide back into the desk when the office ComWeb gave forth with a musical ping. She switched it on.

"Hi, Rak!" she said cheerily. "Anything new?"

The bony-faced young man looking out at her wore the lusterless black uniform of a U-League Junior Scientist. His expression was worried.

He said, "I believe there is, Miss Farn." Rak was the group leader of the thirty-four Junior Scientists the League had installed in the Project. Like all the Juniors, he took his duties very seriously. "Unfortunately it's nothing I can discuss over a communicator. Would it be possible for you to come over and meet with us during the day?"

"That," Trigger stated, "was a ridiculous question, Rak! Want me over right now?"

He grinned. "Thanks, Miss Farn! In twenty minutes then? I'll get my advisory committee together and we can meet in the little conference room off the Exhibition Hall."

Trigger nodded. "I'll be wandering around the Hall. Just send a guard out to get me when you're ready."

3

She switched off the ComWeb and stood up. Rak and his group were stuck with the Plasmoid Project a lot more solidly than she was. They'd been established here, confined to their own wing of the Project area, when she came in from Manon with the Commissioner. Until the present security rulings were relaxed—which might not be for another two years—they would remain on the project.

Trigger felt a little sorry for them, though the Junior Scientists didn't seem to mind the setup. Dedication stood out all over them. Since about half were young women, one could assume that at any rate they weren't condemned to a completely monastic existence.

A couple of workmen were guiding a dozen big cleaning robots around the Plasmoid Exhibition Hall, which wouldn't be open to students or visitors for another few hours. Trigger strolled across the floor of the huge area toward a couple of exhibits that hadn't been there the last time she'd come through. Life-sized replicas of two O.G. Plasmoids—Numbers 1432 and 1433—she discovered. She regarded the waxy-looking, lumpish, partially translucent forms with some distaste. She'd been all over the Old Galactic Station itself, and might have stood close enough to the originals of these models to touch them. Not that she would have.

She glanced at her watch, walked around a scale model of *Harvest Moon*, the O.G. station, which occupied the center of the Hall, and went on among the exhibits. There were views taken on Manon Planet in one alcove, mainly of Manon's aerial plankton belt and of the giant plasmoids called Harvesters which had moved about the belt, methodically engulfing its clouds of living matter. A whale-sized replica of a Harvester dominated one end of the Hall, a giant dark-green sausage in external appearance, though with some extremely fancy internal arrangements.

"Miss Farn . . ."

She turned. A League cop, standing at the entrance of a hallway thirty feet away, pitched her the old flourish and followed it up with a bow. Excellent manners these guard boys had!

Trigger gave him a smile.

"Coming," she said.

Junior Scientist Rak and his advisory committee—two other young men and a young woman—were waiting in the conference room for her. They all stood up when she came in. This room marked the border of their territory; they would have violated several League rules by venturing out into the hall through which Trigger had entered.

And that would have been unthinkable.

Rak did the talking, as on the previous occasions when Trigger had met with this group. The advisory committee simply sat there and watched him. As far as Trigger could figure it, they were present at these sessions only to check Rak if it looked as if he were about to commit some ghastly indiscretion.

"We were wondering, Miss Farn," Rak said questioningly, "whether you have the authority to requisition additional University League guards for the Plasmoid Project?"

Trigger shook her head. "I've got no authority of any kind that I know of, as far as the League is concerned. No doubt Professor Mantelish could arrange it for you."

Rak nodded. "Is it possible for you to contact Professor Mantelish?"

"No," Trigger said. She smiled. "Is it possible for you to contact him?"

Rak glanced around his committee as if looking for approval, then said, "No, it isn't. As a matter of fact, Miss Farn, we've been isolated here in the most curious fashion for the past few weeks."

"So have I," said Miss Farn.

Rak looked startled. "Oh!" he said. "We were hoping you would be willing to give us a little information."

"I would," Trigger assured him, "if I had any to give. I don't, unfortunately." She considered. "Why do you feel additional League guards are required?"

"We heard," Rak remarked cautiously, "that there were raiders in the Colonial School area yesterday."

"Grabbers," Trigger said. "They wouldn't bother you. Your section of the project is supposed to be raid-proof anyway."

Rak glanced at his companions again and apparently received some indetectable sign of consent. "Miss Farn, as you know, our group has been entrusted with the care of two League plasmoids here. Are you aware that six of the plasmoids which were distributed to responsible laboratories throughout the Hub have been lost to unknown raiders?"

She was startled. "No, I didn't know that. I heard there'd been some unsuccessful attempts to steal distributed plasmoids."

"These six attempts," Rak said primly, "were completely successful. One must assume that the victimized laboratories also had been regarded as raid-proof."

Trigger admitted it was a reasonable assumption.

"There is another matter," Rak went on. "When we arrived here, we understood that Plasmoid Unit 112-113 was being brought here. It seems possible that its failure to appear indicates that League Headquarters does not consider the project a sufficiently safe place for 112-113."

"Why don't you ask Headquarters?" Trigger suggested. They stirred nervously.

"That would be a violation of the Principle of the Chain of Command, Miss Farn!" Rak explained.

"Oh," she said. The Juniors were over-disciplined, all right. "Is that 112-113 such a particularly important item?"

Rak said carefully, "I would say yes."

"I remember that 112-113 unit now," she said suddenly. "Big, ugly thing—well, that describes a lot of them, doesn't it?"

Rak and the others looked quietly affronted. In a moment, Trigger realized, one of them was going to go into a lecture on functional esthetics unless she could head them off—and she'd already heard quite enough about functional esthetics in connection with the plasmoids.

"Now, 113," she hurried on, "is a very small plasmoid"—she held her hands fifteen inches or so apart—"like that; and it's attached to the big one. Correct?"

Rak nodded, a little stiffly. "Essentially correct, Miss Farn."

"Well," Trigger said, "I can't blame you for worrying a bit. How about your Guard Captain? Isn't it all right to ask him about reinforcements?"

Rak pursed his lips. "Yes. And I did. This morning. Before I called you."

"What did he say?"

Rak grimaced unhappily. "He implied, Miss Farn, that his present guard complement could handle any emergency. How would he know?"

"That's his job," Trigger pointed out gently. The Juniors did look badly worried. "He didn't have any helpful ideas?"

"None," said Rak. "He said that if someone wanted to put up the money to hire a battle squad of Special Federation Police, he could always find some use for them. But that's hopeless, of course."

Trigger straightened up. She reached out and poked

Rak's bony chest with a fingertip. "You know something?" she said. "It's not!"

The four faces lit up together.

"The fact is," Trigger went on, "that I'm handling the Project budget until someone shows up to take over. So I think I'll just buy you that Federation battle squad, Rak! I'll get on it right away." She stood up. The Juniors bounced automatically out of their chairs. "You go tell your Guard Captain," she instructed them from the hall door, "there'll be a squad showing up in time for dinner tonight."

The Federation Police Office in Ceyce informed Trigger that a Class A Battle Squad—twenty trained men with full equipment—would report for two months' duty at the Colonial School during the afternoon. She made them out a check and gave it the Ruya Farn signature via telewriter. The figure on that check was going to cause some U-League auditor's eyebrows to fly off the top of his head one of these days; but if the League insisted on remaining aloof to the problems of its Plasmoid Project, a little financial anguish was the least it could expect in return.

Trigger felt quite cheerful for a while.

Then she had a call from Precol's Maccadon office. She was requested to stand by while a personal interstellar transmission was switched to her ComWeb.

It looked like her day! She hummed softly, waiting. She knew just one individual affluent enough to be able to afford personal interstellar conversations; and that was Commissioner Tate. Fast work, Plemp, she thought approvingly.

But it was Brule Inger's face that flashed into view on the ComWeb. Trigger's heart jumped. Her breath caught in her throat.

"Brule!" she yelled then. She shot up out of her chair. "Where are you calling from?"

Brule's eyes crinkled around the edges. He gave her

the smile. The good old smile. "Unfortunately, darling, I'm still in the Manon System." He blinked. "What happened to your hair?"

"Manon!" said Trigger. She started to settle back, weak with disappointment. Then she shot up again. "Brule! Lunatic! You're blowing a month's salary a minute on this! I love you! Switch off, fast!"

Brule threw back his head and laughed. "You haven't changed much in two months, anyway! Don't worry. It's for free. I'm calling from the yacht of a friend."

"Some friend!" Trigger said, startled.

"It isn't costing her anything either. She had to transmit to the Hub today anyway. Asked me if I'd like to take over the last few minutes of contact and see if I could locate you . . . Been missing me properly, Trigger?"

Trigger smiled. "Very properly. Well, that was lovely of her! Someone I know?"

"Hardly," said Brule. "Nelauk arrived a week or so after you left. Nelauk Pluly. Her father's the Pluly Lines. Let's talk about you. What's the silver-haired idea?"

"Got talked into it," she told him. "It's all the rage again right now."

He surveyed her critically. "I like you better as a redhead."

"So do I." Oops, Trigger thought. Security, girl! "So I'll change back tonight," she went on quickly. "Golly, Brule. It's nice to see that homely old mug again!"

"Be a lot nicer when it won't have to be over a transmitter."

"Right you are!"

"When are you coming back?"

She shook her head glumly. "Don't know."

He was silent a moment. "I've had to take a bit of chitchat now and then," he remarked, "about you and old Tate vanishing together."

Trigger felt herself coloring. "So don't take it," she said shortly. "Just pop them one!"

The smile returned. "Wouldn't be gentlemanly to pop a lady, would it?"

She smiled back. "So stay away from the ladies!" Somehow Brule and Holati Tate never had worked up a really warm regard for each other. It had caused a little trouble before.

"Okay to tell me where you are?" he asked.

"Afraid not, Brule."

"Precol Home Office apparently knows," he pointed out.

"Apparently," Trigger admitted.

They looked at each other a moment; then Brule grinned. "Well, keep your little secret!" he said. "All I really want to know is when you're getting back."

"Very soon, I hope, Brule," Trigger said unhappily. Then there was a sudden burst of sound from the ComWeb—gusts of laughing, chattering voices; a faint wash of music. Brule glanced aside.

"Party going on," he explained. "And here comes Nelauk! She wanted to say hello to you."

A dozen feet behind him, a figure strolled gracefully into view on the screen and came forward. A slender girl with high-piled violet hair and eyes that very nearly matched the hair's tint. She was dressed in something resembling a dozen blossoms—blossoms which, in Trigger's opinion, had been rather carelessly scattered. But presumably it was a very elegant party costume. She was quite young, certainly not yet twenty.

Brule laid a brotherly hand on a powdered shoulder. "Meet Trigger, Nelauk!"

Nelauk murmured it was indeed an honor, one she had long looked forward to. The violet eyes blinked sleepily at Trigger.

Trigger gave her a great big smile. "Thanks so much for arranging for the call. I've been wondering how Brule was doing."

Wrong thing to say, probably, she thought. She was right. Nelauk reached for it with no effort.

"Oh, he's doing wonderfully!" she assured Trigger without expression. "I'm keeping an eye on him. And this small favor—it was the very least I could do for Brule. For you, too, of course, Trigger dear."

Trigger held the smile firmly.

"Thanks so much, again!" she said.

Nelauk nodded, smiled back and drifted gracefully off the screen. Brule blew Trigger a kiss. "They'll be cutting contact now. See you very, very soon, Trigger, I hope."

His image vanished before she could answer.

She paced her office, muttering softly. She went over to the ComWeb once, reached out toward it and drew her hand back again.

Better think this over.

It might not be an emergency. Brule didn't exactly chase women. He let them chase him now and then. Long before she left Manon, Trigger had discovered, without much surprise, that the wives, daughters and girl friends of visiting Hub tycoons were as susceptible to the Inger charm as any Precol clerks. The main difference was that they were a lot more direct about showing it.

It hadn't really worried her. In fact, she found Brule's slightly startled reports of the maneuverings of various amorous Hub ladies very entertaining. But she had put in a little worrying about something else. Brule's susceptibility seemed to be more to the overwhelming mass display of wealth with which he was suddenly in almost constant contact. Many of the yachts he went flitting around among as Precol's representative were elaborate spacegoing palaces, and it appeared Brule Inger was soon regarded as a highly welcome guest on most of them.

Brule talked about that a little too much.

Trigger resumed her pacing.

Little Nelauk mightn't be twenty yet, but she'd flipped

out a challenge just now with all the languid confidence of a veteran campaigner. Which, Trigger thought cattily, little Nelauk undoubtedly was.

And a girl, she added cattily, whose father represented the Pluly Lines did have some slight reason for confidence . . .

"Meow!" she reproved herself. Nelauk, to be honest about it, was also a dish.

But if she happened to be serious about Brule, the dish Brule might be tempted by was said Pluly Lines.

Trigger went over to the window and looked down at the exercise quadrangle forty floors below.

"If he's that much of a meathead!" she thought.

He could be that much of a meathead. He was also Brule. She went back to her desk and sat down. She looked at the ComWeb. A girl had a right to consider her own interests.

And there was the completely gruesome possibility now that Holati Tate might call in at any moment, give her an entirely reasonable, satisfactory, valid, convincing explanation for everything that had happened lately—and then show her why it would be absolutely necessary for her to stay here a while longer.

If it was a choice between inconveniencing Holati Tate and losing that meathead Brule . . .

Trigger switched on the ComWeb.

4

The head of the personnel department of Precol's Maccadon office said, "You don't want me, Argee. That's not my jurisdiction. I'll connect you with Undersecretary Rozan."

Trigger blinked. "Under—" she began. But he'd already cut off.

She stared at the ComWeb, feeling a little shaken. All she'd done was to say she wanted to apply for a transfer! Undersecretary Rozan was one of Precol's Big Four. For a moment, Trigger had an uncanny notion. Some strange madness was spreading insidiously through the Hub. She shook the thought off.

A businesslike blonde showed up in the screen. She might be about thirty-five. She smiled a small, cold smile.

"Rozan," she said. "You're Trigger Argee. I know about you. What's the trouble?"

Trigger looked at her, wondering. "No trouble," she said. "Personnel just routed me through to you."

"They've been instructed to do so," said Rozan. "Go ahead."

"I'm on detached duty at the moment."

"I know."

"I'd like to apply for a transfer back to my previous job. The Manon System."

"That's your privilege," said Rozan. She half turned, swung a telewriter forward and snapped it into her ComWeb. She glanced out at Trigger's desk. "Your writer's connected, I see. We'll want thumbprint and signature."

She slid a form into her telewriter, shifted it twice as Trigger deposited thumbprint and signature, and drew it out. "The application will be processed promptly, Argee. Good day."

Not a gabby type, that Rozan.

If not gabby, the Precol blonde was a woman of her word. Trigger had just started lunch when the office mail receiver tinkled brightly at her. It was her retransfer application. At the bottom of the form was stamped "Application Denied," followed by the signature of the Secretary of the Department of Precolonization, Home Office, Evalee.

Trigger's gaze shifted incredulously from the signature to the two words, and back. They'd taken the trouble to get that signature transmitted from Evalee just to make it clear that there were no heads left to be gone over in the matter. Precol was not transferring her back to Manon. That was final. Then she realized there was a second sheet attached to the application form.

On it in handwriting were a few more words: "In accordance with the instructions of Commissioner Tate." And a signature, "Rozan." And three final words: "Destroy this note."

Trigger crumpled up the application in one hand. Her other hand darted to the ComWeb.

Then she checked herself. To fire an as-of-now resignation back at Precol had been the immediate impulse. But something, some vague warning chill, was saying it might be a very poor impulse to follow.

She sat back to think it over.

It was very probable that Undersecretary Rozan disliked Holati Tate intensely. A lot of the Home Office big shots disliked Holati Tate. He'd stomped on their toes more than once—very justifiably; but he'd stomped. The Home Office wouldn't go an inch out of its way to do something just because Commissioner Tate happened to want it done.

So somebody else was backing up Commissioner Tate's instructions.

Trigger shook her head helplessly.

The only somebody else who *could* give instructions to the Precolonization Department was the Council of the Federation!

And how could the Federation possibly care what Trigger Argee was doing? She made a small, incredulous noise in her throat.

Then she sat there a while, feeling frightened.

The fright didn't really wear off, but it settled down slowly inside her. Up on the surface she began to think again.

Assume it's so, she instructed herself. It made no sense,

but everything else made even less sense. Just assume it's so. Set it up as a practical problem. Don't worry about the why . . .

The problem became very simple then. She wanted to go to Manon. The Federation—or something else, something quite unthinkable at the moment but comparable to the Federation in power and influence—wanted to keep her here.

She uncrumpled the application, detached Rozan's note, tore up the note and dropped its shreds into the wall disposal. That obligation was cancelled. She didn't have any other obligations. She'd liked Holati Tate. When all this was cleared up, she might find she still liked him. At the moment she didn't owe him a thing.

Now. Assume they hadn't just blocked the obvious route to Manon. They couldn't block all routes to everywhere; that was impossible. But they could very well be watching to see that she didn't simply get up and walk off. And they might very well be prepared to take quite direct action to stop her from doing it.

She would, Trigger decided, leave the method she'd use to get out of the Colonial School unobserved to the last. That shouldn't present any serious difficulties.

Once she was outside, what would she do?

Principally, she had to buy transportation. And that—since she had no intention of spending a few months on the trip, and since a private citizen didn't have the ghost of a chance at squeezing aboard a Federation packet on the Manon run—was going to be expensive. In fact, it was likely to take the bulk of her savings. Under the circumstances, however, expense wasn't important. If Precol refused to give her back her job when she showed up on Manon, a number of the industrial outfits preparing to move in as soon as the planet got its final clearance would be very happy to have her. She'd already turned down a dozen offers at considerably more than her present salary.

So . . . she'd get off the school grounds, take a tube

strip into downtown Ceyce, step into a ComWeb booth, and call Grand Commerce transportation for information on the earliest subspace runs to Manon.

She'd reserve a berth on the first fast boat out. In the name of—let's see—in the name of Birna Drellgannoth, who had been a friend of hers when they were around the age of ten. Since Manon was a Precol preserve, she wouldn't have to meet the problem of precise personal identification, such as one ran into when booking passage to some of the member worlds.

The ticket office would have her thumbprints then. That was unavoidable. But there were millions of thumbprints being deposited every hour of the day on Maccadon. If somebody started checking for her by that method, it should take them a good long while to sort out hers.

Next stop—the Ceyce branch of the Bank of Maccadon. And it was lucky she'd done all her banking in Ceyce since she was a teen-ager, because she would have to present herself in person to draw out her savings. She'd better lose no time getting to the bank either. It was one place where theoretical searchers could expect her to show up.

She could pay for her ship reservation at the bank. Then to a store for some clothes and a suitcase for the trip . . .

And, finally, into some big middle-class hotel where she would stay quietly until a few hours before the ship was due to take off.

That seemed to cover it. It probably wasn't foolproof. But trying to work out a foolproof plan would be a waste of time when she didn't know just what she was up against. This should give her a running start, a long one.

When should she leave?

Right now, she decided. Commissioner Tate presumably would be informed that she had applied for a transfer and that the transfer had been denied. He knew her too well not to become very suspicious if it looked as if she were just sitting there and taking it.

She got her secretary on the ComWeb.

"I'm thinking of leaving the office," she said. "Anything for me to take care of first?"

It was a safe question. She'd signed the day's mail and checks before lunch.

"Not a thing, Miss Farn."

"Fine," said Ruya Farn. "If anyone wants me in the next three or four hours, I'll be either down in the main library or out at the lake."

And that would give somebody two rather extensive areas to look for her, if and when they started to look—along with the fact that, for all anyone knew, she might be anywhere between those two points.

A few minutes later, Trigger sauntered, humming blithely, into her room and gave it a brief survey. There were some personal odds and ends she would have liked to take with her, but she could send for them from Manon.

The Denton, however, was coming along. The little gun had a very precisely calibrated fast-acting stunner attachment, and old Runser Argee had instructed Trigger in its use with his customary thoroughness before he formally presented her with the gun. She had never had occasion to turn the stunner on a human being, but she'd used it on game. If this cloak and dagger business became too realistic, she'd already decided she would use it as needed.

She slipped the Denton into the side pocket of a lightweight rain robe, draped the robe over her arm, slung her purse beside it, picked up the sun hat and left the room.

The Colonial School's kitchen area was on one of the underground levels. Unless they'd modified their guard system very considerably since Trigger had graduated, that was the route by which she would leave.

As far as she could tell they hadn't modified anything. The whole kitchen level looked so unchanged that she had a moment of nostalgia. Groups of students went chattering along the hallways between the storerooms and the cooking and processing plants. The big mess hall, Trigger noticed in passing, smelled as good as it always had. Bells sounded the end of a period and a loudspeaker system began directing Class so and so to Room such and such. Standing around were a few uniformed guards— mainly for the purpose of helping out newcomers who had lost their direction.

She came out on the equally familiar big and brightly lit platform of the loading ramp. Some sixty or seventy great cylindrical vans floated alongside the platform, most of them disgorging their contents, some still sealed.

Trigger walked unhurriedly down the ramp, staying in the background, observing the movements of two ramp guards and marking four vans which were empty and looked ready to go.

The driver of the farthest of the four empties stood in the back of his vehicle, a few feet above the platform. When Trigger came level with him, he was studying her. He was a big young man with tousled black hair and a rough-and-ready look. He was grinning very faintly. He knew the ways of Colonial School students.

Trigger raised her left hand a few inches, three fingers up. His grin widened. He shook his head and raised both hands in a corresponding gesture. Eight fingers.

Trigger frowned at him, stopped and looked back along the row of vans. Then left hand up again—four fingers and thumb.

The driver made a circle with finger and thumb. A deal, for five Maccadon crowns. Which was about standard fare for unauthorized passage out of the school.

Trigger wandered on to the end of the platform, turned and came back, still unhurriedly but now close to the edge of the ramp. Down the line, another van slammed open in back and a stream of crates swooped out, riding a gravity beam from the roof toward a waiting storeroom carrier. The guard closest to Trigger turned to watch the process. Trigger took six quick steps and reached her driver.

He put down a hand to help her step up. She slipped the five-crown piece into his palm.

"Up front," he whispered hoarsely. "Next to the driver's seat and keep down. How far?"

"Nearest tube line."

He grinned again and nodded. "Can do."

Twenty minutes later Trigger was in a downtown ComWeb booth. There had been a minor modification in her plans and she'd stopped off in a store a few doors away and picked up a carefully nondescript street dress and a scarf. She changed into the dress now and bundled the school costume into a deposit box, which she dispatched to Central Deposit with a one-crown piece, getting a numbered slip in return. It had occurred to her that there was a chance otherwise of getting caught in a Colonial School roundup, if it was brought to Doctor Plemponi's attention that there appeared to be considerably more students out on the town at the moment than could be properly overlooked.

Or even, Trigger thought, if somebody simply happened to have missed Trigger Argee.

She slipped the rain robe over her shoulders, dropped a coin into the ComWeb, and covered the silver-blonde hair with the scarf. The screen lit up. She asked for Grand Commerce Transportation.

Waiting, she realized suddenly that so far she was rather enjoying herself. There had been a little argument with the van driver who, it turned out, had ideas of his own about modifying Trigger's plans—a complication she'd run into frequently in her school days too. As usual, it didn't develop into a very serious argument. Truckers who dealt with the Colonial School knew, or learned in one or two briefly horrid lessons, that Mihul's commando-trained charges were prone to ungirlish methods of discouragement when argued with too urgently.

The view screen switched on. The Transportation clerk's glance flicked over Trigger's street dress when she told him her destination. His expression remained bland. Yes, the *Dawn City* was leaving Ceyce Port for the Manon System tomorrow evening. Yes, it was subspace express—one of the newest and fastest, in fact. His eyes slipped over the dress again. Also one of the most luxurious, he might add. There would be only two three-hour stops in the Hub beyond Maccadon—one each off Evalee and Garth. Then a straight dive to Manon unless, of course, gravitic storm shifts forced the ship to surface temporarily. Average time for the *Dawn City* on the run was eleven days; the slowest trip so far had required sixteen.

"But unfortunately, madam, there are only a very few cabins left—and not very desirable ones, I'm afraid." He looked apologetic. "There hasn't been a vacancy on the Manon run for the past three months."

"I can stand it, I imagine," Trigger said. "How much for the cheapest?"

The clerk cleared his throat gently and told her.

She couldn't help blinking, though she was braced for it. But it was more than she had counted on. A great deal more. It would leave her, in fact, with exactly one hundred and twenty-six crowns out of her entire savings, plus the coins she had in her purse.

"Any extras?" she asked, a little hoarsely.

He shrugged. "There's Traveler's Rest," he said negligently. "Nine hundred for the three dive periods. But Rest is optional, of course. Some passengers prefer the experience of staying awake during a subspace dive." He smiled—rather sadistically, Trigger felt—and added, "Till they've lived through one of them, that is."

Trigger nodded. She'd lived through quite a few of them. She didn't like subspace particularly—nobody did—but except for an occasional touch of nausea or dizziness at the beginning of a dive, it didn't bother her much. Many people got hallucinations, went into states of panic or just got very sick. "Anything else?" she asked.

"Just the usual tips and things," said the clerk. He looked surprised. "Do you—does madam wish to make the reservation?"

"Madam does," Trigger told him coldly. "How long will it hold?"

It would be good up to an hour before take-off time, she learned. If not claimed then, it would be filled from the last-minute waiting list.

She left the booth thoughtfully. At least the *Dawn City* would be leaving in less than twenty-six hours. She wouldn't have to spend much of her remaining capital before she got off Maccadon.

She'd skip meals, she decided. Except breakfast next morning, which would be covered by her hotel room fee.

And it wasn't going to be any middle-class hotel.

There was no one obviously waiting for her at the Bank of Maccadon. In fact, since that venerable institution covered a city block, with entrances running up from the street level to the fifty-eighth floor, a small army would have been needed to make sure of spotting her. She had to identify herself to get into the vaults, but there was a solution to that. Seven years ago when Runser Argee died suddenly and she had to get his property and records straightened out, a gray-haired little vault attendant with whom she dealt had taken a fatherly interest in her. When she saw he was still on the job, Trigger was certain the matter would go off all right.

It did. He didn't take a really close look at her until she shoved her signature and Federation identification in front of him. Then his head bobbed up briskly. His eyes lit up.

"Trigger!" He bounced out of his chair. His right hand shot out. "Good to see you again! I've been hearing about you."

They shook hands. She put a finger to her lips. "I'm here incog!" she cautioned in a low voice. "Can you handle this quietly?"

The faded blue eyes widened slightly, but he asked no questions. Trigger Argee's name was known rather widely, as a matter of fact, particularly on her home world. And as he remembered Trigger, she wasn't a girl who'd go look for a spotlight to stand in.

He nodded. "Sure can!" He glanced suspiciously at the nearest customers, then looked down at what Trigger had written. He frowned. "You drawing out everything? Not leaving Ceyce for good, are you?"

"No," Trigger said. "I'll be back. This is just a temporary emergency."

That was all the explaining she had to do. Four minutes later she had her money. Three minutes after that she had paid for the *Dawn City* reservation as Birna Drellgannoth and deposited her thumbprints with the ticket office. Counting what was left, she found it came to just under a hundred and thirty-eight.

Definitely no dinner tonight! She needed a suitcase and a change of clothing. And then she'd just better go sit in that hotel room.

The street level traffic was moderate around the bank, but it began to thicken as she approached a shopping center two blocks farther on. Striding along, neither hurrying nor idling, Trigger decided she had it made. The only real chance to catch up with her had been at the bank. And the old vault attendant wouldn't talk.

Half a block from the shopping center, a row of spacers on planetleave came rollicking cheerily toward her, uniform jackets unbuttoned, three Ceyce girls in arm-linked formation among them, all happily high. Trigger shifted toward the edge of the sidewalk to let them pass. As the line swayed up on her left, there was the shadowy settling of an aircar at the curb to her right.

With loud outcries of glad recognition and whoops of

laughter, the line swung in about her, close. Bodies crowded against her; a hand was clapped over her mouth. Other hands held her arms. Her feet came off the ground and she had a momentary awareness of being rushed expertly forward.

Then she was in the car, half on her side over the rear seat, two very strong hands clamping her wrists together behind her back. As she sucked in her breath for a yell, the door snapped shut behind her, cutting off the rollicking "ha-ha-ha's" and other noises outside.

There was a lurching twist as the aircar shot upward.

5

The man who held Trigger's wrists shifted his grip up her arms, and turned her a little so that she could sit upright on the seat, faced half away from him. She had got only a glimpse of him as he caught her, but he seemed to be wearing the same kind of commercial spacer's uniform as the group which had hustled her into the car. The other man in the car, the driver, sat up front with his back to them. He looked like any ordinary middle-aged civilian.

Trigger let her breath out slowly. There was no point in yelling now. She could feel her legs tremble a little, but she didn't seem to be actually frightened. At least, not yet.

"Spot anything so far?" the man who held her asked. It was a deep voice. It sounded matter-of-fact, quite unexcited.

"Three possibles anyway," the driver said with equal casualness. He didn't turn his head. "Make it two . . . One very definite possible now, I'd say!"

"Better feed it to her then."

The driver didn't reply, but the car's renewed surge

of power pushed Trigger down hard on the seat. She couldn't see much more than a shifting piece of the skyline through the front view plate. Their own car seemed to be rising at a tremendous rate. They were probably, she thought, already above the main traffic arteries over Ceyce. "Now, Miss Argee," the man sitting beside her said, "I'd like to reassure you a little first."

"Go ahead and reassure me," Trigger said unsteadily.

"You're in no slightest danger from us," he said. "We're your friends."

"Nice friends!" remarked Trigger.

"I'll explain it all in a couple of minutes. There may be some fairly dangerous characters on our tail at the moment, and if they start to catch up—"

"Which they seem to be doing," the driver interrupted. "Hang on for a few fast turns when we hit the next cloud bank."

"We'll probably shake them there," the other man explained to Trigger. "In case we don't though, I'll need both hands free to handle the guns."

"So?" she asked.

"So I'd like to slip a set of cuffs on you for just a few minutes. I've been informed you're a fairly tricky lady, and we don't want you to do anything thoughtless. You won't have them on very long. All right?"

Trigger bit her lip. It wasn't all right, and she didn't feel at all reassured so far.

"Go ahead," she said.

He let go of her left arm, presumably to reach for the handcuffs. She twisted around on him and went into fast action.

She was fairly proficient at the practice of unarmed mayhem. The trouble was that the big ape she was trying the stuff on seemed at least as adept and with twice her muscle. She lost a precious instant finding out that the Denton was no longer in her robe pocket. After that she never got back the initiative. It didn't help either that the car suddenly seemed to be trying to fly in three directions at once.

All in all, about forty seconds passed before she was plumped back on the seat, her hands behind her again, linked at the wrists by the smooth plastic cords of the cuffs. The ape stood behind the driver, his hands resting on the back of the seat. He wasn't, Trigger observed bitterly, even breathing hard. The view plate was full of the cottony whiteness of a cloud heart. They seemed to be dropping again.

One more violent swerve and they came flashing out into wet gray cloud-shadow and on into brilliant sunlight.

A few seconds passed. Then the ape remarked, "Looks like you lost them, chum."

"Right," said the driver. "Almost at the river now. I'll turn north there and drop down."

"Right," said the ape. "Get us that far and we'll be out of trouble."

A few minutes passed in silence. Presently Trigger sensed they were slowing and losing altitude. Then a line of trees flashed by in the view plate. "Nice flying!" the ape said. He punched the driver approvingly in the shoulder and turned back to Trigger.

They looked at each other for a few seconds. He was tall, dark-eyed, very deeply tanned, with thick sloping shoulders. He probably wasn't more than five or six years older than she was. He was studying her curiously, and his eyes were remarkably steady. Something stirred in her for a moment, a small chill of fear. Something passed through her thoughts, a vague odd impression, like a half aroused memory, of huge, cold, dangerous things far away. It was gone before she could grasp it more clearly. She frowned.

The ape smiled. It wasn't, Trigger saw, an entirely unpleasant face. "Sorry the party got rough," he said. "Will you give parole if I take those cuffs off and tell you what this is about?"

She studied him again. "Better tell me first," she said shortly.

"All right. We're taking you to Commissioner Tate. We'll be there in about an hour. He'll tell you himself why he wanted to see you."

Trigger's eyes narrowed for an instant. Secretly she felt very much relieved. Holati Tate, at any rate, wouldn't let anything really unpleasant happen to her—and she would find out at last what had been going on.

"You've got an odd way of taking people places," she observed.

He laughed. "The grabber party wasn't scheduled. You'd indicated you wanted to speak to the Commissioner. We were sent to the Colonial School to pick you up and escort you to him. When we found out you'd disappeared, we had to do some fast improvising. Not my business to tell you the reasons for that."

Trigger said hesitantly, "Those people who were chasing this car—"

"What about them?" he asked thoughtfully.

"Were they after *me*?"

"Well," he said, "they weren't after me. Better let the Commissioner tell you about that, too. Now—how about parole?"

She nodded. "Till you turn me over to the Commissioner."

"Fair enough," he said. "You're his problem then." He took a small flat piece of metal out of a pocket and reached back of her with it. He didn't seem to do more than touch the cuffs, but she felt the slick coils loosen and drop away.

Trigger rubbed her wrists, "Where's my gun?" she asked.

"I've got it. I'll give it to the Commissioner."

"How did you people find me so fast?"

"Police keep bank entrances under twenty-four hour visual survey. We had someone watching their screens.

You were spotted going in." He sat down companionably beside her. "I'd introduce myself, but I don't know if that would fit in with the Commissioner's plans."

Trigger shrugged. It still was quite possible, she decided, that her own plans weren't completely spoiled. Holati and his friends didn't necessarily know about that vault account. If they did know she'd had one and had closed it out, they could make a pretty good guess at what she'd done with the money. But if she just kept quiet, there might be an opportunity to get back to Ceyce and the *Dawn City* by tomorrow evening.

"No hard feelings, are there?" the Commissioner's over-muscled henchman inquired amiably.

Trigger glanced at him from the side. Not amiably. "Yes," she said evenly. "There are."

He looked surprised. "Maybe," the driver suggested from the front, "what Miss Argee could do with is a shot of Puya. Flask's in my coat pocket. Left side."

"There's an idea," remarked Trigger's companion. He looked at her. "It's very good Puya."

"So choke on it," Trigger told him gently. She settled back into the corner of the seat and closed her eyes. "You can wake me up when we get to the Commissioner."

6

When Trigger was brought to Commissioner Tate's little private office and inquired with some heat what the devil was up, the tall grabber hadn't come into the office with her. He asked the Commissioner from the door whether he should get Professor Mantelish to the conference room, and the Commissioner nodded. The door closed and the two of them were alone.

Commissioner Tate was a mild-looking little man, well along in years, sparse and spruce in his Precol uniform.

The small gray eyes in the sun-darkened, leathery face weren't really mild, if you considered them more closely, or if you knew the Commissioner.

"I know it's looked odd," the Commissioner admitted, "but the circumstances have been very odd. Still are. And I didn't want to worry you any more than I had to."

"Really? The methods you've used not to worry me have hardly been soothing," said Trigger, unmollified.

"I know that, too," said the Commissioner. "But if I'd told you everything immediately, you would have had reason enough to be worried for the past two months, rather than just for a day or so. The situation has improved now, very considerably. In fact, in another few days you shouldn't have any more reason to worry at all." He smiled briefly. "At least, no more than the rest of us."

Trigger felt a bit dry-lipped suddenly. "I do at present?" she asked.

"You did till today. There's been some pretty heavy heat on you, Trigger girl. We're switching most of it off tonight. For good, I think."

"You mean some heat will be left?"

"In a way," he said. "But that should be cleared up too in the next three or four days." Commissioner Tate got to his feet. "Then let's go join Mantelish."

"Why the professor?"

"He's got a kind of pet I'd like you to look at."

"A pet!" cried Trigger. She shook her head again and stood up resignedly. "Lead on, Commissioner!"

They joined Mantelish and his plasmoid weirdie in what looked like the dining room of what had looked like an old-fashioned hunting lodge when the aircar came diving down on it between two ice-sheeted mountain peaks. Trigger wasn't sure in just what section of the main continent they were; but there were only two or three alternatives—it was high in the mountains, and night came a lot faster here than it did around Ceyce.

She greeted Mantelish and sat down at the table. He was a very big, rather fat but healthy-looking old man with a thick thatch of white hair and a ruddy face.

Then the Commissioner locked the doors and introduced her to the professor's pet.

"In some way," Holati Tate said, "this little item here seems to be at the core of the whole plasmoid problem. Know what it is?"

Trigger looked at the little item with some revulsion. Dark green, marbled with pink streakings, it lay on the table between them, rather like a plump leech a foot and a half long. It was motionless except that the end nearest her shifted in a short arc from side to side, as if the thing suffered from a very slow twitch.

"One of the plasmoids obviously," she said. "A jumpy one." She blinked at it. "Looks like that 113. Is it?"

She glanced around. Commissioner Tate and Professor Mantelish, who sat in an armchair off to her right, were staring at her, eyebrows up, apparently surprised about something. "What's the matter?" she asked.

"We're just wondering," said Holati, "how you happen to remember 113, in particular, out of the thousands of plasmoids on *Harvest Moon.*"

"Oh. One of the Junior Scientists on your Project mentioned the 112-113 unit. That brought it to mind. Is this 113?"

"No," said Holati Tate. "But it appears to be a duplicate of it. It's labeled 113-A. Even the professor isn't certain he could distinguish between the two. Right, Mantelish?"

"That is true," said Mantelish, "at present. Without a physical comparison—" He shrugged.

"What's so important about the critter?" Trigger asked, eyeing the leech again. One good thing about it, she thought—it wasn't equipped to eye her back.

"The plasmoid you mentioned earlier, Unit 112-113,

has been stolen," the Commissioner said. "We don't—" But Holati Tate's attention had shifted suddenly to the table. "Hey, now!" he said in a low voice.

Trigger followed his gaze. After a moment she made a soft, sucking sound of alarmed distaste.

"Ugh!" she remarked. "It's moving!"

"So it is," Holati said.

"Towards me!" said Trigger. "I think—"

"Don't get startled. Mantelish!"

Mantelish already was coming up slowly behind Trigger's chair. "Don't move!" he cautioned her.

"Why not?" said Trigger.

"Hush, my dear." Mantelish laid a large, heavy hand on each of her shoulders and bore down slightly. "It's sensitive! This is very interesting. Very."

Perhaps it was. She kept watching the plasmoid. It had thinned out somewhat and was gliding very slowly but very steadily across the table. Definitely in her direction.

"Ho-ho!" said Mantelish in a thunderous murmur. "Perhaps it likes you, Trigger! Ho-ho!" He seemed immensely pleased.

"Well," Trigger said helplessly, "I don't like it!" She wriggled slightly under Mantelish's hands. "And I'd sooner get out of this chair!"

"Don't be childish, Trigger," said the professor annoyedly. "You're behaving as if it were, in some manner, offensive."

"It is," she said.

"Hush, my dear," Mantelish said absently, putting on a little more pressure. Trigger hushed resignedly. They watched. In about a minute, the gliding thing reached the edge of the table. Trigger gathered herself to duck out from under Mantelish's hands and go flying out of the chair if it looked as if the plasmoid was about to drop into her lap.

But it stopped. For a few seconds it lay motionless. Then it gradually raised its front end and began waving it gently back and forth in the air. At her, Trigger suspected.

"Yipes!" she said, horrified.

The front end sank back. The plasmoid lay still again. After a minute it was still lying still.

"Show's over for the moment, I guess," said the Commissioner.

"I'm afraid so," said Professor Mantelish. His big hands went away from Trigger's aching shoulders. "You startled it, Trigger!" he boomed at her accusingly.

7

The point of it, Holati Tate explained, was that this had been more activity than 113-A normally displayed over a period of a week. And 113-A was easily the most active plasmoid of them all nowadays.

"It is, of course, possible," Mantelish said, arousing from deep thought, "that it was attracted by your body odor."

"Thank you, Mantelish!" said Trigger.

"You're welcome, my dear." Mantelish had pulled his chair up to the table; he hitched himself forward in it. "We shall now," he announced, "try a little experiment. Pick it up, Trigger."

She stared at him. "Pick it up? No, Mantelish. We shall now try some other little experiment."

Mantelish furrowed his Jovian brows. Holati gave her a small smile across the table. "Just touch it with the tip of a finger," he suggested. "You can do that much for the professor, can't you?"

"Barely," Trigger told him grimly. But she reached out and put a cautious fingertip to the less lively far end of 113-A. After a moment she said, "Hey!" She moved the finger lightly along the thing's surface. It had a velvety, smooth, warm feeling, rather like a kitten. "You know," she said surprised, "it feels sort of nice! It just looks disgusting—"

"Disgusting!" Mantelish boomed, offended again.

The Commissioner held up a hand. "Just a moment," he said. He'd picked up some signal Trigger hadn't noticed, for he went over to the wall now and touched something there. A release button apparently. The door to the room opened. Trigger's grabber came in. The door closed behind him. He was carrying a tray with a squat brown flask and four rather small glasses on it.

The Commissioner introduced him: Heslet Quillan— Major Heslet Quillan, of the Subspace Engineers. For a Subspace Engineer, Trigger thought skeptically, he was a pretty good grabber. But there was a qualified truce in the room. There was no really good reason not to include Major Quillan in it. He gave Trigger a grin. She gave him a tentative smile in return.

"Ah, Puya!" Professor Mantelish exclaimed, advancing on the tray as Quillan set it on the table. Mantelish seemed to have forgotten about plasmoid experiments for the moment, and Trigger didn't intend to remind him. She drew her hand back quietly from 113-A. The professor unstoppered the flask. "You'll have some, Trigger, I'm sure? The only really good thing the benighted world of Rumli ever produced."

"My great-grandmother," Trigger remarked, "was a Rumlian." She watched him fill the four glasses with a thin purple liquid. "I've never tried it; but yes, thanks."

Quillan put one of the glasses in front of her.

"And we shall drink," Mantelish suggested, with a suave flourish of his Puya, "to your great-grandmother!"

"We shall also," suggested Major Quillan, pulling a chair up to the table for himself, "advise Trigger to take a very small sip on her first go at the stuff."

Nobody had invited him to sit down. But nobody was objecting either. Well, that fitted, Trigger thought.

She sipped. It was tart and hot. Very hot. She set the glass back on the table, inhaled with difficulty, exhaled quiveringly. Tears gathered in her eyes.

"Very good!" she husked.

"Very good," the Commissioner agreed. He put down his empty glass and smacked his lips lightly. "And now," he said briskly, "let's get on with this conference."

Trigger glanced around the room while Quillan refilled three glasses. The small live coal she had swallowed was melting away; a warm glow began to spread through her. It did look like the dining room of a hunting lodge. The woodwork was dark, old-looking, worn with much polishing. Horned heads of various formidable Maccadon life-forms adorned the walls.

But it was open season now on a different kind of game. Three men had walked briskly past them when Quillan brought her in by the front door. They hadn't even looked at her. There were sounds now and then from some of the other rooms, and that general feeling of a considerable number of people around—of being at an operating headquarters of some sort, which hummed with quiet activity.

Holati glanced at Quillan. "Someone at the door. We'll hold it while you see what they want."

The burly character who had appeared at the door said diffidently that Professor Mantelish had wanted to be present while his lab equipment was stowed aboard. If the professor didn't mind, things were about that far along.

Mantelish excused himself and went off with the messenger. The door closed. Quillan came back to his chair.

"We're moving the outfit later tonight," the Commissioner explained. "Mantelish is coming along—plus around eight tons of his lab equipment. Plus his six special U-League guards."

"Oh?" Trigger picked up the Puya glass. She looked into it. It was empty. "Moving where?" she asked.

"Manon," said the Commissioner. "Tell you about that later."

Every last muscle in Trigger's body seemed to go limp simultaneously. She settled back slightly in the chair, surprised by the force of the reaction. She hadn't realized by half how keyed up she was! She sighed a small sigh. Then she smiled at Quillan.

"Major," she said, "how about a tiny little refill on that Puya—about half?"

Quillan took care of the tiny little refill.

Commissioner Tate said, "By the way, Quillan does have a degree in subspace engineering and gets assigned to the Engineers now and then. But his real job's Space Scout Intelligence."

Trigger nodded. "I'd almost guessed it!" She gave Quillan another smile. She nearly gave 113-A a smile.

"And now," said the Commissioner, "we'll talk more freely. We tell Mantelish just as little as we can. To tell you the truth, Trigger, the professor is a terrible handicap on an operation like this. I understand he was a great friend of your father's."

"Yes," she said. "Going over for visits to Mantelish's garden with my father is one of the earliest things I remember. I can imagine he's a problem!" She shifted her gaze curiously from one to the other of the two men. "What are you people doing?"

Holati Tate said, "We're one of a few hundred Federation groups assigned to the plasmoid project. Each group works at its specialties, and the information gets correlated." He paused. "The Federation Council—they're the ones we're working for directly— the Council's biggest concern is the very delicate political situation that's involved. They feel it could develop suddenly into a dangerous one. They may be right."

"In what way?" Trigger asked.

"Well, suppose that a key unit is lost and stays lost. Unit 112-113, to be precise. Suppose all the other plasmoids put together don't contain enough information to show how the Old Galactics produced the things and got them to operate."

"Somebody would get that worked out pretty soon, wouldn't they?"

"Not necessarily, or even probably, according to Mantelish and some other people who know what's happened. There seem to be too many basic factors missing. It might be necessary to develop a whole new class of sciences first. And that could take a few centuries."

"Well," Trigger admitted, "*I* could get along without the things indefinitely."

"Same here," the plasmoid nabob agreed ungratefully. "Weird beasties! But—let's see. At present there are twelve hundred and fifty-eight member worlds to the Federation, aren't there?"

"More or less."

"And the number of planetary confederacies, subplanetary governments, industrial, financial and commercial combines, assorted power groups, etc. and so on, is something I'd hate to have to calculate."

"What are you driving at?" she asked.

"They've all been told we're heading for a new golden age, courtesy of the plasmoid science. Practically everybody has believed it. Now there's considerable doubt."

"Oh," she said. "Of course—practically everybody is going to get very unhappy, eh?"

"Including," said Holati, "any one of the two hundred and fourteen restricted worlds. Their treaties of limitation wouldn't have let them get into the plasmoid pie until the others had been at it a decade or so. They would have been quite eager . . ."

There was a little pause. Then Trigger said, "Lordy! The thing could even set off another string of wars—"

"That's a point the Council is nervous about," he said.

"Well, it certainly is a mess." Trigger was silent a moment. "Holati, could those things ever become as valuable as people keep saying? It's all sounded a little exaggerated to me."

The Commissioner said he'd wondered about it too. "I'm not enough of a biologist to make an educated guess. What it seems to boil down to is that they might. Which would be enough to tempt a lot of people to gamble very high for a chance to get control of the plasmoid process. We've been working a couple of leads here. Pretty short leads so far, but you work with what you can get." He nodded at the table. "We picked up the first lead through 113-A."

Trigger glanced down. The plasmoid lay there some inches from the side of her hand. "You know," she said uncomfortably, "old Repulsive moved again while we were talking! Towards my hand." She drew the hand away.

"I was watching it," Major Quillan said reassuringly from the end of the table. "I would have warned you, but it stopped when it got as far as it is now. That was around five minutes ago."

Trigger reached back and gave old Repulsive a cautious pat. "Very lively character! He does feel pleasant to touch. Kitty-cat pleasant! How did you get a lead through him?"

"Mantelish brought it back to Maccadon with him, mainly because he couldn't even guess at what its function was. It was just lying there in a cubicle. So he did considerable experimenting with it."

Trigger shook her head. "So what happened with 113-A?"

"Mantelish began to get results with it," the Commissioner said. "One experiment was rather startling. He'd been trying that electrical stimulation business. Nothing happened until he had finished. Then he touched the plasmoid, and it fed the whole charge back to him. Apparently it was a fairly hefty dose."

She laughed delightedly. "Good for Repulsive! Stood up for his rights, eh?"

"Mantelish gained some such impression anyway. He became more cautious with it after that. And then he learned something that should be important. He was visiting another lab where they had a couple of plasmoids which actually moved now and then. He had 113-A in his coat pocket. The two lab plasmoids stopped moving while he was there. They haven't moved since. He thought about that, and then located another moving plasmoid. He dropped in to look it over, with 113-A in his pocket again, and *it* stopped. He did the same thing in one more place and then quit. There aren't that many moving plasmoids around. Those three labs are still wondering what hit their specimens."

She studied 113-A curiously. "A mighty mite! What does Mantelish make of it?"

"He thinks the stolen 112-113 unit forms a kind of self-regulating system. The big one induces plasmoid activity, the little one modifies it. This 113-A might be a spare regulator. But it seems to be more than a spare— which brings us to that first lead we got. A gang of raiders crashed Mantelish's lab one night."

"When was that?"

"Some months ago. Before you and I left Manon. The professor was out, and 113-A had gone along in his pocket as usual. But his two lab guards and one of the raiders were killed. The others got away. The Feds got there fast, and dead-brained the raider. They learned just two things. One, he'd been mind-blocked and couldn't have spilled any significant information even if they had got him alive. The other item they drew from his brain was a clear impression of the target of the raid—the professor's pal here."

"Uh-huh," Trigger said, lost in thought. She poked Repulsive lightly. "Did they want to kill it or grab it?"

The Commissioner looked at her. "Grab it, was the dead-brain report. Why?"

"Just wondering. Would make a difference, wouldn't it? Did they try again?"

"There've been five more attempts," he said.

"And what's everybody concluded from that?"

"They want 113-A in a very bad way. So they need it."

"In connection with the key unit?" Trigger asked.

"Probably."

"That makes everything look very much better, doesn't it?"

"Quite a little," he said. "The unit may not work, or may not work satisfactorily, unless 113-A is in the area. Mantelish talks of something he calls proximity influence. Whatever that is, 113-A has demonstrated it has it."

"So," Trigger said, "whoever stole 112-113 might have two thirds of what everybody wants, and you might have one third. Right here on the table. How many of the later raiders did you catch?"

"All of them," said the Commissioner. "Around forty. We got them dead, we got them alive. It didn't make much difference. They were hired hands. Very expensive hired hands, but still just that. Most of them didn't know a thing we could use. The ones that did know something were mind-blocked again."

"I thought," Trigger said reflectively, "you could *un*block someone like that."

"You can, sometimes. If you're very good at it and if you have time enough. We couldn't afford to wait a year. They died before they could tell us anything."

There was a pause. Then Trigger asked, "How did you get involved in this, personally?"

"More or less by accident," the Commissioner said. "It was in connection with our second lead."

"That's me, huh?" she said unhappily.

"Yes."

"Why would anyone want to grab me? I don't know anything."

He shook his head. "We haven't found out yet. We're hoping we will, in a very few days."

"Is that one of the things you can't tell me about?"

"I can tell you most of what I know at the moment," said the Commissioner. "Remember the night we stopped off at Evalee on the way in from Manon?"

"Yes," she said. "That big hotel!"

8

"About an hour after you'd decided to hit the bunk," Holati said, "I portaled back to your rooms to pick up some Precol reports we'd been setting up."

Trigger nodded. "I remember the reports."

"A couple of characters were working on your doors when I got there. They went for their guns, unfortunately. But I called the nearest Scout Intelligence office and had them dead-brained."

"Why that?" she asked.

"It could have been an accident—a couple of ordinary thugs. But their equipment looked a little too good for ordinary thugs. I didn't know just what to be suspicious of, but I got suspicious anyway."

"That's you, all right," Trigger acknowledged. "What were they?"

"They had an Evalee record which told us more than the brains did. They were high-priced boys. Their brains told us they'd allowed themselves to be mind-blocked on this particular job. High-priced boys won't do that unless they can set their standard price very much higher. It didn't look at all any more as if they'd come to your door by accident."

"No," she admitted.

"The Feds got in on it then. There'd been that business in Mantelish's lab. There were similarities in the pattern. You knew Mantelish. You'd been on *Harvest Moon* with him. They thought there could be a connection."

"But what connection?" she protested. "I *know* I don't know anything that could do anybody any good!"

He shrugged. "I can't figure it either, Trigger girl. But the upshot of it was that I was put in charge of this phase of the general investigation. If there is a connection, it'll come out eventually. In any case, we want to know who's been trying to have you picked up and why."

She studied his face with troubled eyes.

"That's quite definite, is it?" she asked. "There couldn't possibly still be a mistake?"

"No. It's definite."

"So that's what the grabber business in the Colonial School yesterday was about . . ."

He nodded. "It was their first try since the Evalee matter."

"Why do you think they waited so long?"

"Because they suspected you were being guarded. It's difficult to keep an adequate number of men around without arousing doubts in interested observers."

Trigger glanced at the plasmoid. "That sounds," she remarked, "as if you'd let other interested observers feel you'd left them a good opening to get at Repulsive."

He didn't quite smile. "I might have done that. Don't tell the Council."

Trigger pursed her lips. "I won't. So the grabbers who were after me figured I was booby-trapped. But then they came in anyway. That doesn't seem very bright. Or did you do something again to make them think the road was clear?"

"No," he said. "They were trying to clear the road for themselves. We thought they would finally. The deal was set up as a one-two."

"As a what?"

"One-two. You slug into what could be a trap like that with one gang. If it was a trap, they were sacrifices. You hope the opposition will now relax its precautions. Sometimes it does—and a day or so later you're back for the real raid. That works occasionally. Anyway it was the plan in this case."

"How do you know?"

"They'd started closing in for the grab in Ceyce when Quillan's group located you. So Quillan grabbed you first."

She flushed. "I wasn't as smart as I thought, was I?"

The Commissioner grunted. "Smart enough to give us a king-sized headache! But *they* didn't have any trouble finding you. We discovered tonight that some kind of tracer material had been worked into all your clothes. Even the flimsiest. Somebody may have been planted in the school laundry, but that's not important now." He looked at her for a moment. "What made you decide to take off so suddenly?" he asked.

Trigger shrugged. "I was getting pretty angry with you," she admitted. "More or less with everybody. Then I applied for a transfer, and the application bounced—from Evalee! I figured I'd had enough and that I'd just quietly clear out. So I did—or thought I did."

"Can't blame you," said Holati.

Trigger said, "I still think it would have been smarter to keep me informed right from the start of what was going on."

He shook his head. "I wouldn't be telling you a thing even now," he said, "if it hadn't been definitely established that you're already involved in the matter. This could develop into a pretty messy operation. I wouldn't have wanted you in on it, if it could have been avoided. And if you weren't going to be in on it, I couldn't go spilling Federation secrets to you."

"I'm in on it, definitely, eh?"

He nodded. "For the duration."

"But you're still not telling me everything?"

"There're a few things I can't tell you," he said. "I'm following orders in that."

Trigger smiled faintly "That's a switch! I didn't know you knew how."

"I've followed plenty of orders in my time," the Commissioner said, "especially when I thought they made sense. And I think these do."

Trigger was silent a moment. "You said a while ago that most of the heat was to go off me tonight. Can you talk about that?"

"I'll have to tell you something else again first—why we're going to Manon."

She settled back in her chair. "Go ahead."

"By what is, at all events, an interesting coincidence," the Commissioner went on, "we've had word that an outfit called Vishni's Fleet hasn't been heard from for some months. Their Independent Fleet area is a long way out beyond Manon, but Vishni's had his pick of a few hundred uncharted habitable planets and a few thousand very expert outworlders. And Vishni's boys are exactly the kind of people who would get involved in a deal like this."

"You think they stole 112-113?" Trigger asked.

Holati shook his head. "Doesn't look as simple as that, because there were obviously some insiders involved. But I don't want to get into that here." He and Quillan exchanged a quick glance. The Commissioner hurried on.

"Now, what's been done is to hire a few of the other I-Fleets around there and set them and as many Space Scout squadrons as could be kicked loose from duty elsewhere to surveying the Vishni territory. Our outfit is in charge of that operation. And Manon, of course, is a lot better point from which to conduct it than the Hub. If something is discovered that looks interesting enough to investigate in detail, we'll only be a week's run away.

"So we've been ready to move for the past two weeks now, which was when the first reports started coming in from the Vishni area—negative reports so far, by the way. I've kept stalling from day to day, because there were also indications that your grabber friends might be getting set to swing at you finally. It seemed tidier to get that matter cleared up first. Now they've swung, and we'll go."

He rubbed his chin. "The nice thing about it all," he remarked, "is that we're going there with the two items the opposition has revealed it wants. We're letting them know those items will be available in the Manon System henceforward. They might get discouraged and just drop the whole project. If they do, that's fine. We'll go ahead with cleaning up the Vishni phase of the operation.

"But," he continued, "the indications are they can't drop their project any more than we can drop looking for that key unit. So we'll expect them to show up in Manon. When they do, they'll be working in unfamiliar territory and in a system where they have only something like fifty thousand people to hide out in, instead of a planetary civilization. I think they'll find things getting very hot for them very fast in Manon."

"*Very* good," said Trigger. "That I like! But what makes you think the opposition is just one group? There might be a bunch of them by now. Maybe even fighting among themselves."

"I'd bet on at least two groups myself," he said. "And if they're fighting, they've got our blessing. They're still all opposition as far as we're concerned."

She nodded. "How are you letting them know about the move?"

"The mountains around here are lousy with observers. Very cute tricks some of them use—one boy has been sitting in a hollow tree for weeks. We let them see what we want to. This evening they saw you coming in. Later tonight they'll see you climbing into the ship with the rest of the party and taking off. They've already picked up messages to tell them just where the ship's going." He paused. "But you've got a job to finish up here first,

Trigger. That'll take about four days. So it won't really be you they see climbing into the ship."

"What!" She straightened up.

"We've got a facsimile for you," he explained. "Girl agent. She goes along to draw the heat to Manon."

Trigger felt herself tightening up slowly all over.

"What's this job you're talking about?" she asked evenly.

"Can't tell you in too much detail. But around four days from now somebody is coming in to Maccadon to interview you."

"Interview me? What about?"

He hesitated a moment. "There's a theory," he said, "that you might have information you don't know you have. And that the people who sent grabbers after you want that information. If it's true, the interview will bring it out."

Her mouth went dry suddenly. And she'd almost spilled everything, she was thinking. The paid-up reservation. Every last thing.

"I'd like to get this straight," she said. "What you're talking about sounds like it's a mind-search job, Holati."

"It's in that class," he said. "But it won't be an ordinary mind-search. The people who are coming here are top experts at that kind of work."

She nodded. "I don't know much about it . . . Do they think somebody's got to me with a hypno-spray or something? That I've been conditioned? Something like that?"

"I don't know, Trigger," he said. "It may be something in that line. But whatever it is, they'll be able to handle it."

Trigger moistened her lips. "I was thinking, you know," she said. "Supposing I'm mind-blocked."

He shook his head. "I can tell you that, anyway," he said. "We already know you're not."

Trigger was silent a moment. Then she said, "After that interview's over, I'm to ship out to Manon—is that it?"

"That's right."

"But it would depend on the outcome of that interview too, wouldn't it?" Trigger pointed out. "I mean you can't really be sure what those people might decide, can you?"

"Yes, I can," he said. "This thing's been all scheduled out, Trigger. And the next step of the schedule for you is Manon. Nothing else."

She didn't believe him in the least. He couldn't know. She nodded.

"Guess I might as well play along." She looked at him. "I don't think I really have much choice, do I?"

"Afraid not," he admitted. "It's one of those things that just has to be done. But you won't find it at all bad. Your companion, by the way, for the next three days will be Mihul."

"Mihul!" Trigger exclaimed.

"Right here," said Mihul's voice. Trigger swung around in her chair.

Mihul stood in a door which had appeared in the far wall of the room. She gave Trigger a smile. Trigger looked back at the Commissioner.

"I don't get it," she said.

"Oh, Mihul's in Scout Intelligence," he said. "Wouldn't be here if she weren't."

"Been an agent for eighteen years," Mihul said, coming forward. "Hi, Trigger. Surprised?"

"Yes," Trigger admitted. "Very."

"They brought me into this job," Mihul said, "because they figured you and I would get along together just fine."

9

It was really infernally bad luck! Mihul was going to be the least easy of wardens to get away from . . .

particularly in time to catch a liner tomorrow night. Mihul knew her much too well.

"Like to come along and meet your facsimile now?" Mihul inquired. She grinned. "Most people find the first time quite an experience."

Trigger stood up resignedly. "All right," she said. They were being polite about it, but it was clear that it was still a cop and prisoner situation. And old friend Mihul! She remembered something then. "I believe Major Quillan has my gun."

He looked at her thoughtfully, not smiling. "No," he said. "Gave it to Mihul."

"That's right," said Mihul. "Let's go, kid."

They went out through the door that had appeared in the wall. It closed again behind them.

The facsimile stood up from behind a table at which she had been sitting as Trigger and Mihul came into the room. She gave Trigger a brief, impersonal glance, then looked at Mihul.

Mihul performed no introductions.

"Dress, robe and scarf," she said to the facsimile. "The shoes are close enough." She turned to Trigger. "She'll be wearing your street clothes when she leaves," she said. "Could we have the dress now?" Trigger pulled the dress over her head, tossed it to Mihul and stood in her underwear, looking at her double slip out of her street clothes. They did seem to be a very close match in size and proportions. Watching the shifting play of slim muscles in the long legs and smooth back, Trigger decided the similarity was largely a natural one. The silver-blonde hair was the same, of course. The gray eyes seemed almost identical—and the rest of the face was a little *too* identical! They must have used a life-mask there.

It was a bit uncanny. Like seeing one's mirror image start moving about independently. If the girl had talked, it might have reduced the effect. But she remained silent.

She put on the dress Trigger had been wearing and smoothed it down. Mihul surveyed the result. She nodded. "Perfect." She took Trigger's robe and scarf from the back of a chair where someone had draped them and handed them over.

"You won't wear the scarf," she said. "Just shove it into a pocket of the coat."

The girl slung the cloak over her shoulder and stood holding the scarf. Mihul looked her over once more. "You'll do," she said. She smiled briefly. "All right."

The facsimile glanced at Trigger again, turned and moved attractively out of the room. Trigger frowned.

"Something wrong?" Mihul asked. She had gone over to a wall basin and was washing out a tumbler.

"Why does she walk like that?"

"The little swing in the rear? She's studied it." Mihul half filled the tumbler with water, fished a transparent splinter of something out of a pocket and cracked the splinter over the edge of the glass. "Among your friends it's referred to as the Argee Lilt. She's got you down pat, kid."

Trigger didn't comment. "Am I supposed to put on her clothes?"

"No. We've got another costume for you." Mihul came over, holding out the glass. "This is for you."

Trigger looked at the glass suspiciously. "What's in it?"

The blue eyes regarded her mildly. "You could call it a sedative."

"Don't need any. Thanks."

"Better take it anyway." Mihul patted her hip with her other hand. "Little hypo gun here. That's the alternative."

"What!"

"That's right. Same type of charge as in your fancy Denton. Stuff in the glass is easier to take and won't leave you groggy."

"What's the idea?"

"I've known you quite a while," said Mihul. "And I

was watching you the last twenty minutes in that room through a screen. You'll take off again if you get the least chance. I don't blame you a bit. You're being pushed around. But now it's my job to see you don't take off; and until we get to where you're going, I want to be sure you'll stay quiet."

She still held out the glass, in a long, tanned, capable hand. She stood three inches taller than Trigger, weighed thirty-five pounds more. Not an ounce of that additional thirty-five pounds was fat. If she'd needed assistance, the hunting lodge was full of potential helpers. She didn't.

"I never claimed I liked this arrangement," Trigger said carefully. "I did say I'd go along with it. I will. Isn't that enough?"

"Sure," Mihul said promptly. "Give word of parole?"

There was a long pause.

"No!" Trigger said.

"I thought not. Drink or gun?"

"Drink," Trigger said coldly. She took the glass. "How long will it put me out?"

"Eight to nine hours." Mihul stood by watchfully while Trigger emptied the tumbler. After a moment the tumbler fell to the floor. She reached out then and caught Trigger as she started down.

"All right," she said across her shoulder to the open doorway behind her. "Let's move!"

Trigger awoke and instantly went taut with tension. She lay quiet a few seconds, not even opening her eyes. There was cool sunlight on her eyelids, but she was indoors. There was a subdued murmur of sound somewhere; after a moment she knew it came from a news viewer turned low, in some adjoining room. But there didn't seem to be anybody immediately around her. Warily she opened her eyes.

She was on a couch in an airy, spacious room furnished

in the palest of greens and ivory. One entire side of the room was either a window or a solido screen. In it was a distant mountain range with many snowy peaks, an almost cloudless blue sky. Sun at midmorning or midafternoon.

Sun and all had the look of Maccadon—they probably still were on the planet. That was where the interview was to take place. But she also could have been sent on a three-day space cruise, which would be a rather good way to make sure a prisoner stayed exactly where you wanted her. This could be a spaceliner suite with a packaged view of any one of some hundreds of worlds, and with packaged sunlight thrown in.

There was one door to the room. It stood open, and the news viewer talk came from there.

Trigger sat up quietly and looked down at the clothes she wore. All white. A short-sleeved half-blouse of some soft, rather heavy, very comfortable unfamiliar stuff. Bare midriff. White kid trousers which flared at the thighs and were drawn in to a close fit just above the knees and down the calves, vanishing into kid boots with thick, flexible soles.

Sporting outfit . . . That meant Maccadon!

She pulled a handful of hair forward and looked at it. They'd recolored it—this time to a warm mahogany brown. She swung her legs off the couch and stood up quietly. A dozen soft steps across the springy thick-napped turf of ivory carpet took her to the window.

The news viewer clicked and went silent.

"Like the view?" Old Lynx-ears asked from beyond the door.

"Not bad," Trigger said. She saw a long range of woodlands and open heath, rising gradually into the flanks of the mountains. On the far right was the still, silver glitter of two lakes. "Where are we?"

"Byla Uplands Game Preserve. That's the game bird area before you." Mihul appeared in the doorframe, in an outfit almost a duplicate of Trigger's, in pearl-gray tones. "Feel all right?"

"Feeling fine," Trigger said. Byla Uplands—the southern tip of the continent. She could make it back to Ceyce in two hours or less! She turned and grinned at Mihul. "I also feel hungry. How long was I out?"

Mihul glanced at her wristwatch. "Eight hours, ten minutes. You woke up on schedule. I had breakfast sent up thirty minutes ago. I've already eaten mine—took one sniff and plunged in. It's good!" Mihul's hair, Trigger saw, had been cropped short and a streak of gray added over the right side; and they'd changed the color of her eyes to hazel. She wondered what had been done to her along that line. "Want to come in?" Mihul said. "We can talk while you eat."

Trigger nodded. "After I've freshened up."

The bathroom mirror showed they'd left her eyes alone. But there was a very puzzling impression that she was staring at an image considerably plumper, shorter, younger than it should be—a teen-ager around seventeen or eighteen. Her eyes narrowed. If they'd done flesh-sculpting on her, it could cause complications.

She stripped hurriedly and checked. They hadn't tampered with her body. So it had to be the clothes; though it was difficult to see how even the most cunning cut could provide such a very convincing illusion of being more rounded out, heavier around the thighs, larger breasts—just missing being dumpy, in fact. She dressed again, looked again, and came out of the bathroom, still puzzled.

"Choice of three game birds for breakfast," Mihul announced. "Never heard of any of them. All good. Plus regular stuff." She patted her flat midriff. "Ate too much!" she admitted. "Now dig in and I'll brief you."

Trigger dug in. "I had a look at myself in the mirror," she remarked. "What's this now-you-see-it-now-you-don't business of fifteen or so pounds of baby fat?"

Mihul laughed. "You don't really have it."

"I know that too. How do they do it?"

"Subcolor job in the clothes. They're not really white. Anyone looking at you gets his vision distorted a little without realizing it. Takes a wider view of certain areas, for example. You can play it around in a lot of ways."

"I never heard of that one," Trigger said. "You'd think it would be sensational in fashions."

"It would be. Right now it's top secret for as long as Intelligence can keep it that way."

Trigger chewed a savory morsel of something. "Then why did you tell me?"

"You're one of the gang, however reluctant. And you're good at keeping the mouth shut. Your name, by the way, is now Comteen Lod, just turned eighteen. I am your dear mama. You call me Drura. We're from Slyth-Talgon on Evalee, here for a few days shooting."

Trigger nodded. "Do we do any shooting?"

Mihul pointed a finger at a side table. The Denton lay there, looking like a toy beside a standard slender-barrelled sporting pistol. "Bet your life, Comteen!" she said. "I've always been too stingy to try out a first-class preserve on my own money. And this one is *first* class." She paused. "Comteen and Drura Lod really exist. We're a very fair copy of what they look like, and they'll be kept out of sight till we're done here. Now—"

She leaned back comfortably, tilting the chair and clasping her hands around one knee. "Aside from the sport, we're here because you're a convalescent. You're recovering from a rather severe attack of Dykart fever. Heard of it?"

Trigger reflected. "Something you pick up in some sections of the Evalee tropics, isn't it?"

Mihul nodded. "That's what you did, child! Skipped your shots on that last trip we took—and six months later you're still paying for it. You were in one of those

typical Dykart fever comas when we brought you in last
night."

"Very clever!" Trigger commented acidly.

"Very." Mihul pursed her lips. "The Dykart bug causes
temporary derangements, you know—spells during which
convalescents talk wildly, imagine things."

Trigger popped another fragment of meat between her
teeth and chewed thoughtfully, looking over at Mihul.
"Very good duck or whatever!" she said. "Like imagin-
ing they've been more or less kidnapped, you mean?"

"Things like that," Mihul agreed.

Trigger shook her head. "I wouldn't anyway. You types
are bound to have all the legal angles covered."

"Sure," said Mihul. "Just thought I'd mention it. Have
you used the Denton much on game?"

"Not too often." Trigger had been wondering whether
they'd left the stunner compartment loaded. "But it's a
very fair gun for it."

"I know. The other one's a Yool. Good game gun, too.
You'll use that."

Trigger swallowed. She met the calm eyes watching
her. "I've never handled a Yool. Why the switch?"

"They're easy to handle. The reason for the switch is
that you can't just stun someone with a Yool. It's better
if we both stay armed, though it isn't really necessary—
so much money comes to play around here they can
afford to keep the Uplands very thoroughly policed, and
they do. But an ace in the hole never hurts." She considered. "Changed your mind about that parole business
yet?"

"I hadn't really thought about it," Trigger said.

"I'd let you carry your own gun then."

Trigger looked reflective, then shook her head. "I'd
rather not."

"Suit yourself," Mihul said agreeably. "In that case
though, there should be something else understood."

"What's that?"

"We'll have up to three-four days to spend here together before Whatzzit shows up."

"Whatzzit?"

"For future reference," Mihul said, "Whatzzit will be that which—or he or she who—wishes to have that interview with you and has arranged for it. That's in case you want to talk about it. I might as well tell you that I'll do very little talking about Whatzzit."

"I thought," Trigger suggested, "I was one of the gang."

"I've got special instructions on the matter," Mihul said. "Anyway, Whatzzit shows up. You have your interview. After that we do whatever Whatzzit says we're to do. As you know."

Trigger nodded.

"Meanwhile," said Mihul, "we're here. Very pleasant place to spend three-four days in my opinion and, I think, in yours."

"Very pleasant," Trigger agreed. "I've been suspecting it was you who suggested it would be a good place to wait in."

"No," Mihul said. "Though I might have, if anyone had asked me. But Whatzzit's handling all the arrangements, it seems. Now we could have fun here—which, I suspect, would be the purpose as far as you're concerned."

"Fun?" Trigger said.

"To put you into a good frame of mind for that interview, might be the idea," Mihul said. "I don't know. Three days here should relax almost anyone. Get in a little shooting. Loaf around the pools. Go for rides. Things like that. The only trouble is I'm afraid you're nourishing dark notions which are likely to take all the enjoyment out of it. Not to mention the possibility of really relaxing."

"Like what?" Trigger asked.

"Oh," Mihul said, "there're all sorts of possibilities, of course." She nodded her head at the guns. "Like yanking the Denton out of my holster and feeding me a dose of the stunner. Or picking up that coffee pot there and tapping me on the skull with it. It's about the right weight."

Trigger said thoughtfully, "I don't think either of those would work."

"They might," Mihul said. "They just might! You're fast. You've been taught to improvise. And there's something eating you. You're edgy as a cat."

"So?" Trigger said.

"So," Mihul said, "there are a number of alternatives. I'll lay them out for you. You take your pick. For one, I could just keep you doped. Three days in dope won't hurt you, and you'll certainly be no problem then. Another way—I'll let you stay awake, but we stay in our rooms. I can lock you in at night, and that window is escape-proof. I checked. It would be sort of boring, but we can have tapes and stuff brought up. I'd have the guns put away and I'd watch you like a hawk every minute of the day."

She looked at Trigger inquiringly. "Like either of those?"

"Not much," Trigger said.

"They're safe," Mihul said. "Quite safe. Maybe I should. Well, the heat's off, and it's just a matter now of holding you for Whatzzit. There're a couple of other choices. One of them has an angle you won't like much either. On the other hand, it could give you a sporting chance to take off if you're really wild about it. And it's entirely in line with my instructions. I warned them you're tricky."

Trigger stopped eating. "Let's hear that one."

Mihul tilted the chair back a little farther and studied her a moment. "Pretty much like I said before. Everything friendly and casual. Gun a bit, swim a bit. Go for a ride or soar. Lie around in the sun. But because of those notions of yours, there'd be one thing added. An un-incentive."

"An un-incentive?" Trigger repeated.

"Exactly," said Mihul. "*That* isn't at all in line with my instructions. But you're a pretty dignified little character, and I think it should work."

"Just what does this un-incentive consist of?" Trigger inquired warily.

"If you make a break and get away," Mihul said, "that's one thing. Something's eating you, and I'm not sure I like the way this matter's been handled. In fact, I don't like it. So I'll try to stop you from leaving, but if it turns out I couldn't, I won't hold any grudges. Even if I wake up with lumps."

She paused. "On the other hand," she said, "there we are—together for three-four days. I don't want to spend them fighting off attempts to clobber me every thirty seconds. So any time you try and miss, Comteen, mama is going to pin you down fast and hot up your seat with whatever is handiest."

Trigger stared at her.

She cleared her throat.

"While I'm carrying a gun?" she said shakily. "Don't be ridiculous, Mihul!"

"You're not going to gun me for keeps to get out of a licking," Mihul said. "And that's all the Yool can do. How else will you stop me?"

Trigger's fingernails drummed the tabletop briefly. She wet her lips. "I don't know," she admitted.

"Of course," said Mihul, "all this unpleasantness can be avoided very easily. There's always the fourth method."

"What's that?"

"Just give parole."

"No parole," Trigger said thinly.

"All right. Which of the other ways will it be?"

Trigger didn't hesitate. "The sporting chance," she said. "The others aren't choices."

"Fair enough," said Mihul. She stood up and went over to the wall. She selected a holster belt from the pair hanging there and fastened it around her. "I rather thought you'd pick it," she said. She gave Trigger a brief grin. "Just make sure it's a good opening!"

"I will," Trigger said.

Mihul moved to the side table, took up the Denton, looked at it, and slid it into her holster. She turned to gaze out the window. "Nice country!" she said. "If you're done with breakfast, how about going out right now for a first try at the birds?"

Trigger hefted the coffee pot gently. It was about the right weight at that. But the range was a little more than she liked, considering the un-incentive.

Besides, it might crack the monster's skull.

She set the pot gently down again.

"Great idea!" she said. "And I'm all finished eating."

10

Half an hour later there still hadn't been any decent openings. Trigger was maintaining a somewhat broody silence at the moment. Mihul, beside her, in the driver's seat of the tiny sports hopper, chatted pleasantly about this and that. But she didn't appear to expect any answers.

There weren't many half-hours left to be wasted.

Trigger stared thoughtfully out through the telescopic ground-view plate before her, while the hopper soared at a thousand feet toward the two-mile square of preserve area which had been assigned to them to hunt over that morning. Dimly reflected in the view plate, she could see the head of the gun-pup who went with that particular area lifted above the seat-back behind her. He was gazing straight ahead between the two humans, absorbed in canine reflections.

There was plenty of bird life down there. Some were original Terran forms, maintained unchanged in the U-League's genetic banks. Probably many more were inspired modifications produced on Grand Commerce game ranches. At any other time, Trigger would have found herself enjoying the outing almost as much as Mihul.

Not now. Other things kept running through her head. Money, for example. They hadn't returned her own cash to her and apparently didn't intend to—at least not until after the interview. But Mihul was carrying at least part of their spending money in a hip pocket wallet. The rest of it might be in a concealed room safe or deposited with the resort hotel's cashier.

She glanced over at Mihul again. Good friend Mihul never before had looked quite so large, lithe, alert and generally fit for a rough-and-tumble. That un-incentive idea was fiendishly ingenious! It was difficult to plan things through clearly and calmly while one's self-esteem kept quailing at vivid visualizations of the results of making a mistake.

The hopper settled down near the center of their territory, guided the last half mile by Mihul who had fancied the looks of some shrub-cluttered ravines ahead. Trigger opened the door on her side. The gun-pup leaped lightly across the seat and came out behind her. He turned to look over his huntresses and gave them a wag, a polite but perfunctory one. Then he stood waiting for orders.

Mihul considered him. "Guess he's in charge here," she said. She waved a hand at the pup. "Go find 'em, old boy! We'll string along."

He loped off swiftly, a lean brown hound-like creature, a Grand Commerce development of some aristocratic Terran breed and probably a considerable improvement on the best of his progenitors. He curved around a thick clump of shrubs like a low-flying hawk. Two plump feather-shapes, emerald-green and crimson, whirred up out of the near side of the shrubbery, saw the humans before them and rose steeply, picking up speed.

A great many separate, clearly detailed things seemed to be going on within the next four or five seconds. Mihul swore, scooping the Denton out of its holster. Trigger already had the Yool out, but the gun was unfamiliar; she hesitated. Fascinated, she glanced from the speeding, soaring feather-balls to Mihul, watched the tall woman straighten for an overhead shot, left hand grasping right wrist to steady the lightweight Denton—and in that particular instant Trigger knew exactly what was going to happen next.

The Denton flicked forth one bolt. Mihul stretched a little more for the next shot. Trigger wheeled matter-of-factly, dropping the Yool, left elbow close in to her side. Her left fist rammed solidly into Mihul's bare brown midriff, just under the arch of the rib cage.

That punch, in those precise circumstances, would have paralyzed the average person. It didn't quite paralyze Mihul. She dropped forward, doubled up and struggling for breath, but already twisting around toward Trigger. Trigger stepped across her, picked up the Denton, shifted its setting, thumbed it to twelve-hour stunner max, and let Mihul have it between the shoulder blades.

Mihul jerked forward and went limp.

Trigger stood there, shaking violently, looking down at Mihul and fighting the irrational conviction that she had just committed cold-blooded murder.

The gun-pup trotted up with the one downed bird. He placed it reverently by Mihul's outflung hand. Then he sat back on his haunches and regarded Trigger with something of the detached compassion of a good undertaker.

Apparently this wasn't his first experience with a hunting casualty.

The story Trigger babbled into the hopper's communicator a minute later was that Drura Lod had succumbed to an attack of Dykart fever coma—and that an ambulance and a fast flit to a hospital in the nearest city were indicated.

The preserve hotel was startled but reassuring. That the mother should be afflicted with the same ailment as the daughter was news to them but plausible enough. Within eight minutes, a police ambulance was flying Mihul and Trigger at emergency speeds towards a small Uplands city behind the mountains.

Trigger never found out the city's name. Three minutes after she'd followed Mihul's floating stretcher into the hospital, she quietly left the building again by a street entrance. Mihul's wallet had contained two hundred and thirteen crowns. It was enough, barely.

She got a complete change of clothes in the first Automatic Service store she came to and left the store in them, carrying the sporting outfit in a bag. The aircab she hired to take her to Ceyce had to be paid for in advance, which left her eighty-two crowns. As they went flying over a lake a while later, the bag with the sporting clothes and accessories was dumped out of the cab's rear window. It was just possible that the Space Scouts had been able to put that tracer material idea to immediate use.

In Ceyce a short two hours after she'd felled Mihul, Trigger called the interstellar spaceport and learned that the *Dawn City* was open to passengers and their guests.

Birna Drellgannoth picked up her tickets and went on board, mingling unostentatiously with a group in a mood of festive leave-taking. She went fading even more unostentatiously down a hallway when the group stopped cheerfully to pose for a solidopic girl from one of the news agencies. She located her cabin after a lengthy search, set the door to don't-disturb, glanced around the cabin and decided to inspect it in more detail later.

She pulled off her slippers, climbed on the outsized overstuffed divan which passed here for a bunk, and stretched out.

She lay there a while, blinking at the ceiling and worrying a little about Mihul. Even theoretically a stunner-max blast couldn't cause Mihul the slightest permanent damage. It might, however, leave her in a fairly peevish mood after the grogginess wore off, since the impact wasn't supposed to be pleasant. But Mihul had stated she would hold no grudges over a successful escape attempt; and even if they caught up with her again before she got to Manon, this attempt certainly had to be rated a technical success.

They might catch up, of course, Trigger thought. The Federation must have an enormous variety of means at its disposal when it set out seriously to locate one of its missing citizens. But the *Dawn City* would be some hours on its way before Mihul even began to think coherently again. She'd spread the alarm then, but it should be a while before they started to suspect Trigger had left the planet. Maccadon was her home world, after all. If she'd just wanted to hole up, that was where she would have had the best chance to do it successfully.

Evalee, the first Hub stop, was only nine hours' flight away; Garth lay less than five hours beyond Evalee. After that there was only the long subspace run to Manon . . .

They'd have to work very fast to keep her from leaving the Hub this time!

Trigger glanced over at the Denton lying by the bedside ComWeb on a little table at the head of the divanthing. She was aware of a feeling of great contentment, of growing relaxation. She closed her eyes.

By and large, she thought—all things considered—she hadn't come off badly among the cloak and dagger experts! She was on her way to Manon.

Some hours later she slept through the *Dawn City's* thunderous take-off.

When she woke up next she was in semi-darkness. But she knew where she was and a familiar feeling of low-weight told her the ship was in flight. She sat up.

At her motion, the area about her brightened, and the cabin grew visible again. It was rather large, oval-shaped. There were three closed doors in the walls, and the walls themselves were light amber, of oddly insubstantial appearance. A rosy tinge was flowing up from the floor level through them, and as the color surged higher and deepened, there came an accompanying stir of far-off, barely audible music. The don't-disturb sign still reflected dimly from the interior panels of the passage door. Trigger found its control switch on the bedstand and shut it off.

At once a soft chiming sounded from the miniature ComWeb on the bedstand. Its screen filled with a pulsing glow, and there was a voice.

"This is a recording, Miss Drellgannoth," the voice told her. "If Room Service may intrude with an audio message, please be so good as to touch the blue circle at the base of your ComWeb."

Trigger touched the blue circle. "Go ahead," she invited.

"Thank you, Miss Drellgannoth," said the voice. "For the duration of the voyage your personal ComWeb will be opened to callers, for either audio or visual intrusion, only by your verbal permission or by your touch on the blue circle."

It stopped. Another voice picked up. "This is your Personal Room Stewardess, Miss Drellgannoth. Forgive the intrusion, but the ship will dive in one hour. Do you wish to have a rest cubicle prepared?"

"No, thanks," Trigger said. "I'll stay awake."

"Thank you, Miss Drellgannoth. As a formality and in accordance with Federation regulations, allow me to remind you that Federation Law does not permit the bearing of personal weapons by passengers during a dive."

Her glance went to the Denton. "All right," she said. "I won't. It's because of dive hallucinations, I suppose?"

"Thank you very much, Miss Drellgannoth. Yes, it is because of the misapprehensions which may be caused by dive hallucinations. May I be of service to you at this time? Perhaps you would like me to demonstrate the various interesting uses of your personal ComWeb Cabinet?"

Trigger's eyes shifted to the far end of the cabin. A rather large, very elegant piece of furniture stood there. Its function hadn't been immediately obvious, but she had heard of ComWeb Service Cabinets.

She thanked the stewardess but declined the offer. The lady switched off, apparently a trifle distressed at not having discovered anything Birna Drellgannoth's personal stewardess might do for Birna right now.

Trigger went curiously over to the cabinet. It opened at her touch and she sat down before it, glancing over its panels. A remarkable number of uses were indicated, which might make it confusing to the average Hub citizen. But she had been trained in communications, and the service cabinet was as simple as any gadget in its class could get.

She punched in the ship's location diagram. The *Dawn City* was slightly more than an hour out of Ceyce Port, but it hadn't yet cleared the subspace nets which created interlocking and impenetrable fields of energy about the Maccadon System. A ship couldn't dive in such an area without risking immediate destruction; but the nets were painstakingly maintained insurance against a day when subspace warfare might again explode through the Hub.

Trigger glanced over the diagrammed route ahead. Evalee . . . Garth. A tiny green spark in the far remoteness of space beyond them represented Manon's sun.

Eleven days or so. With the money to afford a rest cubicle, the time could be cut to a subjective three or four hours.

But it would have been foolish anyway to sleep through the one trip on a Hub luxury liner she was ever likely to take in her life.

She set the cabinet to a review of the *Dawn City*'s passenger facilities, and was informed that everything would remain at the disposal of waking passengers throughout all dives. She glanced over bars, fashion shows, dining and gaming rooms. The Cascade Plunge, from the looks of it, would have been something for Mihul . . . "Our Large Staff of Traveler's Companions"—just what she needed. The Solido Auditorium. " . . . and the Inferno— our Sensations Unlimited Hall." A dulcet voice informed her regretfully that Federation Law did not permit the transmission of full SU effects to individual cabins. It did, however, permit a few sample glimpses. Trigger took her glimpses, sniffed austerely, switched back to the fashions.

There had been a neat little black suit on display there. While she didn't intend to start roaming about the ship until it dived and the majority of her fellow travelers were immersed in their rest cubicles, she probably still would be somewhat conspicuous in her Automatic Sales dress on a boat like the *Dawn City*. That little black suit hadn't looked at all expensive—

"Twelve hundred forty-two Federation credits?" she repeated evenly a minute later. "I see!"

Came to roughly eight hundred fifty Maccadon crowns, was what she saw.

"May we model it in your suite, madam?" the store manager inquired.

"No, thanks," Trigger told her. "Just looking them over a bit." She switched off, frowned absently at a panel labeled "Your Selection of Personalized Illusion Arrangements," shook her head, snapped the cabinet shut and stood up. It looked like she had a choice between being conspicuous and staying in her cabin and playing around with things like the creation of illusion scenes.

And she was really a little old for that kind of entertainment.

She opened the door to the narrow passageway outside the cabin and glanced tentatively along it. It was very quiet here. One of the reasons this was the cheapest cabin they'd had available presumably was that it lay outside of the main passenger areas. To the right the corridor opened on a larger hall which ran past a few hundred yards of storerooms before it came to a stairway. At the head of the stairway, one came out eventually on one of the passenger levels. To the left the corridor ended at the door of what seemed to be the only other cabin in this section.

Trigger looked back toward the other cabin.

"Oh," she said. "Well . . . hello."

The other cabin door stood open. A rather odd-looking little person sat in a low armchair immediately inside it. She had lifted a thin, green-sleeved arm in a greeting or beckoning gesture as Trigger turned.

She repeated the gesture now. "Come here, girl!" she called amiably in a quavery old-woman voice.

Well, it couldn't do any harm. Trigger put on her polite smile and walked down the hall toward the open door. A quite tiny old woman it was, with a head either shaved or naturally bald, dressed in a kind of dark-green pajamas. Long glassy earrings of the same color pulled down the lobes of her small ears. The oddness of the face was due mainly to the fact that she wore a great deal of make-up, and that the make-up was a matching green.

She twisted her head to the left as Trigger came up, and chirped something. Another woman appeared behind the door, almost a duplicate of the first, except that this one had gone all out for pink. Tiny things. They both beamed up at her.

Trigger beamed back. She stopped just outside the door.

"Greetings," said the pink one.

"Greetings," Trigger replied, wondering what world they came from. The style wasn't exactly like anything she'd seen before.

"We," the green lady informed her with a not unkindly touch of condescension, "are with the Askab of Elfkund."

"Oh!" said Trigger in the tone of one who is impressed. Elfkund hadn't rung any bells.

"And with whom are you, girl?" the pink one inquired.

"Well," Trigger said, "I'm not actually *with* anybody."

The smiles faded abruptly. They glanced at each other, then looked back at Trigger. Rather severely, it seemed.

"Did you mean," the green one asked carefully, "that you are *not* a retainer?"

Trigger nodded. "I'm from Maccadon," she explained. "The name is Birna Drellgannoth."

"Maccadon," the pink one repeated. "You are a commoner then, young Birna?"

"Of course she is!" The green one looked offended. "Maccadon!" She got out of her chair with remarkable spryness and moved to the door. "It's quite drafty," she said, looking pointedly past Trigger. The door closed on Trigger's face. A second later, she heard the lock snap shut. A moment after that, the don't-disturb sign appeared.

Well, she thought, wandering back to her cabin, it didn't look as if she were going to be bothered with excessively friendly neighbors on this trip.

She had a bath and then discovered a mechanical stylist in a recess beside the bathroom mirror. She swung the gadget out into the room, set it for a dye removal operation and sat down beneath it. A redhead again a minute or so later, she switched the machine to Orado styles and left it to make up its electronic mind as to what would be the most suitable creation under the circumstances.

The stylist hovered above her for over a minute, muttering and clucking as it conducted an apparently disapproving survey of the job. Then it went swiftly and silently to work. When it shut itself off, Trigger checked the results in the mirror.

She wasn't too pleased. An upswept arrangement which brought out the bone structure of her face rather well but didn't do much else for her. Possibly the stylist had included the Automatic Sales dress in its computations.

Well, it would have to do for her first tour of the ship.

11

The bedside ComWeb warned her politely that it was now ten minutes to dive point. Waking passengers who experienced subspace distress in any form could obtain immediate assistance by a call on any ComWeb. If they preferred, they could have their cabins kept under the continuous visual supervision of their personal steward or stewardess.

The *Dawn City's* passenger areas still looked rather well populated when Trigger arrived. But some of the passengers were showing signs of regretting their decision to stay awake. Presently she became aware of a faint queasiness herself.

It wasn't bad—mainly a sensation as if the ship were trying continuously to turn over on its axis around her and not quite making it—and she knew from previous experience that after the first hour or so she would be completely free of that. She walked into a low, dimly lit, very swank-looking gambling room, still well patronized by the hardier section of her fellow travelers, searching for a place where she could sit down unobtrusively for a while and let the subspace reaction work itself out.

A couch beside a closed door near the unlit end of the room seemed about right for the purpose.

Trigger sat down and glanced around. There were a variety of games in progress, all unfamiliar to her. The players were mostly men, but a remarkable number of beautiful women, beautifully gowned, stood around the tables as observers. Traveler's Companions, Trigger realized suddenly—the *Dawn City*'s employees naturally would be inured to subspace effects. From the scraps of talk she could pick up, the stakes seemed uniformly high.

A swirl of vertigo suddenly built up in her again. This one was stronger than most; for a moment she couldn't be sure whether she was going to be sick or not. She stood up, stepped over to the door a few feet away, pulled it open and went through, drawing it shut behind her.

There had been a shielding black-light screen in the doorway. On the other side was bottled sunshine.

She found herself on a long balcony which overlooked a formal garden enclosure thirty feet below. There was no one else in sight. She leaned back against the wall beside the door, closed her eyes and breathed slowly and deeply for some seconds. The sickish sensation began to fade.

When she opened her eyes again, she saw the little yellow man.

He stood motionless at the far end of the garden, next to some flowering shrubbery out of which he might have just stepped. He seemed to be peering along the sand path which curved in toward the balcony and vanished beneath it, below the point where Trigger stood.

It was sheer fright which immobilized her at first. Because there was not anything really human about that small, squat, man-shaped figure. A dwarfish yellow demon he seemed, evil and menacing. The garden, she realized suddenly, might be an illusion scene. Or else—

The thing moved in that instant. It became a blur of motion along the curving path and disappeared under the balcony. After a second or so she heard the sound of a door closing, some distance away. The garden lay still again.

Trigger stayed where she was, her knees shaking a little. The fright appeared to have driven every trace of nausea out of her, and gradually her heartbeat began to return to normal. She took three cautious steps forward to the balcony railing, where the tip of a swaying green tree branch was in reach.

She put her hand out hesitantly, felt the smooth vegetable texture of a leaf, grasped it, pulled it away. She moved back to the door and examined the leaf. It was a quite real leaf. Thin sap formed a bead of amber moisture at the break in the stalk as she looked at it.

No illusion structure could be elaborated to that extent.

So she'd just had her first dive hallucination—and it had been a dilly!

Trigger dropped the leaf, pushed shakily at the balcony door, and stepped back through the black-light screen into the reassuring murmur of human voices in the gambling room.

An hour later, the ship's loudspeaker system went on. It announced that the *Dawn City* would surface in fifteen minutes because of gravitic disturbances, and proceed the rest of the way to Evalee in normal space, arriving approximately five hours behind schedule. Rest cubicle passengers would not be disturbed, unless this was specifically requested by a qualified associate.

Trigger turned her attention back to her viewer, feeling rather relieved. She hadn't experienced any further hallucinations, or other indications of subspace distress; but the one she'd had would do her for a while. The little viewer library she was in was otherwise deserted, and she'd been going about her studies there just the least bit nervously.

Subject of the studies were the Hub's principal games of chance. She'd identified a few of those she'd been watching—and one of them did look as if someone who went at it with an intelligent understanding of the odds—

A part of Trigger kept tut-tutting and shaking its head

at such reckless notions. But another part pointed out that they couldn't be much worse off financially than they were right now. So what if they arrived in Manon dead-broke instead of practically? Besides, there was the problem of remaining inconspicuous till they got there. On the *Dawn City* no one whose wardrobe was limited to one Automatic Sales dress was going to remain inconspicuous very long.

Trigger-*in-toto* went on calculating the odds for various possible play combinations. She developed her first betting system, presently discovered several holes in it, and began to develop another.

The loudspeaker system went on again. She was too absorbed to pay much attention to it at first. Then she suddenly straightened up and listened, frowning.

The man speaking now was the liner's First Security Officer. He was being very polite and regretful. Under Section such and such, Number so and so, of the Federation's Legal Code, a cabin-by-cabin search of the passenger area of the *Dawn City* had become necessary. The persons of passengers would not be searched. Passengers might, if they wished, be present while their cabins were inspected; but this was not required. Baggage need not be opened, providing its spy-proofing was not activated. Any information revealed by the search which did not pertain to a violation of the Code Section and Number in question would not be recorded and could not be introduced as future legal evidence under any circumstances. Complaints regarding the search could be addressed to any Planetary Moderator's office.

This wasn't good at all! Trigger stood up. The absence of luggage in her cabin mightn't arouse more than passing interest in the searchers. Her gun was a different matter. Discreet inquiries regarding a female passenger who carried a double-barreled sporting Denton might be one of the check methods used by the Scout Intelligence boys if they started thinking of liners which recently had left Maccadon in connection with Trigger's disappearance. There weren't likely to be more than two or three guns of that type on board, and it was almost certain that she would be the only woman who owned one.

She'd better go get the Denton immediately . . . and then vanish again into the public sections of the ship! Some Security officer with a good memory and a habit of noticing faces might identify her otherwise from the news viewer pictures taken on Manon.

And he just might start wondering then why she was traveling as Birna Drellgannoth—and start to check.

She paused long enough to get the Legal Code article referred to into the viewer.

Somebody on board appeared to have got himself murdered.

She reached the cabin too late. A couple of young Security men already were going over it. Trigger said hello pleasantly. It was too bad, but it wasn't their fault. They just had a job to do.

They smiled back at her, apologized for the intrusion and went on with their business. She sat down and watched them. The Denton was there in plain sight. Dropping it into her purse now would be more likely to fix it in their memory than leaving it where it was.

The gadgets they were using were in concealing casings, and she couldn't guess what they were looking for by the way they used them. It didn't seem that either of them was trying to haul up an identifying memory about her. They did look a little surprised when the second cabin closet was opened and found to be as empty as the first; but no comments were made about that. Two minutes after Trigger had come in, they were finished and bowed themselves out of the cabin again. They turned then toward the cabin occupied by the ancient retainers of the Askab of Elfkund.

Trigger left her door open. This she wanted to hear, if she could.

She heard. The Elfkund door also stayed open, while the racket beyond it grew shriller by the moment. Finally a ComWeb chimed. A feminine voice spoke sternly. The quavering outcries subsided. It looked as if Security had been obliged to call on someone higher up in the Elfkund entourage to come to its aid. Trigger closed her door grinning.

On the screen of her secluded library, she presently watched a great port shuttle swing in from Evalee to meet the hovering *Dawn City*. It would bring another five hundred or so passengers on board and take off the few who had merely been making the short run from Maccadon to Evalee in style. Solidopic operators were quite likely to be on the shuttle, so she had decided to keep away from the entry area.

The transfer operation was carried out very expeditiously, probably to make up for some of the time lost on the surface. When the shuttle shoved off, the loudspeaker announced that normal space flight would be maintained till after the stopover at Garth. Trigger wandered thoughtfully back to her cabin. She closed the door behind her.

Then she saw the man sitting by the ComWeb cabinet. Her breath sucked in. She crouched a little, ready to wheel and bolt.

"Take it easy, Trigger!" Major Quillan said. He was in civilian clothes, of rather dudish cut.

Trigger swallowed. There was, too obviously, no place to bolt to. "How did you find me?"

He shrugged. "Longish story. You're not under arrest."

"I'm not?"

"No," said Quillan. "When we get to Manon, the Commissioner will have a suggestion to make to you."

"Suggestion?" Trigger said warily.

"I believe you're to take back your old Precol job in Manon, but as cover for your participation in our little project. If you agree to it."

"What if I don't?"

He shrugged again. "It seems you'll be writing your own ticket from here on out."

Trigger stared at him, wondering. "Why?"

Quillan grinned. "New instructions have been handed down," he said. "If you're still curious, ask Whatzzit."

"Oh," Trigger said. "Then why are you here?"

"I," said Quillan, "am to make damn sure you get to Manon. I brought a few people with me."

"Mihul, too?" Trigger asked, a shade diffidently.

"No. She's on Maccadon."

"Is she—how's she doing?"

"Doing all right," Quillan said. "She sends her regards and says a little less heft on the next solar plexus you torpedo should be good enough."

Trigger flushed. "She isn't sore, is she?"

"Not the way you mean." He considered. "Not many people have jumped Mihul successfully. In her cockeyed way, she seemed pretty proud of her student."

Trigger felt the flush deepen. "I got her off guard," she said.

"Obviously," said Quillan. "In any ordinary argument she could pull your legs off and tie you up with them. Still, that wasn't bad. Have you talked to anybody since you came on board?"

"Just the room stewardess. And a couple of old ladies in the next cabin."

"Yeah," he said. "Couple of old ladies. What did you talk about?"

Trigger recounted the conversation. He reflected, nodded and stood up.

"I put a couple of suitcases in that closet over there," he said. "Your personal stuff is in them, de-traced.

Another thing—somebody checked over your finances and came to the conclusion you're broke."

"Not exactly broke," said Trigger.

Quillan reached into a pocket, pulled out an envelope and laid it on the cabinet. "Here's a little extra spending money then," he said. "The balance of your Precol pay to date. I had it picked up on Evalee this morning. Seven hundred twenty-eight FC."

"Thanks," Trigger said. "I can use some of that."

They stood looking at each other.

"Any questions?" he asked.

"Sure," Trigger said. "But you wouldn't answer them."

"Try me, doll," said Quillan. "But let's shift operations to the fanciest cocktail lounge on this thing before you start. I feel like relaxing a little. For just one girl, you've given us a fairly rough time these last forty-eight hours!"

"I'm sorry," Trigger said.

"I'll bet," said Quillan.

Trigger glanced at the closet. If he'd brought everything along, there was a dress in one of those suitcases that would have been a little too daring for Maccadon. It should, therefore, be just about right for a cocktail lounge on the *Dawn City*; and she hadn't had a chance to wear it yet. "Give me ten minutes to change."

"Fine." Quillan started toward the door. "By the way, I'm your neighbor now."

"The cabin at the end of the hall?" she asked startled.

"That's right." He smiled at her. "I'll be back in ten minutes."

Well, that was going to be cozy! Trigger found the dress, shook it out and slipped into it, enormously puzzled but also enormously relieved. That Whatzzit!

Freshening up her make-up, she wondered how he had induced the Elfkund ladies to leave. Perhaps he'd managed to have a better cabin offered to them. It must be convenient to have that kind of a pull.

12

"Well, we didn't just leave it up to them," Quillan said. "Ship's Engineering spotted a radiation leak in their cabin. Slight but definite. They got bundled out in a squawking hurry." He added, "They did get a better cabin though."

"Might have been less trouble to get me to move," Trigger remarked.

"Might have been. I didn't know what mood you'd be in."

Trigger decided to let that ride. This cocktail lounge was a very curious place. By the looks of it, there were thirty or forty people in their immediate vicinity; but if one looked again in a couple of minutes, there might be an entirely different thirty or forty people around. Sitting in easy chairs or at tables, standing about in small groups, talking, drinking, laughing, they drifted past slowly; overhead, below, sometimes tilted at odd angles—fading from sight and presently returning.

In actual fact she and Quillan were in a little room by themselves, and with more than ordinary privacy via an audio block and a reconstruct scrambler which Quillan had switched on at their entry. "I'll leave us out of the viewer circuit," he remarked, "until you've finished your questions."

"Viewer circuit?" she repeated.

Quillan waved a hand around. "That," he said. "There are more commercial and industrial spies, political agents, top-class confidence men and whatnot on board this ship than you'd probably believe. A good percentage of them are pretty fair lip readers, and the things you want to talk about are connected with the Federation's hottest current secret. So while it's a downright crime not to put you on immediate display in a place like this, we won't take the chance."

Trigger let that ride too. A group had materialized at an oblong table eight feet away while Quillan was speaking. Everybody at the table seemed fairly high, and two of the couples were embarrassingly amorous; but she couldn't quite picture any of them as somebody's spies or agents. She listened to the muted chatter. Some Hub dialect she didn't know.

"None of those people can see or hear us then?" she asked.

"Not until we want them to. Viewer gives you as much privacy as you like. Most of the crowd here just doesn't see much point to privacy. Like those two."

Trigger followed his glance. At a tilted angle above them, a matched pair of black-haired, black-gowned young sirens sat at a small table, sipping their drinks, looking languidly around.

"Twins," Trigger said.

"No," said Quillan. "That's Blent and Company."

"Oh?"

"Blent's a lady of leisure and somewhat excessively narcissistic tendencies," he explained. He gave the matched pair another brief study. "Perhaps one can't really blame her. One of them's her facsimile. Blent—whichever it is—is never without her fac."

"Oh," Trigger said. She'd been studying the gowns. "That," she said, a trifle enviously, "is why I'm not at all eager to go on display here."

"Eh?" said Quillan.

Trigger turned to regard herself in the wall mirror on the right, which, she had noticed, remained carefully unobscured by drifting viewers and viewees. A thoughtful touch on the lounge management's part.

"Until we walked in here," she explained, "I thought this was a pretty sharp little outfit I'm wearing."

"Hmm," Quillan said judiciously. He made a detailed

appraisal of the mirror image of the slim, green, backless, half-thigh-length sheath which had looked so breath-taking and seductive in a Ceyce display window. Trigger's eyes narrowed a little. The major had appraised the dress in detail before.

"It's about as sharp a little outfit as you could get for around a hundred and fifty credits," he remarked. "Most of the items the girls are sporting here are personality conceptions. That starts at around ten to twenty times as high. I wasn't talking about displaying the dress. Now what were those questions?"

Trigger took a small sip of her drink, considering. She hadn't made up her mind about Major Quillan, but until she could evaluate him more definitely, it might be best to go by appearances. The appearances so far indicated small sips in his company.

"How did you people find me so quickly?" she asked.

"Next time you want to sneak off a civilized planet," Quillan advised her, "pick something like a small freighter. Or hire a small-boat to get you out of the system and flag down a freighter for you. Plenty of tramp captains will make a space stop to pick up a paying passenger. Liners we can check."

"Sorry," Trigger said meekly. "I'm still new at this business."

"And thank God for that!" said Quillan. "If you have the time and the money, it's also a good idea, of course, to zig a few times before you zag towards where you're really heading. Actually, I suppose, the credit for picking you up so fast should go to those collating computers."

"Oh?"

"Yes." Major Quillan looked broodingly at his drink for a moment. "There they sit," he remarked suddenly, "with their stupid plastic faces hanging out! Rows of them. You feed them something you don't understand. They don't understand it either. Nobody can tell me they can. But they kick it around and giggle a bit, and out comes some ungodly suggestion."

"So they helped you find me?" she said cautiously. It was clear that the major had strong feelings about computers.

"Oh, sure," he said. "It usually turns out it was a good idea to do what those CCs say. Anything unusual that shows up in the area you're working on gets chunked into the things as a matter of course. We were on the liners. *Dawn City* reports back a couple of murders. '*Dawn City* to the head of the list!' cry the computers. Nobody asks why. They just plow into the ticket purchase records. And right there are the little Argee thumbprints!"

He looked at Trigger. "My own bet," he said, somewhat accusingly, "was that you were on one of those that had just taken off. We didn't know about that ticket reservation."

"What I don't see," Trigger said, changing the subject, "is why two murders should seem so very unusual. There must be quite a few of them, after all."

"True," said Quillan. "But not murders that look like catassin killings."

"Oh!" she said startled. "Is that what these were?"

"That's what Ship Security thinks."

Trigger frowned. "But what could be the connection—"

Quillan reached across the table and patted her hand. "You've got it!" he said with approval. "Exactly! No connection. Some day I'm going to walk down those rows and give them each a blast where it will do the most good. It will be worth being broken for."

Trigger said, "I thought that catassin planet was being guarded."

"It is. It would be very hard to sneak one out nowadays. But somebody's breeding them in the Hub. Just a few. Keeps the price up."

Trigger grimaced uncomfortably. She'd seen recordings

of those swift, clever, constitutionally murderous creatures in action. "You say it looked like catassin killings. They haven't found it?"

"No. But they think they got rid of it. Emptied the air from most of the ship after they surfaced and combed over the rest of it with life detectors. They've got a detector system set up now that would spot a catassin if it moved twenty feet in any direction."

"Life detectors go haywire out of normal space, don't they?" she said. "That's why they surfaced then."

Quillan nodded. "You're a well-informed doll. They're pretty certain it's been sucked into space or disposed of by its owner, but they'll go on looking till we dive beyond Garth."

"Who got killed?"

"A Rest Warden and a Security officer. In the rest cubicle area. It might have been sent after somebody there. Apparently it ran into the two men and killed them on the spot. The officer got off one shot and that set off the automatic alarms. So pussy cat couldn't finish the job that time."

"It's all sort of gruesome, isn't it?" Trigger said.

"Catassins are," Quillan agreed. "That's a fact."

Trigger took another sip. She set down her glass. "There's something else," she said reluctantly.

"Yes?"

"When you said you'd come on board to see I got to Manon, I was thinking none of the people who'd been after me on Maccadon could know I was on the *Dawn City*. They might though. Quite easily."

"Oh?" said Quillan.

"Yes. You see I made two calls to the ticket office. One from a street ComWeb and one from the bank. If they already had spotted me by that tracer material, they could have had an audio pick-up on me, I suppose."

"I think we'd better suppose it," said Quillan. "You had a tail when you came out of the bank anyway." His glance went past her. "We'll get back to that later. Right now, take a look at that entrance, will you?"

Trigger turned in the direction he'd indicated.

"They do look like they're somebody important," she said. "Do you know them?"

"Some of them. That gentleman who looks like he almost has to be the *Dawn City's* First Captain really is the *Dawn City's* First Captain. The lady he's escorting into the lounge is Lyad Ermetyne. *The* Ermetyne. You've heard of the Ermetynes?"

"The Ermetyne Wars? Tranest?" Trigger said doubtfully.

"They're the ones. Lyad is the current head of the clan."

The history of Hub systems other than one's own became so involved so rapidly that its detailed study was engaged in only by specialists. Trigger wasn't one. "Tranest is one of the restricted planets now, isn't it?" she ventured.

"It is. Restriction is supposed to be a handicap. But Tranest is also one of the wealthiest individual worlds in the Hub."

Trigger watched the woman with some interest as the party moved along a dim corridor, followed by the viewer circuit's invisible pick-up. Lyad Ermetyne didn't look more than a few years older than she was herself. Rather small, slender, with delicately pretty features. She wore something ankle-length and long-sleeved in lusterless gray with an odd, smoky quality to it.

"Isn't she the empress of Tranest or something of the sort?" Trigger asked.

Quillan shook his head. "They've had no emperors there, technically, since they had to sign their treaty with the Federation. She just owns the planet, that's all."

"What would she be doing, going to Manon?"

"I'd like to know," Quillan said. "The Ermetyne's a lady

of many interests. Now—see the plump elderly man just behind her?"

"The ugly one with the big head who sort of keeps blinking?"

"That one. He's Belchik Pluly and—"

"Pluly?" Trigger interrupted. "The Pluly Lines?"

"Yes. Why?"

"Oh—nothing really. I heard—a friend of mine—Pluly's got a yacht out in the Manon System. And a daughter."

Quillan nodded. "Nelauk."

"How did you know?"

"I've met her. Quite a girl, that Nelauk. Only child of Pluly's old age, and he dotes on her. Anyway, he's been on the verge of being blacklisted by Grand Commerce off and on through the past three decades. But nobody's ever been able to pin anything more culpable on him than that he keeps skimming extremely close to the limits of a large number of laws."

"He's very rich, I imagine?" Trigger said thoughtfully.

"Very. He'd be much richer even if it weren't for his hobby."

"What's that?"

"Harems. The Pluly harems rate among the most intriguing and best educated in the Hub."

Trigger looked at Pluly again. "Ugh!" she said faintly.

Quillan laughed. "The Pluly salaries are correspondingly high. Viewer's dropping the group now, so there's just one more I'd like you to notice. The tall girl with black hair, in orange."

Trigger nodded. "Yes. I see her. She's beautiful."

"So she is. She's also Space Scout Intelligence. Gaya. Comes from Farnhart where they use the single name system. A noted horsewoman, very wealthy, socially established. Which is why we like to use her in situations like this."

Trigger was silent a moment. Then she said, "What kind of situation is it? I mean, what's she doing with Lyad Ermetyne and the others?"

"She probably attached herself to the group as soon as she discovered Lyad had come on board. Which," Quillan said, "is exactly what I would have told Gaya to do if I'd spotted Lyad first."

Trigger was silent a little longer this time. "Were you thinking this Lyad could be . . ."

"One of our suspects? Well," said Quillan judiciously, "let's say Lyad has all the basic qualifications. Since she's come on board, we'd better consider her. When something's going on that looks more than usually tricky, Lyad is always worth considering. And there's one point that looks even more interesting to me now than it did at first."

"What's that?"

"Those two little old ladies I eased out of their rightful cabin."

Trigger looked at him. "What about them?"

"This about them. The Askab of Elfkund is, you might say, one of the branch managers of the Ermetyne interests in the Hub. He is also a hard-working heel in his own right. But he's not the right size to be one of the people we're thinking about. Lyad is. He might have been doing a job for her."

"Job?" she asked. She laughed. "Not with those odd little grannies?"

"We know the odd little grannies. They're the Askab's poisoners and pretty slick at it. They were sizing you up while you were having that little chat, doll. Probably not for a coffin this time. You were just getting the equivalent of a pretty thorough medical check-up. Presumably, though, for some sinister ultimate purpose."

"How do you know?" Trigger asked, very uncomfortably.

"One of those little suitcases in their cabin was a diagnostic recorder. It would have been standing fairly close to the door while you were there. If they didn't take your recordings out before I got there, they're still inside. They're being watched and they know it. It seemed like a good idea to keep the Askab feeling fairly nervous until we found out whether those sweethearts of his had been parked next door to you on purpose."

"Apparently they were," Trigger admitted. "Nice bunch of people!"

"Oh, they're not all bad. Lyad has her points. And old Belchik, for example, isn't really a heel. He just has no ethics. Or morals. And revolting habits. Anyway, all this brings up the matter of what we should do with you now."

Trigger set her glass down on the table.

"Refill?" Quillan inquired. He reached for the iced crystal pitcher between them.

"No," she said. "I just want to make a statement."

"State away." He refilled his own glass.

"For some reason," said Trigger, "I've been acting lately—the last two days—in a remarkably stupid manner."

Quillan choked. He set his glass down hastily, reached over and patted her hand. "Doll," he said, touched, "it's come to you! At last."

She scowled at him. "I don't usually act that way."

"That," said Quillan, "was what had me so baffled. According to the Commissioner and others, you're as bright in the head as a diamond, usually. And frankly—"

"I know it," Trigger said dangerously. "Don't rub it in!"

"I apologize," said Quillan. He patted her other hand.

"At any rate," Trigger said, drawing her hands back, "now that I've realized it, I'm going to make up for it. From here on out, I'll cooperate."

"To the hilt?"

She nodded. "To the hilt! Whatever that is."

"You can't imagine," said Quillan, "how much that relieves me." He filled her glass, giving her a relieved look. "I had definite instructions, of course, not to do anything like grabbing you by the back of the neck, flinging you into a rest cubicle and sitting on it, guns drawn, until we'd berthed in Precol Port. But I was tempted, I can tell you."

He paused and thought. "You know," he began again, "that really would be the best."

"No!" Trigger said indignantly. "When I said cooperate, I meant actively. Mihul said I'm considered one of the gang in this project. From now on I'll behave like one. And I'll also expect to be treated like one."

"Hm," said Quillan. "Well, there is something you can do, all right."

"What's that?"

"Go on display here, now."

"What for?" she asked.

"As bait, you sweet ninny! If the boss grabber is on this ship, we should draw a new nibble from him." He appraised the green dress in the mirror again. His expression grew absent. It might be best, Trigger suspected, a trifle uneasily, to keep Major Quillan's thoughts turned away from things like nibbling.

"All right," she said briskly. "Let's do that. But you'll have to brief me."

13

She had felt somewhat self-conscious for the first two or three minutes. But it helped when she caught a glimpse of their own table drifting by among the others and realized that the smiling red-headed viewer image over there looked completely at her ease.

It helped, too, that Major Quillan turned suddenly into the light-but-ardent-conversation type of companion. In the short preceding briefing he had pointed out that a bit of flirting, etc., was a necessary, or at least nearly necessary, part of the act. Trigger was going along with the flirting; he could be right about that. She intended to stay on the alert for the etc.

They got nibbles very promptly. But not quite the right kind.

The concealed table ComWeb murmured, "A caller requests to be connected with Major Quillan. Is it permitted?"

"Oho!" Quillan said poisonously. "I suspected we should have stayed off circuit! Who's the caller?"

"The name given is Keth Deboll."

Quillan laughed. "Give the little wolf Major Quillan's regards and tell him it was a good try. I'll look him up tomorrow."

He gave Trigger a gentle wink. "Let 'em pant," he said. "At a distance!"

She smiled uncertainly. If he had a mustache, she thought, he'd be twirling it.

There were two more calls in the next few minutes, of similar nature. Quillan rebuffed them cheerfully. It was rather flattering in a way. She wondered how so many people in the cocktail lounge happened to know Quillan by name.

When the ComWeb reported the fourth caller, it sounded awed.

"The name given is the Lady Lyad Ermetyne!" it said.

Quillan beamed. "Lyad? Bless her heart! A pleasure. Put her through."

A screen shaped itself on the wall mirror to the right. Lyad Ermetyne's face appeared in it.

"Heslet Quillan!" She smiled. "So you aren't permanently lost to your friends, after all!" It was a light, liquid voice. It suited her appearance perfectly.

"Only to the frivolous ones," Quillan said. His thick black brows went up. His face took on a dedicated look. "I'm headed for Manon on duty."

She nodded. "Still with the Subspace Engineers?"

"And with the rank of major by now," Quillan said.

"Congratulations! But I'd already observed that your

fabulous good fortune hasn't deserted you in the least."
Lyad's glance switched to Trigger; she smiled again. It
was a pleasant, easy smile that showed white teeth.
"Would you shield your ComWeb, Quillan?"

"Shield it?" Quillan looked surprised. "Why, certainly!"
He reached under the edge of the table. The drifting
viewer images vanished. "Go ahead."

Lyad's eyes turned back to Trigger. They were off-color
eyes, like amber or a light wine, fringed with long black
lashes. Very steady, very knowing eyes. Trigger felt herself tensing.

"Forgive me the discourtesy of inquiring directly," the
light voice said. "But you are Trigger Argee, aren't you?"

Quillan's hand slapped the table. He looked at Trigger and laughed. "Better give up, Trigger! I told you you
were much more widely known than you believed."

"Well, Brule," Trigger muttered moodily to the
solidopic propped upright against the pillow before her,
"you'd bug those pretty blue eyes out if you knew who's
invited me to dinner!"

Brule smiled back winningly. She lay on her cabin's
bed, chin on her crossed arms, eyes a dozen inches from
the pretty blue ones. She studied Brule's features soberly.

"Major Heslet Quillan," she announced suddenly in
cold, even tones, "is a completely impossible character!"

It was no more than the truth. She didn't mind so
much that Quillan wouldn't tell her what he thought of
Lyad Ermetyne's standing on the suspect list now—there
hadn't really been much opportunity for open conversation so far. But he and that unpleasant Belchik Pluly had
engaged in some jovial back-slapping and rib-punching
when he and Trigger went over to join Lyad's party at
her request; and Quillan cried out merrily that he and
Belchik had long had one great interest in common—
ha-ha-ha! Then those two great buddies vanished together
for a full hour to take in some very special, not publicly

programmed Sensations Unlimited even in the *Dawn City's* Inferno.

Lyad had smiled after them as they left. "Aren't men disgusting?" she said tolerantly.

That reflected on her, didn't it? She was supposed to be very good friends with somebody like that! Of course Quillan must have some bit of Intelligence business in mind with Pluly, but there should be other ways of going about it. And later, when she'd been just a little stiff with him, Quillan had had the nerve to tell her not to be a prude, doll!

Trigger shoved the solidopic under the pillow. Then she rolled on her side and blinked at the wall.

Naturally, Major Quillan's personal habits were none of her business. It was just that in less than an hour he was to pick her up and take her to the Ermetyne suite for that dinner. She was wondering how she should behave towards him.

Reasonably pleasant but cool, she decided. But again, not too cool, since she'd obligated herself to help him find out what the Tranest tycooness was after. Any obvious lack of friendliness between them might make the job more difficult.

Trigger sighed. Things were getting complicated again.

While Quillan was indulging his baser nature among the questionable attractions of the Inferno, she'd shot three hundred of her Precol credits on a formal black gown . . . on what, yesterday, she would have considered a rather unbelievable gown. Even at an Ermetyne dinner she couldn't actually look dowdy in it. And then, accompanied by Gaya, who had turned out to be a very pleasant but not very communicative companion, she'd headed for a gambling room to make back the price of the gown.

It hadn't worked out. The game she'd particularly studied up on turned out to have a five hundred minimum play. Which finished that scheme. The system she'd planned to use looked very sound, but she needed more than one chance to try it in. She and Gaya sat down at another table, with a different game, where you could get in for fifty credits. In eight minutes Trigger lost a hundred and twenty and quit.

Gaya won seventy-five.

It had been an interesting day, but with some unsatisfactory aspects to it.

She hauled the solidopic out from under the pillow again.

"And you," she told Brule warningly, "seem to be playing around with some *very* bad company, my friend! Just luck I'm coming back to see you don't get into serious trouble!"

She'd showered and was studying the black gown's effect before the mirror when the ComWeb chimed.

"Permission for audio intrusion granted," Trigger said casually without looking around. She was getting used to this sort of thing.

"Thank you, Miss Drellgannoth," said the ComWeb. "A package from the Beldon Shop has been deposited in your mail transmitter." It signed off.

Beldon Shop? Trigger frowned, laid the gown across a chair and went over to the transmitter receptacle. She opened it. A flat small green package, marked "The Styles of Beldon," slid out. A delicate scent came trailing along with it. A small white envelope clung to the package's top.

Inside the envelope was a card. It read:

"A peace offering. Would you wear it to dinner in token of forgiveness? Very humbly, Q."

Trigger found herself smiling and wiped off the smile. Then she let it come back. No point in staying grim with the character! She pulled the package tab and it opened up. There were three smaller packages inside.

She opened the first of these and for a moment gazed doubtfully at four objects like green leaf buds, each the size of her thumb. She laid them down and opened the second package. This one contained a pair of very fancy high heels, green and pale gold.

Out of the third flowed something which was, at all events, extraordinarily beautiful material of some kind. Velvety green . . . shimmeringly alive. Its touch was a caress. Its perfume was like soft whispers. Lifting one end with great care between thumb and finger, Trigger let it unfold itself toward the floor.

Tilting her head to the side, she studied the shimmering featherweight cat's cradle of jewel-green ribbons that hung there.

Wear it?

What *was* it?

She reflected, found her dressing gown in one of the suitcases, slipped it on, sat down before the ComWeb with the mysterious ribbon arrangement, and dialed Gaya's number.

The Intelligence girl was in her cabin and obviously had been napping. But she was wide awake now. "Shielded here!" she said quickly as soon as her image cleared. "Go ahead!"

"It's nothing important," Trigger said hastily. Gaya relaxed. "It's just—" She held up the ribbons. "Major Quillan sent me this."

Gaya uttered a small squeal. "Oh! Beautiful! A Beldon!"

"That's what it says."

Gaya smiled. "He must like you!"

"Oh?" said Trigger. She hesitated. Gaya's face grew questioning. She asked, "Is something the matter?"

"Probably not," said Trigger. She considered. "If you laugh," she warned, "I'll hate you." She indicated the ribbons again. "What is that Beldon really?"

Gaya blinked. "You haven't been around our decadent circles long enough," she said soberly. Then she did laugh. "Don't hate me, Trigger! Anyway, it's very high fashion.

It's also"—her glance went quickly over Trigger—"in excellent taste, in this case. It's a Beldon gown."

A gown!

Some of the beautiful ribbons were wider than others. None of them looked as wide as they should have been. Not for a gown.

Dubiously, Trigger wriggled and fitted herself into the high fashion item. Even before she went over to the mirror in it, she knew it wouldn't do. Not possibly! Styles on many Hub worlds were rather bold of course, but she was sure this effect wasn't what the Beldon's designers had intended.

She stepped in front of the mirror. Her eyes widened. "Brother," she breathed.

That Beldon did go with a woman like stripes went with a tiger! After one look, you couldn't quite understand why nature hadn't arranged for it first. But just as obviously there wasn't nearly enough Beldon around at the moment.

Trigger checked the time and began to feel harried. Probably she'd wind up wearing the black gown anyway, but at least she wanted to get this matter worked out before she decided. She dialed for a drink, took two swallows and reflected that she might have put the thing on backwards. Or upside down.

Five minutes later, she sat at the dresser, tapping her fingers on its glassy surface, gazing at the small pile of green ribbons before her and whistling softly. There was a thoroughly baffled look on her face. Suddenly she stood up and went back to the ComWeb.

"Ribbons?" said the lady who was the Beldon Shop's manager. "That would be 741. A delightful little creation!"

"Delightful," said Trigger. "May I see it on the model?"

"Immediately, madam."

A few moments later, a long-limbed model strolled into the view screen, displaying an exquisite arrangement of burnt sienna ribbons plus four largish leaf-like designs.

Trigger glanced quickly back to the table where she had put down the strange green buds. They had quietly opened out meanwhile.

She thanked the manager, switched off the ComWeb, got into the Beldon again and attached her leaf designs where the model had carried them. They adhered softly, molding themselves to her, neatly completing the costume.

She stepped into the high heels and looked in the mirror again. She breathed "Brother!" again. Maccadon wouldn't have approved. She wasn't sure she approved either.

But one thing was certain—there wasn't the remotest suggestion of dowdiness about a Beldon. Objectively, impersonally considered, the effect was terrific.

Feeling tawny and feline, Trigger slowly lifted one shoulder and lowered it again. She turned and strolled toward the full-length mirror across the cabin, admiring the shifts of the Beldon effect in the flow of motion.

Terrific!

With another drink, she could do it.

She dialed another drink and settled down with it beneath the mechanical stylist for a readjustment in the hairdo department. This time the stylist purred as it surveyed and hummed while it worked. And when the hairdo was done and Trigger moved to get up, its flexible little tool pads pulled her back gently into the seat and tilted up her chin. For a moment she was startled. Then she saw that the stylist had produced a shining make-up kit and was opening it. This time she was getting the works . . .

Twenty minutes later, Quillan's voice informed her via the ComWeb that he could be outside her cabin any time she was ready. Trigger told him cheerily to come right over, picked up her purse and swaggered toward the door, smiling a cool, feline smile.

"Prude, eh?" she muttered.

She opened the door.

"Ya-arghk!" cried Quillan, shaken.

14

They were out on a terrace near the top of an illusion mountainside, in a beautiful evening. Dinner had been old-style and delicious, served by its creators, two slim, brown-skinned, red-lipped girls who looked much too young to have acquired such skills. They were natives of Tranest, Lyad said proudly, and two of the finest food technicians in the Hub. They were, at all events, the two finest food technicians Trigger had run into as yet.

The brandy which followed the dinner seemed to represent no letdown to the connoisseurs around Trigger. She went at it cautiously, though she had swallowed a couple of wake-up capsules just before they walked into the Ermetyne suite. The capsules took effect in the middle of the first course; and what she woke up to was a disconcerting awareness of being the center of much careful attention. The boys were all giving her-plus-Beldon the eye, intensively; even Lyad's giant-sized butler or majordomo or whatever she'd called him, named Virod, ogled coldly out of the background. Trigger gave them the eye back, one after the other, in turn; and that stopped it. Lyad, beautifully wearing something which would have passed muster at the U-League's Annual Presidential Dinner in Ceyce, looked amused.

It wasn't till the end of the second course that Trigger began to feel at ease again. After that she forgot, more or less, about the Beldon. The talk remained light during dinner. When they switched off the illusion background for a look at the goings-on during the Garth stopover, she took the occasion to study her companions in more detail.

There were three men at the table; Lyad and herself. Quillan sat opposite her. Belchik Pluly's unseemly person, in a black silk robe which left his plump arms bare from the elbows down, was on Quillan's right.

The third man fascinated her. It was as if some strange cold creature had walked up out of a polar sea to come on board their ship.

It wasn't so much his appearance, though the green tip of a Vethi sponge lying coiled lightly about his neck probably had something to do with the impression. Trigger knew about Vethi sponges and their addicts, though she hadn't seen either before. It wasn't too serious an addiction, except perhaps in the fact that it was rarely given up again. The sponges soothed jangled nerves, stabilized unstable emotions.

Balmordan didn't look like a man who needed one. He was big, not as tall as Quillan but probably heavier, with strong features, a boldly jutting nose. Bleak, pale eyes. He was about fifty and wore a richly ornamented blue shirt and trousers. The shirt hung loose, perhaps to conceal the flattened contours of his odd companion's body. Lyad had introduced him as a Devagas scientist and in a manner which indicated he was a man of considerable importance. That meant he was almost certainly a member of the Devagas hierarchy, which in itself would have made him very interesting.

Trigger had run into some of the oddball missionaries the Devagas kept sending about the Hub; and she'd sometimes speculated curiously regarding the leaders of that chronically angry, unpredictable nation which, on its twenty-eight restricted worlds, formed more than six percent of the population of the Hub. The Devagas seemed to like nobody; and certainly nobody liked them.

Balmordan didn't fit her picture of a Devagas leader too badly. His manner and talk were easygoing and agreeable. But his particular brand of ogle, when she first became aware of it, had been disquieting. Rather like a biologist planning the details of an interesting vivisection.

Of course he was a biologist.

But Trigger kept wondering why Lyad had invited him to dinner. She was positive, for one thing, that Belchik Pluly wasn't at all happy about Balmordan's presence.

Dinner was over before the Garth take-off, and they switched themselves back to the mountainside and took other chairs. A red-haired, green-eyed, tanned, sinuous young woman called Flam appeared from time to time to renew brandy glasses and pass iced fruits around. She gave Trigger coolly speculative looks now and then.

Then Virod showed up again with a flat tray of what turned out to be a very special brand of tobacco. Trigger declined. The men made connoisseur-type sounds of high appreciation, and everybody, including Lyad, lit up small pipes of a very special brand of coral and puffed away happily. Quillan looked up at Virod.

"Hi, big boy!" he said pleasantly. "How's everything been with you?"

Virod, in a wide-sleeved scarlet jacket and creased black trousers, bowed his shaved bullet head very slightly. "Everything's been fine, Major Quillan," he said. "Thank you." He turned and went out of the place. Trigger glanced after him. Virod awed her a little—he was really huge. Moving about among them, he had seemed like a softly padding elephant. And there was an elephant's steady deftness in the way he held out the tiny tobacco trays.

The Ermetyne winked at Quillan. "Quillan wrestled Virod to a pindown once," she said to Trigger. "A fifty-seven minute round, wasn't it?"

"Thereabouts," Quillan said. He added, "Trigger doesn't know yet that I was a sports bum in my youth."

"Really?" Trigger said.

He nodded. "Come from a long line of sports bums, as a matter of fact. But I broke tradition—went into business for myself finally. Nowadays I'm old and soft. Eh, Belchy?" The two great pals, sitting side by side, dug elbows at each other and ha-ha-ha'd. Trigger winced.

"Still in the same line of business, on the side?" Lyad inquired.

Quillan looked steadily at her and grinned. "More or less," he said.

"We might," Lyad said thoughtfully, "come back to that later. As for that match with Virod," she went on to Trigger, "it was really a terrific event! Virod was a Tranest arena professional before I took him into my personal employ, and he's very, very rarely been beaten in any such contest." She laughed. "And before such a large group of people, too! I'm afraid he's never quite forgiven you for that, Quillan."

"I'll keep out of his way," Quillan said easily.

"Did you people know," Lyad said, "that the trouble on the way between Maccadon and Evalee was caused by a catassin killing?" There was a touch of mischief in the question, Trigger thought.

There were assorted startled responses. The Ermetyne went briefly over some of the details Quillan had told; essentially it was the same story. "And do you know, Belchik, what the creature was trying to do? It was trying to get into the rest cubicle vaults. Just think, it might have been sent after you!"

It was rather cruel. Pluly's head jerked, and he blinked rapidly at Lyad, saying nothing. He was a badly scared little man at that moment. Trigger felt a little sorry for him, but not too sorry. Belchy's ogle had been of the straightforward, loose-lipped, drooling variety.

"You're safe when you're in one of those things, Belchik!" Quillan said reassuringly. "Wouldn't you feel a little safer there yourself, Lyad? If you say they're not even sure they've killed the creature . . ."

"I probably shall have a cubicle set up here," Lyad said. "But not as protection against a catassin. It would never get past Pilli, for one thing." She looked at Trigger. "Oh, I forgot. You haven't met Pilli. Virod!" she called.

Virod appeared at the far end of the terrace.

"Yes, First Lady?"

"Bring in Pilli," she told him.

Virod bowed. "Pilli is in the room, First Lady." He glanced about, went over to a massive easy chair a few dozen feet away, and swung it aside. Something like a huge ball of golden fur behind it moved and sat up.

It was an animal of some sort. Its head seemed turned toward the group, but whatever features it had remained hidden under the fur. Then an arm like the arm of a bear reached out and Trigger saw a great furred hand that in shape seemed completely human clutch the chair's edge.

"He was resting," Lyad said. "Not sleeping. Pilli doesn't sleep. He's a perfect guardian. Come here, Pilli—meet Trigger Argee."

Pilli swung up on his feet. It was an impressively effortless motion. There was a thick wide torso on short thick legs under the golden fur. The structure was gorilla-like. Pilli might weigh around four hundred pounds.

He started silently forward and Trigger felt a tingle of alarm. But he stopped six feet away. She looked at him. "Do I say something to Pilli?"

Lyad looked pleased. "No. He's a biostructure. A very intelligent one, but speech isn't included in his pattern."

Trigger kept looking at the golden-furred nightmare. "How can he see to guard you through all that hair?"

"He doesn't see," Lyad said. "At least not as we do. Pilli's part of one of our Tranest experiments—the original stock came from the Maccadon life banks, a small golden-haired Earth monkey. The present level of the experiment is on the fancy side—it has four hearts, for example, and what amounts to a second brain at the lower half of its spine. But it doesn't come equipped with visual organs. Pilli is one of twenty-three of the type. They have compensatory perception of a kind that is still quite mysterious. We hope to breed them past the speech barrier so they can tell us what they do instead of seeing . . . All right, Pilli. Run along!" She said to

Balmordan, "I believe he doesn't like that Vethi thing of yours very much."

Balmordan nodded. "I had the same impression."

Perhaps, Trigger thought, that was why Pilli had been lurking so close to them. She watched the biostructure move off down the terrace, grotesque and huge. She had got its scent as it went past her, a fresh, rather pleasant whiff, like the smell of ripe apples. An almost amiable sort of nightmare figure, Pilli was; the apple smell went with that, seemed to fit it. But the nightmare was there too. She found herself feeling rather sorry for Pilli.

"In a way," Lyad said, "Pilli brings us to that matter of business I mentioned this afternoon."

The group's eyes shifted over to her. She smiled.

"We have good scientists on Tranest," she said, "as Pilli, I think, demonstrates." She nodded at Balmordan. "There are good scientists in the Devagas Union. And everyone here is aware that the Treaties of Restriction imposed on both our governments have made it impossible for our citizens to engage seriously in plasmoid research."

Trigger nodded briefly as the light-amber eyes paused on her for a moment. Quillan had cautioned her not to show surprise at anything the Ermetyne might say or do. If Trigger didn't know what to say herself, she was merely to look inscrutable. "I'll scrut," he explained. "The others won't. I'll take over then and you just follow my lead. Get it?"

"Balmordan," Lyad said, "I understand you are going to Manon to attend the seminars and demonstrations on the plasmoid station?"

"That is true, First Lady," said Balmordan.

"Now I," Lyad told the company, "shall be more honest. The information released in those seminars is of no value whatever. He"—she nodded at the Devagas scientist—"and I are going to Manon with the same goal in mind. That is to obtain plasmoids for our government laboratories."

Balmordan smiled amiably.

Trigger asked, "How do you intend to obtain them?"

"By offering very large sums of money, or equivalent inducements, to people who are in a position to get them for me," said Lyad.

Quillan tut-tutted disapprovingly. "The First Lady's mind," he told Trigger, "turns readily to illegal methods."

"When necessary," Lyad said undisturbed, "as it is here."

"How about you, sir?" Quillan asked Balmordan. "Are we to understand that you also would be interested in the purchase of a middling plasmoid or two?"

"I would be, naturally," Balmordan said. "But not at the risk of causing trouble for my government."

"Of course not," Quillan said. He thought a moment. "You, Belchy?" he asked.

Pluly looked alarmed. "No! No! No!" he said hastily. He blinked wildly. "I'll stick to the shipping business. It's safer."

Quillan patted him fondly on the shoulder. "That's one law-abiding citizen in this group!" He winked at Trigger. "Trigger's wondering," he told Lyad, "why she and I are being told these things."

"Well, obviously," Lyad said, "Trigger and you are in an excellent position—or will be, very soon—to act as middlemen in the matter."

"Wha . . ." Trigger began, astounded. Then, as all eyes swiveled over to her, she checked herself. "Did you really think," she asked Lyad, "that we'd agree to such a thing?"

"Certainly not," said Lyad. "I don't expect anyone to agree to anything tonight—though it's a safe assumption I'm not the only one here who has made sure this conversation is not being recorded, and will not be available for reconstruction. Well, Quillan?" She smiled.

"How right you are, First Lady!" Quillan said. He tapped a breast pocket. "Scrambler and distorter present and in action."

"And you, Balmordan?"

"I must admit," Balmordan said pleasantly, "that I thought it wise to take certain precautions."

"Very wise!" said Lyad. Her glance shifted, with some amusement in it, to Pluly. "Belchik?"

"You're a nerve-wracking woman, Lyad," Belchik said unhappily. "Yes. I'm scrambling, of course." He shuddered. "I can't afford to take chances. Not when you're around."

"Of course not, and even so," said Lyad, "there are still reasons why an unconsidered word might be embarrassing in this company. So, no, Trigger, I'm not expecting anybody to agree to anything tonight. I'm merely mentioning that I'm interested in the purchase of plasmoids. Incidentally, I'd be very much more interested even in seeing you, and Quillan, enter my employ directly. Yes, Belchik?"

Pluly had begun giggling wildly.

"I was—ha-ha—having the same idea!" he gasped. "About one of—ha-ha—of 'em anyway! I—"

He jerked and came to an abrupt stop, transfixed by Trigger's stare. Then he reached for his glass, blinking at top speed. "Excuse me," he muttered.

"Hardly, Belchik!" said Lyad. She gave Trigger a small wink. "But I can assure you, Trigger Argee, that you'd find *my* pay and working conditions very attractive indeed."

It seemed a good moment to look inscrutable. Trigger did.

"Serious about that, Lyad?" asked Quillan.

The Ermetyne said, "Certainly I'm serious. Both of you could be of great value to me at present." She looked at him a moment. "Did you ever happen to tell Trigger about the manner in which you re-established the family fortune?"

"Not in any great detail," Quillan said.

"A very good hijacker and smuggler went to waste

when you signed up with the Engineers," Lyad said. "But perhaps not entirely to waste."

"Perhaps not," acknowledged Quillan. He grinned. "But I'm a modest man. One fortune's enough for me."

"There was a time, you know," Lyad said, "when I was rather afraid it would be necessary to have you killed."

Quillan laughed. "There was a time," he admitted, "when I suspected you might be thinking along those lines, First Lady! Didn't lose too much, did you?"

"I lost enough!" Lyad said. She wrinkled her nose at him. "But that's all over and done with. And now—no more business tonight. I promise." She turned her head a little. "Flam!" she called.

"Yes, First Lady?" said the voice of the redheaded girl.

"Bring us Miss Argee's property, please."

Flam brought in a small package of flat disks taped together. Lyad took them.

"Sometimes," she told Quillan, "the Askab becomes a little independent. He's been spoken to. Here—you keep them for Trigger."

She tossed the package lightly over to them. Quillan put out a hand and caught it.

"Thanks," he said. He put the package in a pocket. "I'll call off my beagles."

"Suit yourself as to that," said the Ermetyne. "It won't hurt the Askab to stay frightened a little longer."

She checked herself. The room's ComWeb was signaling. Virod went over to it. A voice came through.

" . . . The Garth-Manon subspace run begins in one hour. Rest cubicles have been prepared . . ."

"That means me," Belchik Pluly said. He climbed hastily to his feet. "Can't stand dives! Get hallucinations. Nasty ones." He staggered a little then, and Trigger realized for the first time that Belchy had got pretty thoroughly drunk.

"Better give our guest a hand, Virod," Lyad called over her shoulder. "Happy dreams, Belchik! Are you going by

Rest, Trigger? No? You're not, of course, Quillan. Balmordan?"

The Devagas scientist also shook his head.

"Then by all means," Lyad said, "let's stay together a little while longer."

15

"She," said Trigger, "is a remarkable woman."

"Yeah," said Quillan. "Remarkable."

"May I ask you, finally, a few pertinent questions?" Trigger inquired humbly.

"Not here, sweet stuff," said Quillan.

"You're a bossy sort of slob, Heslet Quillan," she said equably.

Quillan didn't answer. They had come down the stairway to the storerooms level and were walking along the big lit hallway toward their cabins. Trigger felt pleasantly relaxed. But she did have a great many pertinent questions to ask Quillan now, and she wanted to get started on them.

"Oh!" she said suddenly. Just as suddenly, Quillan's hand was on her shoulder, moving her along.

"Hush now," he said. "And keep walking."

"But you saw it, didn't you?" Trigger asked, trying to look back to the small open door into the storerooms they'd just passed.

Quillan sighed. "Certainly," be said. "Guy in space armor."

"But what's he doing there?"

"Checking something, I suppose." His hand left her shoulder; and, for just a moment, his finger rested lightly across her lips. Trigger glanced up at him. He was walking on beside her, not looking at her.

All right, she thought—she could take a hint. But she

felt tense and uncomfortable now. Something was going on again, apparently.

They turned into the side passage and came up to her cabin. Trigger started to turn to face him, and Quillan picked her up and went on without a noticeable break in his stride. Close to her ear, his voice whispered, "Explain in a moment! Dangerous here."

As the door to the end cabin closed behind them, he put her back on her feet. He looked at his watch.

"We can talk here," he said. "But there may not be much time for conversation." He gestured toward a table against the wall. "Take a look at the setup."

Trigger looked. The table was littered with instruments, like an electronic workbench. A visual screen showed a view of both her own cabin and a section of the passage outside it, up to the point where it entered the big hall.

"What is it?" she asked uncertainly.

"Essentially," said Quillan, "we've set up a catassin trap."

"Catassin!" Trigger squeaked.

"That's right. Don't get too nervous though. I've caught them before. Used to be a sort of specialty of mine. And there's one thing about them—they'll blab their pointed little heads off if you can get one alive and promise it its catnip . . ." He'd shucked off his jacket and taken out of it a very large handgun with a bell-shaped mouth. He laid the gun down next to the view screen. "In case," he said, unreassuringly. "Now just a moment."

He sat down in front of the view screen and did something to it.

"All right," he said then. "We're here and set. Probability period starts in three minutes, continues for sixty. Signal on any blip. Otherwise no gabbing. And remember they're *fast*. Don't get sappy."

There was no answer. Quillan did something else to the screen and stood up again. He looked broodingly at

Trigger. "It's those damn computers again!" he said. "I don't see any sense in it."

"In what?" she asked shakily.

"Everything that's happening around here is being fed back to them at the moment," he said. "When they heard about our invite to Lyad's dinner party, and who was to be present, they came up with a honey. In the time period I mentioned a catassin is supposed to show up at your cabin. They give it a pretty high probability."

Trigger didn't say anything. If she had, she probably would have squeaked again.

"Now don't worry," he said, squeezing her shoulder reassuringly between a large thumb and four slightly less large fingers. "Nice muscle!" he said absently. "The cabin's trapped and I've taken other precautions." He massaged the muscle gently. "Probably the only thing that will happen is that we'll sit around here for an hour or so, and then we'll have a hearty laugh together at those foolish computers!" He smiled.

"I thought," Trigger said without squeaking, "that everybody was pretty sure it was dead."

Quillan frowned. "Well, that's something else again! There are at least two ways I know of to sneak it past that search. Jump it out and in with a subtub is one— they could have done that from their own cabin as soon as they had its pattern. So I don't really think it's dead. It's just—"

"Quillan," a tiny voice said from the viewer.

He turned, took two steps, and sat down fast before the viewer. "Go ahead!"

"Fast motion in B section. Going your way."

Fast motion. A thought flicked up. "Quillan—" Trigger began.

He raised a shushing hand. "Get a silhouette?" he asked. His hands went to a set of control switches and stayed there.

"No. Pickup shows a haze like in the reconstruct." An instant's pause. "Leaving B section."

"Motion in C section," said another voice.

Quillan said, "All right. It's coming. No more verbal reports unless it changes direction. If you want to stay alive, don't move unless you're in armor."

There was silence. Quillan sat unmoving, eyes fixed on the screen. Trigger stood just behind him. Her legs had begun to tremble. She'd better tell him.

"Quillan—"

For an instant, in the screen, there was something like heat shimmer at the far end of the passage. Then she saw her cabin door pop open.

The interior of the cabin showed in a brief flare of blue light. In it was a shape. It vanished instantly again.

She heard Quillan make a shocked, incredulous sound. His left hand slashed at a switch on the panel.

Twenty feet from them, just behind the closed door to the passage, was a splatting noise like a tremendous slap. Then another noise, strangely like a brief cloudburst. Then silence again.

She realized Quillan was on his feet beside her, the oversized gun in his hand. It was pointed at the door. His eyes switched suddenly from the door to the screen and back again. She felt him relaxing slowly. Then she discovered she was clutching a handful of his shirt along with a considerable chunk of tough skin. She went on clutching it.

"Fly swatter got it!" he said. "Whew!" He looked down and patted the clutching hand. "That was no catassin! The trap in the cabin wasn't fast enough. Had a gravity mine outside our door, just in case. *That* was barely fast enough!" For once, Quillan looked almost awed.

"L-l-l-like—" Trigger began. She tried again. "Like a little yellow man—"

"You saw it? In the cabin? Yes. Never saw anything just like it before!"

Trigger pressed her lips together to make them stay steady.

"I have," she said. "That's what I was trying to tell you."

Quillan stared at her for an instant. "You'll tell me about it in a couple of minutes. I've got some quick work to do first." He checked himself. A wide grin spread suddenly over his face. "Know something, doll?"

"What?"

"The damn computers!" Major Quillan said happily. "They goofed!"

The gravity mine would have reduced almost any life-form which moved into its field to a rather thin smear, but there wasn't even that left of the yellow demon-shape. Something, presumably something it was carrying, had turned it into a small blaze of incandescent energy as the mine flattened it out. Which explained the sound like a cloudburst. That had been the passage's automatic fire extinguishers going into brief but correspondingly violent action.

Quillan's group stayed out of sight for the time being. He'd barely got the mine put away, along with a handful of warped metal slugs, which was what the mine had left of their attacker's mechanical equipment, and Trigger's cabin door locked again, when three visitors came zooming down the storerooms hall in a small car. A ship's engineer and two assistants had arrived to check on what had started the extinguishers.

"They may," Quillan said hopefully, "just go away again." He and Trigger were watching the engineers through the viewer which had been extended to cover their end of the passage.

They didn't just go away again. They checked the extinguishers, looked at the floor, still wet but rapidly absorbing the last drops of the brief deluge. They exchanged puzzled comment. They checked everything once more. Finally the leader made use of the door announcer and asked if he might intrude.

Quillan switched off the viewer. "Come in," he said resignedly.

The door opened. The three glanced at Quillan, and then at Trigger-plus-Beldon. Their eyes widened only slightly. Duty on the *Dawn City* produced hardened men.

Neither Quillan nor Trigger could offer the slightest explanation as to what had started the extinguishers. The engineers apologized and withdrew. The door closed again.

Quillan switched on the viewer. Their voices came back into the cabin as they climbed into their car.

"So that's how it happened," one of the assistants was saying reflectively.

"Right," said the ship's engineer. "Like to burst into flames myself."

"Ha-ha-ha!" They drove off.

Trigger flushed. She looked at Quillan.

"Perhaps I ought to get into something else," she said. "Now that the party's over."

"Perhaps," Quillan admitted. "I'll have Gaya bring something down. We want to stay out of your cabin for an hour or so till everything's been checked. There'll be a few conferences to go through now."

Gaya arrived next, with clothes. Trigger retired to the cabin's bathroom with them and came out a few minutes later, dressed again. Meanwhile the *Dawn City's* First Security Officer also had arrived and was setting up a portable restructure stage in the center of the cabin. He looked rather grim, but he also looked like a very much relieved man.

"I suggest we run your sequence off first, Major," he said. "Then we can put them on together, and compare them."

Trigger sat down on a couch beside Gaya to watch. She'd been told that the momentary view of the little demon-shape in the cabin had been deleted from Security's copy of their own sequence and wasn't to be mentioned.

Otherwise there really was not too much to see. What the attacking creature had used to blur the restructure wasn't clear, except that it wasn't a standard scrambler. Amplified to the limits of clarity and stepped down in time to the limit of immobility, all that emerged was a shifting haze of energy, which very faintly hinted at a dwarfish human shape in outline. A rather unusually small and heavy catassin, the Security chief pointed out, would present such an outline. That something quite material was finally undergoing devastating structural disorganization on the gravity mine was unpleasantly obvious, but it produced no further information. The sequence ended with the short blaze of heat which had set off the extinguishers.

Then they ran the restructure of the preceding double killing. Trigger watched, gulping a little, till it came to the point where the haze shape actually was about to touch its victims. Then she studied the carpet carefully until Gaya nudged her to indicate the business was over. Catassins almost invariably used their natural equipment in the kill; it was a swift process, of course, but shockingly brutal, and Trigger didn't care to remember what the results looked like in a human being. Both men had been killed in that manner; and the purpose obviously was to conceal the fact that the killer was not a catassin, but something even more efficient along those lines.

It didn't occur to the Security chief to question Trigger. A temporal restructure of a recent event was a far more reliable witness than any set of human senses and memory mechanisms. He left presently, reassured that the catassin incident was concluded. It startled Trigger to realize that Security did not seem to be considering seriously the possibility of discovering the human agent behind the murders.

Quillan shrugged. "Whoever did it is covered three ways in every direction. The chief knows it. He can't psych four thousand people on general suspicions, and he'd hit mind-blocks in every twentieth passenger presently on board if he did. Anyway he knows we're on it, and that we have a great deal better chance of nailing the responsible characters eventually."

"More information for the computers, eh?" Trigger said.

"Uh-huh."

"You got this little chunk the hard way, I feel," she observed.

"True," Quillan admitted. "But we have to get it any way we can till we get enough to move on. Then we move." He looked at her, with an air of regarding a new idea. "You know," he said, "you don't do badly for an amateur!"

"She doesn't do badly," Gaya's voice said behind Trigger, "for anybody. How do you people feel about a drink? I thought I could use one myself after looking at the chief's restructure."

Trigger felt herself coloring. Praise from the cloak and dagger experts! For some reason it pleased her immensely. She turned her head to smile at Gaya, standing there with three glasses on a tray.

"Thanks!" she said. She took one of the glasses. Gaya held the tray out to Quillan and took the third glass herself.

It was some five minutes later when Trigger remarked, "You know, I'm getting sleepy."

Quillan looked around from the viewer equipment he and Gaya were dismantling. "Why not hit the couch over there and take a nap?" he suggested. "It'll be about an hour before the boys can get down here for the real conference."

"Good idea." Trigger yawned, finished her drink, put the glass on a table, and wandered over to the couch.

She stretched out on it. A drowsy somnolence enveloped her almost instantly. She closed her eyes.

Ten minutes later, Gaya, standing over her, announced, "Well, she's out."

"Fine," said Quillan, packaging the rest of the equipment. "Tell them to haul in the rest cubicle. I'll be done here in a minute. Then you and the lady warden can take over."

Gaya looked down at Trigger. There was a trace of regret in her face. "I think," she said, "she's going to be fairly displeased with you when she wakes up and finds she's on Manon."

"Wouldn't doubt it," said Quillan. "But from what I've seen of her, she's going to get fairly displeased with me from time to time on this operation anyway."

Gaya looked at his back.

"Major Quillan," she said, "would you like a tip from a keen-eyed operator?"

"Go ahead, ole keen-eyed op!" Quillan said in kindly tones.

"Not that you don't have it coming, boy," said Gaya. "But watch yourself! This one is dangerous. This one could sink you for keeps."

"You're going out of your mind, doll," said Quillan.

16

The Precol Headquarters dome on Manon Planet was still in the spot where Trigger had left it, looking unchanged; but everything else in the area seemed to have been moved, improved, expanded or taken away entirely, and unfamiliar features had appeared. In the screens of Commissioner Tate's Precol offices, Trigger could see both the new metropolitan-sized spaceport on which the *Dawn City* had set down that morning, and the towering glassy structures of the giant shopping and recreation center, which had been opened here recently by Grand Commerce in its bid for a cut of prospective outworld salaries. The salaries weren't entirely prospective either.

Ten miles away on the other side of Headquarters dome, new squares of living domes were sprouting up daily. At this morning's count they housed fifty-two thousand people. The Hub's major industries and assorted branches of Federation government had established a solid foothold on Manon.

Trigger turned her head as Holati Tate came into the office. He closed the door carefully behind him.

"How's the little critter doing?" he asked.

"Still absorbing the goop," Trigger said. She held Mantelish's small mystery plasmoid cupped lightly between thumbs and fingers, its bottom side down in a shallow bowl half full of something which Mantelish considered to be nutritive for plasmoids, or at least for this one. Its sides pulsed lightly and regularly against her palms. "The level of the stuff keeps going down," she added.

"Good," said Holati. He pulled a chair up to the table and sat down opposite her. He looked broodingly at plasmoid 113-A.

"You really think this thing *likes* me—personally?" Trigger inquired.

Her boss said, "It's eating, isn't it? And moving. There were a couple of days before you got here when it looked pretty dead to me."

"Hard to believe," Trigger observed, "that a sort of leech-looking thing could distinguish between people."

"This one can. Do you get any sensations while holding it?"

"Sensations?" She considered. "Nothing particular. It's just like I said the other time—little Repulsive is rather nice to feel."

"For you," he said. "I didn't tell you everything."

"You rarely do," Trigger remarked.

"I'll tell you now," said Holati. "The day after we left Maccadon, when it started acting first very agitated and then very droopy, Mantelish said it might be missing the female touch it had got from you. He was being facetious, I think. But I couldn't see any reason not to try it, so I called in your facsimile and had her sit down at the table where the thing was lying."

"Yes?"

"Well, first it came flying up to her, crying 'Mama!' Not actually, of course. Then it touched her hand and recoiled in horror."

Trigger raised an eyebrow.

"It looked like it," he insisted. "We all commented on it. So then she reached out and touched it. Then she recoiled in horror."

"Why?"

"She said it had given her a very nasty electric jolt. Apparently like the one it gave Mantelish."

Trigger glanced down dubiously at Repulsive. "Gee, thanks for letting me hold it, Holati! It seems to have stopped eating now, by the way. Or whatever it does. Doesn't look much fatter if any, does it?"

The Commissioner looked. "No," he said. "And if you weighed it, you'd probably find it still weighs an exact three and a half pounds. Mantelish feels the thing turns any food intake directly into energy."

"Then it should be able to produce a very nice jolt at the moment," Trigger commented. "Now, what do I do with Repulsive?"

Holati took a towel from beneath the table and spread it out. "Absorbent material," be said. "Lay it on that and just let it dry. That's what we used to do."

Trigger shook her head. "Next thing, I'll be changing its diapers!"

"It isn't that bad," the Commissioner said. "Anyway, you will adopt baby, won't you?"

"I suppose I have to." She placed the plasmoid on the towel, wiped her hands and stepped back from it. "What happens if it falls on the floor?"

"Nothing," Holati said. "It just moves on in the direction it was going. Pretty hard to hurt those things."

"In that case," Trigger said, "let's check out its container now."

The Commissioner took Repulsive's container out of a desk safe and handed it to her. Its outer appearance was that of a neat modern woman's handbag with a shoulder strap. It had an antigrav setting which would reduce its overall weight, with the plasmoid inside, down to nine ounces if Trigger wanted it that way. It also had a combination lock, unmarked, virtually invisible, the settings of which Trigger already had memorized. Without knowing the settings, a determined man using a high-powered needle blaster might have opened the handbag in around nine hours. A very special job.

Trigger ran through the settings, opened the container and peered inside. "Rather cramped," she observed.

"Not for one of them. We needed room for the gadgetry."

"Yes," she said. "Subspace rotation." She shook her head. "Is that another Space Scout invention?"

"No," said Holati. "They stole it from Subspace Engineers. Engineers don't know we have it yet. Far as I know, nobody else has got it from them. Go ahead—give it a try."

"I was going to." Trigger snapped the container shut, slipped the strap over her shoulder and stood straight, left hand closed over the lower rim of the purse-like object. She shifted the ball of her thumb and the tip of her middle finger to the correct spots and began to apply pressure. Then she started. Handbag and strap had vanished.

"Feels odd!" She smiled. "And to bring it back, I just have to be here—the same place—and say those words."

He nodded. "Want to try that now?"

Trigger waved her left hand gently through the air beside her. "What happens," she asked, "if the thing surfaces exactly where my hand happens to be?"

"It won't surface if there's anything bulkier than a few dust motes in the way. That's one improvement the Sub Engineers haven't heard about yet."

"Well . . ." She glanced around, picked up a plastic ruler from the desk behind her, and moved back a cautious step. She waved the ruler's tip gingerly about in the area where the handbag had been.

"Come, Fido!" she said.

Nothing happened. She drew the ruler back.

"Come, Fido!"

Handbag and strap materialized in mid-air and thumped to the floor.

"Convinced?" Holati asked. He picked up the handbag and gave it back to her.

"It seems to work. How long will that little plasmoid last if it's left in subspace like that?"

He shrugged. "Indefinitely, probably. They're tough. We know that twenty-four hours at a stretch won't bother it in the least, so we've set that as the limit it's to stay rotated except in emergencies."

"And you—and one other person I'm not to know about, but who isn't anywhere near here—can also bring it back?"

"Yes. If we know the place from which it's been rotated. So the agreement is that—again except in absolute emergencies—it will be rotated only from one of the six points specified and known to all three of us."

Trigger nodded. She opened the container and went over to the table where the plasmoid still lay on its towel. It was dry by now. She picked it up.

"You're a lot of trouble, Repulsive!" she told it. "But these people think you must be worth it." She slipped it into the container, and it seemed to snuggle down comfortably inside. Trigger closed the handbag, lightened it to half its normal weight, slipped the strap back over her left shoulder. "And now," she inquired, "what am I to do with the stuff I usually keep in a purse?"

"You'll be in Precol uniform while you're here. We've had a special uniform made for you. Extra pockets."

Trigger sighed.

"Oh, they're quite inconspicuous and convenient," he assured her. "We checked with the girls on that."

"I'll bet!" she said. "Did they okay the porgee pouch too?"

"Sure. Porgee doping is a big thing all over the Hub at the moment. Among the ladies anyway. Shows you're the delicate sort, or something like that. I forget what they said. Want to start carrying it?"

"Hand it over," Trigger said resignedly. "I did see quite a few pouches on the ship. Might as well get people used to thinking I've turned into a porgee sniffer."

Holati went back to the desk safe and took out a flat pouch, the length of his hand but narrower. He gave it to her. It appeared to be worked of gold thread; one side was studded with tiny pearls, the opposite surface was plain. Trigger laid the plain side against the cloth of her skirt, just below the right hip, and let go. It adhered there. She stretched her right leg out to the side and considered the porgee pouch.

"Doesn't look too bad," she conceded. "That's real porgee in the top section?"

"The real article. Close to nine hundred and fifty credits worth."

"Suppose somebody wants to borrow a sniff? Wouldn't be good to have them fumbling around the pouch very much!"

"They can't," said the Commissioner. "That's why we made it porgee. When you buy a supply, it has to be adjusted to your individual chemistry, exactly. That's mainly what makes it expensive. Try using someone else's, and it'll flip you across the room."

"Better get this adjusted to my chemistry then. I might have to take a demonstration sniff now and then to make it look right."

"We've already done that," he said.

"Good," said Trigger. "Now let's see!" She straightened up, left hand closed lightly around the bottom of the purse, right hand loose at her side. Her eyes searched the office briefly. "Some object around here you don't particularly value?" she asked. "Something largish?"

"Several," the Commissioner said. He glanced around. "That overgrown flower pot in the corner is one. Why?"

"Just practicing," said Trigger. She turned to face the flowerpot. "That will do. Now—here I come along, thinking of nothing." She started walking toward the flowerpot. "Then, suddenly, in front of me, there stands a plasmoid snatcher."

She stopped in mid-stride. Handbag and strap vanished, as her right hand slapped the porgee pouch. The Denton popped into her palm. The flowerpot screeched and flew apart.

"Golly!" she said, startled. "Come, Fido!" Handbag and strap reappeared and she reached out and caught the strap. She looked around at Commissioner Tate.

"Sorry about your pot, Holati. I was just going to shake it up a little. I forgot you people had been handling my gun. I keep it switched to stunner myself when I'm carrying it," she added pointedly.

"Perfectly all right about the pot," the Commissioner said. "I should have warned you. Otherwise, I'd say all you'd need is a moment to see them coming."

Trigger spun the Denton to its stunner setting and laid it back inside the slit which had appeared along the side of the porgee pouch. She ran thumb and finger tip along the length of the slit, and the pouch was sealed again.

"That's the part that's worrying me," she admitted, and left.

17

When Trigger presented herself at Commissioner Tate's personal quarters early that evening, she found him alone.

"Sit down," he said. "I've been trying to get hold of Mantelish for the past hour. He's over on the other side of the planet again."

Trigger sat down and lifted an eyebrow. "Should he be?"

"I don't think so," said Holati. "But I've been overruled on that. He's still the best man the Federation has working on the various plasmoid problems, so I'm not to interfere with his investigations any more than I can show is absolutely necessary. It's probably all right. Those U-League guards of his aren't a bad group."

"If they compare with the boys the League had watching the Plasmoid Project, they should be just about tops," Trigger said.

"The Space Scouts thank you for those kind words," the Commissioner told her. "Those weren't League guards. When it came to deciding who was to keep an eye on you, I overruled everybody."

She smiled. "I might have guessed it. What's there for the professor to be investigating on the other side of Manon?"

"He's hunting for some theoretical creatures he calls wild plasmoids."

"*Wild* plasmoids?"

"Uh-huh. His idea is that some of the plasmoids the Old Galactics were using on Manon might have got away from them, or just been left lying around, so to speak, and could have survived till now. He thinks they might even be reproducing themselves. He's looking for them with a special detector he built."

Trigger held up a finger on which was a slim gold ring with a small green stone in it. "Like this one?" she asked.

"He's got a large version of that type of detector with him too. But he thinks that if any wild plasmoids are around, they're likely to be along the lines of 113-A. So he's also constructed a detector which reacts to 113-A."

"I see." Trigger was silent a moment. "Does Mantelish have any idea why Repulsive is the only plasmoid known to which our ring detectors don't react?"

"Apparently he does," Holati said. "But when he starts in on those subjects, I find him difficult to follow." He looked soberly at Trigger. "There are times," he confessed, "when I suspect Professor Mantelish is somewhat daft. But probably he's just so brilliant that he keeps fading beyond my mental range."

Trigger laughed. "My father used to come home from a session with Mantelish muttering the same sort of thing." She glanced at the ring again. "By the way, have any plasmoids actually been stolen around here for us to detect?"

He nodded. "Quite a few have been snitched from *Harvest Moon* and various storage points by now. I wouldn't be surprised if some of them turn up here in the dome eventually. Not that it's a serious loss. Except for 112-113, what the thieves have been getting away with is small stuff—plasmoid nuts and bolts, so to speak. Still, each of those would still fetch around a hundred thousand credits, if you offered them to the right people. Incidentally, if asking you to this conference has interfered with any personal plans, just say so. We can put it off till tomorrow. Especially since it's beginning to look as if Mantelish won't make it here either."

"Either?" Trigger said.

"Quillan's already had to cancel. He got involved with something during the afternoon."

"Oh," she said coolly. She looked at her watch. "I do have a dinner date with Brule Inger in an hour and a half. But you said this meeting wasn't to take more than an hour anyway, didn't you?"

He nodded.

"Then I'm free. My quarters are arranged, and I'm ready to go back on my old job in the morning."

"Fine," said the Commissioner. "There are things I wanted to discuss with you privately anyway. If we can't get through to Mantelish in another ten minutes, we'll go ahead with that. I would have liked to have Quillan here to fill us in with data about some of the top-level crooks in the Hub. They're a specialty of his. I don't know too much about them myself."

He paused. "That Lyad Ermetyne now," he said, "looks as if she either already is part of the main problem or is working very hard to get there. She's had a Tranest warship stationed here for the past two weeks. A thing called the *Aurora*."

Trigger was startled. "But warships aren't allowed in Manon System!"

"It isn't in the system. It's stationed a half light-year away, where it has a legal right to be. Nothing to worry about as such. It's just a heavy armed frigate, which is the limit Tranest is allowed to build. Since it's Lyad's private boat, I imagine it's been souped-up with everything they could throw in. Anyway, the fact that she sent it here ahead of her indicates she isn't just dropping in for a casual visit."

"She made that pretty clear herself!" Trigger said. "Why do you think she's being so open about it?"

He shrugged. "Might have a number of reasons. One could be that she'd get the beady eye anyway as soon as she showed up here. When Lyad goes anywhere, it's usually on business. After Quillan reported on your dinner party, I got all the information I could on her. The First

Lady stacks up as a tough cookie! Also smart. Most of those Ermetynes wind up being dead-brained by some loving relative, and apparently they have to know how to whip up a sharp brew of poison before they're let into kindergarten. Lyad's been top dog among them since she was eighteen—"

His head turned. A bell had begun pinging in the next room. He stood up.

"Probably Mantelish's outfit on the transmitter," he said. "I told them to call as soon as they located him." He stopped at the door. "Care for a drink, Trigger girl? You know where the stuff is."

"Not just now, thanks."

The Commissioner came back in a couple of minutes. "Darn fool got lost in a swamp! They found him finally, but he's too tired to come over now."

He sat down and scratched his chin thoughtfully. "Do you remember the time you passed out on *Harvest Moon?*" he asked.

Trigger looked at him, puzzled. "The time I what?"

"Passed out. Fainted. Went out cold."

"I? You're out of your mind, Holati! I never fainted in my life."

"Reason I asked," he said, "is that I've been told a spell in a rest cubicle—same thing as a rest cubicle anyway, only it's used for therapy—sometimes resolves amnesias."

"Amnesias! What *are* you talking about?"

The Commissioner said, "I'm talking about you. This is bound to be a jolt, Trigger girl. Might have been easier after a drink. But I'll just give it to you straight. About a week after Mantelish and his U-League crew first arrived here, you did pass out on one occasion while we were on *Harvest Moon* with them. And afterwards you didn't remember doing it."

"I didn't?" Trigger said weakly.

"No. I thought it might have cleared up, and you just

had some reason for not wanting to mention it." He got to his feet. "Like that drink now—before I go on with the details?"

She nodded.

Holati Tate brought her the drink and went on with the details. Trigger and he and a dozen or so of the first group of U-League investigators had been in what was now designated as Section 52 of *Harvest Moon*. The Commissioner was by himself, checking over some equipment which had been installed in one of the compartments. Holati had finished the check-up and was about to leave the area, when he saw Trigger lying on the floor in an adjoining compartment.

"You seemed to be in some kind of coma," he said. "I picked you up and put you into a chair by one of the survey screens, and was trying to get out a call to the ambulance boat when you suddenly opened your eyes. You looked at me and said, 'Oh, there you are! I was just going to go looking for you.'"

It was obvious that she didn't realize anything unusual had happened. Then he'd returned to Manon Planet with Trigger immediately, where she was checked over by Precol's medical staff. Physically there wasn't a thing wrong with her.

"And that," said Trigger, feeling a little frightened, "is something else I don't remember!"

"Well, you wouldn't," the Commissioner said. "You were fed a hypno-spray first. You went out for three hours. When you woke up, you thought you'd been having a good nap. Since the medics were sure you hadn't picked up some odd plasmoid infection, I wanted to know just what else had happened on *Harvest Moon*. One of those scientific big shots might also have used a hypno-spray on you, with the idea of turning you into a conditioned assistant for future shenanigans."

Trigger grinned faintly. "You do have a suspicious mind!" The grin faded. "Was that what they were going to find out in that mind-search interview on Maccadon I skipped out on?"

"It's one of the things they might have looked for," he agreed.

Trigger gazed at him very thoughtfully for a moment. "Well, I loused that deal up!" she remarked. "But why is everybody—" She shook her head. "Excuse me. Go on."

The Commissioner went on. "Old Doc Leeharvis was handling the hypnosis herself. She hit what she thought might be a mind-block when she tried to get you to remember what happened. We know now it wasn't a mind-block. But she wouldn't monkey with you any farther, and told me to get in an expert. So I called the Psychology Service's headquarters on Orado."

Trigger looked startled, then laughed. "The eggheads? You went right to the top there, didn't you?"

"Tried to," said Holati Tate. "It's a good idea when you want real service. They told me to stay calm and to say nothing to you. An expert would be shipped out promptly."

"Was he?"

"Yes."

Trigger's eyes narrowed a little. "Same old hypno-spray treatment?"

"Right," said Commissioner Tate. "He came, sprayed, investigated. Then he told me to stay calm, and went off looking puzzled."

"Puzzled?" she said.

"If I hadn't known before that experts come in all grades," the Commissioner said, "I'd know it now. That first one they sent was just sharp enough to realize there might be something involved in the case he wasn't getting. But that was all."

Trigger was silent a moment. "So there've been more of those investigations I don't know about!" she observed, her voice taking on an edge.

"Uh-huh," the Commissioner said cautiously.

"How many?"

"Seven."

Trigger flushed, straightened up, eyes blazing, and pronounced a very unladylike word.

"Excuse me," she added a moment later. "I got carried away."

"Perfectly all right," said the Commissioner.

"I've been getting just a bit fed up anyway," Trigger went on, voice and color still high, "with people knocking me for a loop one way or another whenever they happen to feel like it!"

"Don't blame you a bit," he said.

"And please don't think I don't appreciate your calling in all those experts. I do. It's just their sneaky, underhanded, secretive methods I don't go for!"

"Exactly how I feel about it," said the Commissioner.

Trigger stared at him suspiciously. "You're a pretty sneaky type yourself!" she said. "Well, excuse the blowup, Holati. They probably had some reason for it. Have they found out anything at all with all this spraying and investigating?"

"Oh, yes. They seem to have made considerable progress. The last report I had from them—about a month ago—shows that the original amnesia has been completely resolved."

Trigger looked surprised. "If it's been resolved," she said reasonably, "why don't I remember what happened?"

"You aren't supposed to become conscious of it before the final interview—I don't know the reason for that. But the memory is available now. On tap, so to speak. They'll give you a cue, and then you'll remember it."

"Just like that, eh?" She paused. "So the Psychology Service is Whatzzit."

"Whatzzit?" said the Commissioner.

She explained about Whatzzit. He grinned.

"Yes," he said. "They're the ones who've been giving the instructions, as far as you're concerned."

Trigger was silent a moment. "I've heard," she said, "the eggheads have terrific pull when they want to use it. You don't hear much about them otherwise. Let me think just a little."

"Go ahead," said Holati.

A minute ticked away.

"What it boils down to so far," Trigger said then, "is still pretty much what you told me on Maccadon. The Psychology Service thinks I know something that might help clear up the plasmoid problem. Or at least help explain it."

He nodded.

"And the people who've been trying to grab me very probably are doing it for exactly the same reason."

He nodded again. "That's almost certain."

"Do you think the eggheads might already have figured out what the connection is?"

The Commissioner shook his head. "If they had, we'd be doing something about it. The Federation Council is very nervous!"

"Well . . ." Trigger said. She pursed her lips. "That Lyad . . ." she said.

"What about her?"

"She tried to hire me," said Trigger. "Major Quillan reported it, I suppose?"

"Sure."

"And it wouldn't be just to steal some stupid plasmoid. Especially since you say a number of small ones are already available. Then there're the ones that raiders picked up in the Hub. She probably has a collection by now."

He nodded. "Probably."

"She seems to know quite a bit about what's been going on."

"Very likely she does."

"Let's grab her!" said Trigger. "We can do it quietly. And she's too big to be mind-blocked. We'd get part of the answer. Perhaps all of it!"

Something flared briefly in the Commissioner's small gray eyes. He reached over and patted her knee.

"You're a girl after my own heart, Trigger," he said. "I'm for it. But half the Council would have fainted dead away if they'd heard you make that suggestion!"

"They're as touchy as that?" she asked, disappointed.

"Yes—and you can't quite blame them. Fumbles could be pretty bad. When it comes to someone around Lyad's level, our own group is restricted to defensive counteraction. If we get evidence against her, it'll be up to the diplomats to decide what's to be done about it. Tactfully. We wouldn't be further involved."

Trigger nodded, watching him. "Go on."

"Well, defensive counteraction can cover a lot of things, of course. If we actually run into the First Lady while were engaged in it, we'll hold her—as long as we can. And from all accounts, now that she's showed up to take personal charge of things around here, we can expect some very fast, very direct action from Lyad."

"How fast?"

"My own guess," said the Commissioner, "would be around a week. If she hasn't moved by then, we might help things along a little."

"Make a few of those openings for her, eh? Well, that doesn't sound too bad." Trigger reflected. "Then there's Point Number Two," she said.

"What's that?"

She grimaced. "I'm not real keen on it," she confessed, "but I think we'd better do something about that interview with Whatzzit I ducked out of. If they still want to talk to me—"

"They do. Very much so."

"What's that business about their saying it was okay now for me to go on to Manon?"

Commissioner Tate tugged gently at his left ear lobe. "Frankly," he said, "That's something that shook me a little."

"Shook you? Why?"

"It's that matter of experts coming in grades. The upper ranks in the Psychology Service are extremely busy people, I understand. After your first interview we were shifted upward promptly. A couple of middling high-bracket investigators took over for a while. But after the fourth interview I was told I'd have to bring you to the Hub to let somebody really competent handle the next stage of whatever they've been doing. They said they couldn't spare anybody of that caliber for a trip to Manon."

"Was *that* the real reason we went to Maccadon?" Trigger asked, startled.

"Sure. But we still hadn't got anywhere near the Service's top level then. As I get it, their topnotchers don't spend much time on individual cases. They keep busy with things on the scale of our more bothersome planetary cultures—and there are supposed to be only a hundred or so of them in that category. So I was more than a little surprised when the Service informed me finally one of those people was coming to Maccadon to conduct your ninth interview."

"One of the real eggheads!" Trigger smiled nervously. "And then I just took off! They can't have too good an opinion of me at the moment, you know."

"Apparently that didn't upset them in the least," the Commissioner said. "They told me to stay calm and make sure you got to Manon all right. Then they said they had a ship operating in this area, and they'd route it over to Manon after you arrived here."

"A ship?" Trigger asked.

"I've seen a few of their ships—they looked like over-sized flying mountains. Camouflage jobs. What they actually are is spacegoing superlaboratories, from what I've heard. This one has a couple of those topnotchers on board, and one of them will take you on. It's due here in a day or so."

Trigger had paled somewhat. "You know," she said, "I feel a little shaken myself now."

"I'm not surprised," said the Commissioner.

She shook her head. "Well, if they're topnotchers, they must know what they're doing." She gave him a smile. "Looks like I'm something extremely unusual! Like a bothersome planetary culture . . . Weak joke," she added.

The Commissioner ignored the weak joke. "There's another thing," be said thoughtfully.

"What's that?"

"When I mentioned your reluctance about being interviewed, they told me not to worry about it—that you wouldn't try to duck out again. That's why I was surprised when you brought up the matter of the interview yourself just now."

"Now that is odd," Trigger admitted after a pause. "How would they know?"

"Right," he said. He sighed. "Guess we're both a little out of our depth there. I've come close to getting impatient with them a few times—had the feeling they were stalling me off and holding back information. But presumably they do know what they're doing." He glanced at his watch. "That hour's about up now, by the way."

"Well, if there's something else that should be discussed I can break my dinner date," Trigger said, somewhat reluctantly. "I had a chance to talk with Brule at the spaceport for a while, when we came in this morning."

"I wasn't suggesting that," said Holati. "There still are things to be discussed, but a few hours one way or the other won't make any difference. We'll get together again around lunch tomorrow. Then you'll be filled in pretty well on all the main points of this business."

Trigger nodded. "Fine."

"What I had in mind right now was that the Service people suggested having you look over their last report on you after your arrival. You'd have just enough time for that before going to keep your date. Care to do it?"

"I certainly would!" Trigger said.

The transmitter signaled for attention while she was studying the report. Holati Tate went off to answer it. The report was rather lengthy, and Trigger was still going over it when he got back. He sat down again and waited.

When she looked up finally, he asked, "Can you make much sense of it?"

"Not very much," Trigger admitted. "It just states what seems to have happened. Not how or why. Apparently they did get me to develop total recall of that knocked-out period in the last interview—I even reported hearing you moving around in the next compartment. Then, some time before I actually fell down," she continued, "I was apparently already in that mysterious coma. Getting deeper into it. It started when I walked away from Mantelish's group, without having any particular reason for doing it. I just walked. Then I was in another compartment by myself and still walking, and the stuff kept getting deeper, until I lost physical control of myself and fell down. Then I lay there a while until you came down that aisle and saw me. And after you'd picked me up and put me in that chair—just like that, everything clears up! Except that I don't remember what happened and think I've just left Mantelish to go looking for you. I don't even wonder how I happen to be sitting there in a chair!"

The Commissioner smiled briefly. "That's right. You didn't."

Her slim fingers tapped the pages of the report, the green stone in the ring he'd given her to wear reflecting little flashes of light. "They seem quite positive that nobody else came near me during that period. And that nobody had used a hypno-spray on me or shot a hypodermic pellet into me—anything like that—before the seizure or whatever it was came on. How do you suppose they could be so sure of that?"

"I wouldn't know," Holati said. "But I think we might as well assume they're right."

"I suppose so. What it seems to boil down to is they're saying I was undergoing something like a very much slowed-down, very profound emotional shock—source still undetermined, but profound enough to knock me completely out for a while. Only they also say that—for a whole list of reasons—it couldn't possibly have been an emotional shock after all! And when the effect left, it went instantaneously. That would be just the reverse to the pattern of an emotional shock, wouldn't it?"

"Yes," he said. "That occurred to me too, but it didn't explain anything to me. Possibly it's explained something to the Psychology Service."

"Well," Trigger said, "it's certainly all very odd. Very disagreeable, too!" She laid the report down on the arm of her chair and looked at the Commissioner. "Guess I'd better run now," she said. "See you around lunchtime, Commissioner."

"Right, Trigger," he said, getting up.

He closed the door behind her and went back to the transmitter. He looked rather unhappy.

"Yes?" said a voice in the transmitter.

"She just left," Commissioner Tate said. "Get on the beam and stay there!"

18

"Well," Trigger said, regarding Brule critically, "I just meant to say that you're getting the least little bit plump here and there, under all that tan. I'll admit it doesn't show yet when you're dressed."

Brule smiled tolerantly. In silver swimming trunks and

sandals, he was obviously a very handsome hunk of young man, and he knew it. So did Trigger. So did a quartet of predatory young females eyeing them speculatively from a table only twenty feet away.

"I've come swimming here quite a bit since they opened the Center," be said. He flexed his right arm and regarded his biceps complacently. "That's just streamlined muscle you're looking at, sweetheart!"

Trigger reached over and poked the biceps with a fingertip. "Muscle?" she said, smiling at him. "It dents. See?"

He clasped his other hand over hers and squeezed it lightly.

"Oh, golly, Brule!" she said happily. "I'm so glad I'm back!"

He gave her the smile. "You're not the only glad one!"

She looked around, humming softly. They were having dinner in one of the Grand Commerce Center's restaurants. This one happened to be beneath the surface of the artificial swimming lake installed in the Center—a giant grotto surrounded by green-gold chasms of water on every side. Underwater swimmers and bottom walkers moved past beyond the wide windows. A streak of silvery swiftness against a dark red canyon wall before her was trying to keep away from a trio of pursuing spear fishermen. Even the lake fish were Hub imports, advertised as such by the Center.

Her eyes widened suddenly. "Hey!" she said.

"What?"

"That group of people up there!"

Brule looked. "What about them?"

"No suits, you idiot!"

He grinned. "Oh, a lot of them do that. Okay by Federation law, you know. And seeing Manon's so close to becoming open Federation territory, we haven't tried to enforce minor Precol regulations much lately."

"Well—" Trigger began. He was still smiling. "Have *you* been doing it?" she inquired suspiciously.

"Swimming in the raw? Certainly. Depends on the company. If you weren't such a little prude, I'd have suggested it tonight. Want to try it later?"

Trigger colored. Prude again, she thought. "Nope," she said. "There are limits."

He patted her cheek. "On you it would look cute."

She shook her head, aware of a small fluster of guilt. There had been considerably less actual coverage in the Beldon costume than there was in the minute two-piece counterpart to Brule's silver trunks she wore at the moment. She'd have to tell Brule about the Beldon stunt, since it was more than likely he'd hear about it from others—Nelauk Pluly, for one.

But not now. Things were getting just a little delicate along that line at the moment.

"Leave us change the subject, pig," she said cheerfully. "Tell me what else you've been doing besides acquiring a gorgeous tan."

A couple of hours later, things began to get delicate again. Same subject. Trigger had been somewhat startled at the spaceport when Brule told her he had shifted his living quarters to a Center apartment, and that a large number of Precol's executives were taking similar liberties. Holati's stand-in, Acting Commissioner Chelly, apparently hadn't been too successful at keeping up personnel discipline.

She hadn't said anything. It was true that Manon was still a precolonial planet only as a technicality. They didn't know quite as much about it as they had to know before it could be officially released for unrestricted settling, but by now there was considerable excuse for loosening up on many of the early precautionary measures. For one thing, there were just so many Hub people around nowadays that it would have been a practical impossibility to enforce all Precol rules.

What bothered her mainly about the business of Brule's Center apartment was that it might make the end of the evening less pleasant than she wanted it to be. Brule had become the least bit swacked. Not at all offensively, but he tended to get pretty ambitious then. And during the past few hours she'd noticed that something had changed in his attitude toward her. He'd always been confident of himself when it came to women, so it wasn't that. It was perhaps, Trigger thought, like an unspoken ultimatum along those lines. And she'd felt herself freezing up a little in response to the thought.

The apartment was very beautiful. Nelauk, she guessed. Or somebody else like that. Brule's taste was good, but he simply wouldn't have thought of a lot of the details here. Neither, Trigger conceded, would she. Some of the details looked pretty expensive.

He came back into the living room in a dressing gown, carrying a couple of drinks. It was going to get awkward, all right.

"Like it?" he asked, waving a hand around.

"It's beautiful," Trigger said honestly. She smiled. She sipped at the drink and placed it on the arm of her chair. "Somebody like an interior decorator help you with it?"

Brule laughed and sat down opposite her with his drink. The laugh had sounded the least bit annoyed. "You're right," he said. "How did you guess?"

"You never went in for art exactly," she said. "This room is a work of art."

He nodded. He didn't look annoyed any more. He looked smug. "It is, isn't it?" he said. "It didn't even cost so very much. You just have to know how, that's all."

"Know how about what?" Trigger asked.

"Know how to live," Brule said. "Know what it's all about. Then it's easy."

He was looking at her. The smile was there. The warm, rich voice was there. All the old charm was there. It was Brule. And it wasn't. Trigger realized she was twisting

her hands together. She looked down at them. The little
jewel in the ring Holati Tate had given her to wear
blinked back with crimson gleamings.

Crimson!

She drew a long, slow breath.

"Brule," she said.

"Yes?" said Brule. At the edge of her vision she saw
the smile turn eager.

Trigger said, "Give me the plasmoid." She raised her
eyes and looked at him. He'd stopped smiling.

Brule looked back at her a long time. At least it
seemed a long time to Trigger. The smile suddenly
returned.

"What's that supposed to mean?" he asked, almost
plaintively. "If it's a joke, I don't get it."

"I just said," Trigger repeated carefully, "give me the
plasmoid. The one you stole."

Brule took a swallow of his drink and put the glass
down on the floor. "Aren't you feeling well?" he asked
solicitously.

"Give me the plasmoid."

"Honestly, Trigger." He shook his head. He laughed.
"What *are* you talking about?"

"A plasmoid. The one you took. The one you've got
here."

Brule stood up. He studied her face, blinking, puzzled.
Then he laughed, richly. "Trigger, I've fed you one drink
too many! I never thought you'd let me do it. Be sensible now—if I had a plasmoid here, how could you tell?"

"I can tell. Brule, I don't know how you took it or why
you took it. I don't really care." And that was a lie, Trigger
thought dismally. She cared. "Just give it to me, and I'll
put it back. We can talk about it afterwards."

"Afterwards," Brule said. The laugh came again, but
it sounded a little hollow. He moved a step toward her,
stopped again, hands on his hips. "Trigger," he said
soberly, "if I've ever done anything you mightn't approve

of, it was done for both of us. You realize that, don't you?"

"I think I do," Trigger said warily. "Yes. Give it to me, Brule."

Brule leaped forward. She slid sideways out of the chair to the floor as he leaped. She was crying inside, she realized vaguely. Brule was going to kill her now, if he could.

She caught his left foot with both hands as he came down, and twisted viciously.

Brule shouted something. His red, furious face swept by above. He thumped to the floor beside her, one leg flung across her thighs, gripping.

In colonial school Brule had received the same basic training in unarmed combat that Trigger had. He was close to eighty pounds heavier than Trigger, and it was still mostly muscle. But it was nearly four years now since be had bothered himself with drills.

And he hadn't been put through Mihul's advanced students' courses lately.

He stayed conscious a little less than nine seconds.

The plasmoids were in a small electronic safe built into a music cabinet. The stamp to the safe was in Brule's billfold.

There were three of them, about the size of mice, starfish-shaped lumps of translucent, hard, colorless jelly. They didn't move.

Trigger laid them in a row on the polished surface of a small table, and blinked at them for a moment from a streaming left eye. The right eye was swelling shut. Brule had got in one wild wallop somewhere along the line. She picked up a small jar, emptied some spicy-smelling, crumby contents out on the table, dropped the plasmoids inside, closed the jar and left the apartment with it. Brule was just beginning to stir and groan.

Commissioner Tate hadn't retired yet. He let her in without a word. Trigger put the jar down on a table.

"Three of your nuts and bolts in there," she said.

He nodded. "I know."

"I thought you did," said Trigger. "Thanks for the quick cure. But right at the moment I don't like you very much, Holati. We can talk about that in the morning."

"All right," said the Commissioner. He hesitated. "Anything that should be taken care of before then?"

"It's been taken care of," Trigger said. "One of our employees has been moderately injured. I dialed the medics to go pick him up. They have. Good night."

"You might let me do something for that eye," he said.

Trigger shook her head. "I've got stuff in my quarters."

She locked herself into her quarters, got out a jar of quick-heal and anointed the eye and a few other minor bruises. She put the jar away, made a mechanical check of the newly installed anti-intrusion devices, dimmed the lights and climbed into her bunk. For the next twenty minutes she wept violently. Then she fell asleep.

An hour or so later, she turned over on her side and said without opening her eyes, "Come, Fido!"

The plasmoid purse appeared just above the surface of the bunk between Trigger's pillow and the wall. It dropped with a small thump and stood balanced uncertainly. Trigger slept on.

Five minutes after that, the purse opened itself. A little later again, Trigger suddenly shifted her shoulder uneasily, frowned and made a little half-angry, half-whimpering cry. Then her face smoothed out. Her breathing grew quiet and slow.

Major Heslet Quillan of the Subspace Engineers came breezing into Manon Planet's spaceport very early in the morning. A Precol aircar picked him up and let him out on a platform of the Headquarters dome near Commissioner Tate's offices. Quillan was handed on toward the offices through a string of underlings and reached the door just as it opened and Trigger Argee stepped through.

He grasped her cordially by the shoulders and cried out a cheery hello. Trigger made a soft growling sound in her throat. Her left hand chopped right, her right hand chopped left. Quillan grunted and let go.

"What's the matter?" he inquired, stepping back. He rubbed one arm, then the other.

Trigger looked at him, growled again, walked past him, and disappeared through another door, her back very straight.

"Come in, Quillan," Commissioner Tate said from within the office.

Quillan went in and closed the door behind him. "What did I do?" he asked bewilderedly.

"Nothing much," said Holati. "You just share the misfortune of being a male human being. At the moment, Trigger's against 'em. She blew up the Brule Inger setup last night."

"Oh!" Quillan sat down. "I never did like that idea much," he said.

The Commissioner shrugged. "You don't know the girl yet. If I'd hauled Inger in, she would never have really forgiven me for it. I had to let her handle it herself. Actually she understands that."

"How did it go?"

"Her cover reported it was one hell of a good fight for some seconds. If you'd looked closer, you might have just spotted the traces of the shiner Inger gave her. It was a beaut' last night."

Quillan went white.

"But if you're thinking of having a chat with Inger *re* that part of it," the Commissioner went on, "forget it." He glanced at a report form from the medical department on his desk. "Dislocated shoulder . . . broken thumb . . . moderate concussion. And so on. It was the throat punch that finished the matter. He can't talk yet. We'll call it square."

Quillan grunted. "What are you going to do with him now?"

"Nothing," Holati said. "We know his contacts. Why bother? He'll resign end of the month."

Quillan cleared his throat and glanced at the door. "I suppose she'll want him put up for rehabilitation—seemed pretty fond of him."

"Relax, son," said the Commissioner. "Trigger's an individualist. If Inger goes up for rehabilitation, it will be because he wants it. And he doesn't, of course. Being a slob suits him fine. He's just likely to be more cautious about it in the future. So we'll let him go his happy way. Now—let's get down to business. How does Pluly's yacht harem stack up?"

A reminiscent smile spread slowly over Quillan's face. He shook his head. "Awesome, brother!" he said. "Plain awesome!"

"Pick up anything useful?"

"Nothing definite. But whenever Belchy comes out of the esthetic trances, he's a worried man. Count him in."

"For sure?"

"Yes."

"All right. He's in. Crack the *Aurora* yet?"

"No," said Quillan. "The girls are working on it, But the Ermetyne keeps a mighty taut ship and a mighty disciplined crew. We'll have a couple of those boys wrapped up in another week. No earlier."

"A week might be soon enough," said the Commissioner. "It also might not."

"I know it," said Quillan. "But the *Aurora* does look a little bit obvious, doesn't she?"

"Yes," Holati Tate admitted. "Just a little bit."

19

By lunchtime, Trigger was acting almost cordial again. "I've got the Precol job lined up," she reported to Holati Tate. "I'll handle it like I used to, whenever I can. When I can't, the kids will shift in automatically." The kids were the five assistants among whom her duties had been divided in her absence.

"Major Quillan called me up to Mantelish's lab around ten," she went on. "The prof wanted to see Repulsive, so I took him up there. Then it turned out Mantelish wanted to take Repulsive along on a field trip this afternoon."

Holati looked startled. "He can't do that, and he knows it!" He reached for the desk transmitter.

"Don't bother, Commissioner. I told Mantelish I'd been put in charge of Repulsive, and that he'd lose an arm if he tried to walk out of the lab with him."

Holati cleared his throat. "I see! How did Mantelish react?"

"Oh, he huffed a bit. Like he does. Then he calmed down and agreed he could get by without Repulsive out there. So we stood by while he measured and weighed the thing, and so on. After that he got friendly and said you'd asked him to fill me in on current plasmoid theory."

"So I did," said Holati. "Did he?"

"He tried, I think. But it's like you say. I got lost in about three sentences and never caught up." She looked curiously at the Commissioner. "I didn't have a chance to talk to Major Quillan alone, so I'm wondering why Mantelish was told the I-Fleets in the Vishni area are hunting for planets with plasmoids on them. I thought you felt he was too wooly-minded to be trusted."

"We couldn't keep that from him very well," Holati said. "He was the boy who thought of it."

"You didn't have to tell him they'd found some possibles, did you?"

"We did, unfortunately. He's had those plasmoid detectors of his for about a month, but he didn't happen to think of mentioning them. The reason he was to come back to Manon originally was to sort over the stuff the Fleets have been sending back here. It's as weird a collection of low-grade life-forms as I've ever seen, but not plasmoid. Mantelish went into a temper and wanted to know why the idiots weren't using detectors."

"Oh, Lord!" Trigger said.

"That's what it's like when you're working with him," said the Commissioner. "We started making up detectors wholesale and rushing them out there, but the new results haven't come in yet."

"Well, that explains it." Trigger looked down at the desk a moment, then glanced up and met the Commissioner's eye. She colored slightly.

"Incidentally," she said, "I did take the opportunity to apologize to Major Quillan for clipping him a couple this morning. I shouldn't have done that."

"He didn't seem offended," said Holati.

"No, not really," she agreed.

"And I explained to him that you had very good reason to feel disturbed."

"Thanks," said Trigger. "By the way, was he really a smuggler at one time? And a hijacker?"

"Yes—very successful at it. It's excellent cover for some phases of Intelligence work. As I heard it, though, Quillan happened to scramble up one of the Hub's nastier dope rings in the process, and was broken two grades in rank."

"Broken?" Trigger said. "Why?"

"Unwarranted interference with a political situation. The Scouts are rough about that. You're supposed to see those things. Sometimes you don't. Sometimes you do and go ahead anyway. They may pat you on the back privately, but they also give you the axe."

"I see," she said. She smiled.

His desk transmitter buzzed and Trigger took it on an earphone extension.

"Argee," she said. She listened a moment. "All right. Coming over." She stood up, replacing the earphone. "Office tangle," she explained. "Guess they feel I'm fluffing off, now I'm back. I'll get back here as soon as it's straightened out. Oh, by the way."

"Yes?"

"The Psychology Service ship messaged in during the morning. It'll arrive some time tomorrow and wants a station assigned to it outside the system, where it won't be likely to attract attention. Are they really as huge as all that?"

"I've seen one or two that were bigger," the Commissioner said. "But not much."

"When they're stationed, they'll send someone over in a shuttle to pick me up."

The Commissioner nodded. "I'll check on the arrangements for that. The idea of the interview still bothering you?"

"Well, I'd sooner it wasn't necessary," Trigger admitted. "But I guess it is." She grinned briefly. "Anyway, I'll be able to tell my grandchildren some day that I once talked to one of the real eggheads!"

The Psychology Service woman who stood up from a couch as Trigger came into the small spaceport lounge next evening looked startlingly similar to Major Quillan's *Dawn City* assistant, Gaya. Standing, you could see that she was considerably more slender than Gaya. She had all of Gaya's good looks.

"The name is Pilch," she said. She looked at Trigger and smiled. It was a good smile, Trigger thought; not the professional job she'd expected. "And everyone who knows Gaya," she went on, "thinks we must be twins."

Trigger laughed. "Aren't you?"

"Just first cousins." The voice was all right, too—clear and easy. Trigger felt herself relax somewhat. "That's one reason they picked me to come and get you. We're already almost acquainted. Another is that I've been assigned to take you through the preliminary work for your interview after we get to the ship. We can chat a bit on the way, and that should make it seem less disagreeable. Boat's in the speedboat park over there."

They started down a short hallway to the park area. "Just how disagreeable is it going to be?" Trigger asked.

"Not at all bad in your case. You're conditioned to the processes more than you know. Your interviewer will just pick up where the last job ended and go on from there. It's when you have to work down through barriers that you have a little trouble."

Trigger was still mulling that over as she stepped ahead of Pilch into the smaller of two needle-nosed craft parked side by side. Pilch followed her in and closed the lock behind them. "The other one's a combat job," she remarked. "Our escort. Commissioner Tate made very sure we had one, too!" She motioned Trigger to a low soft seat that took up half the space of the tiny room behind the lock, sat down beside her and spoke at a wall pickup. "All set. Let's ride!"

Blue-green tinted sky moved past them in the little room's viewer screen; then a tilted landscape flashed by and dropped back. Pilch winked at Trigger. "Takes off like a scared yazong, that boy! He'll race the combat job to the ship. About those barriers. Supposing I told you something like this. There's no significant privacy invasion in this line of work. We go directly to the specific information we're looking for and deal only with that. Your private life, your personal thoughts, remain secret, sacred and inviolate. What would you say?"

"I'd say you're a liar," Trigger said promptly.

"Supposing I told you very sincerely that no recording

will be made of any little personal glimpses we may get?"

"Lying again."

"Right again," said Pilch. "You've been scanned about as thoroughly as anyone ever gets to be outside of a total therapy. Your personal secrets are already on record, and since I'm doing most of the preparatory work with you, I've studied all the significant-looking ones very closely. You're a pretty good person, for my money. All right?"

Trigger studied her face uncomfortably. Hardly all right, but . . .

"I guess I can stand it," she said. "As far as you're concerned, anyway." She hesitated. "What's the egghead like?"

"Old Cranadon?" said Pilch. "You won't mind her a bit, I think. Very motherly old type. Let's get through the preparations first, and then I'll introduce you to her. If you think it would make you more comfortable, I'll just stay around while she's working. I've sat in on her interviews before. How's that?"

"Sounds better," Trigger said. She did feel a good deal relieved.

They slid presently into a tunnel-like lock of the space vehicle Holati Tate had described as a flying mountain. From what Trigger could see of it in the guide lights on the approach, it did rather closely resemble a very large mountain of the craggier sort. They went through a series of lifts, portals and passages, and wound up in a small and softly lit room with a small desk, a very large couch, a huge wall-screen, and assorted gadgetry. Pilch sat down at the desk and invited Trigger to make herself comfortable on the couch.

Trigger lay down on the couch. She had a very brief sensation of falling gently through dimness.

Half an hour later she sat up on the couch. Pilch switched on a desk light and looked at her thoughtfully.

Trigger blinked. Then her eyes widened, first with surprise, then in comprehension.

"Liar!" she said.

"Hm-m-m," said Pilch. "Yes."

"That *was* the interview!"

"True."

"Then you're the egghead!"

"Tcha!" said Pilch. "Well, I believe I can modestly describe myself as being something like that. Yes. You're another, by the way. We're just smart about different things. Not so very different."

"You were smart about this," Trigger said. She swung her legs off the couch and regarded Pilch dubiously. Pilch grinned.

"Took most of the disagreeableness out of it, didn't it?"

"Yes," Trigger admitted, "it did. Now what do we do?"

"Now," said Pilch, "I'll explain."

The thing that had caught their attention was a quite simple process. It just happened to be a process the Psychology Service hadn't observed under those particular circumstances before.

"Here's what our investigators had the last time," Pilch said. "Lines and lines of stuff, of course. But there's a simple continuity which makes it clear. No need to go into details. As classes—you've stepped now and then on things that squirmed or squashed. Bad smells. Etcetera. How do you feel about plasmoids?"

Trigger wrinkled her nose. "I just think they're unpleasant things. All except—"

Oops! She checked herself.

"—Repulsive," said Pilch. "It's quite all right about Repulsive. We've been informed of that supersecret little item you're guarding. If we hadn't been told, we'd know now, of course. Go ahead."

"Well, it's odd!" Trigger remarked thoughtfully. "I just

said I thought plasmoids were rather unpleasant. But that's the way I used to feel about them. I don't feel that way now."

"Except again," said Pilch, "for that little monstrosity on the ship. If it was a plasmoid. You rather suspect it was, don't you?"

Trigger nodded. "That would be pretty bad!"

"Very bad," said Pilch. "Plasmoids generally, you feel about them now as you feel about potatoes . . . rocks . . . neutral things like that?"

"That's about it," Trigger said. She still looked puzzled.

"We'll go over what seems to have changed your attitude there in a minute or so. Here's another thing—" Pilch paused a moment, then said, "Night before last, about an hour after you'd gone to bed, you had a very light touch of the same pattern of mental blankness you experienced on that plasmoid station."

"While I was asleep?" Trigger said, startled.

"That's right. Comparatively very light, very brief. Five or six minutes. Dream activity, etcetera, smooths out. Some blocking on various sense lines. Then, normal sleep until about five minutes before you woke up. At that point there may have been another minute touch of the same pattern. Too brief to be actually definable. A few seconds at most. The point is that this is a continuing process."

She looked at Trigger a moment. "Not particularly alarmed, are you?"

"No," said Trigger. "It just seems very odd."

"Yes, I know."

Pilch was silent for some moments again, considering the wall-screen as if thinking about something connected with it.

"Well, we'll drop that for now," she said finally. "Let me tell you what's been happening these months, starting with that first amnesia-covered blankout on *Harvest*

Moon. When you got the first Service check-up at Commissioner Tate's demand, there was very little to go on. The amnesia didn't lift immediately—not very unusual. The blankout might be interesting because of the circumstances. Otherwise the check showed you were in a good deal better than normal condition. Outside of total therapy processes—and I believe you know that's a long haul—there wasn't much to be done for you, and no particular reason to do it. So an amnesia-resolving process was initiated and you were left alone for a while.

"Actually something already was going on at the time, but it wasn't spotted until your next check. What it's amounted to has been a relatively minor but extremely precise and apparently purposeful therapy process. The very interesting thing is that this orderly little process appears to have been going on all by itself. And that just doesn't happen. You disturbed now?"

Trigger nodded. "A little. Mainly I'm wondering why somebody wants me to not-dislike plasmoids."

"So am I wondering," said Pilch. "Somebody does, obviously. And a very slick somebody it is. We'll find out by and by. Incidentally, this particular part of the business has been concluded. Apparently, our 'somebody' doesn't intend to make you wild for plasmoids. It's enough that you don't dislike them."

Trigger smiled. "I can't see anyone making me wild for the things, whatever they tried!"

Pilch nodded. "Could be done," she said. "Rather easily. You'd be bats, of course. But that's very different from a simple neutralizing process like the one we've been discussing . . . Now here's something else. You were pretty unhappy about this business for a while. That wasn't 'somebody's' fault. That was us.

"Your investigators could have interfered with the little therapy process in a number of ways. That wouldn't have taught them a thing, so they didn't. But on your third check they found something else. Again it wasn't in the least obtrusive; in someone else they mightn't have given it a second look. But it didn't fit at all with your major personality patterns. You wanted to stay where you were."

"Stay where I was?"

"In the Manon System."

"Oh!" Trigger flushed a little. "Well—"

"I know. Let's go on a moment. We had this inharmonious inclination. So we told Commissioner Tate to bring you to the Hub and keep you there, to see what would happen. And on Maccadon, in just a few weeks, you'd begun working that moderate inclination to be back in the Manon System up to a dandy first-rate compulsion."

Trigger licked her lips. "I—"

"Sure," said Pilch. "You had to have a good sensible reason. You gave yourself one."

"Well!"

"Oh, you were fond of that young man, all right. But that was the first time you hadn't been able to stand a couple of months away from him. It was also the first time you'd started worrying about competition. You now had your justification. And we," Pilch said darkly, "had a fine, solid compulsion with no doubt very revealing ramifications to it to work on. Just one thing wrong with that, Trigger. You don't have the compulsion any more."

"Oh?"

"You don't even," said Pilch, "have the original moderate inclination. Now one might have some suspicions there! But we'll let them ride for the moment."

She did something on the desk. The huge wall-screen suddenly lit up. A soft, amber-glowing plane of blankness, with a suggestion of receding depths within it.

"Last night, shortly before you woke up," Pilch said, "you had a dream. Actually you had a series of dreams during the night which seem pertinent here. But the earlier ones were rather vague preliminary structures. In one way and another, their content is included in this final symbol grouping. Let's see what we can make of them."

A shape appeared on the screen.

Trigger started, then laughed.

"What do you think of it?" Pilch asked.

"A little green man!" she said. "Well, it could be a sort of counterpart to the little yellow thing on the ship, couldn't it? The good little dwarf and the very bad little dwarf."

"Could be," said Pilch. "How do you feel about the notion?"

"Good plasmoids and bad plasmoids?" Trigger shook her head. "No. It doesn't feel right."

"Right," Pilch said. "Let's see what you can do with this one."

Trigger was silent for almost a minute before she said in a subdued voice, "I just get what it shows. It doesn't seem to mean anything?"

"What does it show?"

"Laughing giants stamping on a farm. A tiny sort of farm. It looks like it might be the little green man's farm. No, wait. It's not his! But it belongs to other little green people."

"How do you feel about that?"

"Well—I hate those giants!" Trigger said. "They're cruel. And they laugh about being cruel."

"Are you afraid of them?"

Trigger blinked at the screen for a few seconds. "No," she said in a low, sleepy voice. "Not yet."

Pilch was silent a moment. She said then, "One more."

Trigger looked and frowned. Presently she said, "I have a feeling that does mean something. But all I get is that it's the faces of two clocks. On one of them the hands are going around very fast. And on the other they go around slowly."

"Yes," Pilch said. She waited a little. "No other thought

about those clocks? Just that they should mean something?"

Trigger shook her head. "That's all."

Pilch's hand moved on the desk again. The wall-screen went blank, and the light in the little room brightened slowly. Pilch's face was reflective.

"That will have to do for now," she said. "Trigger, this ship is working on an urgent job somewhere else. We'll have to go back and finish that job. But I'll be able to return to Manon in about ten days, and then we'll have another session. And I think that will get this little mystery cleared up."

"All of it?"

"All of it, I'd say. The whole pattern seems to be moving into view. More details will show up in the ten-day interval; and one more cautious boost then should bring it out in full."

Trigger nodded. "That's good news. I've been getting a little fed up with being a kind of walking enigma."

"Don't blame you at all," Pilch said, sounding almost exactly like Commissioner Tate. "Incidentally, you're a busy lady at present, but if you do have half an hour to spare from time to time, you might just sit down comfortably somewhere and listen to yourself thinking. The way things are going, that should bring quite a bit of information to view."

Trigger looked doubtful. "Listen to myself thinking?"

"You'll find yourself getting the knack of it rather quickly," Pilch said. She smiled. "Just head off in that general direction whenever you find the time, and don't work too hard at it. Are there any questions now before we start back to Manon?"

Trigger studied her a moment. "There's one thing I'd like to be sure about," she said. "But I suppose you people have your problems with Security too."

"Who doesn't?" said Pilch. "You're secure enough for me. Fire away."

"All right," Trigger said. "So I am involved with the plasmoid mess?"

"You're right in the middle of it, Trigger. That's definite. In just what way is something we should be able to determine next session."

Pilch turned off the desk light and stood up. "I always hate to run off and leave something half finished like this," she admitted, "but I'll have to run anyway. The plasmoids are nowhere near the head of the Federation's problem list at present. They're just coming up mighty fast."

20

When Trigger reached her office next morning, she learned that the Psychology Service ship had moved out of the Manon area within an hour after she'd been returned to the Headquarters dome the night before.

None of the members of the plasmoid team were around. The Commissioner, who had a poor opinion of sleep, had been up for the past three hours; he'd left word Trigger could reach him, if necessary, in the larger of his two ships, parked next to the dome in Precol Port. Presumably he had the ship sealed up and was sitting in the transmitter cabinet, swapping messages with the I-Fleets in the Vishni area. He was likely to be at that for hours more. Professor Mantelish hadn't yet got back from his latest field trip, and Major Heslet Quillan just wasn't there.

It looked, Trigger decided, not at all reluctantly, like a good day to lean into her Precol job a bit. She told the staff to pitch everything not utterly routine her way, and leaned.

A set of vitally important reports from Precol's Giant

Planet Survey Squad had been mislaid somewhere around
Headquarters during yesterday's conferences. She soothed
down the GP Squad and instituted a check search. A
team of Hub ecologists, who had decided for themselves
that outworld booster shots weren't required on Manon,
called in nervously from a polar station to report that their
hair was falling out. Trigger tapped the "Manon Fever"
button on her desk, and suggested toupees.

The ecologists were displeased. A medical emergency
skip-boat zoomed out of the dome to go to their rescue;
and Trigger gave it its directions while dialing for the
medical checker who'd allowed the visitors to avoid their
shots. She had a brief chat with the young man, and left
him twitching as the GP Squad came back on to inquire
whether the reports had found yet. Trigger began
to get a comfortable feeling of being back in the good
old groove.

Then a message from the Medical Department
popped out on her desk. It was addressed to Commissioner Tate and stated that Brule Inger was now
able to speak again.

Trigger frowned, sighed, bit her lip and thought a
moment. She dialed for Doctor Leehaven. "Got your
message," she said. "How's he doing?"

"All right," the old medic said.

"Has he said anything?"

"No. He's scared. If he could get up the courage, he'd
ask for a personnel lawyer."

"Yes, I imagine. Tell him this then—from the Commissioner; not from me—there'll be no charges, but
Precol expects his resignation, end of the month."

"That on the level?" Doctor Leehaven demanded
incredulously.

"Of course."

The doctor snorted. "You people are getting soft-
headed! But I'll tell him."

The morning went on. Trigger was suspiciously

studying a traffic control note stating that a Devagas missionary ship had checked in and berthed at the spaceport when the GC Center's management called in to report, with some nervousness, that the Center's much advertised meteor-repellent roof had just flipped several dozen tons of falling Moon Belt material into the spaceport area. Most of it, unfortunately, had dropped around and upon a Devagas missionary ship.

"Not damaged, is it?" she asked.

The Center said no, but the Missionary Captain insisted on speaking to the person in charge here. To whom should they refer him?

"Refer him to me," Trigger said expectantly. She switched on the vision screen.

The Missionary Captain was a tall, gray-haired, gray-eyed, square-jawed man in uniform. After confirming to his satisfaction that Trigger was indeed in charge, he informed her in chilled tones that the Devagas Union would hold her personally responsible for the unprovoked outrage unless an apology was promptly forthcoming.

Trigger apologized promptly. He acknowledged with a curt nod.

"The ship will now require new spacepaint," he pointed out, unmollified.

Trigger nodded. "We'll send a work squad out immediately."

"We," the Missionary Captain said, "shall supervise the work. Only the best grade of paint will be acceptable!"

"The very best only," Trigger agreed.

He gave her another curt nod, and switched off.

"Ass," she said. She cut in the don't-disturb barrier and dialed Holati's ship.

It took a while to get through; he was probably busy somewhere in the crate. Like Belchik Pluly, the Commissioner, while still a very wealthy man, would have been a very much wealthier one if it weren't for his hobby. In his case, the hobby was ships, of which he now owned two. What made them expensive was that they had been tailor-made to the Commissioner's specifications, and his specifications had provided him with two rather exact duplicates of the two types of Scout fighting ships in which Squadron Commander Tate had made space hideous for evildoers in the good old days. Nobody as yet had got up the nerve to point out to him that private battlecraft definitely were not allowable in the Manon System.

He came on finally. Trigger told him about the Devagas. "Did you know those characters were in the area?" she asked.

The Commissioner knew. They'd stopped in at the system check station three days before. The ship was clean. "Their missionaries all go armed, of course; but that's their privilege by treaty. They've been browsing around and going hither and yon in skiffs. The ship's been on orbit till this morning."

"Think they're here in connection with whatever Balmordan is up to?" Trigger inquired.

"We'll take that for granted. Balmordan, by the way, attended a big shindig on the Pluly yacht yesterday. Unless his tail goofed, he's still up there, apparently staying on as a guest."

"Are you having these other Devagas watched?"

"Not individually. Too many of them, and they're scattered all over the place. Mantelish got back. He checked in an hour ago."

"You mean he's upstairs in his quarters now?" she asked.

"Right. He had a few more crates hauled into the lab, and he's locked himself in with them and spy-blocked the place. May have got something important, and may just be going through one of his secrecy periods again. We'll find out by and by. Oh, and here's a social note. The First Lady of Tranest is shopping in the Grand Commerce Center this morning."

"Well, that should boost business," said Trigger. "Are you going to be back in the dome by lunchtime?"

"I think so. Might have some interesting news, too, incidentally."

"Fine," she said. "See you then."

Twenty minutes later the desk transmitter gave her the "to be shielded" signal. Up went the barrier again.

Major Quillan's face looked out at her from the screen. He was, Trigger saw, in Mantelish's lab. Mantelish stood at a workbench behind him.

"Hi!" he said.

"Hi, yourself. When did you get in?"

"Just now. Could you pick up the whoosis-and-whichis and bring it up here?"

"Right now?"

"If you can," Quillan said. "The professor's got something new, he thinks."

"I'm on my way," said Trigger. "Take about five minutes."

She hurried down to her quarters, summoned Repulsive's container into the room and slung the strap over her shoulder.

Then she stood still a moment, frowning slightly. Something—something like a wisp of memory, something she *should* be remembering—was stirring in the back of her mind. Then it was gone.

Trigger shook her head. It would keep. She opened the door and stepped out into the hall.

She fell down.

As she fell, she tried to give the bag the send-off squeeze, but she couldn't move her fingers. She couldn't move anything.

There were people around her. They were doing things swiftly. She was turned over on her back and, for a few moments then, she saw her own face smiling down at her from just a few feet away.

21

She was, suddenly, in a large room, well lit, with elaborate furnishings—sitting leaned back in a soft chair before a highly polished little table. On the opposite side of the table two people sat looking at her with expressions of mild surprise. One of them was Lyad Ermetyne. The other was a man she didn't know.

The man glanced aside at Lyad. "Very fast snap-back!" he said. He looked again at Trigger. He was a small man with salt-and-pepper hair, a deeply lined face, beautiful liquid-black eyes.

"Very!" Lyad said. "We must remember that. Hello, Trigger!"

"Hello," Trigger said. Her glance went once around the room and came back to Lyad's amiably observant face. Repulsive's container was nowhere around. There seemed to be nobody else in the room. An ornamental ComWeb stood against one wall. Two of the walls were covered with heavy hangings, and a great gold-brocaded canopy bellied from the ceiling. No doors or portals in sight; they might be camouflaged, or behind those hangings. Any number of people could be in call range—and a few certainly must be watching her right now, because that small man was no rough-and-tumble type.

The small man was regarding her with something like restrained amusement.

"A cool one," he murmured. "Very cool!"

Trigger looked at him a moment, then turned her eyes back to Lyad. She didn't feel cool. She felt tense and scared cold. This was probably very bad!

"What did you want to see me about?" she asked.

Lyad smiled. "A business matter. Do you know where you are?"

"Not on your ship, First Lady."

The light-amber eyes barely narrowed. But Lyad had become, at that moment, very alert.

"Why do you think so?" she asked pleasantly.

"This room," said Trigger. "You don't gush, I think. What was the business matter?"

"In a moment," Lyad said. She smiled again. "Where else might you be?"

Trigger thought she could guess. But she didn't intend to. Not out loud. She shrugged. "It's no place I want to be." She settled back a little in her chair. Her right hand brushed the porgee pouch.

The porgee pouch.

It would have been like the Ermetyne to investigate the pouch carefully, take out the gun and put the pouch back. But they might not have.

Somebody was bound to be watching. She couldn't find out—not until the instant after she decided to try the Denton.

"I can believe that," Lyad said. "Forgive me the discourtesy of so urgent an invitation, Trigger. A quite recent event made it seem necessary. As to the business—as a start, this gentleman is Doctor Veetonia. He is an investigator of extraordinary talents along his line. At the moment, he is a trifle tired because of the very long hours he worked last night."

Doctor Veetonia turned his head to look at her. "I did, First Lady? Well, that does explain this odd weariness. Did I work well?"

"Splendidly," Lyad assured him. "You were never better, Doctor."

He nodded, smiled vaguely and looked back at Trigger. "This must go, too, I suppose?"

"I'm afraid it must," Lyad said.

"A great pity!" Doctor Veetonia said. "A great pity. It would have been a pleasant memory. This very cool one!" The vague smile shifted in the lined face again. "You are so beautiful, child," he told Trigger, "in your anger and terror and despair. And above it still the gaging purpose, the strong, quick thinking. You will not give in easily. Oh, no! Not easily at all. First Lady," Doctor Veetonia said plaintively, "I should like to remember this one! It should be possible, I think."

Small, icy fingers were working up and down Trigger's spine. The Ermetyne gave her a light wink.

"I'm afraid it isn't, Doctor," she said. "There are such very important matters to be discussed. Besides, Trigger Argee and I will come to an amicable agreement very quickly."

"No." Doctor Veetonia's face had turned very sullen.

"No?" said Lyad.

"She will agree to nothing. Any fool can see that. I recommend, then, a simple chemical approach. Your creatures can handle it. Drain her. Throw her away. I will have nothing to do with the matter."

"Oh, but, Doctor!" the Ermetyne protested. "That would be so crude. And so very uncertain. Why, we might be here for hours still!"

He shook his head.

Lyad smiled. She stroked the lined cheek with light fingertips. "Have you forgotten the palace at Hamal Lake?" she asked. "The great library? The laboratories? Haven't I been very generous?"

Doctor Veetonia turned his face toward her. He smiled thoughtfully.

"Now that is true!" he admitted. "For the moment I did forget." He looked back at Trigger. "The First Lady gives," he told her, "and the First Lady takes away. She has given me wealth and much leisure. She takes from me now and then a memory. Very skillfully, since she was my pupil. But still the mind must dim by a little each time it is done."

His face suddenly grew concerned. He looked at Lyad again. "Two more years only!" he said. "In two years I shall be free to retire, Lyad?"

Lyad nodded. "That was our bargain, Doctor. You know I keep bargains."

Doctor Veetonia said, "Yes. You do. It is strange in an Ermetyne. Very well! I shall do it." He looked at Trigger's face. The black-liquid eyes blinked once or twice. "She is almost certain she is being watched," he said, "but she has been thinking of using the ComWeb. The child, I believe, is prepared to attack us at any opportune moment." He smiled. "Show her first why her position is hopeless. Then we shall see."

"Why, it's not in the least hopeless," Lyad said. "And please feel no concern about the Doctor, Trigger. His methods are quite painless and involve none of the indignities of a chemical investigation. If you are at all reasonable, we'll just sit here and talk for twenty minutes or so. Then you will tell me what sum you wish to have deposited for you in what bank, and you will be free to go."

"What will we talk about?" Trigger said.

"Well, for one," said the Ermetyne, "there is that rather handsome little purse you've been carrying about lately. My technicians inform me there may be some risk of damaging its contents if they attempt to force it open. We don't want that. So we'll talk a bit about the proper way of opening it." She gave Trigger her little smile. "And Doctor Veetonia will verify the accuracy of any statements made on the matter."

She considered. "Oh, and then I shall ask a few questions. Not many. And you will answer them. It really will be quite simple. But now let me tell you why I so very much wanted to see you today. We had a guest here last night. A gentleman whom you've met—Balmordan. He was mind-blocked on some quite important subjects, and so—though the doctor and I were very patient and careful—he died in the end. But before he died, he had told me as much as I really needed to know from him.

"Now with that information," she went on, "and with

the contents of your purse and with another little piece of information, which you possess, I shall presently go away. On Orado, a few hours later, Tranest's ambassador will have a quiet talk with some members of the Federation Council. And that will be all, really." She smiled. "No dramatic pursuit! No hue and cry! A few treaties will be very considerably revised. And the whole hubbub about the plasmoids will be over." She nodded. "Because they can be made to work, you know. And very well!"

Doctor Veetonia hadn't looked away from Trigger while Lyad was speaking. He said now, "My congratulations, First Lady! But the girl has not been convinced in the least that she should cooperate. She may hope to be rescued before the information you want can be forced from her."

The Ermetyne sighed. "Oh, really now, Trigger!" She very nearly pouted. "Well, if I must explain about that to you, too, I shall."

She considered a moment.

"Did you see your facsimile?"

Trigger nodded. "Very briefly."

Lyad smiled. "How she and my other people passed in and out of that dome, and how it happened that your room guards were found unconscious and were very hurriedly taken to the medical department's contagious ward, makes an amusing little story. But it would be too long in the telling just now. Your facsimile is one of Tranest's finest actresses. She's been studying and practicing being you for months. She knows where to go and what to do in that dome to avoid contact with people who know you too intimately. If it seems that discovery is imminent, she needs only a minute by herself to turn into an entirely different personality. So hours might pass without anyone even suspecting you were gone.

"But on the other hand," Lyad admitted fairly, "your double might be caught immediately or within minutes. She would not be conscious then, and I doubt your fierce little Commissioner would go to the unethical limits of dead-braining a live woman. If he did, of course, he would learn nothing from her.

"Let's assume, nevertheless, that for one reason and another your friends suspect me immediately, and only me. At the time you were being taken from the dome, I was observed leaving the Grand Commerce Center. I'd shopped rather freely; a number of fairly large crates and so forth were loaded into my speedboat. And we were observed returning to the *Aurora*."

"Not bad," Trigger admitted. "Another facsimile, I suppose?"

"Of course." The Ermetyne glanced at a small jeweled wristwatch. "Now the *Aurora*, if my orders were being followed, and they were, dived approximately five minutes ago—unless somebody who might be your wrathful rescuers approached her before that time, in which case she dived then. In either case, the dive was seen by the Commissioner's watchers; and the proper conclusions sooner or later will be drawn from that."

"Supposing they dive after her and run her down?" Trigger said.

"They might! The *Aurora* is not an easy ship to run down in subspace; but they might. After some hours. It would be of no consequence at all, would it?" The amber eyes regarded Trigger with very little expression for a moment. "How many hours or minutes do you think you could hold out here, Trigger Argee, if it became necessary to put on real pressure?"

"I don't know," Trigger admitted. She moistened her lips.

"I could give you a rather close estimate, I think," the Ermetyne said. "But forgive me for bringing up that matter. It was an unnecessary discourtesy. Let's assume instead that the rather clever people with whom you've been working are quite clever enough to see through all these little maneuverings. Let's assume further that they

are even able to conclude immediately where you and
I must be at the moment.

"We are, as it happens, on the *Griffin*, which is
Belchik Pluly's outsized yacht, and which is orbiting
Manon at present. This room is on a sealed level of
the yacht, where Belchik's private life normally goes on
undisturbed. I persuaded him two days ago to clear
out this section of it for my own use. There is only
one portal entry to the level, and that entry is locked
and heavily guarded at the moment. There are two
portal exits. One of them opens into a special lock in
which there is a small speedboat of mine, prepared to
leave. It's a very fast boat. If there have been faster
ones built in the Hub, I haven't heard of them yet.
And it can dive directly from the lock."

She smiled at Trigger. "You have the picture now,
haven't you? If your friends decide to board the *Griffin*, they'll be able to do it without too much argument.
After all, we don't want to be blown up accidentally. But
they'll have quite a time working their way into this level.
If a boarding party is reported, we'll just all quietly go
away together with no fuss or hurry. I can guarantee that
no one is going to trace or overtake that boat. You see?"

"Yes," Trigger said disconsolately, slumping back a little.
Her right hand dropped to her lap. Well, she thought,
last chance!

Doctor Veetonia frowned. "First—" he began.

Trigger slapped the porgee pouch. And the Denton's
soundless blast slammed the talented investigator back
and over in his chair.

"Gun," Trigger explained unnecessarily.

The Ermetyne's face had turned white with shock. She
flicked a glance down at the man, then looked back at
Trigger.

"There're guns on me too, I imagine," Trigger said.
"But this one goes off very easily, First Lady! It would
take hardly any jolt at all."

Lyad nodded slightly. "They're no fools! They won't risk shooting. Don't worry." Her voice was careful but quite even. A tough cookie, as the Commissioner had remarked.

"We won't bother about them at the moment," Trigger said. "Let's stand up together."

They stood up.

"We'll stay about five feet apart," Trigger went on. "I don't know if you're the gun-grabbing type."

The Ermetyne almost smiled. "I'm not!" she said.

"No point in taking chances," Trigger said. "Five feet." She gave Doctor Veetonia a quick glance. He did look very unpleasantly dead.

"We'll go over to that ComWeb in a moment," she told Lyad. "I imagine you wouldn't have left it on open circuit?"

Lyad shook her head. "Calls go through the ship's communication office."

"Your own people on duty there?"

"No. Pluly's."

"Will they take your orders?"

"Certainly!"

"Can they listen in?" Trigger asked.

"Not if we seal the set here."

Trigger nodded. "You'll do the talking," she said. "I'll give you Commissioner Tate's personal number. Tell them to dial it. The Precol transmitters pick up ComWeb circuits. Switch on the screen after the call is in; he'll want to see me. When he comes on, just tell him what's happened, where we are, what the layout is. He's to come over with a squad to get us. I won't say much, if anything. I'll just keep the gun on you. If there's any fumble, we both get it."

"There won't be any fumble, Trigger," Lyad said.

"All right. Let's set up the rest of it before we move. After the Commissioner signs off, he'll be up here in three minutes flat. Or less. How about this ship's officers—do they take your orders too?"

"With the obvious exception of yourself," Lyad said, "everyone on the *Griffin* takes my orders at the moment."

"Then just tell whoever's in charge of the yacht to let the squad in before there's any shooting. The Commissioner can get awfully short-tempered. Then get the guards away from that entry portal. That's for their own good."

The Ermetyne nodded. "Will do."

"All right. That covers it, I think."

They looked at each other for a moment.

"With the information you got from Balmordan," Trigger remarked, "you should still be able to make a very good dicker with the Council, First Lady. I understand they're very eager to get the plasmoid mess straightened out quietly."

Lyad lifted one shoulder in a brief shrug. "Perhaps," she said.

"Let's move!" said Trigger.

They walked toward the ComWeb rather edgily, not very fast, not very slow, Trigger four or five steps behind. There had been no sound from the walls and no other sign of what must be very considerable excitement nearby. Trigger's spine kept tingling. A needlebeam and a good marksman could pluck away the Denton and her hand along with it, without much real risk to the Ermetyne. But probably even the smallest of risks was more than the Tranest people would be willing to take when the First Lady's person was involved.

Lyad reached the ComWeb and stopped. Trigger stopped too, five feet away. "Go ahead," she said quietly.

Lyad turned to face her. "Let me make one last—well, call it an appeal," she said. "Don't be an over-ethical fool, Trigger Argee! The arrangement I've planned will do no harm to anybody. Come in with me, and you can write your own ticket for the rest of your life."

"No ticket," Trigger said. She waggled the Denton slightly. "Go ahead! You can talk to the Council later."

Lyad shrugged resignedly, turned again and reached toward the ComWeb.

Trigger might have relaxed just a trifle at that moment. Or perhaps there was some other cue that Pilli could pick up. There came no sound from the ceiling canopy. What she caught was a sense of something moving above her. Then the great golden bulk landed with a terrifying lightness on the thick carpet between Lyad and herself.

The eyeless nightmare head wasn't three feet from her own.

The lights in the room went out.

Trigger flung herself backwards, rolled six feet to one side, stood up, backed away and stopped again.

22

The blackness in the room was complete. She spun the Denton to kill. There was silence around her and then a soft rustling at some distance. It might have been the cautious shuffle of a heavy foot over thick carpeting. It stopped again. Where was Lyad?

Her eyes shifted about, trying to pierce the darkness. Black-light, she thought. She said, "Lyad?"

"Yes?" Lyad's voice came easily in the dark. She might be standing about thirty feet away, at the far end of the room.

"Call your animal off," Trigger said quietly. "I don't want to kill it." She began moving in the direction from which Lyad had spoken.

"Pilli won't hurt you, Trigger," the Ermetyne said. "He's been sent in to disarm you, that's all. Throw your gun away and he won't even touch you." She laughed. "Don't bother shooting in my direction either! I'm not in the room any more."

Trigger stopped. Not because of what that hateful,

laughing voice had said. But because in the dark about her a fresh, pungent smell was growing. The smell of ripe apples.

She moistened her lips. She whispered, "Pilli—keep away!" Eyeless, the dark would mean nothing to it. Seconds later, she heard the thing breathing.

She faced the sound. It stopped for a moment, then it came again. A slow animal breathing. It seemed to circle slowly to her left. After a little it stopped. Then it was coming toward her.

She said softly, almost pleadingly, "Pilli, stop! Go back, Pilli!"

Silence. Pilli's odor lay heavy all around. Trigger heard her blood drumming in her ears, and, for a second then, she imagined she could feel, like a tangible fog, the body warmth of the monster standing in the dark before her.

It wasn't imagination. Something like a smooth, heavy pad of rubber closed around her right wrist and tightened terribly.

The Denton went off two, three, four times before she was jerked violently sideways, flung away, sent stumbling backward against some low piece of furniture and, sprawling, over it. The gun was lost.

As she scrambled dizzily to her feet, Pilli screamed. It was a thin, high, breathless sound like the screaming of a terrified human child. It stopped abruptly. And, as if that had been a signal, the room came full of light again.

Trigger blinked dazedly against the light. Virod stood before her, looking at her, a pair of opaque yellow goggles shoved up on his forehead. Black-light glasses. The golden-haired thing lay in a great shapeless huddle on the floor twenty feet to one side. She couldn't see her gun. But Virod held one, pointing at her.

Virod's other hand moved suddenly. Its palm caught the side of her face in a hefty slap. Trigger staggered dumbly sideways, got her balance, and stood facing him again. She didn't even feel anger. Her cheek began to burn.

"Stop amusing yourself, Virod!" It was Lyad's voice. Trigger saw her then, standing in a small half-opened door across the room, where a wall hanging had been folded away.

"She appeared to be in shock, First Lady," Virod explained blandly.

"Is Pilli dead?"

"Yes. I have her gun. He got it from her." Virod slapped a pocket of his jacket, and some part of Trigger's mind noted the gesture and suddenly came awake.

"So I saw. Well—too bad about Pilli. But it was necessary. Bring her here then. And be reasonably gentle." Lyad still sounded unruffled. "And put that gun in a different pocket, fool, or she'll take it away from you."

She looked at Trigger impersonally as Virod brought her to the little door, his left hand clamped on her arm just above the elbow.

She said, "Too bad you killed my expert, Trigger! We'll have to use a chemical approach now. Flam and Virod are quite good at that, but there will be some pain. Not too much, because I'll be watching them. But it will be rather undignified, I'm afraid. And it will take a great deal longer."

Tanned, tall, sinuous Flam stood in the small room beyond the door. Trigger saw a long, low, plastic-covered table, clamps and glittering gadgetry. That would have been where cold-fish Balmordan hadn't been able to make it against his mind-blocks finally. There was still one thing she could do. The yacht was orbiting.

"That sort of thing won't be at all necessary!" she said shakily. Her voice shook with great ease, as if it had been practicing it all along.

"No?" Lyad said.

"You've won," Trigger said resignedly. "I'll play along now. I'll show you how to open that handbag, to start with."

Lyad nodded. "How do you open it?"

"You have to press it in the right places. Have them bring it here. I'll show you."

Lyad laughed. "You're a little too eager. And much too docile, Trigger! Considering what's in that handbag, it's not at all likely it will detonate if we brightly hand it to you and let you start pressing. But something or other of a very undesirable nature would certainly happen! Flam—"

The tall redhead nodded and smiled. She went over to a wall cabinet, unlocked it and took out Repulsive's container.

Lyad said, "Put it on that shelf for the moment. Then bring me Virod's gun, and hers."

She laid the Denton on the shelf beside the handbag and kept Virod's gun in her hand.

"I'm afraid you'll have to go up on that table now, Trigger," she said. "If you've really decided to cooperate, it won't be too bad. And, by and by, you'll start telling us very exactly what should be done with that handbag. And a few other things."

She might have caught Trigger's expression then. She added dryly, "I was informed a few nights ago that you're quite an artist in rough-and-tumble tactics. So are Virod and Flam. So if you want to give Virod an opportunity to amuse himself a little, go right ahead!"

At that point, the graceful thing undoubtedly would have been to just smile and get up on the table. Trigger discovered she couldn't do it. She gave them a fast, silent, vicious tussle, mouth clenched, breathing hard through her nose. It was quite insanely useless. They weren't letting her get anywhere near Lyad. After Virod had amused himself a little, he picked her up and plunked her down on the table. A minute later, she was stretched out on it, face down, wrists and ankles secured with padded clamps to its surface.

Flam took a small knife and neatly slit the back of the Precol uniform open along the line of her spine. She folded the cloth away. Then Trigger felt the thin icy touches of some vanilla-smelling spray walk up her, ending at the base of her skull.

It wasn't so very painful; Lyad had told the truth about that. But presently it became extremely undignified. Then her thoughts were speeding up and slowing down and swirling around in an odd, confusing fashion. And at last her voice began to say things she didn't want it to say.

After this, there might have been a pause. She seemed to be floating up out of a small pool of sleep when Lyad's voice said somewhere, with cold fury in it: "There's *nothing* inside?"

A whole little series of memory-pictures popped up suddenly then, like a chain of firecrackers somebody had set off. They formed themselves into a pattern; and there the pattern was in Trigger's mind. She looked at it. Her eyes flew open in surprise. She began to laugh weakly.

Light footsteps came quickly over to her. "Where is that plasmoid, Trigger?"

The Ermetyne was in a fine, towering rage. She'd better say something.

"Ask the Commissioner," she said, mumbling it a little.

"It's wearing off, First Lady," said Flam. "Shall I?"

Trigger's thoughts went eddying away for a moment, and she didn't hear Lyad's reply. But then the vanilla smell was there again, and the thin icy touches. This time, they stopped abruptly, halfway.

And then there was a very odd stillness all around Trigger. As if everybody and everything had stopped moving together.

A deep, savage voice said, "I hope there'll be no trouble, folks. I just want her a lot worse than you do."

Trigger frowned in puzzlement. Next came an angry roar, some thumping sounds, a sudden sharp crack.

"Oops!" the deep voice said happily. "A little too hard, I'm afraid!"

Why, of course, Trigger thought. She opened her eyes and twisted her head around.

"Still awake, Trigger?" Quillan asked from the door of the room. He looked pleasantly surprised. There was a very large bell-mouthed gun in his hand.

That was an odd-looking little group in the doorway, Trigger felt. On his knees before Quillan was a fat, elderly man, blinking dazedly at her. He wore a brilliantly purple bath towel knotted about his loins and nothing else. It was a moment before she recognized Belchik Pluly. Old Belchy! And on the floor before Belchy, motionless as if in devout prostration, Virod lay on his face. Dead, no doubt. He shouldn't have got gay with Quillan.

"Yes," Trigger said then, remembering Quillan's question. "I've got a very fast snap-back—but they fed me a fresh load of dope just a moment ago."

"So I saw," said Quillan. His glance shifted beyond Trigger.

"Lyad," he said, almost gently.

"Yes, Quillan?" Lyad's voice came from the other side of Trigger. Trigger turned her head toward it. Lyad and Flam both stood at the far side of the room. Their expressions were unhappy.

"I don't like at all," Quillan said, "what's been going on here. Not one bit! Which is why Big Boy got the neck broken finally. Can the rest of us take a hint?"

"Certainly," the Ermetyne said.

"So the Flam girl quits ogling those guns on the shelf and stays put, or they'll amputate a leg. First Lady, you come up to the table and get Trigger unclamped."

Trigger realized her eyes had fallen shut again. She left them that way for the moment. There was motion near her, and the wrist clamps came off in turn. Lyad moved down to her feet.

"The fancy-looking little gun is Trigger's?" Quillan inquired.

"Yes," said Lyad.

"Is that what happened to Pilli and the other gent out there?"

"Yes."

"Imagine!" said Quillan thoughtfully. "Uh—got something to seal up the clothes?"

"Yes," Lyad said. "Bring it here, Flam."

"Toss it, Flam!" cautioned Quillan. "Remember the leg."

Lyad's hands did things to the clothes at her back. Then they went away.

"You can sit up now, Trigger!" Quillan's voice informed her loudly. "Sort of slide down easy off the table and see if you can stand."

Trigger opened her eyes, twisted about, slid her legs over the edge of the table, came down on her feet, stood.

"I want my gun and the handbag," she announced. She saw them again then, on the shelf, walked over and picked up the plasmoid container. She looked inside, snapped it shut and slung the strap over her shoulder. She picked up the Denton, looked at its setting, spun it and turned.

"First Lady—" she said.

Lyad went white around the lips. Quillan made some kind of startled sound. Trigger shot.

Flam ran at her then, screaming, arms waving, eyes wild and green like an animal's. Trigger half turned and shot again.

She looked at Quillan. "Just stunned," she explained. She waited.

Quillan let his breath out slowly. "Glad to hear it!" He glanced down at Pluly. "Purse was open," be remarked significantly.

"Uh-huh," Trigger agreed.

"How's doohinkus?"

She laughed. "Safe and sound! Believe me."

"Good," he said. He still looked somewhat puzzled.

"Put the eye on Belchy for a few seconds then. We're taking Lyad along. I'll have to carry her now."

"Right," Trigger said. She felt rather jaunty at the moment. She put the eye on Belchik. Belchik moaned.

They started out of the little room, Pluly in the van, clutching his towel. The Ermetyne, dangling loosely over Quillan's left shoulder, looked fairly gruesomely dead. "You walk this side of me, Trigger," Quillan said. "Still all right?"

She nodded. "Yes." Actually she wasn't, quite. It was mainly a problem with her thoughts, which showed a tendency now to move along in odd little leaps and bounds, with short stops in between, as if something were trying to freeze them up. But if it was going to be like the first time, she should last till they got to wherever they were going.

Halfway across the big room, she saw the golden thing like a huge furry sack on the carpet and shivered. "Poor Pilli!" she said.

"Alas!" Quillan said politely. "I gather you didn't just stun Pilli?"

She shook her head. "Couldn't," she said. "Too big. Too fast."

"How about the other one?"

"Oh, him. Stunned. He's an investigator. They thought he was dead, though. That's what scared Lyad and Flam."

"Yeah," Quillan said thoughtfully. "It would."

Another section of wall hanging had folded aside, and a wide door stood open behind it. They went through the door and turned into a mirrored passageway, Pluly still tottering rapidly ahead. "Might keep that gun ready, Trigger," Quillan warned. "We just could get jumped here. Don't think so, though. They'd have to get past the Commissioner."

"Oh, he's here, too?"

She didn't hear what Quillan answered, because things faded out around then. When they faded in again, the passageway with the mirrors had disappeared, and they were coming to the top of a short flight of low, wide stairs and into a very beautiful room. This room was high and long, not very wide. In the center was a small square swimming pool, and against the walls on either side was a long row of tall square crystal pillars through which strange lights undulated slowly. Trigger glanced curiously at the nearest pillar. She stopped short.

"Galaxy!" she said, startled.

Quillan reached back and grabbed her arm with his gun hand. "Keep moving, girl! That's just how Belchik keeps his harem grouped around him when he's working. Not too bad an idea—it does cut down the chatter. This is his office."

"Office!" Then she saw the large business desk with prosaic standard equipment which stood on the carpet on the other side of the pool. They moved rapidly past the pool, Quillan still hauling at her arm. Trigger kept staring at the pillars they passed. Long-limbed, supple and languid, they floated there in their crystal cages, in tinted, shifting lights, eyes closed, hair drifting about their faces.

"Awesome, isn't it?" Quillan's voice said.

"Yes," said Trigger. "Awesome. One in each—he *is* a pig! They look drowned."

"He is and they aren't," said Quillan. "Very lively girls when he lets them out. Now around this turn and . . . oops!"

Pluly had reached the turn at the end of the row of pillars, moaned again and fallen forwards.

"Fainted!" Quillan said. "Well, we don't need him any more. Watch your step, Trigger—dead one just behind Pluly."

Trigger stretched her stride and cleared the dead one behind Pluly neatly. There were three more dead ones lying inside the entrance to the next big room. She went past them, feeling rather dreamy. The sight of a squat, black subtub parked squarely on the thick purple carpeting ahead of her, with its canopy up, didn't strike her as unusual. Then she saw that the man leaning against the canopy, a gun in one hand, was Commissioner Tate. She smiled.

She waved her hand at him as they came up. "Hi, Holati!"

"Hi, yourself," said the Commissioner. He asked Quillan, "How's she doing?"

"Not bad," Quillan said. "A bit ta-ta at the moment. Double dose of ceridim, by the smell of it. Had a little trouble here, I see."

"A little," the Commissioner acknowledged. "They went for their guns."

"Very uninformed gentlemen," said Quillan. He let Lyad's limp form slide off his shoulder, and bent forward to lower her into the subtub's back seat. Trigger had been waiting for a chance to get into the conversation.

"Just who," she demanded now, frowning, "is a bit ta-ta at the moment?"

"You," said Quillan. "You're doped, remember? You'll ride up front with the Commissioner. Here." He picked her up, plasmoid purse and all, and set her down on the front seat. Holati Tate, she discovered then, was already inside. Quillan swung down into the seat behind her. The canopy snapped shut above.

The Commissioner shifted the tub's controls. In the screens, the room outside vanished. A darkness went rushing downwards past them.

A thought suddenly popped to mind again, and Trigger burst into tears. The Commissioner glanced over at her.

"What's the matter, Trigger girl?"

"I'm so s-sorry I killed Pilli. He s-screamed."

Then her mind froze up with a jolt, and thinking stopped completely. Quillan reached over the back of the seat and eased her over on her side.

"Got to her finally!" he said. He sat down again. He brooded a moment. "She shouldn't get so disturbed about that Pilli thing," he remarked then. "It couldn't have lived anyway."

"Eh?" the Commissioner said absently, watching the screens. "Why not?"

"Its brains," Quillan explained, "were too far apart."

The Commissioner blinked. "It's getting to you too, son!" he said.

23

Trigger came out of the ceridim trance hours before Lyad awoke from the stunner blast she'd absorbed. The Commissioner was sitting in a chair beside her bunk, napping.

She looked around a moment, feeling very comfortable and secure. This was her personal cabin on Commissioner Tate's ship, the one he referred to as the Big Job, modeled after the long-range patrol ships of the Space Scouts. It wasn't actually very big, but six or seven people could go traveling around in it very comfortably. At the moment it appeared to be howling through subspace at its hellish rate again, going somewhere.

Well, that could keep.

Trigger reached out and poked the Commissioner's knee. "Hey, Holati!" she whispered. "Wake up."

His eyes opened. He looked at her and smiled. "Back again, eh?" he said.

Trigger motioned at the door. "Close it," she whispered. "Got something to tell you."

"Talk away," he said. "Quillan's piloting, the First Lady's out cold, and Mantelish got dive-sick and I doped him. Nobody else on board."

Trigger lay back and looked at him. "This is going to sound pretty odd!" she warned him. Then she told him what Repulsive had done and what he was trying to do.

The Commissioner looked badly shaken.

"You sure of that, Trigger?"

"Sure, I'm sure."

"Trying to talk to you?"

"That's it."

He blinked at her. "I looked in the bag," he said, "and the thing was gone."

"Lyad knows it was gone," Trigger said. "So in case she gets a chance to blab to someone, we'll say you had it."

He nodded and stood up. "You stay here," he said. "Prescription for the kind of treatment you've had is a day of bed rest."

"Where are you going?"

"I'm going to go talk to that Psychology ship," he said. "And just let 'em try to stall me this time!"

He went off up the passage toward the transmitter cabinet in the forward part of the ship. Some minutes passed. Then Trigger suddenly heard Commissioner Tate's voice raised in great wrath. She listened. It appeared the Psychology Service had got off on the wrong foot by advising him once more to stay calm.

He came back presently and sat down beside the bunk, still a little red in the face. "They're going to follow us," he said. "If they hadn't, I would have turned back and gunned our way on board that lopsided disgrace of theirs."

"Follow us? Where?"

He grunted. "A place called Luscious. We'll be there in under a week. It'll take them about three. But they're starting immediately."

Trigger blinked. "Looks like the plasmoids have made it to the head of the problem list!"

"I wouldn't be surprised," said the Commissioner. "I was put through to that Pilch after a while. She said to remind you to listen to your thinking whenever you can get around to it. Know what she meant?"

"I'm not sure I do," Trigger said hesitantly. "But she's mentioned it. I'll give it a whirl. Why are we going to Luscious?"

"Selan's Fleet found plasmoids on it. It's in the Vishni area."

"What kind of plasmoids?"

He shrugged. "They don't amount to much, from what I heard. Small stuff. But definitely plasmoid. It looks like somebody might have done some experimenting there for a while. And not long ago."

"Did they find the big one?"

"Not yet. No trace of any people on Luscious either." He chewed his lip thoughtfully for a moment. "About an hour after we picked you and Lyad up," he said, "we had a Council Order transmitted to the ship. Told us to swing off course a bit and rendezvous with a fast courier boat of theirs."

"What for?"

"The order said the courier was to take Lyad on board and head for the Hub with her. Some diplomatic business." He scratched his chin. "It also instructed us to treat the First Lady of Tranest with the courtesy due to her station meanwhile."

"Brother!" Trigger said, outraged.

"Just too bad I couldn't read that message," said Holati Tate. "Some gravitic disturbance! Rendezvous point's hours behind us. They'll never catch up."

"Ho-ho!" said Trigger. "But that's being pretty insubordinate, Holati!"

"It was till just now," he said. "I mentioned that we had Lyad on board to that Pilch person. She said she'd speak to the Council. We're to hang on to Lyad, and when Pilch gets to Luscious she'll interview her."

Trigger grinned. "Now that," she remarked, "gives me a feeling of great satisfaction, somehow. When Pilch gets her little mitts on someone, there isn't much left out."

"I had that impression. Meanwhile, we'll put the Ermetyne through a routine questioning ourselves when she gets over being groggy. Courtesy will be on the moderate side. She'll probably spill part of what she knows, especially if you sit there and hand her the beady stare from time to time."

"That," Trigger assured him, "will be hardly any effort at all!"

"I can imagine. You're pretty sure that thing will show up again?"

Trigger nodded. "Just leave the handbag with me."

"All right." He stood up. "I've got a hot lunch prepared for you. I'll bring the bag along. Then you can tell me what happened after they grabbed you."

"How did you find out I was gone?" Trigger asked.

"Your fac," he said. "The girl was darn good actually. I talked to you—her—on office transmitter once and didn't spot a sour note. Mostly she just kept out of everybody's way. Very slick at it! We would have got her fairly fast because we were preparing for take-off to Luscious by then. But she spilled it herself."

"How?"

"I located her finally again, on transmitter screen. There was no one on her side to impress. She took a sniff of porgee."

Trigger laughed delightedly. "Good old porgee pouch! It beat them twice. But how did you know where I was?"

"No problem there. We knew Lyad had strings on Pluly. Quillan knew about that sealed level on Pluly's yacht and got Pluly to invite him over to admire the harem right after the *Dawn City* arrived. While he was admiring, he was also recording floor patterns for a subtub jump. That gimmick's pretty much of a spilled secret now, but on a swap for you and Lyad it was worth it. We came aboard five minutes after we'd nabbed your fac."

"The Ermetyne figured you'd go chasing after the *Aurora*," Trigger said.

"Well," the Commissioner said tolerantly, "the Ermetyne's pretty young. The *Aurora* was a bit obvious."

"How come Quillan didn't start wondering when I didn't show up in Mantelish's lab with Repulsive?"

"So that's what he was for!" Holati said. He rubbed the side of his jaw. "I was curious about that angle! That wasn't Quillan. That was Quillan's fac."

"In Mantelish's lab?" Trigger said, startled.

"Sure. That's how they all got in. In those specimen crates Mantelish has been lugging into the dome the past couple of days. It looks like the prof's been hypnotized up to his ears for months."

The last five hours of her day of recuperative rest Trigger spent asleep, her cabin door locked and the plasmoid purse open on the bunk beside her. Holati had come by just before to report that the Ermetyne was now awake but very groggy, apparently more than a little shocked, and not yet quite able to believe she was still alive. He'd dose her with this and that, and interrogations would be postponed until everybody was on their feet.

When Trigger woke up from her five-hour nap, the purse was shut. She opened it and looked inside. Repulsive was down there, quietly curled up.

"Smart little bugger, aren't you?" she said, not entirely with approval. Then she reached in and gave him a pat. She locked the purse, got dressed and went up to the front of the ship, carrying Repulsive along.

All four of the others were up in the lounge area which included the partitioned control section. The partition had been slid into the wall and the Commissioner, who was at the controls at the moment, had swung his seat half around toward the lounge.

He glanced at the plasmoid purse as Trigger came in, grinned and gave her a small wink.

"Come in and sit down," he said. "We've been waiting for you."

Trigger sat down and looked at them. Something apparently had been going on. Quillan's tanned face was thoughtful, perhaps a trifle amused. Mantelish looked very red and angry. His shock of white hair was wildly rumpled. The Ermetyne appeared a bit wilted.

"What's been going on?" Trigger asked.

It was the wrong question. Mantelish took a deep breath and began bellowing like a wounded thunder-ork. Trigger listened, with some admiration. It was one of the best jobs of well-verbalized huffing she'd heard, even from the professor. He ran down in less than five minutes, though—apparently he'd already let off considerable steam.

Lyad had dehypnotized him, at the Commissioner's suggestion. It had been a lengthy job, requiring a couple of hours, but it was a complete one. Which was understandable, since it was the First Lady herself, Trigger gathered gradually from the noise, who had put Mantelish under the influence, back in his own garden on Maccadon, and within two weeks after his first return from *Harvest Moon*.

It was again Lyad who had given Mantelish his call to bemused duty via a transmitted verbal cue on her arrival in Manon, and instructed him to get lost from his League guards for a few hours in Manon's swamps. There she had met and conferred with him and pumped him of all he could tell her. As the final outrage, she had instructed him to lug her crated cohorts, preserved like Pluly's harem ladies, into the Precol dome—to care for them tenderly there and at the proper cued moment to release them for action—all under the illusion that they were priceless biological specimens!

Mantelish wasn't in the least appeased by the fact that—again at the Commissioner's suggestion—Lyad had installed one minor new hypno-command which, she said, would clear up permanently his tendency toward attacks of dive sickness. But he just ran down finally and sat there, glowering at the Ermetyne now and then.

"Well," the Commissioner remarked, "this might be as good a time as any to ask a few questions. Got your little quizzer with you, Quillan?"

Quillan nodded. Lyad looked at both of them in turn and then, briefly and for the first time, glanced in Trigger's direction.

It wasn't exactly an appealing glance. It might have been a questioning one. And Trigger discovered suddenly that she felt just a little sympathy for Lyad. Lyad had lost out on a very big gamble. And, each in his own way, these were three very formidable males among whom she was sitting. None of them was friendly; two were oversized, and the undersized one had a fairly blood-chilling record for anyone on the wrong side of law and order. Trigger decided to forget about beady stares for the moment.

"Cheer up, Lyad!" she said. "Nobody's going to hurt you. Just give 'em the answers!"

She got another glance. Not a grateful one, exactly. Not an ungrateful one either. Temporary support had been acknowledged.

"Commissioner Tate has informed me," the Ermetyne said, "that this group does not recognize the principle of diplomatic immunity in my case. Under the circumstances I must accept that. And so I shall answer any questions I can." She looked at the pocket quizzer Quillan was checking over unhurriedly. "But such verification instruments are of no use in questioning me."

"Why not?" Quillan asked idly.

"I've been conditioned against them, of course," Lyad said. "I'm an Ermetyne of Tranest. By the time I was twelve years old, that toy of yours couldn't have registered a reaction from me that I didn't want it to show."

Quillan slipped the toy back in his pocket.

"True enough, First Lady," he said. "And that's one small strike in your favor. We thought you might try to gimmick the gadget. Now we'll just pitch you some questions. A recorder's on. Don't stall on the answers."

And he and the Commissioner started flipping out questions. The Ermetyne flipped back the answers. So far as Trigger could tell, there wasn't any stalling. Or any time for it.

Along with Mantelish, Doctors Gess Fayle and Azol had been the three big U-League boys in charge of the initial investigation on *Harvest Moon*. Doctor Azol had been her boy from the start. After faking his own death, he was now on Tranest. The main item in his report to her had been the significance of the 112-113 plasmoid unit. He'd also reported that Trigger Argee had become unconscious on *Harvest Moon*. They'd considered the possibility that somebody was controlling Trigger Argee, or attempting to control her, because of her connections with the plasmoid operations.

Lyad had not been able to buy Gess Fayle. So far as she knew, nobody had been able to buy him. Doctor Fayle had appeared to intend to work for himself. Lyad was convinced he was the one who had actually stolen the 112-113 unit. He was at present well outside the Hub's area of space. He still had 112-113 with him. Yes, she could become more specific about the location—with the help of star maps.

"Let's get them out," said Commissioner Tate.

They got them out. The Ermetyne presently circled a largish section of the Vishni Fleet's area. The questions began again.

113-A: Professor Mantelish had told her of his experiments with this plasmoid—

There was an interruption here while Mantelish huffed reflexively. But it was very brief. The professor wanted to learn more about the First Lady's depravities himself.

—and its various possible associations with the main unit. But by the time this information became available to her, 113-A had been placed under heavy guard. Professor Mantelish had made one attempt to smuggle it out to her.

Huff-huff!

—but had been unable to walk past the guards with it. Tranest agents had made several unsuccessful attempts to pick up the plasmoid. She knew that another group had made similarly unsuccessful attempts. The Devagas. She did not yet know the specific nature of 113-A's importance. But it was important.

As for the rest of it . . .

Trigger: Trigger Argee might be able to tell them why Trigger was important. Doctor Fayle certainly could. So could the top ranks of the Devagas hierarchy. Lyad, at the moment, could not. She did know that Trigger Argee's importance was associated directly with that of plasmoid 113-A. This information had been obtained from a Devagas operator, now dead. Not Balmordan. The operator had been in charge of the attempted pickup on Evalee. The much more elaborate affair at the Colonial School had been a Tranest job. A Devagas group had made attempts to interfere with it, but had been disposed of.

Pluly: Lyad had strings on Belchik. He was afraid of the Devagas but somewhat more terrified of her. His fear of the Devagas was due to the fact that he and an associate had provided the hierarchy with a very large quantity of contraband materials. The nature of the materials indicated the Devagas were constructing a major fortified outpost on a world either airless or with poisonous atmosphere. Pluly's associate had since been murdered. Pluly believed he was next in line to be silenced.

Balmordan: Balmordan had been a rather high-ranking Devagas Intelligence agent. Lyad had heard of him only recently. He had been in charge of the attempts to obtain 113-A. Lyad had convinced him that she would make a very dangerous competitor in the Manon area. She also had made information regarding her activities there available to him.

So Balmordan and a select group of his gunmen had attended Pluly's party on Pluly's yacht. They had been allowed to force their way into the sealed level and were there caught in a black-light trap. The gunmen had been killed. Balmordan had been questioned.

The questioning revealed that the Devagas had found Doctor Fayle and the 112-113 unit. They had succeeded in creating some working plasmoids. To go into satisfactory operation, they still needed 113-A. Balmordan had not known why. But they no longer needed Trigger Argee. Trigger Argee was now to be destroyed at the earliest opportunity. Again Balmordan had not known why. Fayle and his unit were in the fortress dome the Devagas had been building. It was in the area Lyad had indicated. It was supposed to be very thoroughly concealed. Balmordan might or might not have known its exact coordinates. His investigators made the inevitable slip finally and triggered a violent mind-block reaction. Balmordan had died. Dead-braining him had produced no further relevant information.

The little drumfire of questions ended abruptly. Trigger glanced at her watch. It had been going on for only fifteen minutes, but she felt somewhat dizzy by now. The Ermetyne just looked a little more wilted.

After a minute, Commissioner Tate inquired politely whether there was any further information the First Lady could think of to give them at this time.

She shook her head. No.

Only Professor Mantelish believed her.

But the interrogation was over, apparently.

24

Quillan took over the ship controls, and the Commissioner and Trigger went with the recorder into the little office back of the transmitter cabinet, to slam out some fast reports to the Hub and other points. Lyad was apologizing profoundly to Mantelish as they left the lounge. The professor was huffing back at her, rather mildly.

A little while later, Lyad, showing indications of restrained surprise, was helping Trigger prepare dinner. They took it into the lounge. Quillan remained at the controls while the others started eating. Trigger fixed up a tray and brought it to him.

"Thanks for the rescue, Major!" she said.

He grinned up at her. "It was a pleasure."

Trigger glanced back at the little group in the lounge. "Think she was fibbing a bit?"

"Sure. Mainly she'd decided in advance how much to tell and how much not. She thinks fast in action though! No slips. What she told of what she knows makes a solid story, and with angles we can check on fast. So it's bound to have plenty of information in it. It'll do for the moment."

"She's already started buttering up Mantelish," said Trigger.

"She'll do that," Quillan said. "By the time we reach Luscious, the prof probably might as well be back in the trances. The Commissioner intends to give her a little rope, I think."

"How close is Luscious to that area she showed?"

Quillan flicked on their course screen and superimposed the map Lyad had marked. "Red dot's well inside," he pointed out. "That bit was probably quite solid info." He looked up at her. "Did it bother you much to hear the Devagas have dropped the grab idea and are out to do you in?"

Trigger shook her head. "Not really," she said. "Wouldn't make much difference one way or the other, would it?"

"Very little." He patted her hand. "Well, they're not going to get you, doll—one way or the other!"

Trigger smiled. "I believe you," she said. "Thanks." She

looked back into the lounge again. Just at present she did have a feeling of relaxed, unconcerned security. It probably wasn't going to last, though. She glanced at Quillan.

"Those computers of yours," she said. "What did they have to say about that not-catassin you squashed?"

"The crazy things claim now it was a plasmoid," Quillan said. "Revolting notion! But it makes some sense for once. Checks with some of the things Lyad just told us, too. Do you remember that Vethi sponge Balmordan was carrying?"

"Yes."

"It didn't come off ship with him. He checked it out as having died en route."

"That is a revolting notion!" Trigger said after a moment. "Well, at least we've got detectors now."

But the feeling of security had faded somewhat again.

Before dinner was half over, the long-range transmitters abruptly came to life. For the next thirty minutes or so, messages rattled in incessantly, as assorted Headquarters here and there reacted to the Ermetyne's report. The Commissioner sat in the little office and sorted over the incoming information. Trigger stayed at the transmitters, feeding it to him as it arrived. None of it affected them directly—they were already headed for the point in space a great many other people would now start heading for very soon.

Then business dropped off again almost as suddenly as it had picked up. A half dozen low priority items straggled in, in as many minutes. The transmitters puffed idly. Then the person-to-person buzzer sounded.

Trigger punched the screen button. A voice pronounced the ship's dial number.

"Acknowledging," Trigger said. "Who is it?"

"Orado, ComWeb Center," said the voice. "Stand by for contact with Federation Councilman Roadgear."

Trigger whacked the panic button. Roadgear was a NAME! "Standing by," she said.

Commissioner Tate came in through the door and slipped into the chair she'd already vacated. Trigger took another seat a few feet away. She felt a little nervous, but she'd always wanted to see a high-powered diplomat in action.

The screen lit up. She recognized Roadgear from his pics. Tall, fine-looking man of the silvered sideburns type. He was in an armchair in a very plush office.

"Congratulations, Commissioner!" he said, smiling. "I believe you're aware by now that your latest report has set many wheels spinning rapidly!"

"I rather expected it would," the Commissioner admitted. He also smiled.

They pitched it back and forth a few times, very chummy. Roadgear didn't appear to be involved in any specific way with the operations which soon would center about Luscious. Trigger began to wonder what he was after.

"A few of us are rather curious to know," Roadgear said, "why you didn't acknowledge the last Council Order sent you."

Trigger didn't quite start nervously.

"When was this?" asked the Commissioner.

Roadgear smiled softly and told him.

"Got a record here of some scrambled item that arrived about then," the Commissioner said. "Very good of you to call me about it, Councilman. What was the order content?"

"It's dated now, as it happens," Roadgear said. "Actually I'm calling about another matter. The First Lady of Tranest appears to have been very obliging about informing you of some of her recent activities."

The Commissioner nodded. "Yes, very obliging."

"And in so short a time after her, ah, detainment. You must have been very persuasive?"

"Well," Holati Tate said, "no more than usually."

"Yes," said Councilman Roadgear. "Now there's been some slight concern expressed by some members of the Council—well, let's say they'd just like to be reassured that the amenities one observes in dealing with a Head of State actually are being observed in this case. I'm sure they are, of course."

The Commissioner was silent a moment. "I was informed a while ago," he said, "that full responsibility for this Head of State has been assigned to my group. Is that correct?"

The Councilman reddened very slightly. "Quite," he said. "The official Council Order should reach you in a day or so."

"Well, then," said the Commissioner, "I'll assure you and you can assure the Councilmen who were feeling concerned that the amenities are being observed. Then everybody can relax again. Is that all right?"

"No, not quite," Roadgear said annoyedly. "In fact, the Councilmen would very much prefer it, Commissioner, if I were given an opportunity to speak to the First Lady directly to reassure myself on the point."

"Well," Commissioner Tate said, "she can't come to the transmitters right now. She's washing the dishes."

The Councilman reddened very considerably this time. He stared at the Commissioner a moment longer. Then he said in a very soft voice, "Oh, the hell with it!" He added, "Good luck, Commissioner—you're going to need it some time."

The screen went blank.

25

The scouts of Selan's Independent Fleet, who had first looked this planet over and decided to call it Luscious, had selected a name, Trigger thought, which probably would stick. Because that was what it was, at least in the area where they were camping.

She rolled over from her side to her face and gave herself a push away from the rock she'd been regarding contemplatively for the past few minutes. Feet first, she went drifting out into a somewhat deeper section of Plasmoid Creek.

None of it was very deep. There were pools here and there, in the stretch of the creek she usually came to, where she could stand on her toes in the warm clear water and, arms stretched straight up, barely tickle the surface with her fingertips. But along most of the stretch the bigger rocks weren't even submerged.

She came sliding over the sand to another rock, turned on her back and leaned up against the rock, blinking at sun reflections along the water. Camp was a couple of hundred yards down the valley, its sounds cut off by a rise of the ground. The Commissioner's ship was there, plus a half dozen tents, plus a sizable I-Fleet unit with lab facilities which Selan's outfit had loaned Mantelish for the duration. There were some fifteen, twenty people in all about the camp at the moment. They knew she was loafing around in the water up here and wouldn't disturb her.

Strictly speaking, of course, she wasn't loafing. She was learning how to listen to herself think. She didn't feel she was getting the knack of it too quickly; but it was coming. The best way seemed to be to let go mentally as much as possible; to wait without impatience, really to more-or-less listen quietly within yourself, as if you were looking around in some strange forest, letting whatever wanted to come to view come, and fade again, as something else rose to view instead. The main difficulty was with the business of relaxing mentally, which wasn't at all her natural method of approaching a problem.

But when she could do it, information of a kind that was beginning to look very interesting was likely to come filtering into her awareness. Whatever was at work deep in her mind—and she could give a pretty fair guess at what it was now—seemed as weak and slow as the Psychology Service people had indicated. The traces of its work were usually faint and vague. But gradually the traces were forming into some very definite pictures.

Lazing around in the waters of Plasmoid Creek for an hour or so every morning had turned out to be a helpful part of the process. On the flashing, all-out run to Luscious, subspace all the way, with the Commissioner and Quillan spelling each other around the clock at the controls, the transmitters clattering for attention every half hour, the ship's housekeeping to be handled, and somebody besides Mantelish needed to keep a moderately beady eye on the Ermetyne, she hadn't even thought of acting on Pilch's suggestion.

But once they'd landed, there suddenly wasn't much to keep her busy, and she could shift priority to listening to herself think. It was one of those interim periods where everything was being prepared and nothing had got started. As a plasmoid planet, Luscious was pretty much of a bust. It was true that plasmoids were here. It was also true that until fairly recently plasmoids were being produced here.

By the simple method of looking where they were thickest, Selan's people even had located the plasmoid which had been producing the others, several days before Mantelish arrived to confirm their find. This one, by the plasmoid standards of Luscious, was a regular monster, some twenty-five feet high; a gray, mummy-like thing, dead and half rotted inside. It was the first plasmoid—with the possible exception of whatever had flattened itself out on Quillan's gravity mine—known to have died. There had been very considerable excitement when it was first discovered, because the description made it sound very much as if they'd finally located 112-113.

They hadn't. This one—if Trigger had followed Mantelish correctly—could be regarded as a cheap imitation of 112. And its productions, compared with the working plastic life of *Harvest Moon*, appeared to be strictly on a kindergarten level: nuts and bolts and less than that. To Trigger, most of the ones that had been collected looked like assorted bugs and worms, though one at least was the size of a small pig.

"No form, no pattern," Mantelish rumbled. "Was the thing practicing? Did it attempt to construct an assistant and set it down here to test it? Well, now!" He went off again into incomprehensibilities, apparently no longer entirely dissatisfied. "Get me 112!" he bellowed. "Then this business will be solved! Meanwhile we now at least have plasmoid material to waste. We can experiment boldly! Come, Lyad, my dear."

And Lyad followed him into the lab unit, where they went to work again, dissecting, burning, stimulating, inoculating and so forth great numbers of more or less pancake-sized subplasmoids.

This morning Trigger wasn't getting down to the best semi-drowsy level at all readily. And it might very well be that Lyad-my-dear business. "You know," she had told the Commissioner thoughtfully the day before, "by the time we're done, Lyad will know more about plasmoids than anyone in the Hub except Mantelish!"

He didn't look concerned. "Won't matter much. By the time we're done, she and the rest of the Ermetynes will have had to cough up control of Tranest. They've broken treaty with this business."

"Oh," Trigger said. "Does Lyad know that?"

"Sure. She also knows she's getting off easy. If she were a Federation citizen, she'd be up for compulsory rehabilitation right now."

"She'll try something if she gets half a chance!" Trigger warned.

"She sure will," the Commissioner said absently. He went on with his work.

It didn't seem to be Lyad that was bothering her. Trigger lay flat on her back on the shallow sand bar, arms behind her head, feeling the sun's warmth on her closed eyelids. She watched her thoughts drifting by slowly.

It just might be Quillan.

Ole Major Quillan. The rescuer in time of need. The not-catassin smasher. Quite a guy. The water murmured past her.

On the ride out here they'd run by one another now and then, going from job to job. After they'd arrived, Quillan was gone three quarters of the time, helping out in the hunt for the concealed Devagas fortress. It was still concealed; they hadn't yet picked up a trace.

But every so often he made it back to camp. And every so often when he was back in camp and didn't think she was looking, he'd be sitting there looking at her.

Trigger grinned happily. Ole Major Quillan—being bashful! Well now!

And that did it. She could feel herself relaxing, slipping down and away, drifting down through her mind . . . farther . . . deeper . . . toward the tiny voice that spoke in such a strange language and still was becoming daily more comprehensible.

"Uh, say, Trigger!"

Trigger gasped. Her eyes flew open. She made a convulsive effort to vanish beneath the surface of the creek. Being flat on the sand as it was, that didn't work. So she stopped splashing about and made rapid covering-up motions here and there instead.

"You've got a nerve!" she snapped as her breath came back. "Beat it. Fast!"

Ole bashful Quillan, standing on the bank fifteen feet above her, looked hurt. He also looked.

"Look!" he said plaintively. "I just came over to make sure you were all right—wild animals around! I wasn't studying the color scheme."

"*Beat it! At once!*"

Quillan inhaled with apparent difficulty.

"Though now it's been mentioned," he went on, speaking rapidly and unevenly, "there is all that brown and that sort of pink and that lovely white." He was getting more enthusiastic by the moment; Trigger became afraid he would fall off the bank and land in the creek beside her. "And the—ooh-ummh!—wet red hair and the freckles!" he rattled along, his eyes starting out of his head. "And the lovely—"

"Quillan!" she yelled. "Please!"

Quillan checked himself. "Uh!" he said. He drew a deep breath. The wild look faded. Sanity appeared to return. "Well, it's the truth about those wild animals. Some sort of large, uncouth critter was observed just now ducking into the forest at the upper end of the valley."

Trigger darted a glance along the bank. Her clothes were forty feet away, just beside the water.

"I'm observing some sort of large, uncouth critter right here," she said coldly. "What's worse, it's observing me. Turn around!"

Quillan sighed. "You're a hard woman, Argee," he said. But he turned. He was carrying a holstered gun, as a matter of fact; but he usually did that nowadays anyway. "This thing," he went on, "is supposed to have a head like a bat, three feet across. It flies."

"Very interesting," Trigger told him. She decided he wasn't going to turn around again. "So now I'll just get into my clothes, and then—"

It came quietly out of the trees around the upper bend of the creek sixty feet away. It had a head like a bat, and was blue on top and yellow below. Its flopping wing tips barely cleared the bank on either side. The three-foot mouth was wide open, showing very long thin white teeth. It came skimming swiftly over the surface of the water toward her.

"Quiiiii-LLAN!"

26

They walked back along the trail to camp. Trigger walked a few steps ahead, her back very straight. The worst of it had been the smug look on his face.

"Heel!" she observed. "Heel! Heel! Heel!"

"Now, Trigger," Quillan said calmingly behind her. "After all, it was you who came flying up the bank and wrapped yourself around my neck. All wet, too."

"I was scared!" Trigger snarled. "Who wouldn't be? You certainly didn't hesitate an instant to take full advantage of the situation!"

"True," Quillan admitted. "I'd dropped the bat. There you were. Who'd hesitate. I'm not out of my mind."

She did two dance steps of pure rage and spun to face him. She put her hands on her hips. Quillan stopped warily.

"Your mind!" she said. "I'd hate to have one like it. What do you think I am? One of Belchik's houris?"

For a man his size, he was really extremely quick. Before she could move, he was there, one big arm wrapped about her shoulders, pinning her arms to her sides. "Easy, Trigger," he said softly.

Well, others had tried to hold her like that when she didn't want to be held. A twist, a jerk, a heave—and over and down they went. Trigger braced herself quietly. If she was quick enough now—She twisted, jerked, heaved. She stopped, discouraged. The situation hadn't altered appreciably.

She *had* been afraid it wasn't going to work with Quillan.

"Let go!" she said furiously, aiming a fast heel at his instep. But the instep flicked aside. Her shoe dug into the turf of the path. The ape might even have an extra pair of eyes on his feet!

Then his free palm was cupped under her chin, tilting it carefully. His other eyes appeared above hers. Very close. Very dark.

"I'll bite!" Trigger whispered fiercely. "I'll bi-mmph!"

"Mmmph-grrmm!"

"Grr-mm-mhm . . . Hm-m-m . . . mhm!"

They walked on along the trail, hand in hand. They came up over, the last little rise. Trigger looked down on the camp. She frowned.

"Pretty dull!" she observed.

"Eh?" Quillan asked, startled.

"Not that, ape!" she said. She squeezed his hand. "Your morals aren't good, but dull it wasn't. I meant, generally. We're just sitting here now waiting. Nothing seems to be happening."

It was true, at least on the surface. There were a great number of ships and men around and near Luscious, but they weren't in view. They were ready to jump in any direction, at any moment, but they had nothing to jump at yet. The Commissioner's transmitters hadn't signaled more than two or three times in the last two days. Even the short communicators remained mostly silent.

"Cheer up, doll!" said Quillan. "Something's bound to break pretty soon."

That evening, a Devagas ship came zooming in on Luscious.

They were prepared for it, of course. That somebody came around from time to time to look over the local plasmoid crop was only to be expected. As the ship surfaced in atmosphere on the other side of the planet, four one-man Scout fighters flashed in on it from four points of the horizon, radiation screens up. They tacked holding beams on it and braced themselves. A Federation destroyer appeared in the air above it.

The Devagas ship couldn't escape. So it blew itself up.

They were prepared for that, too. The Devagas pilot was being dead-brained three minutes later. He didn't know a significant thing except the exact coordinates of an armed, subterranean Devagas dome, a three days' run away.

The Scout ships that had been hunting for the dome went bowling in toward it from every direction. The more massive naval vessels of the Federation followed behind. There was no hurry for the heavies. The captured Devagas ship's attempt to beam a warning to its base had been smothered without effort. The Scouts were getting in fast enough to block escape attempts.

"And now we split forces," the Commissioner said. He was the only one, Trigger thought, who didn't seem too enormously excited by it all. "Quillan, you and your group get going! They can use you there a whole lot better than we can here."

For just a second, Quillan looked like a man being dragged violently in two directions. He didn't look at Trigger. He asked, "Think it's wise to leave you people unguarded?"

"Quillan," said Commissioner Tate, "that's the first time in my life anybody has suggested I needed guarding."

"Sorry, sir," said Quillan.

"You mean," Trigger said, "we're not going? We're just staying here?"

"You've got an appointment, remember?" the Commissioner said.

Quillan and company were gone within the hour. Mantelish, Holati Tate, Lyad and Trigger stayed at camp.

Luscious looked very lonely.

❖   ❖   ❖

"It isn't just the king plasmoid they're hoping to catch there," the Commissioner told Trigger. "And I wouldn't care, frankly, if the thing stayed lost the next few thousand years. But we had a very odd report last week. The Federation's undercover boys have been scanning the Devagas worlds and Tranest very closely of late, naturally. The report is that there isn't the slightest evidence that a single one of the top members of the Devagas hierarchy has been on any of their worlds for the past two months."

"Oh," she said. "They think they're out here? In that dome?"

"That's what's suspected."

"But why?"

He scratched his chin. "If anyone knows, they haven't told me. It's probably nothing nice."

Trigger pondered. "You'd think they'd use facsimiles," she said. "Like Lyad."

"Oh, they did," he said. "They did. That's one of the reasons for being pretty sure they're gone. They're nowhere near as expert at that facsimile business as the Tranest characters. A little study of the recordings showed the facs were just that."

Trigger pondered again. "Did they find anything on Tranest?"

"Yes. One combat-strength squadron of those souped-up frigates of the *Aurora* class they're allowed by treaty can't be accounted for."

Trigger cupped her chin in her hands and looked at him. "Is that why we've stayed on Luscious, Holati—the four of us?"

"It's one reason. That Repulsive thing of yours is another."

"What about him?"

"I have a pretty strong feeling," he said, "that while they'll probably find the hierarchy in that Devagas dome, they won't find the 112-113 item there."

"So Lyad still is gambling," Trigger said. "And we're gambling we'll get more out of her next play than she does." She hesitated. "Holati—"

"Yes?"

"When did you decide it would be better if nobody ever got to see that king plasmoid again?"

Holati Tate said, "About the time I saw the reconstruct of that yellow monster of Balmordan's. Frankly, Trigger, there was a good deal of discussion of possibilities along that line before we decided to announce the discovery of *Harvest Moon*. If we could have just kept it hidden away for a couple of centuries—until there was considerably more good sense around the Hub—we probably would have done it. But somebody was bound to run across it sometime. And the stuff did look as if it might be extremely valuable. So we took the chance."

"And now you'd like to untake it?"

"If it's still possible. Half the Fed Council probably would like to see it happen. But they don't even dare think along those lines. There could be a blowup that would throw Hub politics back into the kind of snarl they haven't been in for a hundred years. If anything is done, it will have to look as if it had been something nobody could have helped. And that still might be bad enough."

"I suppose so. Holati—"

"Yes?"

She shook her head. "Nothing. Or if it is, I'll ask you later." She stood up. "I think I'll go have my swim."

She still went loafing in Plasmoid Creek in the mornings. The bat had been identified as an innocent victim of appearances, a very mild mannered beast dedicated to the pursuit and engulfment of huge moth-like bugs which hung around watercourses. Luscious still looked like the safest of all possible worlds for any creature as vigorous as a human being. But she kept the Denton near now, just in case.

She stretched out again in the sun-warmed water,

selected a smooth rock to rest her head on, wriggled into the sand a little so the current wouldn't shift her, and closed her eyes. She lay still, breathing slowly. Contact was coming more easily and quickly every morning. But the information which had begun to filter through in the last few days wasn't at all calculated to make one happy.

She was afraid now she was going to die in this thing. She had almost let it slip out to Holati, which wouldn't have helped in the least. She'd have to watch that in the future.

Repulsive hadn't exactly said she would die. He'd said, "Maybe." Repulsive was scared too. Scared badly.

Trigger lay quiet, her thoughts, her attention drifting softly inward and down. Creek water rippled against her cheek.

It was all because that one clock moved so slowly. That was the thing that couldn't be changed. Ever.

27

Three mornings later, the emergency signal called her back to camp on the double.

Trigger ran over the developments of the past days in her mind as she trotted along the path, getting dressed more or less on the way. The Devagas dome was solidly invested by now, its transmitters blanked out. It hadn't tried to communicate with its attackers. On their part, the Fed ships weren't pushing the attack. They were holding the point, waiting for the big, slow wrecking boats to arrive, which would very gently and delicately start uncovering and opening the dome, taking it apart, piece-by-piece. The hierarchy could surrender themselves and whatever they were hiding in there at any point in the process. They didn't have a chance. Nobody and nothing had escaped. The Scouts had swatted down a few Devagas vessels on the way in; but those had been headed toward the dome, not away from it.

Perhaps the Psychology Service ship had arrived, several days ahead of time.

The other three weren't in camp, but the lock to the Commissioner's ship stood open. Trigger went in and found them gathered up front. The Commissioner had swung the transmitter cabinet aside and was back there, prowling among the power leads.

"What's wrong?" Trigger asked.

"Transmitters went out," he said. "Don't know why yet. Grab some tools and help me check."

She slipped on her work gloves, grabbed some tools and joined him. Lyad and Mantelish watched them silently.

They found the first spots of the fungus a few minutes later.

"Fungus!" Mantelish said, startled. He began to fumble in his pockets. "My microscope—"

"I have it." Lyad handed it to him. She looked at him with concern. "You don't think—"

"It seems possible. We did come in here last night, remember? And we came straight from the lab."

"But we had decontaminated," Lyad said puzzledly.

"Don't try to walk in here, Professor!" Trigger warned as he lumbered forward. "We might have to de-electrocute you. The Commissioner will scrape off a sample and hand it out. This stuff—if it's what you think it might be—is it poisonous?"

"Quite harmless to life, my dear," said the professor, bending over the patch of greenish-gray scum the Commissioner had reached out to him. "But ruinous in delicate instruments! That's why we're so careful."

Holati Tate glanced at Trigger. "Better look in the black box, Trig," he said.

She nodded and wormed herself farther into the

innards of the transmitters. A minute later she announced, "Full of it! And that's the one part we can't repair or replace, of course. Is it your beast, Professor?"

"It seems to be," Mantelish said unhappily. "But we have, at least, a solvent which will remove it from the equipment."

Trigger came sliding out from under the transmitters, the detached black box under one arm. "Better use it then before the stuff gets to the rest of the ship. It won't help the black box." She shook it. It tinkled. "Shot!" she said. "There went another quarter million of your credits, Commissioner."

Mantelish and Lyad headed for the lock to get the solvent. Trigger slipped off her work gloves and turned to follow them. "Might be a while before I'm back," she said.

The Commissioner started to say something, then nodded and climbed back into the transmitters. After a few minutes, Mantelish came puffing in with sprayers and cans of solvent. "It's at least fortunate you tried to put out a call just now," he said. "It might have done incalculable damage."

"Doubt it," said Holati. "A few more instruments might have gone. Like the communicators. The main equipment is fungus-proof. How do you attach this thing?"

Mantelish showed him.

The Commissioner thanked him. He directed a fine spray of the solvent into the black box and watched the fungus melt. "Happen to notice where Trigger and Lyad went?" he asked.

"Eh?" said Mantelish. He reflected. "I saw them walking down toward camp talking together as I came in," he recalled. "Should I go get them?"

"Don't bother," Holati said. "They'll be back."

They came walking back into the ship around half an hour later. Both faces looked rather white and strained.

"Lyad has something she wants to tell you, Holati," Trigger said. "Where's Mantelish?"

"In his lab. Taking a nap, I believe."

"That's good. We don't want him here for this. Go ahead, Lyad. Just the important stuff. You can give us the details after we've left."

Three hours later, the ship was well away from Luscious, traveling subspace, traveling fast. Trigger walked up into the control section.

"Mantelish is still asleep," she said. They'd fed the professor a doped drink to get him aboard without detailed explanation and argument about how much of the lab should be loaded on the ship first. "Shall I get Lyad out of her cabin for the rest of the story or wait till he wakes up?"

"Better wait," said the Commissioner. "He'll come out of it in about an hour, and he might as well hear it with us. Looks like navigating's going to be a little rough for a spell anyway."

Trigger nodded and sat down in the control seat next to his. After a while he glanced over at her.

"How did you get her to talk?" he asked.

"We went back into the woods a bit. I tied her over a stump and broke two sticks across the first seat of Tranest. Got the idea from Mihul, sort of," Trigger added vaguely. "When I picked up a third stick, Lyad got awfully anxious to keep things at just a fast conversational level. We kept it there."

"Hm," said the Commissioner. "You don't feel she did any lying this time?"

"I doubt it. I tapped her one now and then, just to make sure she didn't slow down enough to do much thinking. Besides I'd got the whole business down on a pocket recorder, and Lyad knew it. If she makes one more goof till this deal is over, the recording gets released to the Hub's news viewer outfits, yowls and all. She'd sooner lose Tranest than risk having that happen. She'll be good."

"Yeah, probably," he said thoughtfully. "About that substation—would you feel more comfortable if we went after the bunch around the Devagas dome first and got us an escort for the trip?"

"Sure," Trigger said. "But that would just about kill any chances of doing anything personally, wouldn't it?"

"I'm afraid so. Scout Intelligence will go along pretty far with me. But they couldn't go that far. We might be able to contact Quillan individually though. He's a topnotch man in a fighter."

"It doesn't seem to me," Trigger said, "that we ought to run any risk of being spotted till we know exactly what this thing is like."

"Well," said the Commissioner, "I'm with you there. We shouldn't."

"What about Mantelish and Lyad? You can't let them know either."

The Commissioner motioned with his head. "The rest cubicle back of the cabins. If we see a chance to do anything, we'll pop them both into Rest. I can dream up something to make that look plausible afterwards, I think."

Trigger was silent a moment. Lyad had told them she'd dispatched the *Aurora* to stand guard over a subspace station where the missing king plasmoid presently was housed, until both she and the combat squadron from Tranest could arrive there. The exact location of that station had been the most valuable of the bits of information she had extracted so painstakingly from Balmordan. The coordinates were centered on the Commissioner's course screen at the moment.

"How about that Tranest squadron?" Trigger asked. "Think Lyad might have risked a lie, and they could get out here in time to interfere?"

"No," said the Commissioner. "She had to have some idea of where to send them before starting them out of the Hub. They'll be doing fine if they make it to the substation in another two weeks. Now the *Aurora*—if they started for Luscious right after Lyad called them last night, at best they can't get there any sooner than we can get to the substation. I figure that at four days. If they turn right around then, and start back—"

Trigger laughed. "You can bet on that!" she said. The Commissioner had used his ship's guns to brand the substation's coordinates in twenty-mile figures into a mountain plateau above Plasmoid Creek. They'd left much more detailed information in camp, but there was a chance it would be overlooked in too hurried a search.

"Then they'll show up at the substation again four or five days behind us," the Commissioner said. "So they're no problem. But our own outfit's fastest ships can cut across from the Devagas dome in less than three days after their search party messages from Luscious to tell them why we've stopped transmitting and where we've gone. Or the Psychology ship might get to Luscious before the search party does and start transmitting about the coordinates."

"In any case," said Trigger, "it's our own boys who are likely to be the problem."

"Yes. I'd say we *should* have two days, give or take a few hours, after we get to the station to see if we can do anything useful and get it done. Of course, somebody might come wandering into Luscious right now and start wondering about those coordinate figures, or drop in at our camp and discover we're gone. But that's not very likely, after all."

"Couldn't be helped anyway," Trigger said.

"No. If we knock ourselves out on this job, somebody besides Lyad's Tranest squadron and the Devagas has to know just where the station is." He shook his head. "That Lyad! I figured she'd know how to run the transmitters, so I gave her the chance. But I never imagined she'd be a good enough engineer to get inside them and mess them up without killing herself."

"Lyad has her points," Trigger said. "Too bad she grew

up a rat. You had a playback attachment stuck in there then?"

"Naturally."

"Full of the fungus, I suppose?"

"Full of it," said the Commissioner. "Well, Lyad still lost on that maneuver. Much less comfortably then she might have, too."

"I think she'd agree with you there," Trigger said.

Lyad's first assignment after Professor Mantelish came out of the dope was to snap him back into trance and explain to him how he had once more been put under hypno control and used for her felonious ends by the First Lady of Tranest. They let him work off his rage while he was still under partial control. Then the Ermetyne woke him up.

He stared at her coldly.

"You are a deceitful woman, Lyad Ermetyne!" he declared. "I don't wish to see you about any of my labs again! At any time. Under any pretext. Is that understood?"

"Yes, Professor," Lyad said. "And I'm sorry that I believed it necessary to—"

Mantelish snorted. "Sorry! Necessary! Just to be certain it doesn't happen again, I shall make up a batch of anti-hypno pills. If I can remember the prescription."

"I happen," the Ermetyne ventured, "to know a very good prescription for the purpose, Professor. If you will permit me."

Mantelish stood up. "I'll accept no prescriptions from you!" he said icily. He looked at Trigger as he turned to walk out of the cabin. "Or drinks from you either, Trigger Argee!" he growled. "Who in the great spiraling galaxy is there left to trust!"

"Sorry, Professor," Trigger said meekly.

In half an hour or so, he calmed down enough to join the others in the lounge, to get the final story on

Gess Fayle and the missing king plasmoid from the
Ermetyne.

Doctor Gess Fayle, Lyad reported, had died very
shortly after stealing the 112-113 unit and leaving the
Manon System. And with him had died every man on
board the U-League's transport ship. It might be sim-
plest, she went on, to relate the first series of events from
the plasmoid's point of view.

"Point of view?" Professor Mantelish interrupted. "The
plasmoid has awareness then?"

"Oh, yes. That one does."

"Self-awareness?"

"Definitely."

"Oho! But then—"

"Professor," Trigger interrupted politely in turn, "may
I get you a drink?"

He glared at her, growled, then grinned. "I'll shut up,"
he said. Lyad went on.

Doctor Fayle had resumed experimentation with the
112-113 unit almost as soon as he was alone with it; and
one of the first things he did was to detach the small
113 section from the main one. The point Doctor Fayle
hadn't adequately considered when he took this step was
that 113's function appeared to be that of a restraining,
limiting or counteracting device on its vastly larger partner. The Old Galactics obviously had been aware of
dangerous potentialities in their more advanced creations,
and had used this means of regulating them. That the
method was reliable was indicated by the fact that, in
the thirty thousand years since the Old Galactics had
vanished, plasmoid 112 had remained restricted to the
operations required for the maintenance of *Harvest Moon*.

But it hadn't liked being restricted.

And it had been very much aware of the possibilities
offered by the new life-forms which lately had intruded
on *Harvest Moon*.

The instant it found itself free, it attempted to take control of the human minds in its environment.

"Mind-level control?" Mantelish exclaimed, looking startled. "Not unheard-of, of course. And we'd been considering . . . But of *human* minds?"

Lyad nodded. "It can contact human minds," she said, "though, perhaps rather fortunately, it can project that particular field effect only within a quite limited radius. A little less, the Devagas found later, than five miles."

Mantelish shook his head, frowning. He turned toward the Commissioner. "Holati," he said emphatically, "I believe that thing could be dangerous!"

For a moment, they all looked at him. Then the Commissioner cleared his throat. "It's a possibility, Mantelish," he admitted. "We will give it thought later."

"What," Trigger asked Lyad, "killed the people on the ship?"

The attempt to control them, Lyad said. Doctor Fayle apparently had died as he was leaving the laboratory with the 113 unit. The other men died wherever they were. The ship, running subspace and pilotless, plowed headlong into the next gravitic twister and broke up.

A Devagas ship's detectors picked up the wreckage three days later. Balmordan was on board the Devagas ship and in charge.

The Devagas, at that time, were at least as plasmoid-hungry as anybody else, and knew they were not likely to see their hunger gratified for several decades. The wreck of a U-League ship in the Manon area decidedly was worth investigating.

If the big plasmoid hadn't been capable of learning from its mistakes, the Devagas investigating party also would have died. Since it could and did learn, they lived. The searchers discovered human remains and the crushed remnants of the 113 unit in a collapsed section of the ship. Then they discovered the big plasmoid—alive in subspace, undamaged and very conscious of the difficulties it now faced.

It had already initiated its first attempt to solve the difficulties. It was incapable of outward motion and could not change its own structure, but it was no longer alone. It had constructed a small work-plasmoid with visual and manipulating organs, as indifferent to exposure to subspace as its designer. When the boarding party encountered the twain, the working plasmoid apparently was attempting to perform some operation on the frozen and shriveled brain of one of the human cadavers.

Balmordan was a scientist of no mean stature among the Devagas. He did not understand immediately what he saw, but he realized the probable importance of understanding it. He had the plasmoids and their lifeless human research object transferred to the Devagas ship and settled down to observe what they did.

Released, the working plasmoid went back immediately to its task. It completed it. Then Balmordan and, presumably, the plasmoids waited. Nothing happened.

Finally, Balmordan investigated the dead brain. Installed in it he found what appeared to be near-microscopic energy receivers of plasmoid material. There was nothing to indicate what type of energy they were to—or could—receive.

Devagas scientists, when they happened to be of the hierarchy, always had enjoyed one great advantage over most of their colleagues in the Federation. They had no difficulty in obtaining human volunteers to act as subjects for experimental work. Balmordan appointed three of his least valuable crew members as volunteers for the plasmoid's experiments.

The first of the three died almost immediately. The plasmoid, it turned out, lacked understanding of, among other things, the use and need of anesthetics. Balmordan accordingly assisted obligingly in the second operation.

He was delighted when it became apparent that his assistance was being willingly and comprehendingly accepted. This subject did not die immediately. But he did not regain consciousness after the plasmoid devices had been installed; and some hours later he did die, in convulsions.

Number Three was more fortunate. He regained consciousness. He complained of headaches and, after he had slept, of nightmares. The next day he went into shock for a period of several hours. When he came out of it, he reported tremblingly that the big plasmoid was talking to him, though he could not understand what it said.

There were two more test operations, both successful. In all three cases, the headaches and nightmares stopped in about a week. The first subject in the series was beginning to understand the plasmoid. Balmordan listened to his reports. He had his three surviving volunteers given very extensive physical and psychological tests. They seemed to be in fine condition.

Balmordan now had the operation performed on himself. When he woke up, he disposed of his three predecessors. Then he devoted his full attention to learning what the plasmoid was trying to say. In about three weeks it became clear . . .

The plasmoid had established contact with human beings because it needed their help. It needed a base like *Harvest Moon* from which to operate and on which to provide for its requirements. It did not have the understanding to permit it to construct such a base.

So it made the Devagas a proposition. It would work for them, somewhat as it had worked for the Old Galactics, if—unlike the Old Galactics—they would work for it.

Balmordan, newly become a person of foremost importance, transmitted the offer to the hierarchy in the Hub. With no hesitation it was accepted, but Balmordan was warned not to bring his monster into the Hub area. If it was discovered on a Devagas world, the hierarchy would be faced with the choice between another war with the Federation and submission to more severely restrictive Federation controls. It didn't care for either alternative; it had lost three wars with the Federated worlds in the past and each time had been reduced in strength.

They contacted Vishni's Independent Fleet. Vishni's area was not too far from Balmordan's ship position, and the Devagas had had previous dealings with him and his men. This time they hired the I-Fleet to become the plasmoid's temporary caretaker. Within a few weeks it was parked on Luscious, where it devoted itself to the minor creative experimentation which presently was to puzzle Professor Mantelish.

The Devagas, meanwhile, toiled prodigiously to complete the constructions which were to be a central feature in the new alliance. On a base very far removed from the Hub, securely anchored and concealed among the gravitic swirlings and shiftings of a subspace turbulence area, virtually indetectable, the monster could make a very valuable partner. If it was discovered, the partnership could be disowned. So could the fact that they had constructed the substation for it—in itself a grave breach of Federation treaties.

They built the substation. They built the armed subterranean observer's dome three days' travel away from it. The plasmoid was installed in its new quarters. It then requested the use of the Vishni Fleet people for further experimentation.

The hierarchy was glad to grant the request. It would have had to get rid of those too well informed hirelings in any case.

Having received its experimental material, the plasmoid requested the Devagas to stay away from the substation for a while.

28

The Devagas, said Lyad, while not too happy with their ally's increasingly independent attitude, were more anxious than ever to see the alliance progress to the working stage. As an indication of its potential usefulness, the monster had provided them with a variety of working plasmoid robots, built to their own specifications.

"What kind of specifications?" Trigger inquired.

Lyad hadn't learned in detail, but some of the robots appeared to have demonstrated rather alarming possibilities. Those possibilities, however, were precisely what intrigued the hierarchy most.

Mantelish smacked his lips thoughtfully and shook his head. "Not good!" he said. "Not at all good! I'm beginning to think—" He paused a moment. "Go on, Lyad."

The hierarchy was now giving renewed consideration to a curious request the plasmoid had made almost as soon as Balmordan became capable of understanding it. The request had been to find and destroy plasmoid 113-A.

The Ermetyne's amber eyes switched to Trigger. "Shall I?" they asked.

Trigger nodded.

And a specific human being. The Devagas already had established that this human being must be Trigger Argee.

"*What?*" Mantelish's thick white eyebrows shot up. "113-A we can understand—it is afraid of being in some way brought back under control. But why Trigger?"

"Because," Lyad said carefully, "112 was aware that 113-A intended to condition Trigger into being *its* interpreter."

Professor Mantelish's jaw dropped. He swung his head toward Trigger. "Is that true?"

She nodded. "It's true, all right. We've been working

on it, but we haven't got too far along. Tell you later. Go ahead, Lyad."

The Devagas, naturally, hadn't acted on the king plasmoid's naive suggestion. Whatever it feared was more than likely to be very useful to them. Instead they made preparations to bring both 113-A and Trigger Argee into their possession. They would then have a new, strong bargaining point in their dealings with their dubious partner. But they discovered promptly that neither Trigger nor 113-A were at all easy to come by.

Balmordan now suggested a modification of tactics. The hierarchy had seen to it that a number of interpreters were available for 112; Balmordan in consequence had lost much of his early importance and was anxious to regain it. His proposal was that all efforts should be directed at obtaining 113-A. Once it was obtained, he himself would volunteer to become its first interpreter. Trigger Argee, because of the information she might reveal to others, should be destroyed—a far simpler operation than attempting to take her alive.

This was agreed to; and Balmordan was authorized to carry out both operations.

Mantelish had begun shaking his head again. "No!" he said suddenly and loudly. He looked at Lyad, then at Trigger. "Trigger!" he said.

"Yes?" said Trigger.

"Take that deceitful woman to her cabin," Mantelish ordered. "Lock her up. I have something to say to the Commissioner."

Trigger arose. "All right," she said. "Come on, Lyad."

The two of them left the lounge. Mantelish stood up and went over to the Commissioner. He grasped the Commissioner's jacket lapels.

"Holati, old friend!" he began emotionally.

"What is it, old friend?" the Commissioner inquired.

"What I have to say," Mantelish rumbled. "will shock you. Profoundly."

"No!" exclaimed the Commissioner.

"Yes," said Mantelish. "That plasmoid 112—it has, of course, an almost inestimable potential value to civilization."

"Of course," the Commissioner agreed.

"But it also," said Mantelish, "represents a quite intolerable threat to civilization."

"Mantelish!" cried the Commissioner.

"It does. You don't comprehend these matters as I do. Holati, that plasmoid must be destroyed! Secretly, if possible. And *by us!*"

"Mantelish!" gasped the Commissioner. "You can't he serious!"

"I am."

"Well," said Commissioner Tate, "sit down. I'm open to suggestions."

Space-armor drill hadn't been featured much in the Colonial School's crowded curriculum. But the Commissioner broke out one of the ship's two heavy-duty suits; and when Trigger wasn't at the controls, eating, sleeping, or taking care of the ship's housekeeping with Lyad and Mantelish, she drilled.

She wasn't at the controls too often. When she was, they had to surface and proceed in normal space. But Lyad, not too surprisingly, turned out to be a qualified subspace pilot. Even less surprisingly, she already had made a careful study of the ship's controls. After a few hours of instruction, she went on shift with the Commissioner along the less rugged stretches. In this area, none of the stretches were smooth.

When not on duty, Lyad lay on her bunk and brooded. Mantelish tried to be useful.

Repulsive might have been brooding too. He didn't make himself noticeable.

Time passed. The stretches got rougher. The last ten hours, the Commissioner didn't stir out of the control seat. Lyad had been locked in her cabin again as the critical period approached. In normal space, the substation should have been in clear detector range by now. Here, the detectors gave occasional blurry, uncertain indications that somewhere in the swirling energies about them might be something more solidly material. It was like creeping through jungle thickets towards the point where a dangerous quarry lurked.

They eased down on the coordinate points. They came sliding out between two monstrous twisters. The detectors leaped to life.

"Ship!" said the Commissioner. He swore. "Frigate class," he said an instant later. He turned his head toward Trigger. "Get Lyad! They're in communication range. We'll let her communicate."

Trigger, heart hammering, ran to get Lyad. The Commissioner had the short-range communicator on when they came hurrying back to the control room together.

"That the *Aurora*?" he asked.

Lyad glanced at the outline in the detectors. "It is!" Her face went white.

"Talk to 'em," he ordered. "Know their call number?"

"Of course." Lyad sat down at the communicator. Her hands shook for a moment, then steadied. "What am I to say?"

"Just find out what's happened, to start with. Why they're still here. Then we'll improvise. Get them to come on screen if you can."

Lyad's fingers flew over the tabs. The communicator signaled contact.

Lyad said evenly, "Come in, *Aurora*! This is the Ermetyne."

There was a pause, a rather unaccountably long pause, Trigger thought. Then a voice said, "Yes, First Lady?"

Lyad's eyes widened for an instant. "Come in on visual, Captain!" There was the snap of command in the words.

Again a pause. Then suddenly the communicator was looking into the *Aurora*'s control room. A brown-bearded, rather lumpy-faced man in uniform sat before the other screen. There were other uniformed men behind him. Trigger heard the Ermetyne's breath suck in and turned to watch Lyad's face.

"Why haven't you carried out your instructions, Captain?" The voice was still even.

"There was a difficulty with the engines, First Lady."

Lyad nodded. "Very well. Stand by for new instructions."

She switched off the communicator. She twisted around toward the Commissioner. "Get us out of here!" she said, chalk-faced. "*Fast!* Those aren't my men."

Flame bellowed about them in subspace. The Commissioner's hand slapped a button. The flame vanished and stars shone all around. The engines hurled them forward. Twelve seconds later, they angled and dived again. Subspace reappeared.

"Guess you were right!" the Commissioner said. He idled the engines and scratched his chin. "But what were they?"

"Everything about it was wrong!" Lyad was saying presently, her face still white. "Their faces, in particular, were deformed!" She looked at Trigger. "You saw it?"

Trigger nodded. She suspected she was on the white-faced side herself. "The captain," she said. "I didn't look at the others. It looked as if his cheeks and forehead were pushed out of shape!"

There was a short silence. "Well," said the Commissioner, "seems like that plasmoid has been doing some more experimenting. Question is, how did it get to them?"

They didn't find any answers to that. Lyad insisted the *Aurora* had been given specific orders to avoid the immediate vicinity of the substation. Its only purpose there was to observe and report on anything that seemed

to be going on in the area. She couldn't imagine her crew
disobeying the orders.

"That mind-level control business," Trigger said finally.
"Maybe *it* found a way of going out to *them*."

She could see by their faces that the idea had occurred,
and that they didn't like it. Well, neither did she.

They pitched a few more ideas around. None of them
seemed helpful.

"Unless we just want to hightail it," the Commissioner
said finally, "about the only thing we can do is go back
and slug it out with the frigate first. We can't risk snoop-
ing around the station while she's there and likely to start
pounding on our backs any second."

Mantelish looked startled. "Holati," he cautioned,
"that's a warship!"

"Mantelish," the Commissioner said, a trifle coldly,
"what you've been riding in isn't a canoe." He glanced
at Lyad. "I suppose you'd feel happier if you weren't
locked up in your cabin during the ruckus?"

Lyad gave him a strained smile. "Commissioner," she
said, "you're so right!"

"Then keep your seat," he said. "We'll start prowling."

They prowled. It took an hour to recontact the *Aurora*,
presumably because the *Aurora* was also prowling for
them. Suddenly the detectors came alive.

The ship's guns went off at once. Then subspace went
careening crazily past in the screens. Trigger looked at
the screens for a few seconds, gulped and started studying
the floor.

Whatever the plasmoid had done to the frigate's crew,
they appeared to have lost none of their ability to give
battle. It was a very brisk affair. But neither had the one-
time Squadron Commander Tate lost much of his talent
along those lines. The frigate had many more guns but
no better range. And he had the faster ship. Four minutes after the first shots were exchanged, the *Aurora* blew
up.

❖   ❖   ❖

The ripped hunk of the *Aurora*'s hull which the Commissioner presently brought into the lock appeared to have had three approximately quarter-inch holes driven at a slant through it, which subsequently had been plugged again. The plugging material was plasmoid in character.

"There were two holes in another piece," the Commissioner said, very thoughtfully. "If that's the average, she was punched in a few thousand spots. Let's go have a better look."

He and Mantelish maneuvered the gravity crane carrying the holed slab of steel-alloy into the ship's workshop. Lyad was locked back into her cabin, and Trigger went on guard in the control room and looked out wistfully at the stars of normal space.

Half an hour later, the two men came up the passage and joined her. They appeared preoccupied.

"It's an unpleasant picture, Trigger girl," the Commissioner said. "Those holes look sort of chewed through. Whatever did the chewing was also apparently capable of sealing up the portion behind it as it went along. What it did to the men when it got inside we don't know. Mantelish feels we might compare it roughly to the effects of ordinary germ invasion. It doesn't really matter. It fixed them."

"Mighty large germs!" Trigger said. "Why didn't their meteor reflectors stop them?"

"If the ship was hove to and these things just drifted in gradually—"

"Oh, I see. That wouldn't activate the reflectors. Then, if we keep moving ourselves—"

"That," said the Commissioner, "was what I had in mind."

29

Trigger couldn't keep from staring at the subspace station. It was unbelievable.

One could still tell that the human construction gangs had put up a standard type of armored station down there. A very big, very massive one, but normally shaped, nearly spherical. One could tell it only by the fact that at the gun pits the original material still showed through. Everywhere else it had vanished under great black masses of material which the plasmoids had added to the station's structure.

All over that black, lumpy, lava-like surface the plasmoids crawled, walked, soared and wriggled. There were thousands of them, perhaps hundreds of different types. It looked like a wet, black, rotten stump swarming with life inside and out.

Neither she nor the two men had made much mention of its appearance. All you could say was that it was horrible.

The plasmoids they could see ignored the ship. They also gave no noticeable attention to the eight space flares the Commissioner had set in a rough cube about the station. But for the first two hours after their arrival, the ship's meteor reflectors remained active. An occasional tap at first, then an almost continuous pecking, finally a twenty-minute drumfire that filled the reflector screens with madly dancing clouds of tiny sparks. Suddenly it ended. Either the king plasmoid had exhausted its supply of that particular weapon or it preferred to conserve what it had left.

"Might test their guns," the Commissioner muttered. He looked very unhappy, Trigger thought.

He circled off, put on speed, came back and flicked the ship past the station's flank. He drew bursts from two pits with a promptness which confirmed what already had been almost a certainty—that the gun installations operated automatically. They seemed remarkably feeble weapons for a station of that size. The Devagas apparently had

had sense enough not to give the plasmoid every advantage.

The Commissioner plunked a test shot next into one of the black protuberances. A small fiery crater appeared. It darkened quickly again. Out of the biggest opening, down near what would have been the foot of the stump if it had been a stump, something long, red and worm-like wriggled rapidly. It flowed up over the structure's surface to the damaged point and thrust the tip of its front end into the crater. Black material began to flow from the tip. The plasmoid moved its front end back and forth across the damaged area. Others of the same kind came out and joined it. The crater began to fill out.

They hauled away a little and surfaced. Normal space looked clean, beautiful, homelike, calmly shining. None of them except Lyad had slept for over twenty hours, "What do you think?" the Commissioner asked.

They discussed what they had seen in subdued voices. Nobody had a plan. They agreed that one thing they could be sure of was that the Vishni Fleet people and any other human beings who might have been on the station when it was turned over to the king plasmoid were no longer alive. Unless, of course, something had been done to them much more drastic than had happened to the *Aurora*'s crew. The ship had passed by the biggest opening, like a low wide black mouth, close enough to make out that it extended far back into the original station's interior. The station was open and airless as *Harvest Moon* had been before the humans got there.

"Some of those things down there," the Commissioner said, "had attachments that would crack any suit wide open. A lot of them are big, and a lot of them are fast. Once we were inside, we'd have no maneuverability to speak of. If the termites didn't get to us before we got inside. Suits won't do it here." He was a gambler, and a gambler doesn't buck impossible odds.

"What could you do with the guns?" Trigger asked.

"Not too much. They're not meant to take down a fortress. Scratching around on the surface with them would just mark the thing up. We can widen that opening by quite a bit, and once it's widened, I can flip in the bomb. But it would be just blind luck if we nailed the one we're after that way. With a dozen bombs we could break up the station. But we don't have them."

They nodded thoughtfully.

"The worst part of that," he went on, "is that it would be completely obvious. The Council's right when it worries about fumbles here. Tranest and the Devagas know the thing is in there. If the Federation can't produce it, both those outfits have the Council over a barrel. Or we could be setting the Hub up for fifty years of fighting among the member worlds, sometime in the next few hours."

Mantelish and Trigger nodded again. More thoughtfully.

"Nevertheless—" Mantelish began suddenly. He checked himself.

"Well, you're right," the Commissioner said. "That stuff down there just can't be turned loose, that's all! The thing's still only experimenting. We don't know what it's going to wind up with. So I guess we'll be trying the guns and the bomb finally, and then see what else we can do . . . Now look, we've got—what is it?—nine or ten hours left. The first of the boys are pretty sure to come helling in around then. Or maybe something's happened we don't know about, and they'll be here in thirty minutes. We can't tell. But I'm in favor of knocking off now and just grabbing a couple of hours' sleep. Then we'll get our brains together again. Maybe by then somebody has come up with something like an idea. What do you say?"

"Where," Mantelish said, "is the ship going to be while we're sleeping?"

"Subspace," said the Commissioner. He saw their

expressions. "Don't worry! I'll put her on a wide orbit and I'll stick out every alarm on board. I'll also sleep in the control chair. But in case somebody gets here early, we've got to be around to tell them about that space termite trick."

Trigger hadn't expected she would be able to sleep, not where they were. But afterwards she couldn't even remember getting stretched out all the way on the bunk.

She woke up less than an hour later, feeling very uncomfortable. Repulsive had been talking to her.

She sat up and looked around the dark cabin with frightened eyes. After a moment, she got out of the bunk and went up the passage toward the lounge and the control section.

Holati Tate was lying slumped back in his chair, eyes closed, breathing slowly and evenly. Trigger put out a hand to touch his shoulder and then drew it back. She glanced up for a moment at the plasmoid station in the screen, seeming to turn slowly as they went orbiting by it. She noticed that one of the space flares they'd planted there had gone out, or else it had been plucked away by a passing twister's touch. She looked away quickly again, turned and went restlessly back through the lounge, and up the passage, toward the cabins. She went by the two suits of space armor at the lock without looking at them. She opened the door to Mantelish's cabin and looked inside. The professor lay sprawled across the bunk in his clothes, breathing slowly and regularly.

Trigger closed his door again. Lyad might be wakeful, she thought. She crossed the passage and unlocked the door to the Ermetyne's cabin. The lights in the cabin were on, but Lyad also lay there placidly asleep, her face relaxed and young looking.

Trigger put her fist to her mouth and bit down hard on her knuckles for a moment. She frowned intensely at nothing. Then she closed and locked the cabin door, went back up the passage and into the control room. She sat down before the communicator, glanced up once more at the plasmoid station in the screen, got up restlessly and went over to the Commissioner's chair. She stood there, looking down at him. The Commissioner slept on.

Then Repulsive said it again.

"No!" Trigger whispered fiercely. "I won't. I can't. You can't make me do it!"

There was a stillness then. In the stillness, it was made very clear that nobody intended to make her do anything.

And then the stillness just waited.

She cried a little.

So this was it.

"All right," she said.

The armor suit's triple light-beam blazed into the wide, low, black, wet-looking mouth rushing toward her. It was much bigger than she had thought when looking at it from the ship. Far behind her, the fire needles of the single gun pit which her passage to the station had aroused still slashed mindlessly about. They weren't geared to stop suits, and they hadn't come anywhere near her. But the plasmoids looked geared to stop suits.

They were swarming in clusters in the black mouth like maggots in a rotting skull. Part of the swarms had spilled out over the lips of the mouth, clinging, crawling, rippling swiftly about. Trigger shifted the flight controls with the fingers of one hand, dropping a little, then straightening again. She might be coming in too fast. But she had to get past that mass at the opening.

Then the black mouth suddenly yawned wide before her. Her left hand pressed the gun handle. Twin blasts stabbed ahead, blinding white, struck the churning masses, blazed over them. They burned, scattered, exploded, and rolled back, burning and exploding, in a double wave to meet her.

"Too fast!" Repulsive said anxiously. "Much too fast!"

She knew it. But she couldn't have forced herself to do it slowly. The armor suit slammed at a slant into a piled, writhing, burning hardness of plasmoid bodies, bounced upward. She went over and over, yanking down all the way on the flight controls. She closed her eyes for a moment.

When she opened them again, the suit hung poised a little above black uneven flooring, turned back half toward the entrance mouth. A black ceiling was less than twenty feet above her head.

The plasmoids were there. The suit's light beams played over the massed, moving ranks: squat bodies and sinuous ones, immensities that scraped the ceiling, stalked limbs and gaping nutcracker jaws, blurs of motion her eyes couldn't step down to define into shapes. Some still blazed with her guns' white fire. The closest were thirty feet away.

They stayed there. They didn't come any closer.

She swung the suit slowly away from the entrance. The ring was closed all about her. But it wasn't tightening.

Repulsive had thought he could do it.

She asked in her mind, "Which way?"

She got a feeling of direction, turned the suit a little more and started it gliding forward. The ranks ahead didn't give way, but they went down. Those that could go down. Some weren't built for it. The suit bumped up gently against one huge bulk, and a six-inch pale blue eye looked in at her for a moment as she went circling around it. "Eyes for what?" somebody in the back of her mind wondered briefly. She glanced into the suit's rear view screen and saw that the ones who had gone down were getting up again, mixed with the ones who came crowding after her. Thirty feet away!

Repulsive was doing it.

So far there weren't any guns. If they hit guns, that would be her job and the suit's. The king plasmoid should be regretting by now that it had wasted its experimental human material. Though it mightn't have been really wasted; it might be incorporated in the stuff that came crowding after her, and kept going down ahead.

Black ceiling, black floor seemed to stretch on endlessly. She kept the suit moving slowly along. At last the beams picked up low walls ahead, converging at the point toward which the suit was gliding. At the point of convergence there seemed to be a narrow passage.

Plasmoid bodies were wedged into it.

The suit pulled them out one by one, its steel grippers clamping down upon things no softer than itself. But it had power to work with and they didn't, at the moment. Behind the ones it pulled out there were presently glimpses of the swiftly weaving motion of giant red wormshapes sealing up the passage. After a while, they stopped weaving each time the suit returned and started again as it withdrew, dragging out another plasmoid body.

Then the suit went gliding over a stilled tangle of red worm bodies. And there was the sealed end of the passage.

The stuff was still soft. The guns blazed, bit into it, ate it away, their brilliance washing back over the suit. The sealing gave way before the suit did. They went through and came out into . . .

She didn't know what they had come out into. It was like a fog of darkness, growing thicker as they went sliding forward. The light beams seemed to be dimming. Then, they quietly went out as if they'd switched themselves off.

In blackness, she fingered the light controls and knew they weren't switched off.

"Repulsive!" she cried in her mind.

Repulsive couldn't help with the blackness. She got the feeling of direction. The blackness seemed to be soaking behind her eyes. She held the speed throttle steady in fingers slippery with sweat, and that was the only way she could tell they were still moving forward.

After a while, they bumped gently against something

that had to be a wall, it was so big, though at first she wasn't sure it was a wall. They moved along it for a time, then came to the end of it and were moving in the right direction again.

They seemed to be in a passage now, a rather narrow one. They touched walls and ceiling from time to time. She thought they were moving downward.

There was a picture in front of her. She realized suddenly that she had been watching it for some time. But it wasn't until this moment that she became really aware of it.

The beast was big, strong and angry. It bellowed and screamed, shaking and covered with foam. She couldn't see it too clearly, but she had the impression of mad, staring eyes and a terrible lust to crush and destroy.

But something was holding it. Something held it quietly and firmly, for all its plunging. It reared once more now, a gross, lumbering hugeness, and came crashing down to its knees. Then it went over on its side.

The suit's beams flashed on. Trigger squeezed her eyes tight shut, blinded by the light that flashed back from black walls all around. Then her fingers remembered the right drill and dimmed the lights. She opened her eyes again and stared for a long moment at the great gray mummy-shape before one of the black walls.

"Repulsive?" she asked in her mind.

Repulsive didn't answer. The suit hung quietly in the huge black chamber. She didn't remember having stopped it. She turned it now slowly. There were eight or nine passages leading out of here, through walls, ceiling, floor.

"Repulsive!" she cried plaintively.

Silence.

She glanced once more at the king plasmoid against the wall. It stayed silent too. And it was as if the two silences cancelled each other out.

She remembered the last feeling of moving downward and lifted the suit toward a passage that came in through the ceiling. She hung before it, considering. Far up and back in its darkness, a bright light suddenly blazed, vanished, and blazed again. Something was coming down the passage, fast . . .

Her hand started for the gun handle. Then it remembered another drill and flashed to the suit's communicator. A voice crashed in around her.

"Trigger, Trigger, Trigger!" it sobbed.

"Ape!" she screamed. "You aren't hurt?"

30

Mantelish's garden in the highlands south of Ceyce had a certain renown all over the Hub. It had been donated to the professor twenty-five years ago by the populace of another Federation world. That populace had negligently permitted a hideous pestilence of some kind to be imported, and had been saved in the nick of time by the appropriate pestilence-killer, hastily developed and forwarded to it by Mantelish. In return, a lifetime ambition had been fulfilled for him—his own private botanical garden plus an unlimited fund for stocking and upkeep.

To one side of the big garden house, where Mantelish stayed whenever he found the time to go puttering around among his specimens, stood a giant sequoia, generally reputed to be the oldest living thing in the Hub outside of the Life Banks. It was certainly extremely old, even for a sequoia. For the last decade there had been considerable talk about the advisability of removing it before it collapsed and crushed the house and everyone in it. But it was one of the professor's great favorites, and so far he had vetoed the suggestion.

Elbows propped on the broad white balustrade of the porch before her third-story bedroom, Trigger was studying the sequoia's crown with a pair of field glasses when

Pilch arrived. She laid the glasses down and invited her guest to pull up a chair and help her admire the view.

They admired the view for a little in silence. "It certainly is a beautiful place!" Pilch said then. She glanced down at Professor Mantelish, a couple of hundred yards from the house, dressed in a pair of tanned shorts and busily grubbing away with a spade around some new sort of shrub he'd just planted, and smiled. "I took the first opportunity I've had to come see you," she said.

Trigger looked at her and laughed. "I thought you might. You weren't satisfied with the reports then?"

Pilch said, "Of course not! But it was obvious the emergency was over, so I was whisked away to something else." She frowned slightly.

"Sometimes," she admitted, "the Service keeps me the least bit busier than I'd prefer to be. So now it's been six months!"

"I would have come in for another interview if you'd called me," Trigger said.

"I know," said Pilch. "But that would have made it official. I can keep this visit off the record." Her eyes met Trigger's for a moment. "And I have a feeling I will. Also, of course, I'm not pushing for any answers you mightn't care to give."

"Just push away," Trigger said agreeably.

"Well, we got the Commissioner's call from his ship. A worried man he was. So it seems now that we've had one of the Old Galactics around for a while. When did you first find out about it?"

"On the morning after our interview. Right after I got up."

"How?"

Trigger laughed. "I watch my weight. When I noticed I'd turned three and a half pounds heavier overnight than I'd averaged the past four years, I knew all right!"

Pilch smiled faintly. "You weren't alarmed at all?"

"No. I guess I'd been prepared just enough by that

time. But then, you know, I forgot all about it again until Lyad and Flam opened that purse—and he wasn't inside. Then I remembered, and after that I didn't forget again."

"No. Of course." Pilch's slim fingers tapped the surface of the table between them. She said then, paying Repulsive the highest compliment Pilch could give, "It—he—was a good therapist!" After a moment, she added, "I had a talk with Commissioner Tate an hour or so ago. He's preparing to leave Maccadon again, I understand."

"That's right. He's been organizing that big exploration trip of Mantelish's the past couple of months. He'll be in charge of it when they take off."

"You're not going along?" Pilch asked.

Trigger shook her head. "Not this time. Ape and I—Captain Quillan and I, that is—"

"I heard," Pilch said. She smiled. "You picked a good one on the second try!"

"Quillan's all right," Trigger agreed. "If you watch him a little."

"Anyway," said Pilch, "Commissioner Tate seems to be just the least bit worried about you still."

Trigger put a finger to her temple and made a small circling motion. "A bit ta-ta?"

"Not exactly that, perhaps. But it seems," said Pilch, "that you've told him a good deal about the history of the Old Galactics, including what ended them as a race thirty-two thousand years ago."

Trigger's face clouded a little. "Yes," she said. She sat silent for a moment. "Well, I got that from Repulsive somewhere along the line," she said then. "It didn't really come clear until some time after we'd got back. But it was there in those pictures in the interview."

"The giants stamping on the farm?"

Trigger nodded. "And the fast clock and the slow one. He was trying to tell it then. The Jesters—that's the giants—they're fast and tough like us. Apparently," Trigger said thoughtfully, "they're a good deal like us in a lot of ways. But worse. Much worse! And the Old Galactics were just slow. They thought slow; they moved slow— they did almost everything slow. At full gallop, old Repulsive couldn't have kept up with a healthy snail. Besides, they just liked to grow things and tinker with things and so on. They didn't go in for fighting, and they never got to be at all good at it. So they just got wiped out, practically."

"The Jesters were good at fighting, eh?"

Trigger nodded. "Very good. Like us, again."

"Where did they come from?"

"Repulsive thought they were outsiders. He wasn't sure. He and that other O.G. were on the sidelines, running their protein collecting station, when the Jesters arrived; and it was all over and they were gone before he had learned much about it."

"From outside the galaxy!" Pilch said thoughtfully. She cleared her throat. "What's this business about they might be back again?"

"Well," Trigger said, "he thought they might be. Just might. Actually he believed the Jesters got wiped out too."

"Eh?" Pilch said. "How's that?"

"Quite a lot of the Old Galactics went along with them like Repulsive went along with me. And one of the things they did know," Trigger said, "was how to spread diseases like nobody's business. About like we use weed-killers. Wholesale. They could clean out the average planet of any particular thing they didn't want there in about a week. So it's not really too likely the Jesters will be back."

"Oh!" said Pilch.

"But if they are coming, Repulsive thought they'd be due in this area in about another eight centuries. That looked like a very short time to him, of course. He thought it would be best to pass on a warning."

"You know," Pilch said after a brief pause, "I find myself agreeing with him there, Trigger! I might turn in a short report on this, after all."

"I think you should, really," Trigger said. She smiled suddenly. "Of course, it might wind up with people thinking both of us are ta-ta!"

"I'll risk that," said Pilch. "It's been thought of me before."

"If they did come," Trigger said, "I guess we'd take them anyway. We've taken everything else like that that came along. And besides—"

Her voice trailed off thoughtfully. She studied the tabletop for a moment. Then she looked up at Pilch.

"Well," she said, smiling, "any other questions?"

"A few," said Pilch, passing up the "and besides—" She considered. "Did you ever actually see him make contact with you?"

"No," Trigger said. "I was always asleep, and I suppose he made sure I'd stay asleep. They're built sort of like a leech, you know. I guess he knew I wouldn't feel comfortable about having something like that go oozing into the side of my neck or start oozing out again. Anyway, he never did let me see it."

"Considerate little fellow!" said Pilch. She sighed. "Well, everything came out very satisfactorily—much more so than anyone could have dared hope at one time. All that's left is a very intriguing mystery which the Hub will be chatting about for years . . . What happened aboard Doctor Fayle's vanished ship that caused the king plasmoid to awaken to awful life?" she cried. "What equally mysterious event brought about its death on that strangely hideous structure it had built in subspace? *What was it planning to do there?* Etcetera." She smiled at Trigger. "Yes, very good!"

"I saw they camouflaged out what was still visible of the original substation before they let in the news viewers," Trigger remarked. "Bright idea somebody had there!"

"Yes. It was I. And the Devagas hierarchy is broken, and the Ermetynes run out of Tranest. Two very bad spots, those were! I don't recall having heard what they did to your friend Pluly."

"I heard," Trigger said. "He just got black-listed by Grand Commerce finally and lost all his shipping concessions. However, his daughter is married to an up and coming young businessman who happened to be on hand and have the money and other qualifications to pick up those concessions." She laughed. "It's the Inger Lines now. They're smart characters, in a way!"

"Yes," said Pilch. "In a way. Did you know Lyad Ermetyne put in for voluntary rehabilitation with us, and then changed her mind and joined the Service?"

"I'd heard of it." Trigger hesitated. "Did you know Lyad paid me a short visit about an hour before you got here this morning?"

"I thought she would," Pilch said. "We came in to Maccadon together."

Trigger had been a little startled when she answered the doorchime and saw Lyad standing there. She invited the Ermetyne in.

"I thought I'd thank you personally," Lyad said casually, "for a recording which was delivered to me some months ago."

"That's quite all right," Trigger said, also casually. "I was sure I wasn't going to have any use for it."

Lyad studied her face for a moment. "To be honest about it, Trigger Argee," she said, "I still don't feel entirely cordial toward you! However, I did appreciate the gesture of letting me have the recording. So I decided to drop by to tell you there isn't really too much left in the way of hard feelings, on my part."

They shook hands restrainedly, and the Ermetyne sauntered out again.

"The other reason she came here," Pilch said, "is to take care of the financing of Mantelish's expedition."

"I didn't know that!" Trigger said, surprised.

"It's her way of making amends. Her legitimate Hub holdings are still enormous, of course. She can afford it."

"Well," Trigger said, "that's one thing about Lyad—she's wholehearted!"

"She's that," said Pilch. "Rarely have I seen anyone rip into total therapy with the verve displayed by the Ermetyne. She mentioned on one occasion that there simply had to be some way of getting ahead of you again."

"Oh," said Trigger.

"Yes," said Pilch. "By the way, what are your own plans nowadays? Aside from getting married."

Trigger stretched slim tanned arms over her head and grinned. "No immediate plans!" she said. "I've resigned from Precol. Got a couple of checks from the Federation. One to cover my expenses on that plasmoid business—that was the *Dawn City* fare mainly—and the other for the five weeks special duty they figured I was on for them. So I'm up to around five thousand crowns again, and I thought I'd just loaf around and sort of think things over till Quillan gets back from his current assignment."

"I see. When is Major Quillan returning?"

"In about a month. It's Captain Quillan at present, by the way."

"Oh?" said Pilch. "What happened?"

"That unwarranted interference with a political situation business. They'd broadcast a warning against taking individual action of any kind against the plasmoid station. But when he got there and heard the Commissioner was in a kind of coma, and I wasn't even on board, he lost his head and came charging into the station after me, flinging grenades and so on around. The plasmoids would have finished him off pretty quick, except most of them had started slowing down as soon as Repulsive turned off the main one. The lunatic was lucky the termites didn't get to him before he even reached the station!"

Pilch said, "Termites?"

Trigger told her about the termites.

"Ugh!" said Pilch. "I hadn't heard about those. So they broke him for that. It hardly seems right."

"Well, you have to have discipline," Trigger said tolerantly. "Ape's a bit short on that end anyway. They'll be upgrading him again fairly soon, I imagine. I might just be going into Space Scout Intelligence myself, by the way. They said they'd be glad to have me."

"Not at all incidentally," remarked Pilch, "my Service also would be glad to have you."

"Would they?" Trigger looked at her thoughtfully. "That includes that total therapy process, doesn't it?"

"Usually," said Pilch.

"Well, I might some day. But not just yet." She smiled. "Let's let Lyad get a head start! Actually, it's just I've found out there are so many interesting things going on all around that I'd like to look them over a bit before I go charging seriously into a career again." She reached across the table and tapped Pilch's wrist. "And I'll show you one interesting thing that's going on right here! Take Mantelish's big tree out there!"

"The sequoia?"

"Yes. Now just last year it was looking so bad they almost talked the professor into having it taken away. Hardly a green branch left on it."

Pilch shaded her eyes and looked at the sequoia's crown far above them. "It looks," she observed reflectively, "in fairly good shape at the moment, I'd say!"

"Yes, and it's getting greener every week. Mantelish brags about a new solvent he's been dosing its roots with. You see that great big branch like an L turned upward, just a little above the center?"

Pilch looked again. "Yes," she said after a moment, "I think so."

"Just before the L turns upward, there's a little cluster of green branches," Trigger said.

"I see those, yes."

Trigger picked up the field glasses and handed them

to her. "Get those little branches in the glasses," she said.

Pilch said presently, "Got them."

Trigger stood up and faced up to the sequoia. She cupped her hands to her mouth, took a deep breath, and yelled, "Yoo-hoo! Reeeepul-sive!"

Down in the garden, Mantelish straightened and looked about angrily. Then he saw Trigger and smiled.

"Yoo-hoo yourself, Trigger!" he shouted, and turned back to his spading.

Trigger watched Pilch's face from the side. She saw her give a sudden start.

"Great Galaxies!" Pilch breathed. She kept on looking. "That's one for the book, isn't it?" Finally she put the glasses down. She appeared somewhat stunned. "He really is a little green man!"

"Only when he's trying to be. It's a sort of sign of friendliness."

"What's he doing up there?"

"He moved over into the sequoia right after we got back," Trigger said. "And that's where he'll probably stay indefinitely now. It's just the right kind of place for Repulsive."

"Have you been doing any more—well, talking?"

"No. Too strenuous both ways. Until a few days before we got back here, there wasn't even a sign from him. He just about knocked himself out on that big plasmoid."

"Who else knows about this?" asked Pilch.

"Nobody. I would have told Holati, except he's still mad enough about having been put into a coma, he might go out and chop the sequoia down."

"Well, it won't go into the report then," Pilch said. "They'd just want to bother Repulsive!"

"I knew it would be all right to tell you. And here's something else very interesting that's going on at present."

"What's that?"

"The real hush-hush reason for Mantelish's expedition,"

Trigger explained, "is, of course, to scout around this whole area of space with planetary plasmoid detectors. They don't want anybody stumbling on another setup like *Harvest Moon* and accidentally activating another king plasmoid."

"Yes," Pilch said. "I'd heard that."

"It was Mantelish's idea," said Trigger. "Now Mantelish is very fond of that sequoia tree. He's got a big, comfortable bench right among its roots, where he likes to sit down around noon and have a little nap when he's out here."

"Oh!" said Pilch. "Repulsive's been up to his old tricks, eh?"

"Sure. He's given Mantelish very exact instructions. So they're going to find one of those setups, all right. And they won't come back with any plasmoids. But they will come back with something they don't know about."

Pilch looked at her for a moment. "*You* say it!"

Trigger's grin widened. "A little green woman," she said.

Sour Note on Palayata

[Editor's note: This story is not directly part of the Trigger Argee and Heslet Quillan cycle of tales. It relates an early adventure of the same Pilch who, many years later, features so prominently in Trigger's history and appears once, in "Compulsion," in the Telzey saga.]

1

Bayne Duffold, Assistant Secretary of the Hub Systems' Outposts Department, said that the entire proposed operation was not only illegal but probably unethical. Conceivably, it might lead to anything from the scientific murder of a single harmless Palayatan native to open warfare with an opponent of completely unknown potential.

Pilch, acting as spokesman for the Hub's Psychological Service Ship stationed off Palayata, heard him out patiently. "All that is very true, Excellency," she said then. "That is why you were instructed to call in the Service."

Assistant Secretary Duffold bit his thumb tip and frowned. It was true that the home office had instructed him, rather reluctantly, to call in the Service; but he had made no mention of that part of it to Pilch. And the girl already had jolted him with the information that a Psychological Service operator had been investigating the Palayatan problem on the planet itself during the past four months. "We figured Outposts was due to ask for a little assistance here about this time," was the way she had put it.

"I can't give my consent to your plan," Duffold said with finality, "until I've had the opportunity to investigate every phase of it in person."

The statement sounded foolish as soon as it was out. The remarkably outspoken young woman sitting on the other side of his desk was quite capable of reminding him that the Psychological Service, once it had been put on an assignment, did not need the consent of an Outposts assistant secretary for any specific operation. Or anybody else's consent, for that matter. It was one reason that nobody really liked the Service.

But Pilch said pleasantly, "Oh, we've arranged to see that you have the opportunity, of course! We'll be having a conference on the ship, spaceside"—she glanced at her timepiece—"four hours from now, for that very purpose. We particularly want to know what Outposts' viewpoint on the matter is."

And that was another reason they were disliked: they invariably did try to get the consent of everyone concerned for what they were doing! It made it difficult to accuse them of being arbitrary.

"Well—" said Duffold. There was really no way for him to avoid accepting the invitation. Besides, while he shared the general feeling of distaste for Psychological Service and its ways, he found Pilch herself and the prospect of spending a half-day or so in her company very attractive.

The Outposts Station's feminine complement on Palayata, while a healthy lot, hadn't been picked for good looks; and there was something about Pilch, something bright and clean, that made him regret momentarily that she wasn't connected with a less morbid line of work. "Kidnapping and enforced interrogation of a friendly alien on his own world!" Duffold shook his head. "That's being pretty heavy-handed, you know."

"No doubt," said Pilch. "But you know nobody has been able to persuade a Palayatan to leave the planet, so why waste time trying? We need the ship's equipment for the investigation, and it might be safer if the ship is a long way out from Palayata while it's going on." She stood up. "Will you be ready to hop as soon as I've picked up Wintan?"

"Hop? Wintan?" Duffold, getting to his feet, looked startled. "Oh, I see. Wintan's the operator you've had working on the planet. All right. Where will I meet you?"

"Space transport," said Pilch. "Ramp Nineteen. Half an hour from now." She was at the office entrance by then; and he said hurriedly, "Oh, by the way—"

Pilch looked back. "Yes?"

"You've been here two days," Duffold said. "Have they bothered you at all?"

She didn't ask what he meant. "No," she said. Black-fringed gray eyes looked at him out of a face from which every trace of expression was suddenly gone, as she added quietly, "But of course I've had a great deal of psychological conditioning—"

There hadn't been any need to rub that in, Duffold thought, flushing angrily. She knew, of course, how he felt about the Service—how any normal human being felt about it! Wars had been fought to prevent the psychological control of Hub citizens on any pretext; and then, when the last curious, cultish cliques of psychologists had been dissolved, it had turned out to be a matter of absolute necessity to let them resume their activities. So they were still around, with their snickering questioning of the dignity of Man and his destiny, their eager prying and twisted interpretations of the privacies and dreams of the mind. Of course, they weren't popular! Of course, they were limited now to the operations of Psychological Service! And to admit that one had, oneself—

Duffold grimaced as he picked up the desk-speaker. He distributed sparse instructions to cover his probable period of absence from the Station, and left the office. There wasn't much time to waste, if he wanted to keep within Pilch's half-hour limit. In the twelve weeks he had been on Palayata, he had avoided direct contact with the natives after his first two or three experiences with the odd emotional effects they produced in human beings. But since he had been invited to the Service conference, it seemed advisable to confirm that experience once more personally.

The simple way to do that was to walk out to Ramp Nineteen, instead of taking the Station tube.

The moment he stepped outside the building, the remembered surges of acute uneasiness came churning up in him again. The port area was crowded as usual by sightseeing Palayatans. Duffold stopped next to the building for a few moments, watching them.

The uneasiness didn't abate. The proximity of Palayatans didn't affect all humans in the same way; some reported long periods of a kind of euphoria when around them, but that sensation could shift suddenly and unaccountably to sharp anxiety and complete panic. Any one of several dozen drugs gave immunity to those reactions; and the members of the Station's human personnel whose work brought them into contact with the natives were, therefore, given chemical treatment as a regular procedure. But Duffold had refused to resort to drugs.

He started walking determinedly toward the ramp area, making no attempt to avoid the shifting streams of the Palayatan visitors. They drifted about in chattering groups, lending the functional terminal an air of cheerful holiday. If his jangling nerves hadn't told him otherwise, Duffold could have convinced himself easily that he was on a purely human world. Physically, Palayatans were humanoid to the n'th degree, at least as judged by the tolerant standards of convergent evolution. They also loved Hub imports, which helped strengthen the illusion. Male and female tended to wander about their business in a haze of Hub perfumes; and at least one in every five adults in sight wore clothes of human manufacture.

But Duffold's nerves were yammering that these creatures were more alien than so many spiders—their generally amiable attitude and the fact that they looked like human beings could be only a deliberate deception, designed to conceal some undefined but sinister purpose. He broke off that unreassuring line of thought, and clamped his mind down purposefully on a more objective consideration of the odd paradoxes presented by these pseudo-people. Palayatans were even more intrigued, for example, by the Hub humans' spectacular technological achievements than by Hub styles and perfumes. Hence their presence in swarms about the Station where they could watch the space transports arrive and depart. But, in twelve years, they hadn't shown the slightest inclination to transplant any significant part of Hub technology to their own rather rural though semi-mechanized civilization.

At an average I.Q. level of seventy-eight in the population, that wasn't surprising, of course. What was not only surprising but completely improbable, when you really considered it, was that they had not only developed a civilization at all, but that it had attained a uniform level everywhere on the planet.

It simply made no sense, Duffold thought bitterly. Outposts' sociological experts had made the same comment over a year ago, when presented with the available data on Palayata. They had suggested either a detailed check on the accuracy of the data, or a referral of the whole Palayatan question to Psychological Service.

The data had been checked, exhaustively. It was quite accurate. After that, Outposts had had no choice—

"My, you're perspiring, Excellency!" Pilch said, as he stepped up on the platform of Ramp Nineteen. "This is Wintan. You've met before, I believe. But you really needn't have hurried so." She glanced at her timepiece. "Why, you're hardly even two minutes late."

Wintan was a stocky fair-haired man, and Duffold did recall having met him some months before, when his credentials—indicating a legitimate scholarly interest in sociology—were being checked at the Station.

They shook hands, and Duffold turned to greet the other man.

Only—it wasn't a man.

Mentally, Duffold recoiled in a kind of frenzy. Physically, he reached out and clasped the elderly Palayatan's palm with a firm if clammy grip, shook it twice, and dropped it, his mouth held taut in what he was positive was an appalling grin. Wintan was saying something about, "Albemarl . . . guide and traveling companion—" Then Pilch tapped Duffold's shoulder.

"The records you sent by tube have arrived, Excellency. Perhaps you'd better check them."

Gratefully, he followed her into the ship. Inside the lock, she stopped and looked at him quizzically. "Hits you pretty hard, doesn't it?" she murmured. "Great Suns, why don't you take one of those drugs?"

Duffold mopped his brow. "Don't like the idea," he said stubbornly. He indicated the two outside the lock. "Don't tell me you got a volunteer for the investigation?"

Pilch's gleaming black hair swung about her shoulders as she turned to look. "No," she smiled. "Albemarl came along to see Wintan off. You've been honored, by the way. He's an itinerant sage of sages among Palayatans—I.Q.

one hundred and nine! He and Wintan have been working together for months. Of course, Wintan's immune to the emotional reactions—"

"I see," Duffold said coldly. "No doubt he's also had thorough psychological conditioning?"

Pilch grinned at him. "Not many," she said, "have had as much."

2

The Psychology Service ship that swallowed up the transport a few hours later was a camouflaged monstrosity moving along with the edge of an asteroid flow halfway across the system. For all practical purposes, it looked indistinguishable from the larger chunks of planetary debris in its neighborhood, and from its size, it might have had a complement of several thousand people. Duffold was a little surprised that out of that potential number, only five Service members attended the conference, two of whom were Wintan and Pilch. It suggested an economy and precision in organization he had somehow failed to expect here.

The appearance of Buchele, the senior commander in charge of the conference, was almost shocking. He had the odd, waxy skin and cautious motion of a man on whom rejuvenation treatments had taken an incomplete effect, but there was no indication of the mental deterioration that was supposed to accompany that condition. His voice was quick, and he spoke with the easy courtesy of a man to whom command was too natural a thing to be emphasized. He introduced Cabon, the ship's captain, a tall man of Pilch's dark slender breed, who said almost nothing throughout the next few hours, and a red-haired woman named Lueral who was, she said, representing Biology Section. Then the conference was under way with a briskness that made Duffold glad he had decided to bring Outposts' full records on Palayata along for the meeting.

They went over the reasons why Outposts was interested in maintaining a Station on Palayata. They were sound reasons: Palayata was a convenient take-off point for the investigation and control of an entire new sector of space, the potential center of a thousand-year, many-sided project. Except for the doubtful factor of the natives, it was as favorable for human use as a world could be expected to become without a century-long conditioning program. The natives themselves represented an immediate new trade outlet for Grand Commerce, whose facilities would make the project enormously less expensive to Government than any similar one on a world that did not attract the organized commercial interests.

Buchele nodded. "Assuming, Excellency, that the Service might be able to establish that the peculiarities of the Palayatan natives are in no way dangerous to human beings, but that the emotional disturbances they cause will have to continue to be controlled by drugs—would Outposts regard that as a satisfactory solution?"

Duffold was convinced that under the circumstances Outposts would be almost tearfully thankful for such a solution, but he expressed himself a little more conservatively. He added, "Is there any reason to believe that they actually are harmless?"

Buchele's dead-alive face showed almost no expression. "No," he said, "there isn't. Your records show what ours do. The picture of this Palayatan culture isn't fully explainable in the terms of any other culture, human or non-human, that we know of. There's an unseen controlling factor—well, call it X. That much is almost definitely established. With the information we have, we could make a number of guesses at its nature; and that's all."

Duffold stared bleakly at him. No one in Outposts had

cared to put it into so many words, but that was what they had been afraid of.

Buchele said softly, "We have considered two possible methods of procedure. With your assistance, Excellency, we should like to decide between them now."

With his assistance! Duffold became suddenly enormously wary. "Go ahead, commander," he requested affably.

"Very well. Let's assume that X actually is a latent source of danger. The section of your records covering the recent deaths of two human beings on the planet might suggest that the danger has become active, but there is no immediate reason to connect those deaths with X."

Duffold nodded hesitantly.

"The point that the Service and, I'm sure, Outposts are most concerned with," the gentle voice of the dead-alive man went on, "is that there is absolutely no way of estimating the possible extent of the assumed danger. As we sit here, we may be members of a race which already has doomed itself by reaching out for one new world that should have been left forever untouched. On the basis of our present information, that is exactly as possible as that the Palayatan X may turn out to be a completely innocuous factor. Where X lies on the scale between those two possibilities can almost certainly be determined, however. The question is simply whether we want to employ the means that will determine it."

"Meaning," said Duffold, "that the rather direct kind of investigation I understand you're planning—kidnapping a native, bringing him out to this ship, and subjecting him to psychological pressures—could start the trouble?"

"It might."

"I agree," Duffold said. "What was the other procedure?"

"To have Outposts and Grand Commerce withdraw all human personnel from Palayata."

"Abandon the planet permanently?" Duffold felt his face go hot.

"Yes," said Buchele.

Duffold drew a slow breath. A spasm of rage shook through him and went away. "We can't do that, and you know it!" he said.

Lusterless eyes hooded themselves in the waxy face. "If you please, Excellency," Buchele said quietly, "there is nothing in the records given us by your Department to indicate that this is an impossibility."

It was true enough. Duffold said sourly, "No need to underline the obvious! We're committed to remain on Palayata until the situation is understood. If there is no danger there, or only ordinary danger—nothing that reaches beyond the planet itself—we can stay or not as we choose. But we can't leave, now that we've brought ourselves to the attention of this X factor, before we know whether or not it constitutes a potential danger to every human world in the galaxy. We can't even destroy the planet, since we don't know whether that would also destroy X, or simply irritate it!"

"Is the destruction of Palayata being seriously considered?" the Service man said.

"Not at the moment," Duffold said grimly.

For the first time then, Buchele shifted his glance slowly about at the other Service members. "It seems that we are in agreement so far," he said, as if addressing them. He looked back at Duffold.

That was when the thought came to Duffold. It startled him, but he didn't stop to consider it. He said, "My Department obviously has been unable to work out a satisfactory solution to the problem. I'm authorized to say that Outposts will give the Service any required support in solving it, providing I'm allowed to observe the operation."

There was a momentary silence. It was bluff, and it wasn't fooling them; but the Service was known to go to considerable lengths to build up good will in the other Departments.

Pilch said suddenly, "We accept the condition—with one qualification."

Duffold hesitated, surprised. Buchele's gaze was on Pilch; the others seemed to be studying him reflectively, but nobody appeared to question Pilch's acceptance. "What's the qualification?" he asked.

"We should have your agreement," she said, "that you will accept any safety measures we feel are required."

"I assume those safety measures are for my benefit," Duffold said gravely.

"Well, yes—"

"Why," said Duffold, "in that case I thank you for your concern. And, of course, you have my agreement."

The others stirred and smiled. Pilch looked rueful. "It's just that—"

"I know," Duffold nodded. "It's just that I haven't had any psychological conditioning."

Pilch was called from the conference room immediately afterwards. This time Duffold was not surprised to discover that she appeared to be in charge of the actual kidnapping project and that she was arranging to include him in the landing party. There seemed to be a constant easy shifting of authority among these people which did not correspond too well with the rank they held.

Others came in. He began to get a picture of unsuspected complexities of organization and purpose within this huge, ungainly ship. There was talk of pattern analysis and factor summaries at the table at which Buchele remained in charge, and Duffold stayed there, since they were dealing with material with which he was in part familiar. It appeared that Wintan, the Service operator who had been working planetside on Palayata, had provided the ship's Integrators with detailed information not included in previous reports; and the patterns were still being revised. So far, Buchele seemed to feel that the revisions indicated no significant changes.

Somebody came to warn Duffold that the landing operation was to get underway in eighty minutes. He hurried off to contact the Outposts Station on Palayata and extend the period he expected to be absent.

When he came back, they were still at it—

There seemed to be no permanent government or permanent social structure of any sort on Palayata; not even, as a rule, anything resembling permanent family groups. On the other hand, some family groups maintained themselves for decades—almost as if someone were trying to prove that no rule could be applied too definitely to the perverse planet! Children needing attention attached themselves to any convenient adult or group of adults and were accepted until they decided to wander off again.

There were no indications of organized science or of scientific speculation. Palayatan curiosity might be intense, but it was brief and readily satisfied. Technical writings on some practical application or other of the scientific principles with which they were familiar here could be picked up almost anywhere and were used in the haphazard instruction that took the place of formal schooling. There wasn't even the vaguest sort of recorded history, but there were a considerable number of historical manuscripts, some of them centuries old and lovingly preserved, which dealt with personal events of intense interest to the recorder and of very limited usefulness to his researcher. It had been the Hub's own archaeological workers who eventually turned up evidence indicating that Palayata's present civilization had been drifting along in much the same fashion for at least two thousand years and perhaps a good deal longer.

Impossible . . . impossible . . . impossible—if things were what they seemed to be!

So they weren't what they seemed to be. Duffold became aware of the fact that by now Buchele and Wintan and he were the only ones remaining at that table. The others presumably had turned their attention to more promising work; and refreshments had appeared.

They ate thoughtfully until Duffold remarked, "They're still either very much smarter than they act—smarter than we are, in fact—or something is controlling them. Right?"

Buchele said that seemed to be about it.

"And if they're controlled," Duffold went on, "the controlling agency is something very much smarter than human beings."

Wintan shook his short-cropped blond head. "That wouldn't necessarily be true."

Duffold looked at him. "Put it this way," he said. "Does the Service think human beings, using all the tricks of your psychological technology, could control a world to the extent Palayata seems to be controlled?"

"Oh, certainly!" Wintan said cheerfully; and Buchele nodded. "Given one trained operator to approximately every thousand natives, something quite similar could be established," the senior commander said dryly. "But who would want to go to all that trouble?"

"And keep it up for twenty centuries or so!" Wintan added. "It's a technical possibility, but it seems a rather pointless one."

Duffold was silent for a moment, savoring some old suspicions. Even if the Service men had a genuine lack of interest in the possibilities of such a project, the notion that Psychology Service felt it was capable of that degree of control was unpleasant. "What methods would be employed?" he said. "Telepathic amplifiers?"

"Well, that would be one of the basic means, of course," Wintan agreed. "Then, sociological conditioning—business of picking off the ones that were getting too bright to be handled. Oh, it would be a job, all right!"

Telepathic amplifiers—Outposts was aware, as was
everyone else, that the Service employed gadgetry in that
class; but no one outside the Service took a very serious view of such activities. History backed up that opinion
with emphasis: the psi boys had produced disturbing
effects in various populations from time to time, but in
the showdown the big guns always had cleaned them up
very handily. Duffold said hopefully, "Does it seem to be
telepathy we're dealing with here?"

Wintan shook his head. "No. If it were, we could spot
it and probably handle whoever was using it. You missed
that part of the summary, Excellency. Checking for tele-
impulses was a major part of the job I was sent to do."
He looked at Buchele, perhaps a trifle doubtfully.
"Palayatans appear to be completely blind to any telepathic form of approach; at least, that's the report of my
instruments."

"Or shut-off," Buchele said gently.

"Or shut-off," Wintan agreed. "We can't determine that
with certainty until we get our specimen on board. We
know the instruments would have detected such a resis-
tance in any human being."

Buchele almost grinned. "In any human being we've
investigated," he amended.

Wintan looked annoyed. From behind Duffold, Pilch's
voice announced, "I'll be wanting his Excellency at
Eighty-two Lock in"—there was something like a
millisecond's pause, while he could imagine her glancing at her timepiece again—"seventeen minutes. But
Lueral wants him first."

As Duffold stood up, she added, "You two had better come along. Biology has something to add to your
discussion on telepathy."

"Significant?" Buchele asked, coming stiffly to his feet.

"Possibly. The Integrators should finish chewing it
around in a few more minutes."

Duffold had been puzzling about what Lueral and the

Biology Section could be wanting of him, but the moment he stepped out of a transfer lock and saw the amplification stage set up, with a view of a steamy Palayatan swamp floating in it, he knew what it was and he had a momentary touch of revulsion. The incident with the keff creature, which had cost the lives of two Outposts investigators, had been an unlovely one to study in its restructure; and he had studied it carefully several times in the past few days, in an attempt to discover any correlation with the general Palayatan situation. He had been unsuccessful in that and, taking the seat next to the stage that was indicated to him, he wondered what Biology thought it had found.

Lueral, the red-headed woman who had attended the earlier part of the general conference, introduced him to a fat, elderly man, whose name Duffold did not catch, but who was Biology's Section Head. He was operating the amplifier and remained in his seat. Lueral said into the darkened room:

"This is the record of an objective restructure his Excellency brought shipward with him. The location of the original occurrence was at the eastward tip of Continent Two; the date, one hundred thirty-eight standard, roughly one hundred hours ago. To save time, we would like his Excellency to give us a brief explanation of the circumstances."

Duffold cleared his throat. "The circumstances," he said carefully, "are that we have investigators working in that area. Ostensibly, they are archaeologists. Actually, they're part of an Outposts project, checking the theory that Palayata is operating under some kind of secret government. There is a concentration of the deserted settlements we find all over the planet around those swamps. The two men involved in the restructure were working through such a settlement—or supposed to be working through it—when the accident occurred."

He added, "If it was an accident. I brought the record

along because of the possibility that it was something else."

The Section Head said in a heavy voice, "The restructure appears to have been made within two hours after the actual incident."

"A little less than two hours," Duffold agreed. "There were hourly position checks. When the team failed to check in, a restructure heli began to track them. By the time they reached this keff animal, some natives already had killed it—with a kind of harpoon gun, as the restructure shows. Some portions of the bodies of our investigators were recovered."

"Had the natives observed the incident?" Lueral inquired.

"They said they had—too far off to prevent it. They claim they kill a keff whenever they find one, not because they regard them as a danger to themselves but because they are highly destructive to food animals in the area. They hadn't realized a keff might also be destructive to human beings."

The Section Head said, "This is a view of the keff some minutes after the killing of the two men. The promptness with which the restructure was made permits almost limitless detail."

Duffold felt himself wince as the colors in the amplification stage between them blurred and ran briefly and cleared again. The keff appeared, half-submerged in muddy water, a mottled green and black hulk, the eyeless head making occasional thrusting motions, with an unpleasant suggestion of swallowing.

"Weight approximately three tons," said the Section Head. "The head takes up almost a third of its length. Motions very slow. Normally, this would indicate a vegetarian or omnivorous animal with a limitless food supply, such as these mile-long swamp stretches would provide. Possibly aggressive when attacked, but not dangerous to any reasonably alert and mobile creature."

He added, "However, we were able to pick up tele-impulses at this point, which indicate that the natives' description of its food habits is correct. I suggest using tel-dampers. The impulses are rather vivid."

Pilch's voice said, "Hold still!" behind Duffold, and something like a pliable ring slipped down around his skull. Soft clamps fastened it here and there, and then he was aware of her settling down in the chair beside him. Her whisper reached him again, "If you don't like what you're getting, say so! They don't really need you for this."

Duffold made a grunting sound, indicating complete contentment with his situation and a desire not to be disturbed, but not entirely turning down the suggestion. There were crawling feelings along his spine.

He felt good. He felt drowsy but purposeful, because now there were only a few more steps to go, and then the great pink maw would open before him, and he could relax right into it. Relax and—

He jerked upright in his chair, horror prickling through his nerves. Pilch was tapping his arm.

"Outside!" she whispered. "Keep the damper on." They moved through the dim room; a door clicked ahead of Duffold, then clicked again behind him, and light flooded around them.

He pulled the tel-damper off his head like some small, unclean, clinging animal. "Whew!" he breathed. "Should have taken your advice, I think!"

"Well, you didn't know. We should have thought of it. There are ways of letting stuff like that come at you, and you—"

"Don't say it," he warned. "I'm learning my limitations." He was silent a moment. "Was that how it felt to them?" He described his sensations.

"They felt something like that," she said. "You gave the impulses your individual interpretations, of course, because you'd seen the restructure and knew what the keff was like. Cabon will be out in a moment, by the way. They got the Integrators' report back on this. I gather there's nothing definite enough in it to change our plans."

"I see," Duffold said absently. Mentally, he was reliving that section of the restructure in which the two investigators had come walking and wading right up to the keff, looking about as if searching for something, and apparently not even aware of each other's presence. Then they had stood still, while the huge head came slowly up out of the water before them—and the wet, pink maw opened wide and slapped shut twice.

Cabon stepped out of the room behind them. He grinned faintly. "Raw stuff," he remarked. "You've got a fine restructure team, Excellency."

"Any delays indicated?" Pilch inquired.

"No. You'd better go ahead on schedule. It's almost certain we'll still need our average Palayatan—and the one we've got spotted isn't going to hold still for us forever."

3

Yunnan, the average Palayatan, had finished the satisfactory third day of his solitary camping hike with a satisfactory meal composed largely of a broiled platterful of hard-shelled and hard-to-catch little water creatures, famed for their delicacy. The notion of refreshing his memory of that delicacy had been in his mind for some weeks and had finally led him up to this high mountain plateau and its hundreds of quick, cold streams where they were to be found at their best.

Having sucked out the last of the shells and pitched it into his camp fire, he sat on for a while under the darkening sky, watching the stars come out and occasionally glancing across the plateau at the dark, somber mass of the next mountain ridge. Two other campfires had become very distantly visible there, indicating the presence of other soqua spearers. He would stay here two more days, Yunnan thought, and then turn back, towards the valleys and the plain, and return to his semi-permanent house in his semi-permanent settlement, to devote himself again for a while to his semi-permanent occupation of helping local unbannut-growers select the best seeds for next season's crop.

It was all a very pleasant prospect. Life, Yunnan told himself, with a sense of having summed it up, was a pretty good thing! It was a conclusion he had come to before under similar circumstances.

Presently he rebuilt the fire, stretched out on some blankets close to it, and pulled a few more blankets on top of him. He blinked up at the stars a few more times and fell sound asleep.

Far overhead, a meteor that was not a meteor hit the atmosphere, glowed yellow, and vanished. A survey heli of the Hub Station's Planetary Geographers outfit, which had been moving high and unobtrusively above the plateau all day, came in closer to a point almost directly above Yunnan's camp, remained there a few minutes, and moved off again across the plateau and on beyond the mountain ridges to the east.

A dark spherical body, the size of a small house, sank swiftly and silently toward the plateau and came to a halt finally a hundred yards above Yunnan's camp and a little more than that to one side of it. Presently a breeze moved from that direction across the camp, carrying traces of a chemical not normally found in such concentration in Palayata's air. Yunnan inhaled it obligingly. A few minutes later, the breeze grew suddenly into a smooth, sustained rush of air, like the first moan of an approaching storm. Sparks flew from the fire, and leaves danced out of the trees. Then the wind subsided completely, and three people came walking into the camp. They bent above Yunnan.

"Perfect reaction!" Pilch's voice said. She straightened and glanced up. The spherical object had come gliding along at treetop level behind them and was now stationed directly overhead. Various and sundry clicking, buzzing, and purring sounds came out of its open lock. "Take them two or three more minutes to get a complete reproduction," she remarked. "Nothing to do but wait."

Duffold grunted. He was feeling uncomfortable again, and not entirely because of the presence of a Palayatan. Pilch had explained what had happened to Yunnan; the patterns of external sensory impressions that had been sifting into his brain at the moment the trace-chemical reached it through his blood stream were fixed there now, and no new impressions were coming through. He would remain like that, his last moment of sleep-sensed external reality extending itself unchangingly through the hours and days until the blocking agent was removed. What worried Duffold was that the action was a deliberate preliminary prod at the mysterious X factor, and if X felt prodded, there was no telling at all just how it might respond.

He looked down at their captive. Yunnan certainly looked quietly asleep, but the mild smile on his humanoid features might have expressed either childlike innocence or a rather sinister enjoyment of the situation, depending on how you felt about Palayatans.

And assuming Yunnan was harmless, at least for the moment, was somebody—or something—else, far off or perhaps quite close in the thickening night around them, aware by now that untoward and puzzling things were going on in a Palayatan mind?

Duffold knew they were trying to check on that, too. A voice began murmuring presently from one of the talkie gadgets Pilch wore as earrings. When it stopped, she said briefly, "All right." And then, to Duffold, "Not a pulse coming through the tele-screens that wouldn't be normal here! Just animals—" She sounded disappointed about it.

"Too bad!" Duffold said blandly. His nerves unknotted a trifle.

"Well, it's negative evidence anyway!" Pilch consoled him. The voice murmured from the same earring again, and she said, "All right. Put down the carrier then!" and to her two companions, "They're all done in the shuttle. Let's go."

A grav-carrier came floating down through the dark air toward them, and the crewman who had accompanied them into the camp began to extinguish the fire. He was conscientious and thorough about it. Pilch stepped up on the carrier. Duffold looked at her, at the busy crewman, and at Yunnan. Then he set his teeth, wrapped the Palayatan up in his blankets, picked him up, and laid him down on the carrier.

"Hm-m-m!" said Pilch. "Not bad, Excellency!"

Duffold thought a bad word and hoped she wasn't being telepathic.

"Of course not!" said Pilch, reaching up for the earring that hadn't come into noticeable use so far. She began to unscrew it. "Besides, I'm shutting off the pickup right now, Excellency—"

Almost two hours later, Yunnan awakened briefly. He blinked up at the familiar star-patterns overhead, gazed out across the plateau, and noted that one of the campfires there had gone out. Thus reminded, he yawned and scratched himself, stood up, and replenished his own fire. Then he lay down again, listened for a half-minute or so to the trilling night-cries of two small tree creatures not far away, and drifted back to sleep.

"He's completely out of the sensory stasis now, of course," Wintan explained to Duffold as the view of Yunnan's camp faded out before them. "How did you like the staging job?"

Duffold admitted it was realistic. He was wondering, however, he added, what would have happened if the Palayatan had decided to go for a stroll and walked off the stage?

"Well," Wintan said reflectively, "if he'd done that, we would have known he was ignoring the five or six plausible reasons against doing it that were planted in his awareness. In that case, we could have counted on his being an individual embodiment of the X factor, so to speak. The staff was prepared for the possibility."

Duffold knew that Psychological Service as such was, as a matter of fact, prepared for the possibility that they had hauled a super-being on board which conceivably could destroy or take control of this huge ship—and distant weapons were trained on the ship to insure that it wouldn't be under alien control for more than an instant. Even more distantly, out in the nothingness of space somewhere, events on the ship were being subjected to a moment-to-moment scrutiny and analysis.

Nor was *that* all. The Outposts patrol ships at Palayata had been relieved from duty by a Supreme Council order from the Hub; and, in their places, heavily armed cruisers of a type none of the patrol commanders could identify had begun to circle the planet.

"They won't break up Palayata unless they have to, of course!" Cabon had said, in reporting that matter to Duffold. "But that's no worry of ours at the moment. Our job is to trace out, record, and identify every type of thought, emotion, and motivation that possibly could go ticking through this Yunnan's inhuman little head. If we find out he's exactly what he seems to be, that eliminates one possible form of X."

And if Yunnan was something other than the not too intelligent humanoid he seemed to be, they had X neatly isolated for study. Whether or not they completed the study then depended largely on the nature of the subject.

Rationally, Duffold couldn't disagree with the method.

It was drastic; the casually icy calculation behind the preparations made by the Service had, in fact, shocked him as nothing else had done in his life. But, at one stage or another, it would bring X into view. If X was both hostile and more than a match for man, man at least had avoided being taken by surprise. If X was merely more than a match for man—

"Mightn't hurt us at all to learn how to get along with our superiors for a while," Wintan had observed thoughtfully.

It was a notion Duffold found particularly difficult to swallow.

He had noticed, in this last hour while they completed their preparations to invade the Average Palayatan's mind, occasional traces of a tingling excitement in himself—something close to elation. By and by, it dawned on him that it was the kind of elation that comes from an awareness of discovery.

He was engaged in an operation with the most powerful single organization of the Hub Systems. The despised specialists of Psychology Service, the errand boys of the major Departments, were, as a matter of fact, telling everyone, apparently including the Hub's Supreme Council, just what should be done about Palayata and how to do it.

Probably, it hadn't always been that way, Duffold decided; but the regular Departments of the Hub were getting old. For a decade, Outposts—one of the most brisk of the lot—had been gathering evidence that Palayatan civilization wasn't so much quaint as incomprehensible. For an equal length of time, it had been postponing recognition of the fact that the incomprehensibility might have a deadly quality to it—that, quite possibly, something very strange and very intelligent was in concealment on Palayata, observing human beings and perhaps only tolerating their presence here for its unknown purposes.

Even after the recognition had been forced on it, the Department had been unwilling to make any move at all on its own responsibility, for fear it might make the wrong one. Instead, it called in Psychology Service—

For the same reason that Psychology Service always was called in when there was an exceptionally dirty and ticklish job to be done—the Service People showed an unqualified willingness to see any situation exactly as it was and began dealing with it immediately in the best possible manner, to the limits of human ability. It was an attitude that guaranteed in effect that any problem which was humanly resolvable was going to get resolved.

The excitement surged up in Duffold again. And that, he added to himself, was why they didn't share the normal distaste for the notion of encountering a superior life form. The most superior of life forms couldn't improve on that particular attitude! Here or elsewhere, the Service eventually might be defeated, but it could never be outclassed.

He wondered at that difference in organizations that were equally human and decided it was simply that the Service now attracted the best in human material that happened to be around. At other times in history, the same type of people might have been engaged in very different activities—but they would always be found moving into the front ranks of humanity and moving out of the organizations that were settling down to the second-rate job of maintaining what others had gained.

As for himself—well, he'd gone fast and far in Outposts. He knew he was brainier than most. If it took some esoteric kind of mental training to get himself into mankind's real front ranks, he was going to take a look at it—

Providing, that was, that the lives of everyone on the ship didn't get snuffed out unexpectedly sometime in the next few hours!

✧   ✧   ✧

Wintan: *Pilch, your lad has just bucked his way through simultaneously to the Basis of Self-Esteem and the Temptations of Power and Glory! I'm a little in awe of him. What to do?*

Pilch: *Too early for a wide-open, I think! It could kill him. If we tap anything, we're going to have trouble. Buchele isn't—*

Cabon: *Make it wide-open, Wintan. My responsibility.*

Pilch: *No!*

Voice from Somewhere Far Out: *Agreement with Cabon's decision. Proceed!*

Wintan had left the pick-up room for the time being; and Duffold had it all to himself.

It was an odd place. Almost the most definite thing you could say about it was that it was somewhere within the vast bulk of the Service ship. Duffold sat in something like a very large and comfortable armchair with his feet up on a cushioned extension; and so far as he could tell, the armchair might have been floating slowly and endlessly through the pale-green, luminous fog which started about eight feet from his face in every direction. The only other thing visible in the room was another chair off to his right, in which Wintan had been sitting. Even the entrance by which they had come in was indetectable in the luminosity; when Wintan left, he appeared to vanish in cool green fire long before he reached it.

There wasn't much more time before the work on the captured Palayatan began, and Duffold started running the information he'd been given regarding the operation and his own role as an observer through his mind. Some of the concepts involved were unfamiliar; but, on the whole, it sounded more comprehensible than he had expected. They were acting on the assumption that, with the exception of the X factor, the structure of a Palayatan's mental personality was similar to the human one. They reacted to outside stimuli in much the same way and appeared to follow the same general set of basic motivations.

It was already known that there were specific differences. The Palayatan mind was impermeable to telepathic impulses at the level of sensory and verbal interpretations, which was the one normally preferred by human telepaths when it could be employed, since it involved the least degree of individual garbling of messages. Palayatans, judging by the keff creature's inability to affect them, were also impermeable to telepathed emotional stimuli. In spite of the effect they themselves produced on most untrained humans, it had been demonstrated that they also did not radiate at either of these levels, as against the diffused trickling of mental and emotional impulses normally going out from a human being.

At least, that was the picture at present. It might change when the ship's giant amplifiers, stimulators, and microscanners were brought into play upon Yunnan's sleeping brain. If X was a concealed factor of the Palayatan's personality, it would show up instantly. In that case, the investigation as such would be dropped, and the Service would switch its efforts into getting X into communication. It should at least be possible to determine rather quickly whether or not X was hostile and how capable it was of expressing hostility effectively, either here or on the planet.

But if it was found that Yunnan, as he knew himself, was Yunnan and nothing else, the search would drop below the levels of personality toward the routine mechanisms of the mind and the organic control areas. Somewhere in those multiple complexities of interacting structures of life must be a thing that was different enough from the standard humanoid pattern to make Palayata what it was. They had talked of the possibility that the X influence, if it was an alien one, did not extend actively beyond the planet. But the traces of its action would still be there and could be interpreted.

Duffold's impressions of the possibilities at that stage became a little vague, and he shifted his attention to a consideration of what Wintan had said regarding himself. There was apparently always some risk involved in an investigation of this kind, not to the subject, but to the investigator.

Or, in this case, to the observer.

The trouble was, according to Wintan, that the human mind—or any other type of mind the Service had studied so far, for that matter—was consciously capable of only a very limited form of experience. "A practical limitation," Wintan had said. "Most of what's going on in the universe isn't really any individual's concern. If he were trying to be aware of it all the time, he couldn't walk across the room without falling on his face. Besides, it would kill him."

And when Duffold looked questioningly at him, he added, "Did you ever go in for the Sensational Limitations vogue, Excellency?"

"No," Duffold said shortly.

"Well," Wintan acknowledged, "they get a little raw, at that! However, they do show that a human being can tolerate only a definitely limited impact of emotion—artificially induced or otherwise—at any one time, before he loses awareness of what's going on. Now, the more or less legitimate material the Sensationalists use is drawn from emotions that other human beings have at one time or another consciously experienced, sometimes under extreme stimulation, of course. However, as a rather large number of Sensationalists have learned by now, the fact that a sensation came originally from a human mind doesn't necessarily make its re-experience a safe game for another human being."

He was silent for a moment. "That keff animal," he

said then. "You saw it. Can you imagine yourself thinking and feeling like a keff, Excellency?"

Duffold grinned. "I hadn't thought of it," he said. He considered and shook his head. "Probably not too well."

"It appears to be a fairly complicated creature," Wintan said. "Stupid, of course. It doesn't need human intelligence to get along. But it's not just a lump of life responding to raw surges of emotion. There are creatures that aren't much else, a good deal farther down on the scale. They haven't developed anything resembling a calculating brain, and what we call emotion is what guides them and keeps them alive. To be effective guides to something like that, those emotions have to be pretty strong. As a matter of fact, they're quite strong enough to wreck anything as complex and carefully balanced as a conscious human mind very thoroughly, if it contacts them for more than a very short time."

"How do you know?" Duffold inquired.

"So far, our Hub Sensationalists haven't learned how to bottle anything like that," Wintan said. "At least, we haven't run into any indications of it. However, Psychology Service did learn how, since it was required for a number of reasons. In the process, we might have discovered that emotion can kill the body by destroying the mind in a matter of seconds if we hadn't been made aware of the fact a good deal earlier—"

"Yes?" Duffold said politely.

"Excellency," Wintan said, "civilized man is—with good reason, I think—a hellishly proud creature. Unfortunately, his achievements often make it difficult for him to accept that his remote ancestors—and the remote ancestors of every other mobile and intelligent life form we've come across—were, at one period, specks of appetite in the mud, driven by terrors and a brainless lust for survival, ingestion, and procreation that are flatly inconceivable to the conscious human mind today."

Duffold laughed. "I'll accept it," he said agreeably.

"In that case," said Wintan, "you might consider accepting that precisely the same pattern is still present in each of our intelligent life forms and is still basically what motivates them as organisms. Self-generated or not, emotions like that can still shock the mind that contacts them consciously in full strength to death. Normally, of course, that's a flat impossibility—our mental structure guarantees that what filters through into consciousness is no more than the trace of a shadow of the basic emotions . . . no more than consciousness needs to guide it into reasonably intelligent conduct and, usually, at any rate, no more than consciousness can comfortably tolerate. But in an investigation of this kind, we'll be playing around the edges of the raw stuff sooner or later. We'll try to keep out of it, of course."

Duffold said thoughtfully that he was beginning to see the reason for safeguards. "What makes it possible for you to get into trouble here?"

"Something like a cubic mile of helpful gadgetry," Wintan said. "It's quite an accomplishment."

"It is," Duffold said. "So it's not all conditioning then. Can you—conditioned—people get along without safeguards?"

Wintan said amiably that to some extent they could. On reflection, it didn't sound too bad to Duffold. The particular type of safeguard that had been provided for him in the pick-up room was to the effect that as he approached an emotional overload, he would be cut out of contact automatically with the events in the ship. Otherwise, he would remain an observer-participant, limited only by his lack of understanding of the progress of the operation.

Wintan: *I've given him fair warning, Pilch.*

Pilch, grudgingly: *There's no such thing in this game! I suppose you did what you could.*

❖   ❖   ❖

Pictures moved now and then through the luminous mist. Some were so distinct that it seemed to Duffold he was looking straight through the bulk of the ship at the scene in question. Most were mere flickers of form and color, and a few a tentative haziness in which a single detail might assume a moment of solidity before the whole faded out.

"Cabon's checking the final arrangements," Wintan said from the chair to Duffold's right.

Duffold nodded, fascinated by the notion that he was observing the projected images of a man's mind, and disappointed that the meaning of much of it apparently was wasted on him. Buchele's waxy face showed up briefly, followed by the picture of a thick-necked man whose cheekbones and jaw were framed by a trimmed bristle of red beard.

"Our primary investigators, those two," Wintan said briefly. "The other one's Ringor—head of Pattern Analysis." The mind-machines and their coordinators did what they could; they supplied power and analyzed a simultaneous wealth of detail no human mentality could begin to grasp in the same span of time. To some degree, they also predicted the course that should be followed. But the specific, moment to moment turns of the search for X were under the direction of human investigators. Eight or nine others would trace the progress of the leading two but would not become immediately involved unless they were needed. Pilch was one of these.

The reconstruction of Yunnan's camp area came gradually into sight now, absorbing the pick-up medium as it cleared and spread about and behind the two observers. Presently, it seemed to Duffold that he was looking down at the sleeping figure near the fire from a point about forty feet up in Palayata's crisp night air. The illusion would have been perfect except for two patches of something like animated smoke to either side of Yunnan. He studied the phenomenon for a moment and was startled by a sudden impression that the swirling vapory lines of one of those patches was the face of the red-bearded investigator. It changed again before he could be sure. He glanced over at Wintan, suspended incongruously in his chair against the star-powdered night.

The Service man grinned. "Saw it, too," he said in a voice that seemed much too loud here to Duffold. "The other one is Buchele—or the projector's impression of Buchele at the moment. They're designed to present what they get in a form that makes some meaning in human perceptions, but they have peculiar notions about those! You'll get used to it."

He was, Duffold decided, speaking of one of the machines. He was about to inquire further when the scene became active.

Something a little like a faint, brief gleaming of planetary auroras . . . then showers of shooting stars . . . played about the horizons. For a moment he forgot he was watching a reconstruction. The lights and colors flowed together and became the upper part of the body of a blond woman smiling down over the distant mountains at the sleeping Palayatan, her hands resting on the tops of the ridges. Briefly, the face blurred into an unpleasantly grimacing mask and cleared again. Then the woman was gone, and in her place was a brightly lit, perfectly ordinary looking room, in which a man in the uniform of the Service sat at a table.

"What's all this?" Duffold breathed.

"Eh?" Wintan said absently. "Oh!" He turned his head and laughed. "Our investigators were tuning in on each other. They've worked together before, but it takes a moment or so—Ah, here we go!"

Duffold blinked. The universe all around them was suddenly an unquiet grayness, a vaguely disturbing grayness because there was motion in it which couldn't be identified. A rapid shifting and flowing of nothing into nothing that just missed having significance for him.

"About as good a presentation as the projector can manage," Wintan's voice said, almost apologetically—and Wintan, too, Duffold noticed now, was invisible in the grayness. He felt uncomfortably isolated. "You're looking at . . . well, it would be our Palayatan's consciousness, if he were awake."

Duffold said nothing. He had been seized by the panicky notion that breathing might become difficult in this stuff, and he was trying to dismiss that notion. A splash of blue, a beautiful, vivid blue, blazed suddenly in the grayness and vanished. "They're moving," Wintan's voice murmured. "Dream level now!"

Breathing *was* difficult! If only that blue would come back—

It came. Duffold gasped with relief, as gray veils exploded about him and a bright blue sky, deep with cloudbanks, spread overhead and all about. Wintan spoke from somewhere, with a touch of concern, "If this is bothering you at all, I can shut you out of it instantly, you know!"

"No," Duffold said. He broke out laughing. "I just discovered I'm not here!"

It was true in a peculiar way. There wasn't a trace of Wintan or himself or of their supporting chairs in sight here. He looked down through empty space where his body should have been and laughed again. But he could still feel himself and the pressure of the chair against him, at any rate; so he hadn't become disembodied.

"Dreams are odd." Wintan's voice sounded as if he might be smiling, too, but the concern hadn't quite left it. "Especially when they're somebody else's. And especially again when that someone isn't human. Incidentally, this is a visual pick-up for you. All you have to do to break it is to close your eyes."

Duffold closed his eyes experimentally and patted the side of the chair. Then he opened them again—

Yunnan's dream had changed in that instant. He was

looking down now into a section of a shallow stream, swift-moving and clear, through which a creature like a mottled egg darted behind a silver lure. Another one showed up beyond it, both flashingly quick, propelled by a blurred paddling of red legs.

"Mountain soquas," said Wintan. "Our friend was spearing them during the day." His voice sounded thoughtful. "No trace of anything that might indicate X, so far. I imagine they'll stimulate a different type of sequence—"

The scene flowed, as he spoke, into something entirely different again. This was, Duffold decided, apparently an angular caricature of a Palayatan town-street, presented in unpleasantly garish colors. Something that was in part a red-legged soqua and in part an extremely stout Palayatan was speaking excitedly to a small group of other Palayatans. The next moment, they had all turned and were staring straight at Duffold. Their eyes seemed to contain some terrible accusation. Involuntarily, he cringed—just as the scene flickered out of existence.

The green luminescence was about them again. From the other chair, Wintan grinned briefly at him.

"Tapped a nightmare layer," he explained. "It woke him up. So our little friends have bad dreams, too, occasionally!" He studied Duffold quizzically. "Did you get the guilt in that one?"

"Guilt?" Duffold repeated.

"He'd been killing soquas," Wintan said. "Naughty thing to do, according to his subconscious, so it punished him." He added, "No luck at all, so far, unless there was something I missed. An orderly, childish mind. No real guile in it—and it does fit the way they look and act."

"Could it be faked?"

"Well," Wintan said, "*we* couldn't do it. Not to that extent. They'll hit the Deep Downs next, I imagine. Should become more interesting now."

A riot of color blazed up about them—color that was

too rich and in meaningless flux and motion, or frozen into patterns that stirred Duffold uncomfortably. Something came to his memory and he turned and spoke in Wintan's direction.

"Yes," Wintan's voice replied, "it's not surprising that it makes you think of some forms of human art. We have a comparable layer." He was silent for a moment. "How do you feel?"

"Slight headache," Duffold said, surprised. "Why?"

"It might affect you that way. Just close your eyes a while. I'll let you know if we run into something significant."

Duffold closed his eyes obediently. Now that his attention was on it, the headache seemed more than slight. He began to massage his forehead with his fingertips. Wintan's voice went on, "It's a nearly parallel complex of mental structures, as one would expect, considering the physical similarities. This particular area originates when the brain's visual centers are developing in the zygote. It's pure visual experience, preceding any outside visual stimulus. Later on, in humans anyway, it can become a fertile source of art . . . also of nightmares, incidentally." His voice stopped, then resumed sharply, "Buchele's tracing something—there!"

Duffold opened his eyes. Instantly, he had a sensation that *was* pure nightmare—of being sucked forward, swept up and out of his chair, up and into—

The sensation stopped, and a velvety blackness swam in front of him like an intangible screen. He was still in his chair. He drew in a quivering breath. The only reason he hadn't shouted in fright was that he hadn't been capable of making a sound.

"That—!" he gasped.

"Easy," Wintan said quietly. "I've shut you off."

"But that was that keff animal!"

"Something very like it," Wintan said, and Duffold

realized that he could see the Service man again now. Wintan was watching something that was behind the area of screening blackness for Duffold, and if he felt any of the effects that had paralyzed Duffold, he didn't show it. He added, "It's very interesting. We'd been wondering about the keff!"

"I thought," Duffold said, "that Palayatans weren't bothered by the animal."

Wintan glanced at him. "Our present Palayatans aren't. Did you notice the stylized quality of that image and the feeling of size—almost like a monument?"

Duffold said shortly that he hadn't been in a frame of mind to observe details. His vulnerability was still irritating. "It looked like a keff to me. Why should it be in this fellow's mind?"

"Ancestral image," Wintan said, "or I miss my guess! And that means—it almost *has* to mean that at one time the Palayatans weren't immune to . . . ah, wait!"

"Something new?" Duffold said quickly.

Wintan seemed to hesitate. "Yes," he said.

"Then cut me in again. I don't want to miss more than I have to."

For a moment, Duffold thought Wintan hadn't responded. Then he realized that the blackness before him wasn't quite what it had been a few seconds ago.

He stared uncomprehendingly. An eerie shiver went over him. "What's this?" he demanded, his voice unaccountably low.

"Something really new!" Wintan said quietly. "I think, Excellency, that they've found X!"

For the moment, that seemed to have no meaning to Duffold. The pale thing swimming in the dark before them was roughly circular and quite featureless. He had a feeling it was nothing tangible, a dim light—but his hair was bristling at the back of his neck. The thought came to him that if this was what the projectors were making of the thing that had been tracked down, the mind-machines were as puzzled as he was. "Something really new—" Wintan had said.

He realized that the thing wasn't alone.

To right and left of it, like hounds cautiously circling a strange beast they had overtaken, moved two lesser areas of light. The human investigators hadn't withdrawn.

They're trying to make contact with it, he thought. And some of the sense of awe and oppression left him. If they could face this strangeness at first hand—

It happened quickly. One of the smaller areas of light moved closer to the large one, hesitated, and moved closer again. And something like a finger of brightness stabbed out from the large one and touched the other.

Instantly, there was only blackness. Duffold heard Wintan catch his breath, and started to ask what had happened. He checked himself, appalled.

A face swam hugely before them. It was Buchele's, and it was the face of a personality sagging out of existence. The eyes were liquid, and the mouth slid open and went lax. Across the fading image flashed something sharp and decisive; and Duffold knew, without understanding how he knew it, that Cabon had given a command and that it had been acknowledged.

In the next instant, as the scene of darkness and its pale inhabitant reshaped itself, he knew also by whom the command had been acknowledged.

"No!" he shouted. He was struggling to get up out of the chair, as Wintan called out something he didn't understand. But it was over by then.

Again there had been three areas of light, two small and one large. Again, a small one came gliding in towards the large one; and again light stabbed out to meet it.

This time, it was like a jarring dark explosion all around him. Dazed, Duffold seemed to hang suspended for a moment over a black pit, and then he was dropping towards it. It was, he sensed suddenly, like dropping into a living volcano. Its terrors, stench, and fury boiled up horribly to engulf him.

4

The office seemed stuffy. Duffold reached back and turned the refresher up a few notches, simultaneously switching the window view to the spaceport section where the shuttles and transports stood ramped. Since he'd got back, that was the only available outside view he'd cared to look at. Except for that guide of Wintan's—Albemarl or whatever his name was—four days ago, no Palayatan ever had been allowed into that area. They hadn't sense enough to insure they would remain un-cindered there.

He noticed the Service transport had landed at Ramp Thirteen. They were punctual, as usual. A few figures moved about it, too far off to be recognized. Duffold picked up the sheaf of Service reports from a corner of the desk, flicked through them, and hauled out a sheet. There were some points he wanted to refresh his mind on before the coming interview with—well, with whomever it was they'd decided to send down. He hadn't specified Pilch, though he imagined it was the kind of job she would be likely to take on.

He read hurriedly, skipping sections here and there. " . . . Originally, then, it was the class of creatures of which the present-day keff is the only surviving species that forced the divergence in mental development on the proto-humanoids. Their evolutionary response was a shift of the primary center of awareness from the level of sensory interpretation to that of organic control, which has remained a semiautomatic, unconscious area of mind in any similar species. The telepathic bands on which the keff-like carnivores operated could stimulate only the sensory-response areas of the brain. The controlling central mind of the humanoid was no longer affected by them. The continuing inflow of keff-impulses on the upper telepathic bands became a meaningless irritation, and the brain eventually sealed off its receptors to them . . .

"To an observer of the period, it might have seemed that the Palayatan humanoid species now had trapped itself in an evolutionary pocket. Animal intelligence must isolate itself from the full effect of the primitive emotional storms of the unconscious if it is to develop rationality and the ability of abstract thought. In doing this, it reduces its awareness of the semiautomatic levels of mind which remain largely in the area of the unconscious. In this case, however, it was losing contact with the level of sensory interpretation which normally is the indicated area of intellectual development . . . For many hundreds of thousands of years, the Palayatan humanoid remained superficially an animal. His brain was, in fact, continuing to evolve at a rate comparable to the proto-human one; but the increase in consciousness and potential of organization was being absorbed almost entirely by the internal mind to which he as a personality had retreated . . ."

Duffold put that sheet down, shook his head, and selected another one. " . . . The fairly well-developed civilization we now find on Palayata . . . of comparatively recent date . . . The humanoid being with whom we have become familiar conveniently might be regarded as a secondary personality, subordinate to the internal one. However, the term is hardly more justified than if it were applied to the human sympathetic nervous system . . .

"The Palayatan superficial mind has become an increasingly complex structure because the details of its required activities are complex. It has awareness of its motivations, but is not aware that an internal mind is the source of those motivations. It has no understanding of the fact that its individual desires and actions are a considered factor in the maintenance of the planetary civilization which it takes for granted.

"On the other hand, the internal personality, at this stage of its development, is still capable of only a generalized comprehension of the material reality in which it exists as an organism. It employs its superficial mind as an agent which can be motivated to act towards material goals that will be beneficial to itself and its species. By human standards, the goals have remained limited ones since the possibility of achieving them depends on the actual degree of intelligence developed at present by the superficial minds. They are limited again by the internal minds' imperfect concept of the nature of material reality. As an example, the fact that space might extend beyond the surface of their planet has had no meaning to them, though it has been presented as a theoretical possibility by some abstract thinkers . . ."

Duffold shoved the sheets back into the stack. He couldn't argue with the reports or with the Service's official conclusion regarding Palayata, and he didn't doubt that the Hub Departments would accept them happily. So we're dealing with a native race of split personalities this time—no matter, so long as the Service guarantees they're harmless! The emotional disturbance they caused human beings couldn't be changed, unfortunately; but any required close contacts could be handled by drug-fortified personnel.

Everybody was going to feel satisfied with the outcome— except Duffold. He was reaching for another section of the reports when the desk communicator murmured softly up at him.

"Oh!" he said. "Why, yes. Send her right in."

He studied Pilch curiously after she was seated. Objectively, she looked as attractive as ever, with her long, clean lines and a profile almost too precisely perfect. Otherwise, she stirred no feeling in him this time; and he was a little relieved about that.

"I understand," she said, "that you weren't entirely pleased with our reports?"

"I did have a few questions," Duffold said. "It was very good of you to come. The original reports, of course, have been transmitted to my headquarters."

She nodded briefly.

"Personally," Duffold said hesitantly, "I find all this a little difficult to believe. Of course, I blacked out before the investigation was concluded. The reports simply state what you found, not how you got the information."

"That's right," said Pilch. "How we got it wouldn't mean much to someone who wasn't familiar with our methods of operation. What part can't you believe? That the real Palayatan is so far inside himself that he hardly knows we're around when we meet him?"

"Oh, I'll accept that that's the way it is," Duffold said irritably. "But how did you find out?"

"One of those inner minds told us," said Pilch. "Not the one inside Yunnan—he was scared to death by the time we got done with him and yelled for help. So another one reached out far enough from the planet to see what was wrong—a colleague of ours, so to speak. At least, he regards himself as a psychologist—a specialist in mental problems."

Duffold shook his head helplessly.

"Well, it's an odd sort of existence, by our standards," Pilch said. "I don't think I'd go for it myself. But they like it well enough." She thought a moment and added, "The feeling I had was as if you were a deep-sea animal, intensely aware of yourself and of everything else in a big, dark ocean all around you. Actually, there was a sort of richness in the feeling. I'd say their life-experience is at least as varied as the average human one."

"What scared Yunnan?" Duffold asked.

"He knew something was wrong. He didn't realize he'd been removed bodily from the planet, but to use our terms, he felt as if he had suddenly grown almost deaf—

and invisible. He couldn't understand the other Palayatans very well anymore, and they didn't seem to be too aware of him. And then our investigators suddenly were *talking* to him! Do you know what human beings seem like to those inside Palayatans? Something like small sleepy animals that have mysteriously turned up in their world. I imagine our degree of organic intelligence can't be too impressive at that! So when two of those animals began to address him—conscious minds like himself, but *not* his kind of mind—Yunnan panicked."

"So he killed Buchele," Duffold said.

Pilch said impassively, "It would be correct to say that Buchele killed himself. There were sections of his mind that he had never been able to accept as part of himself. Buchele was an idealist in his opinion of himself, and in Service work that's a risk. Of course, he had a right to insist on taking that risk if he chose."

"Exactly what did happen to him?" Duffold said carefully.

"The Palayatan jolted a sealed-off section of Buchele's mind into activity, and Buchele met its impact in full consciousness. It killed him."

"No matter how you phrase it," Duffold said, "it seems that one human being, at least, has been murdered by a Palayatan!"

She shook her head. "Not if murder is in the intention. Because it was only trying to frighten Buchele off. It's the way they deal with another mind that is annoying them."

"Frighten him off?" Duffold repeated incredulously.

"Look," Pilch said, "every time you felt that anxiety you mentioned, you'd been jolted by some Palayatan in exactly the same way. Every human being, every intelligent life-form we know about, keeps that stuff out of awareness by layers and layers of mental padding. Our heavy-duty civilized emotions are just trickles of the real thing. It takes the kind of power equipment we have on the ship to drive ourselves down consciously, with full awareness, to the point where we're close enough to it that a Palayatan could topple us in. So it can't ever happen on the planet."

Duffold looked like a man who has suddenly come upon a particularly distasteful notion.

"Some people reported euphorias," he said.

Pilch nodded. "I didn't mention that because I knew you wouldn't care for it. Well, I told you they've been regarding us as some sort of small strange animal. Some of them become quite fond of the little beasts. So they stimulate us pleasantly—till we take a nip out of them or whatever it is we do that annoys them. Tell me something," she went on before he could reply. "Just before you blacked out during the investigation, what were the sensations you hit—terror, self-disgust, rage?"

He looked at her carefully. "Well—all of that," he said. "The outstanding feeling was that I was in close contact with something incredibly greedy, devouring . . . foul! I can appreciate Buchele's attitude." He hesitated. "How did it happen that I wasn't aware of what got Buchele?"

"Automatic switch-off for the instant it lasted. It was obvious that it was going over the level of emotional tolerance that had been set for you. We told you there'd be safeguards."

"I see," said Duffold. "Then what about the other thing?"

Pilch looked faintly surprised. "Wintan would have cut you out of it, if he'd had the time," she said. "But obviously you did tolerate it even if you blacked out for a while. That was still well within the safe limit."

Duffold felt a slow stirring of rage. "When you took Buchele's place, it seemed to me that the Palayatan struck at you in the same way he had at Buchele. Is that correct?"

Pilch nodded. "It is."

"But because of your superior conditioning, it didn't disturb you?"

"Not enough to keep me from making use of it," Pilch said.

"In what way?"

"I opened it up on the Palayatan. That," said Pilch, "was when he yelled for help. But it was too bad you picked it up!"

Duffold carefully traced a large, even circle on the desk top with a fingertip. "And you could accept *that* as being part of your mind?" he said with a note of mild wonder. "Well, I suppose you should be congratulated on such an unusual ability."

She looked a little pale as she walked out of the office. But, somehow, Duffold couldn't find any real satisfaction in that.

Wintan was leaning against the side of the central Outpost building as Pilch came out of the entrance. She stopped short.

"Thought you'd be at the transport," she said.

"I was," Wintan said. "Twelve slightly stunned keffs in good shape have been loaded, and I was making a last tour of the area."

"Albemarl?" she asked as they started walking back to the ramps. "Or the psychologist?"

"Both," Wintan said. "I'd have liked to say good-by to Albemarl, but there's still no trace of the old tramp anywhere. He'd have enjoyed the keff hunt, too! Too bad he had to wander off again."

"How about the other one?"

"Well, there's very little chance he'll actually contact us, of course," Wintan said. "However"—he held his right hand up—"observe the new wrist adornment! If he's serious about it, that's to help him locate me."

She looked at two polished black buttons set into a metal wrist-strap. "What's it supposed to do?"

"Theoretically, it sets up a small spot of static on *their* awareness band. Tech hasn't had a chance to test it, of course, but it seems to be working. I've been getting some vaguely puzzled looks from our local friends as I wander about, but that's as much interest as they've shown. How did it go with his Excellency?"

"Satisfactorily, I suppose," Pilch said grudgingly. "No heavy dramatics. But for a while there, you know, that little man had me feeling mighty unclean!"

"Self-defense," Wintan said tolerantly. "Give him time to shake it down. Basically, he already knows it was one of his own little emotional volcanoes he dropped into, not yours. But it'll be a year or two before he's really able to admit it to himself, and meanwhile he can let off steam by sitting around and loathing you thoroughly from time to time."

"I read the Predictor's report on him, too," Pilch said. "I still don't agree it was the right way to handle it."

Wintan shrugged. "Cabon can estimate them. If we'd jolted this one much heavier, it might have broken him up. But if the jolt had been a little too light, he could have buried it permanently away and forgotten about it again. As it is, he knows what's inside him, and eventually he'll know it consciously. When he does, he'll be ready for Service work without qualifications—and that means he won't go out some day like Buchele did."

They walked on in silence for a while, through the drifting crowds of visiting Palayatans. Assorted Hub perfumes tinged the air, soft voices chattered amiably, faces turned curiously after the passing humans. "What makes you all so sure Duffold will be back?" Pilch said finally. "Even if he realizes what happened, the rap on the nose he got could be discouraging."

"It could be, for someone else," Wintan said. "But there're some you can't keep away, once they learn where the biggest job really is. For his Excellency, the rap on the nose will turn out eventually to have been Stage One of conditioning."

"Well, maybe. But an idealist like that," said Pilch, "always strikes me as peculiar! They never want to look at the notion that the real reason Man rates some slight cosmic approval is that he can act as well as he does, in spite of the stuff he's evolving from."

"Can't really blame them," Wintan remarked. "As you probably discovered in your own conditioning, some of that stuff just isn't good to look at."

"Now there for once," Pilch agreed darkly, "you spoke a fair-sized truth. Incidentally, that static you're spreading doesn't seem to meet with everyone's approval around here. I've been jolted three times in the last ten seconds."

"Small boy about six steps behind us," Wintan reported. "He's scowling ferociously—but mama's leading him off now. I wonder what he made of it consciously?"

"He'll probably grow up with a vague but firmly held notion that Hub humans don't smell good," Pilch estimated. They were coming up to a long, low wall from which the ramp-ways led into the sunken take-off section. The crowds were thinning out. "Have you noticed anyone acting as if he might conceivably be our psychologist?"

Wintan said he hadn't. "If he's in the area, as he said he would be, he's still got about ten minutes to make up his mind to go space-faring. Let's stop here and give him a last chance to show up before we go out on the ramp."

They leaned back against the wall surveying passing natives hopefully. "He was excited about the idea at first," Wintan said, "but I imagine it seemed like too big a change when he'd had time to think about it. After all, he would have lost contact with all his kind before the ship was out of the system."

Pilch shivered. "Like a man living in a solitary dream for years, listening to the voices of strange entities. Isn't it odd—two intelligent races, physically side by side, but each blocked from any real contact with the other by the fears of its own mind!"

"It needn't have stayed that way," Wintan said regretfully. "Lord, the things we could have learned! We working down towards his awareness band, and he working up towards ours. Wish we had time to experiment here for a year or so! But the Great God Schedule has got us. It's likely to be a half century before the Service can spare another look at Palayata."

Pilch glanced at her timepiece. "The same Schedule also says we start moving towards Ramp Thirteen right now, Wintan."

They moved, reluctantly. As they came up the stairs to the locked platform gate, a lanky figure that had been sitting beside it stood up without unseemly haste.

Pilch darted a wild glance at Wintan. "Great Suns!" she said as they both came to a stop. Wintan was clearing his throat. "Ah, Albemarl—" His voice sounded shaky. "I greet you!"

"And I greet you, Wintan!" the elderly Palayatan said benignly. "I must ask your forgiveness for not having met you here as I promised, but I have had a very strange experience."

"Ah, yes?" Wintan said.

"Yes, indeed! For forty long years, I have wandered over the face of the world, welcome everywhere because of my great wisdom and the free flow of my advice. When you asked me some time ago whether I would like to enter your ship and go out of the world in it, into that strange emptiness overhead from which you people come, I laughed at you. Because—forgive me again, Wintan— we all think here that it is very foolish to leave a fair and familiar world and the comfort of many, many friends, in order, at best and after a long time, to reach another world that cannot be so very different, where friends must be made again. Also, you spoke of risks."

"Yes," Wintan said, "there are always risks, of course."

Albemarl nodded. "But on the night after you left," he said, "I had a dream. A strong voice spoke to me, which I know as the voice of my True Self"—Pilch gulped—"and it told me of a thing I had overlooked. I knew then it was true, but it disturbed me greatly. So for these days and nights I have been wandering about the hills, thinking of what it said. But in the end I have come here with a calm heart to ask whether I may now enter the ship and go wandering with you and your friends through all the years and the strangeness that is beyond the world."

"You may, indeed, Albemarl!" Wintan said.

"And we leave now? I am ready."

"We leave now." Wintan gave Pilch a look, still incredulous but shining; then he stepped up to the gate and put the ball of his thumb against the lock that would open only to a human pattern.

"Albemarl," Pilch said gently, as the gate hissed open, "would you mind very much telling me what the thing was that you had overlooked?"

Albemarl blinked at her benevolently with his somewhat muddy Palayatan eyes. "Why, not at all. It is a simple thing but a great one—that wisdom accepts no limits. So when a wise man hears of a new thing that may be learned, beyond anything he knew before, it may not seem as comforting as the familiar things he knows, but he must learn it or he will never be content."

Wintan had moved back from the gate to let Pilch through. She put her hand on Albemarl's elbow and stepped up to the gate with him. Then she stopped.

"After you, brother!" Pilch said.

Afterword

by Eric Flint

James Schmitz's Hub tales revolve around a central core. Or, it might be better to say, a tandem axle—the adventures of Telzey Amberdon and Trigger Argee. Those core stories, with two exceptions ("The Searcher" and "A Nice Day for Screaming"), have all been assembled in the first three volumes of this four-volume series.

Depending on whether you approach the "core" from a Telzey or a Trigger angle, the volumes can be read in different orders. The early adventures of Telzey are collected in *Telzey Amberdon* and those of Trigger in *Trigger & Friends*—respectively, volumes 1 and 3 of the series. Volume 2, *T'nT: Telzey and Trigger*, serves as the sequel either way. Telzey stars in all seven stories collected in volume 2, although in "The Symbiotes" she plays a distinctly secondary role. Trigger features in three of them: "Compulsion," "Glory Day," and "The Symbiotes."

But the core stories involve more than just Telzey and

461

Trigger. In addition, there are a number of secondary characters who frequently appear in Telzey and Trigger's adventures. Many of these "secondary" characters are quite prominent in their own right, and they are as much a part of the "core" as Telzey and Trigger. In fact, most of them get at least one story in which they are the protagonist rather than the spear-carrier.

Holati Tate, for instance, is actually the hero in the opening story of this volume, "Harvest Time"—and Trigger is *his* supporting character.

Pilch stars in "Sour Note," as the other lead character with Bayne Duffold (who never appears anywhere else).

Wellan Dasinger, the head of the Kyth Interstellar Detective Agency who figures as Telzey's sidekick in "Undercurrents" and "Resident Witch", is the lead character of "The Star Hyacinths." (All three of those stories being included in the first volume.)

Heslet Quillan, in addition to being the other main character in *Legacy,* is the protagonist of the novella "Lion Loose." He also stars in "Forget It," of course, but . . .

"Forget It" is actually an adaptation by Guy Gordon of a non-Hub story called "Planet of Forgetting." In the course of assembling the stories for this volume, I remarked to Guy that it was unfortunate that Schmitz only wrote one independent Quillan story. Guy sent me a copy of "Planet of Forgetting," pointing out that with just a change of names, a slight addition to the dialogue (Quillan's ubiquitous "doll") and changing a few paragraphs of background information, it *was* a Quillan story. I read the story, saw that he was right, and we decided to include Guy's adaptation as part of this volume. That was very "impure" of us, true, but I can't say I feel in the least apologetic about it. In either version, it's a nice story, and Schmitz's original would not have been included in this series anyway.

We are now almost finished with the core stories of

Schmitz's Hub universe. But not quite—and one of the very best is still to come.

That is "The Searcher," which will open Volume 4 of this series. "The Searcher" stars Danestar Gems and Corvin Wergard, two detectives from the Kyth agency. (Wergard also appears in the Telzey story "Resident Witch" in Volume 2.)

In addition, there's "A Nice Day For Screaming," which stars Keth Deboll. Deboll was the reporter whom Telzey allied with in "Company Planet," and he had a very minor off-stage role in *Legacy*. (He's the one who calls Quillan in the *Dawn City*'s lounge and tries to get introduced to Trigger—to no avail.)

And that will be it, for what I'm calling the "core stories" of the Hub. Most of Volume 4 shifts focus entirely, and except for the two stories mentioned none of the core characters appear. Yet, in a way, Volume 4 also revolves around a tandem axle of its own—and a central character.

The character is Nile Etland, who is the most important character Schmitz developed for his Hub universe other than Telzey and Trigger. Nile features in two stories, the novelette "Trouble Tide" and the novel entitled *The Demon Breed* (which was originally serialized in *Analog* magazine under the title "The Tuvela"). *The Demon Breed* is, in many ways, the best piece of fiction that James Schmitz ever wrote. Together with "Trouble Tide"—which has never been re-issued since its original appearance in *Astounding Science Fiction* in September of 1958—the Nile Etland "saga" comprises about half the material in the last volume of the Hub series.

And the "tandem axle" I spoke of earlier is perhaps better exemplified by *The Demon Breed* than any of the stories in Volume 4, although it can be found in all of them:

Ecology, as a theme, stands at the center of most of

the stories in Volume 4. Two of them, in fact—"Grandpa" and "Balanced Ecology"—are quite possibly the best ecology-oriented stories ever written in the history of science fiction.

The other "axle" is another staple of science fiction: *alien invasion.* In one way or another, most of the stories in Volume 4 deal with a threat posed by intelligent aliens to the human society of the Hub. The nature of that threat varies widely, from the inimical ("The Searcher," "The Winds of Time" and *The Demon Breed*) through the casually accidental ("A Nice Day for Screaming") all the way to threats which are not really threats at all, as we discover in "The Other Likeness."

The special approach which Schmitz took to the theme of alien menace—which is perhaps unique to his writings—is that he almost always couched it in broad ecological terms. True, in "The Searcher" and "The Winds of Time" the alien menace is presented in a simple and straight-forward manner. (In fact, they are among the handful of all-time classic SF *Alien Menace!* stories—and it is amazing to me that no-one in Hollywood seems to have noticed that either story would make 99% of all science fiction horror movies pale in comparison.)

But, for the most part, Schmitz presents aliens as simply another factor in the ecology of an inhabited galaxy. And so, for all the excitement of the adventures, there is also a certain serenity in his approach. Serenity, and a kind of warm and relaxed humanism which shines through these stories perhaps even more than any others he wrote.

All of which is a roundabout editor's way of assuring readers who have read and enjoyed the first three volumes that the last one is *not* the "rag, tag and bobtail" of the Hub series. By no means. On average, in fact, the quality of the stories in Volume 4 is perhaps the highest of any of the volumes.

So, yes—we now leave our familiar and beloved Telzey and Trigger behind. But Nile Etland is still to come. She, and her Parahuan enemies and her mutant otter friends—and all the other wonderful characters whom you will find in Volume 4: ranging from monsters like the goyal and the janandra to the benign figure at the center of the diamondwood forest.

And, of course, my personal favorites: the slurp with whom plucky young Ilf contemplates a friendly duel in "Balanced Ecology," and the mysterious creature with whom plucky young Cord *does* fight a duel in "Grandpa"—and a deadly one, nothing friendly about it.

I won't go quite as far as saying "the best is yet to come." But I'm tempted, despite my great fondness for the Telzey and Trigger cycle—and could easily argue the case, either way.

The Psychology Service: Immune System of the Hub

by Guy Gordon

If the Federation of the Hub is the common setting of the stories in these four volumes, *psi* is the thread weaving together Schmitz's entire literary works. The idea of psi (psychic abilities) and the Psychology Service appears throughout his writing, even in non-Hub stories.

In his Agent of Vega series (all of which predate the Hub writings) Schmitz based his Vegan Agents on E. E. "Doc" Smith's Lensmen, except that psi was the advantage held by the agents of the Vegan Confederation instead of Arisian Lenses. Many of Schmitz's non-series stories, such as *The Witches of Karres*, "Gone Fishing," and "Beacon to Elsewhere," have similar psi agencies.

However, Schmitz really hit his stride with the invention of the Psychology Service.

From a surface reading of Schmitz's work, he seems to have little to say about the origin of the Psychology Service. At least, there is little expository material about it in the stories. But if we dig deeper, we can find that background material.

"At one time I made an extensive investigation of this subject in the Federation. My purpose was to test a theory that the emergence of a species from its native world into space and the consequent impact of a wide variety of physical and psychic pressures leads eventually to a pronounced upsurge in its use of Uld powers [psi]." (Lord Gulhad, *The Demon Breed*)

This is exactly what we find in "Blood of Nalakia," the very first story that mentions the Hub. At first, it appears that Frome is using hypnosis and conditioning to an ultrasonic signal to control his captives. But Frome was only using "mechanical means" to enhance his psi talent. When he attacks Frazer, we learn that there is real psi involved. The Elaigar were bred for psi abilities, and at the end of the story, Lane is headed back to the Hub Systems carrying Frome's child.

Not much more than two centuries ago the Hub still had been one of the bloodiest human battle-grounds of all time. It was the tail end of the War Centuries. A thousand governments were forming and breaking interstellar alliances, aiming for control of the central clusters or struggling to keep from being overwhelmed. (*The Demon Breed*)

One thing that happened during the War Centuries is that entire planets died, including Earth—though

Schmitz never explicitly states this. Prior to that period, stories such as "Blood of Nalakia" and "Grandpa" contain people from Earth. In all the later stories, Earth is only mentioned as the source of species that were "preserved in the Life Banks on Maccadon." Every human in the Hub is aware of Man's planet of origin, but nobody mentions its fate.

The War Centuries intervene between "Blood of Nalakia" and "A Sour Note on Palayata." The Federation of the Hub has been founded, and it is significant that the first Federation story written is about the Psychology Service. If it weren't for the details hidden in this story, we probably would never know what caused the War Centuries.

There is a trick involved in understanding the background in "A Sour Note on Palayata"—you have to realize that it's essentially the same story as "The Illusionists" from the Agent of Vega series. Laying these two stories side-by-side clarifies all sorts of cryptic references.

The War Centuries were caused by the rise of psi power in human beings. Pre-war human societies had no defense against psis—they had not yet developed an organization or institution to control them.

A Class Two psi (telep-2) such as Telzey is a serious danger to an unprepared society. In fact, "catastrophic" would be a better word. Consider the first thing Telzey does with her newfound power in "Novice." As soon as the Baluit crest cat crisis is over, she starts experimenting with her Aunt Halet's mind. Halet has no defense and doesn't even know she is being controlled.

The next step for a psi as powerful as Telzey would be to take control of the people around her. She would soon find that she can only control a handful of the billions of people on a planet, so she would try to find a way to extend her control. Schmitz calls these "telepathic amplifiers" or "psychimpulse-multipliers." Using such devices, a sufficiently skilled telepath could start a chain-letter of control called the "Pyramid Effect" in the Agent of Vega series. A single telep-2 could end up controlling the entire planetary population.

The controlled population would have no more defense than Aunt Halet. Those with strong minds that might be able to resist would be destroyed. The average IQ then falls. Eventually, any psychoses in the ruling mind would be transferred to and amplified in the population, leading to ritualized serial murder and mass suicide. When the controlling mind died, the entire planet would die as well. That's what the Psychology Service was worried might be happening on Palayata. It's hard to believe that Schmitz wrote all this before Jim Jones founded Jonestown in Guyana.

In the War Centuries, this happened not once, but hundreds of times. It kept several thousand planets in turmoil not for years, but for centuries. Finally, a defense was found against the psis. It consisted of an organization of both psis and non-psis protected by mind shields. With a defense in hand, physical force was sufficient to defeat the psis.

> Wars had been fought to prevent the psychological control of Hub citizens on any pretext; and then, when the last curious, cultish cliques of psychologists had been dissolved, it had turned out to be a matter of absolute necessity to let them resume their activities. So they were still around . . . Of course, they were limited now to the operations of the Psychological Service. ("A Sour Note on Palayata")

With the end of the War Centuries, the group that won the war founded the Federation. To prevent another psi war, they created the Psychology Service. Their number one job was to prevent rogue psis from causing trouble in the Hub.

❖   ❖   ❖

One thing that bothers many people about the Federation is the autocracy of the Psychology Service. They censor the news. They spy on the citizens. They even have a policy to mind-wipe any Federation official who finds out what they are doing and disagrees with it. The rest of Hub society is so libertarian, how does Schmitz justify the actions of the Service? In fact, he never explicitly defends it. It is left to the reader to realize that the Psychology Service is fighting a plague that threatens the entire human race.

"You make that child sound rather dangerous!" ("Undercurrents")

Let's return to the case of Telzey Amberdon. On the trip back to Orado, she discovers "tele-hypnosis" and uses it to take control of her Aunt Halet. As soon as she steps off the ship, she's spotted, hooked, tagged, and tracked by the Psychology Service. This girl is a danger and they know it. So what do they do? Do they kidnap or murder her? No, they implant a suggestion that she limit her psi activity and seek out the proper authorities.

This is the true Schmitz touch. The Psychology Service is not out to protect society by eliminating psis. Quite the contrary. They will protect the Federation by *immunization*. To eliminate psis would leave the Federation defenseless against external threats (such as the Elaigar), and internal threats such as undetected psis. Instead, Telzey is left free to find her own way of handling her new abilities. She will be tracked, and harsher means will be used only if she becomes a problem. If she can control herself and fit into society, she will be left alone.

Because of this, the Psychology Service is not presented as some dark repressive Gestapo-like organization hiding behind the friendly façade of the Federation. They are   instead   controlling   a   serious   problem   as nondestructively as possible. More than that, they are trying to turn this serious problem into a strength.

> "I think the Overgovernment prefers the species to continue to evolve in its own way. On the record, it's done well. They don't want to risk eliminating genetic possibilities which may be required eventually to keep it from encountering some competitive species as an inferior." (Ticos Cay, *The Demon Breed*)

The Service is also pushing the use of psionic machines in the Federation. People with no psi talent of their own will be empowered to deal with psis. Mind shields are available for defense, and powerful mind-reading machines, such as the ones at the Orado City Space Terminal or Transcluster Finance, will provide the advantages of psi to ordinary people.

As part of their plan to introduce psi to the Hub on a larger scale, one job of the Psychology Service is to control the fear of psis. We see them doing this in several ways. They clean up after psis (like Telzey) by providing believable ordinary explanations for extraordinary events (such as in "Resident Witch"). If a psi won't keep under cover, they arrange to ship them off to someplace like Askanam ("Glory Day"), or the psis disappear into rehab—as happens to Wakote Ti and Alicar Troneff.

The Service also disseminates false stories, minimizing the effectiveness of psi. For example, Assistant Secretary Duffold believes that "the psi boys had produced disturbing effects in various populations from time to time, but in the showdown the big guns always had cleaned them up very handily."

The psis themselves have a different point of view. "The way the Alattas have worked it out, the human psis of the time, and especially the variations in them, had a good deal to do with defeating the Elaigar at Nalakia."

"The function of the Overgovernment is strategy.
In part its strategies are directed at the universe
beyond the Federation. But that is a small part."
(Lord Batras, *The Demon Breed*)

Only a small part of the Psychology Service's attention is directed outward—toward possible enemies beyond the Hub. We'll see more of those in Volume 4 of this series. But you've already read about the top-secret Service Group called Symbiote Control, whose job is to watch over aliens living among the Hub population. With typical Service attitude, symbiotes are left alone as long as they don't make trouble—after all, some of them are actually useful. The Service is watchful, but only takes action when they find a harmful parasite instead of a symbiote.

"We can say in general now that the Federation is
a biological fortress armed by the nature of its
species." (Lord Batras, *The Demon Breed*)

This attitude pervades the top level of the Federation Overgovernment. They treat the human species as an evolving animal and the Federation as an ecology. They aren't out to create perfection. If *survival* is a good enough goal for nature, it's good enough for the Federation and the Psychology Service.

What kind of animal does the Overgovernment want man to be? Aggressively competitive, but intelligently aggressive. Anything less, and they will be swamped from the outside. Anything more, and they risk a return to the War Centuries. Their solution is to give men an outlet for their aggression within the bounds of society. Private wars are allowed. Crime is only lightly controlled, and local governments are encouraged to handle crime themselves. Nile Etland suggests this is a substitute for open warfare.

"It's really more than a substitute," Ticos said. "A society under serious war stresses tends to grow rigidly controlled and the scope of the average individual is correspondingly reduced. In the kind of balanced anarchy in which we live now, the individual's scope is almost as wide as he wants to make it or his peers will tolerate." (*The Demon Breed*)

External threats are met with a very Hub-centric view. While the threat itself is handled expeditiously, the Overgovernment is more worried that such attacks will upset this carefully maintained balance. The Hub is deliberately being kept at the very edge of exploding into violence.

The Overgovernment has shown it is afraid of the effects continuing irritations of the kind might have on its species. We too should be wise enough to be afraid of such effects. (Lord Batras, *The Demon Breed*)